A QUESTION OF WILL

THE ALIOMENTI SAGA
BOOK 1

ALEX ALBRINCK

A QUESTION OF WILL
By Alex Albrinck (www.alexalbrinck.com)

ISBN: 1481894730
ISBN-13: 978-1481894739

http://www.AlexAlbrinck.com
alex@alexalbrinck.com

Cover Art by Karri Klawiter (http://artbykarr.com)
Stock Images by Melissa Offutt (http://melyssah6-stock.deviantart.com/)
Interior Design by Alex Albrinck

Dedicated to my family
Who teach me every day about unconditional love

CONTENTS

ACKNOWLEDGMENTS

Many thanks to my family; you have all provided incredible support throughout the writing process. There's no way I could have finished writing these books without your love and support.

To all of the authors who have, unknowingly, shown me that my dream of writing and publishing my novels needn't remain just a dream: Thank you.

PROLOGUE

Will Stark ran toward his home as fast as he could, despondent at the likelihood that his wife and son would already be dead when he got there. And it would all be his fault. He ran, not for enjoyment or accomplishment, but in a desperate attempt, no matter how futile, to prevent his wife and son from being brutally murdered.

He had turned thirty-five years old today, an age at which running just over a mile should be simple. He'd focused on his business and his family, though, and his fitness levels had suffered as a result. The lack of exercise and the resulting bit of flab around his midsection weren't the only physical symptoms that might make one think him older. Wire-rimmed glasses that enhanced his green eyes perched dangerously on the bridge of his nose, the sweat of exertion and terror threatening to jar them from his face and leave him blind in his pursuit of his target. Noticeable patches of gray mixed in with his normally pitch-black hair. The stressful events of this day were unlikely to keep his hair from growing whiter.

The sharp pains wracking his body weren't entirely due to physical neglect. He'd needed to break into his own highly-secure gated community, climbing over a building and dropping to the ground. He'd twisted his ankle upon hitting the ground, but he'd pressed on. There would be time to deal with that type of pain later. He had to get to his house. The lives of Hope and Josh hung in the balance.

You're already too late, a voice whispered in his head. *The killer had too much of a head start.* Visions of their lifeless faces floated before his eyes, causing him to slow momentarily. *No*, he thought. *I will not quit on them. Ever.* He pushed on, ignoring the stitch growing in his side, and the screaming ankle that wanted rest and ice, not the pounding of an all-out sprint. He tried to distract himself by finding humor in the fact that he was running at full speed in a suit, tie, and overcoat; his shoes were highly polished gems meant for business, not racing. It wasn't ideal.

None of this was ideal.

Desperate times made people do crazy things, to be sure. There had been numerous attempts to abduct him off busy public streets in broad daylight. His car had been shot at on many occasions. People in the press seemed to forget that he was human, and that he had no more interest in losing his freedom or his life than anyone else. The press enjoyed highlighting his "extravagant expenditures" like the cars with armor-plating and bulletproof glass, the fortress-style walls surrounding his community, or the security system in his neighborhood that seemed more extensive than many military bases. They opined that such vast sums of money could have been better spent on other things, implying that the desire of the young multi-billionaire to protect his family from harm was driven by pure selfishness.

He wondered what such people would write about the next day, if his fears became realized.

He knew what *he'd* write. That he'd failed. He had vowed to keep his family safe, no matter the expense. He'd consulted every security expert he could find, hired the best construction crew, paid for double- and triple-redundancies in every person and system charged with the security of those he loved most. Yet it hadn't been enough. A killer had gotten inside his sanctuary and was traveling along an unguarded driveway to his house. Will's wife and son were at risk due to his failure.

He ran faster than he'd ever run before, his feet in misery from the brick-like shoes covering them, as he slammed them repeatedly to the ground. His ankle finally gave out, and he was forced to cover ground in a limping hop that he tried desperately to turn into a sprint.

You should have let them meet you at the restaurant. Then they would not have been at home, waiting to be attacked. The inner voice gnawed away at his determination, seeking to replace it with guilt and self-loathing, and it was succeeding. He refocused, and refused to listen. There could be only one way to mitigate those feelings, and that required getting to his house. Quickly.

He rounded the final bend, his home visible in the fading sunlight. It was a large structure, to be sure, though probably smaller than most might suspect from one so wealthy. The brick and stone exterior of the home continued his theme of security, giving the sense of a castle inside the giant walls surrounding it. He looked inside, through the expansive bay window and into the living room. On most days, he'd see his son Josh standing there, waiting for him, silent as always. On others, he'd see Hope, a chair pulled up by the window while she waited for him, reading.

Today, he saw something that made his stomach spasm.

A man stood in his house, his back to Will. He was dressed in black, his head clean-shaven, the skin marked by dozens of large scars. Will experienced a powerful sensation of hopelessness and dread, as if the mere presence of this man was sufficient to eliminate the will to live of anyone who came near him. On closer examination, he noticed something even more terrifying: the short sword held in the man's right hand, the steel glinting from the lights in the house, and the blood dripping from the blade.

At the sight of the blood, Will passed through the denial stage of grief and went straight to anger. His pain was forgotten in a surge of adrenaline, and his whole body cooperated in moving him towards the house. He would kill that man, the man who had ended the lives of his wife and son.

A bright light burst from the window, blinding him, slowing him down as he twisted away. He blinked his eyes rapidly, forcing them to refocus.

He heard and felt the explosion a few seconds later. The glass exploded from the front windows and lacerated his skin, the damage lessened by the thick overcoat he wore against the late winter chill. The force of the blast knocked him to the ground, hurling him back several yards and knocking his glasses from his face. He felt the heat before he could turn around, and felt his skin burning. He realized that his coat had caught fire, and from his knees he pulled it off, hissing in pain as shards of glass were pulled from his skin in the process. His hands felt the frozen earth, seeking his glasses, in the desperate need to restore his sight. He found the glasses, put them on, and turned, still on his knees.

He could not see his house, even *with* his glasses on. The walls of flame leaped out of the windows and doorways, somehow hot enough to ignite even the brick and stone of the exterior.

He lowered his head to the ground, weeping. Then he screamed out the names of his dead wife and child in a tone of pure, agonizing mourning.

THE FOUR OATHS
OF THE ALIOMENTI

Most recent transcription
Prepared by the Hunter Aramis

As a member of the Aliomenti, and in recognition of the special knowledge, technology, and power inherent in my position, I do hereby swear to abide by and uphold the following Oaths:

OATH NUMBER ONE: I vow to never knowingly share with any non-Aliomenti human the unique knowledge, technology, and power of the Aliomenti, directly or indirectly, nor shall I permit any non-Aliomenti human to acquire any of the same of his own accord. I understand and agree that the penalty for violation of Oath Number One is ten years imprisonment, stripped of all rights, privileges, and power for the duration.

OATH NUMBER TWO: I vow to never knowingly share with any non-Aliomenti human the existence of the Aliomenti, either directly or indirectly, nor shall I permit any non-Aliomenti human to acquire knowledge of the same of his own accord. I understand and agree that the penalty for violation of Oath Number Two is twenty years imprisonment, stripped of all rights, privileges, and power for the duration.

OATH NUMBER THREE: I vow to never enter into a committed relationship of any type, most notably marriage, with any non-Aliomenti human, and likewise vow to avoid such relationships within the Aliomenti community, lest termination of such relationship lead to distrust and disunity among our kind. I understand and agree that the penalty for violation of Oath Number Three is fifty years imprisonment, stripped of all rights, privileges, and power for the duration.

OATH NUMBER FOUR: Concerning the nature of the relationship and the potential for abnormally advanced abilities, I vow never to be the biological parent to any child, regardless of the Aliomenti status of the second parent, regardless of the nature of the conception of the child. I understand and agree that the penalty for violation of Oath Number Four is death.

I hereby state my understanding that any humans involved in the breaking of the Four Oaths shall suffer death at the hand of an Aliomenti assassin.

I affirm my Oaths and vows, and do so of sound mind and body, without compulsion, of my own free will, as evidenced by my signature below in the presence of my Leader.

I
INFILTRATION

Two hours earlier.

"I'll never get tired of this view, Mark." Deron McLean spoke to his colleague through the radio connecting the two guard stations for the exclusive De Gray Estates community. "When you've got a few billion dollars, you can build things like that."

Mark Arnold laughed, taking in the view of the massive dome covering the city of Pleasanton. With darkness approaching, the dome had started to glow, a beacon to all seeking prosperity. "No kidding. Wonder how *those* conversations went?"

"Well, probably something like: 'Hi, I'm Will Stark. I'm buying your city, and with my purchase, I want a tax and regulation-free zone, and then I am going to build a giant dome over it that glows at night, and it will have so many job opportunities in it during this awful economy that I can afford to pay people to move here to work, and businesses to move here and set up shop. Oh, yeah. Then I'm going to build an old-fashioned castle wall and moat around 2,500 acres outside that dome, and hire two dudes named Deron and Mark to keep the nasty stuff away from me.'"

Mark laughed again, with feeling. "Hey, if I had his money, I'd do the same thing. Well, I'd never think of doing *that*, but then again, I'm not Will Stark."

"Nobody is, my friend. Nobody is. Half the time, I'm not even sure that *he* is Will Stark."

"Seems too good to be true, doesn't he?"

"Indeed he does."

The banter stopped, and the two men resumed the standard routine of their guard duties.

Three men appeared on the sidewalk outside the De Gray Estates. Had anyone been watching, they would have sworn that the three men had materialized out of the twilight descending on the town.

They marched with purpose outside the massive walls which surrounded the neighborhood, footsteps partially muffled by the sounds of the water flowing in the moat. Small puffs of smoke emerged from their mouths, the condensation forming in the crisp winter air. The only light came from the two buildings framing the massive concrete gate used to control access into the community. The walls could not be scaled; the gate could not be breached. The wealthy residents of the exclusive community slept secure and comfortable at night, knowing that no one got in without their permission.

Mark worked in what his security team referred to as the Guard Station, a ground-level building which enforced the various security processes allowing residents and non-residents to enter inside the enormous walls. Without Mark, the massive gate would remain above ground, preventing vehicles from entering the premises. Without Mark, those looking to enter the community on foot, through a smaller double-door system known as a man-trap, would be thwarted in their efforts, even if they were a known resident of the community. Mark's team maintained a list of non-residents expected to request access during a given time period, and tracked the comings and goings of residents. Mark knew that, at this time, only two residents were outside the premises — Myra VanderPoole and Will Stark. There were no expected visits from non-residents on the schedule this day.

He thus watched the three men with great interest.

Each man wore black, the expensive-looking shirts sporting a golden emblem with a circle and an upside-down letter V. One man wore a top hat and wire-rimmed glasses, and a second wore what appeared to be a dark cloak. The third man wore no accessories, but his handsome face was marred by a thick scar running horizontally across his right cheek, just under his eye.

Their purposeful facial expressions, devoid of any humor, gave Mark a very bad feeling.

The men passed the Guard Station, and then turned left, heading up the driveway, passed the window with a sign reading "Guests Check In Here First," and proceeded to the outer door of the mantrap.

Mark tapped a button on his control panel. "Deron, are you seeing our uninvited guests?"

After a brief pause, Deron replied. "Got them. Is that guy wearing a top hat?"

"Yeah, and his friend's got a cloak. They went straight to the door without stopping here first to check in."

"I've got a bad feeling about these guys."

"Yeah. Same here."

"I'll call our friends in the Dome."

"Thanks."

That was their procedure for dealing with unapproved guests. Mark, at ground level, would attempt to speak with anyone seeking unauthorized entry. Deron, his partner on this shift, worked in the Guard Tower, and he'd notify the police, stationed inside the massive Dome covering the nearby corporate city of Pleasanton, Ohio, of the potential trespassers. Located on the opposite side of the driveway and concrete gate from the Guard Station, the Tower enabled a guard, located forty feet off the ground, to survey the surrounding territory and perform visual scans of the neighborhood. In the nearly impossible event that someone would breach the walls, the roles would be reversed. Deron would track the perpetrators, and Mark would notify the police.

They'd never had to execute that procedure. No one had ever bothered to try scaling these walls. Several people would try to break in by ramming the gate each year, which generally resulted in a totaled vehicle and, if the foolish driver was lucky, nothing more than whiplash for injuries.

These men clearly desired entry, and his gut told him it wasn't a case of a resident forgetting to phone in the access authorization. The guidelines required him to proceed as if such a mistake had occurred until evidence proved otherwise. He left the speaker on, maintaining contact with Deron, and moved to the window the men had passed. Pressing a button, he activated a speaker on the exterior of the building. "Excuse me, gentlemen. Access to this community is available only to those authorized by current residents, and at present we have no standing authorizations for today. Please step away from the door, and contact the resident you wish to visit to initiate your access requests."

The men ignored him. Not one of them even turned to acknowledge hearing his statement.

Mark sighed. These men were clearly the arrogant guests of one of the wealthy residents of this fortress, no doubt too deluded with self-importance to worry about such trivial matters as security processes. He knew the type. These men would expect him to eventually give in and allow them entry. Mark recalled an approved dinner guest of Myra VanderPoole several years prior. The man, who was severely obese, had entered the first door of the man-trap, and could not close the door behind him. That left the circuit open, and the system was, in such a circumstance, coded to assume a second person was attempting entry at the same time. The man had demanded that they open the doors, and threatened to sue if Mark did not come to manually open the inner door. Mark refused. Myra VanderPoole had come to the front gate herself and they had agreed to open the concrete gate so that the man could walk in. The man had complained loudly about the horrific treatment he'd received at Mark's hands. Myra had apparently set her guest straight on that matter, for he'd apologized for his behavior with great fervor later upon his exit from the community.

Mark began to repeat his statement to the men, but paused. He'd heard something odd from the open communication link with Deron. It had almost sounded like a gasp, an inhalation of breath so sudden that it sounded like a noise of terror. He walked back to the control panel in order to listen more closely. "Deron? Everything all right up there?"

There was no reply. Mark was suddenly overwhelmed by a powerful sensation of pure evil, an effect so strong that he nearly lost his footing. "Deron?"

A thunderous crash sounded from outside, resembling the noise of shattering glass. Mark whirled back toward the driveway, and saw what looked like small pieces of ice fall from the sky. He'd just had time to register this oddity when a second, far louder crash sounded above and behind him. Mark whirled toward the center of the Station and looked up, just as a hole exploded in the ceiling and a large mass fell through. The mass landed in a heap on the floor.

Still feeling the overwhelming sensation of evil, Mark took one step toward the mass of debris, and then stopped, reeling in horror.

The mass that had crashed through the ceiling was Deron. The man looked to be dead. His throat had been slashed away with vicious power, the wound so gaping that the man had already bled out. Deron's eyes were wide and lifeless, his mouth open as if to protest this cruelty. He lay on top of a pile of wood and shingles from the roof and ceiling that he'd crashed through, pieces of timber impaling him, his arms and legs bent at impossible angles.

Mark was numb with shock. He turned back to his control panel, prepared to phone the police and ambulance, when the sensation of evil and foreboding ratcheted up to such a degree that his limbs seemed incapable of moving. When he heard a thumping noise behind him, it took every bit of effort remaining in him to merely turn around.

A man stood in the room, straddling Deron's body. He was dressed in black, with a logo similar to that worn by the three men outside. He was of an average height and build. The man's head was clean-shaven, with dozens of scars of various sizes marring his otherwise handsome face. His eyes, though, turned Mark's legs to jelly, and the guard fell to the ground, suddenly unable to stand. They were completely blood-red, both cornea and iris, and he found himself morbidly fascinated by them. The eyes were devoid of any type of human emotion, full only of malice. He held in his right hand a short sword, blood dripping from the blade. This man exuded the aura of a cold-blooded killer, as evidenced by his execution of Deron.

He needed to get away, he needed to tell somebody, anybody, to help him avoid death at this man's hands. The killer walked toward Mark, a predator who had cornered its weakened prey, and the tip of the sword was suddenly at Mark's throat, the blood — Deron's blood — dripping into Mark's lap.

"Cooperation means Gena Adams lives." The voice was almost a whisper, the tone having the effect of fingernails scratching a chalkboard. Mark's insides chilled at the sound. This man knew about Gena. They were due to be married in a month, but Mark knew this man meant to kill him, just as he'd killed Deron, and therefore that wedding would never happen. He was a security guard in name only, his job that of processing access requests, but as per current law in the country he did not carry a gun. He doubted that it would matter against this man; his hands would fail to steady enough to pull the trigger.

Mark vowed to spend his remaining moments of life ensuring that Gena would live. Over the past few weeks, he'd been starting to think he wasn't good enough for her, because she was simply that sweet and generous a soul. She would hear nothing of such concerns, laughing them off as a case of cold feet. It was a moot concern now.

Mark forced himself to look directly into the eyes of Death and nod once.

The killer backed away, giving Mark room to climb to his feet. Mark never took his eyes from the man. If he was going to die, he wouldn't be a coward and look away.

The killer pointed at the three men standing at the outer door of the man-trap. "Let them in."

Full realization hit Mark. The four men had worked together; three had distracted the guards while the fourth eliminated the first and then subdued the second. How had he missed seeing this man? Had he been hiding in the Tower all this time? Guilt tore at him, and then morphed into steely resolve. He was going to save as many people as possible this day.

He forced himself to look directly into those blood-red eyes and took a deep breath. "No."

The tip of the sword lashed across his face, and he felt the warm blood trickle down both cheeks out of the two lacerations now marking his skin. He had enough time to register this before he found himself on his back, the edge of the sword against his throat. The man had speed Mark could not hope to match.

"Wrong answer," the killer hissed. He rose to his feet, the sword never breaking contact with Mark. At his full height, he used the sword to gesture toward the control panel, where the man-trap authorization buttons were located. The killer had done his homework. The buttons were fingerprint-activated and sensed blood pressure and pulse rate, and only the on-duty guards could activate them. Each guard had his pulse rate and blood pressure measured upon starting his shift. If the measurements at the time they tried to open the man-trap were significantly higher or lower than the baseline, the interior door wouldn't open. Mark had asked why it wouldn't open if the numbers were lower than the baseline, since that would likely represent someone calm and relaxed. "They could also be dead or dying," the security expert had noted. With that memory, Mark was glad his fingers would be of no use to the killer unless they were still attached to Mark.

He climbed to his feet again, trying to calm himself from the violent attack. "The buttons won't work if I'm highly stressed," Mark told the killer. "Leave me alone so I can calm down."

The killer, somehow recognizing this as truth rather than a carefully orchestrated lie, walked to the opposite side of the room and turned his back to Mark. He was clearly unconcerned that Mark would try to flee. Both men knew Mark couldn't outrun him.

Mark took several deep breaths and exhaled slowly. *I am not confined in a room with a superman ninja with a bloody sword. Deron is not lying dead ten feet away. I am going to see Gena again soon.*

He somehow calmed himself, and then pressed the man-trap button. The man with the scar on his right cheek entered the community after the inner door opened in front of him. Mark winced. He could relate to the scar.

The second man, the one wearing a top hat, entered the man-trap, the outer door locking behind him. Mark paused for a moment before he opened the inner door. "What are they going to do?" He glanced behind him at the killer, who had not moved from his spot.

"One of the residents has something he should not possess. We will remedy the situation."

A simple robbery? *That's* what this was about? Surely there were better ways to make money. Will Stark and his wife, for example, tended to be rather generous souls; they'd provided Mark and Gena gifts sufficient to cover the cost of their honeymoon. You could get money without resorting to robbery. Or murder.

Still, he needed to be sure. "So... you aren't going to hurt anyone else?"

There was a pause. "No."

Mark wondered if he'd asked the correct question. He elected not to press the matter against the skilled killer, convincing himself that he had all the assurances he was going to get. He pushed the man-trap button again, allowing the second man inside. The third man, the man wearing the cloak, gave a bow with a bit of a flourish, and then entered the man-trap before being admitted into the neighborhood by Mark.

He glanced at the section of the control panel nearest the man-trap section. It contained a panic button, which would alert the police to a problem at De Gray Estates for which telephone communication was impossible. He could click on that button, and perhaps the police would arrive quickly enough to apprehend these men. That meant Gena would no longer be at any risk. He shifted slightly to the left.

The killer seized him and threw him to the floor, the malevolent blood-red eyes alternately searing a hole through him and freezing every cell of his being. The man's sword pointed at him, unerring, the finger on his left hand waving as he tsked at Mark. He then waved at Mark with the sword, motioning him away from the man-trap and panic buttons, and to the opposite side of the Station, facing the community rather than the street.

He watched the three men he'd just allowed into the community. Three men who were going to rob one of the residents of something these men believed they shouldn't possess. Men willing to kill to accomplish their goals. He glanced at Deron again, a graphic reminder of that fact. Deron would never again return home to his wife and young son. As he looked outside, he saw smoke. The half-dozen covered golf carts residents and guests could use to cover the distance from the front gate to their homes were all in flames. Anyone entering the community on foot would have a longer journey home than they'd expected.

The men reached a central cul-de-sac just inside the gate area, where the residents ceased to be neighbors and traveled upon long, isolated driveways to their secluded homes, as much as a mile away. The men veered sharply left, indicating that they were off to rob the Starks.

Mark cringed inwardly. The Starks were the family in this neighborhood he would least want to see harmed. The other four families residing here represented every negative stereotype of wealth imaginable: old, arrogant, condescending, cheap, and stingy. The Starks were the polar opposites. They were young, in their thirties at most, which made them young enough to be the children or grandchildren of the other residents. Both were active in the community, with far more trips outside the fortress due to community and charitable activities than commutes to Will's office building or personal outings. Most importantly, they were exceptionally generous with their wealth, always looking for excuses to give money away, funding new business ventures to such a degree that the domed city of Pleasanton had become an entrepreneurial haven. The children in the community played sports and engaged in various activities on fields, courts, and diamonds funded by the Starks, an endeavor likely driven by baseball-enthusiast Will. Rumor was that the Starks furnished uniforms, handled fees for umpires and officials, and generally made sure that a lack of funds was never a reason to deny a child the chance to participate in athletics.

Mark was cringing for another reason. Hope Stark was at home, and the three men were likely to encounter her as they searched for whatever item they wanted to take. Given what had happened to Deron already, it was difficult to see Hope surviving their raid on her home.

He needed to do something to help Hope, without appearing to help her. "What do the Starks have that you don't want them to possess?"

The killer didn't respond.

"I've been to their house. I don't think they keep much money there, and they really don't keep many possessions in the house either, at least nothing of any value. Surely, men of your skills can find better places to rob? What do they have that you don't *think* they should have?"

The soulless red eyes turned to him. "Freedom. Life."

"What?" Mark spluttered. "I... I thought you said you weren't going to hurt anyone?"

"Those men will deprive Mr. Stark of freedom." He smiled, a look which chilled the air in the room. "And I will deprive Mrs. Stark of life. She will not suffer."

"You... you can't do that!" Mark shouted, surprising himself. "I'll stop you!"

The killer snorted.

Mark charged him. He once again found himself on the ground, face-down, with his arms pinned behind his back. "Listen closely," the killer hissed. "I am tolerating your presence solely because you will yet be of service to me. Your cooperation for the remainder of your useless life determines whether Gena Adams lives... or how slowly she dies." He paused, the scars seeming to sear more deeply into his face. "I am not pleased at the moment."

The killer walked to the control panel and placed his left hand on the panic button, his right hand still holding the sword. He never took his eyes off Mark, but Mark watched the control panel, puzzled. A small burst of fire erupted from the man's hand — no, that was impossible, wasn't it? — and suddenly the circuitry for the panic button was in flames.

"Not pleased at all." The threat was clear. This man could do more than hurt Gena with a sword; he could burn her until she was in excruciating pain.

Mark would do what he could to save Hope Stark's life, but he was terrified of a man who could kill with such efficiency, attack with such swiftness... and who could somehow shoot flames from his hands at will. With his own death now imminent, though, his courage would be focused on preventing any harm to Gena... even if that meant sacrificing Hope Stark. Courage was in short supply at present. "What do I do now, then?" he asked, his voice timid.

"Wait."

"Wait? For what?"

"A phone call."

And he waited.

II
APPEASEMENT

The man wore a black shirt with a golden circle emblem, black pants, and matching black boots. On his belt was a sheath that held a short, sharp sword, a weapon the man had used to kill on many occasions. Killing was something which provided him great satisfaction, especially those kills affecting the group he referred to as humans. It was rumored that each of the scars marring his head signified a single authorized kill, and his bald head was littered with dozens of such markings. He had earned his title: Assassin. His blood-red eyes were a testament to his skill, and to the overwhelming hatred he bore toward humans.

The Assassin crept along the outside of the massive concrete wall surrounding the community called De Gray Estates, moving slowly so as to avoid detection by the many cameras watching for intruders. As he neared each camera, he would hold out his hand, and a small flash of light would render the camera inoperable. He reached the base of the giant Guard Tower flanking one side of the wide driveway serving as the vehicular entry to the community. The driveway was blocked by a massive concrete gate that lowered into the ground only when a resident passed fingerprint and retinal scan tests, at which point the on-duty guard acknowledged their identity and opened the gate. Guards were able to allow entry via a double-door "man-trap" as well. Guests could enter using the same procedures, provided that a resident had previously authorized the visit.

Three men walked toward the ground-level Guard Station on the other side of the driveway, traveling on the well-lit sidewalk. The guards in the Station and Tower both watched these men, and neither of them noticed The Assassin as he reached the base of the Tower. The Assassin scaled the outside of the Tower, gripping the mortar gaps with his fingertips as he moved upward. Upon reaching

17

the top of the Tower, The Assassin paused momentarily, and an instant later he was inside. Below, the Station guard ordered the three men to comply with procedures for entering the community. His partner in the Tower turned away from the window to contact the police about the situation.

The guard saw the scar-faced Assassin, sensed the aura of pure evil about the killer, and saw the blood-red eyes. He opened his mouth to scream, to yell out a warning to the man on the ground. The sword was faster, though. The Assassin removed it from the sheath and slashed out, his movements a blur, and the guard could not cry out a warning as the blade severed his windpipe and jugular vein at once. The guard clutched his throat, but it was a futile gesture. The blood gushed from the fatal wound, and the guard's eyes widened as he was unable to get air into his screaming lungs. He collapsed face-first to the ground, his body in shock and twitching as it desperately fought to live. It was a fight he would lose.

The Assassin seemed distressed. He moved to the dying man, and using his boot rolled the guard over, in order to see the man's face, and watch his eyes as the light signaling life slowly faded. It took only a few moments, and a hideous smile crossed The Assassin's face. He was overjoyed, drunk on the thrill of the kill, and was eager for more. But he knew he must follow the plan, and must get his companions inside the walls so that they could set the trap for the man known as Will Stark. He must get down to the ground-level Guard Station, prevent the guard there from notifying the human authorities, and coerce him into letting his men inside. He could eliminate all human police that came at him, but the group's rules were clear: do not be seen, and kill as few humans as possible. The first rule was inviolate; all other portions of the plan must be adapted to ensure there was no trace of their presence.

It would take too long to climb down the stairs to the ground, and doing so would give the guard the opportunity to hit his panic button and notify his police. The Assassin needed to get inside the building before the second guard recognized trouble. The man would eventually realize his partner wasn't responding over the microphone link established a few moments earlier between the two buildings. The Assassin's blood-red eyes fell upon the dead body, and the large glass-sided wall nearest the Guard Station. A cruel smile invaded his scarred face, his evil eyes lighting up in anticipation.

He'd never launched a missile before.

He picked up the dead body at his feet, got a running start, and hurled the body through the glass, shattering the window into thousands of pieces. He watched as the body arced through the air, sailed over the driveway, and crashed into the Guard Station roof, falling into the single room below.

The Assassin's emotions were a rising thrill of anticipation as he contemplated *the two remaining deaths he would initiate this day. He raced to the opening in the glass with a burst of adrenaline and leaped through, covering the distance across the driveway as he fell. He landed, catlike, on the roof, where he could already sense the terror in the guard below. The man had seen his friend's corpse. The Assassin dropped through the opening...*

Hope Stark woke, her breaths short, and she sat straight up in her bed. She'd only meant to take a short nap after a long day working with her son, enough to re-energize her for the evening, but a glance at the clock told her she'd overslept. Tonight, she and her son would join her husband, Will, for dinner at Will's favorite steakhouse. It was Will's thirty-fifth birthday.

Right now, though, she was having trouble getting the nightmare out of her mind. In that nightmare, four men dressed in black had worked together to kill one guard at the entrance to her gated community, and those men planned to use the second guard to gain entry and kill at least one other person. Was it her? Her son? Her husband, once he arrived home? She wouldn't have the dream if a member of her family wasn't the intended victim, would she? She tried to convince herself it was nothing more than a bad dream, but the images and sounds were incredibly vivid. Worse, she was still sensing the emotion of the killer, feeling his thrill in killing one man and the joyous anticipation he had at the prospect of causing more deaths. She shuddered.

Hope stretched, rose from the bed, and marched into her bathroom. She glanced at her reflection, deciding that she presently met the definition of frumpy: jeans, an over-sized sweatshirt, and her golden hair pulled back in a ponytail. She splashed cold water on her face, both in an effort to fully wake up from her nap, and to shake the dream and the ongoing sense of dread from her mind. Though a success in terms of waking her up, the cold water had no impact on her tense mood. Why would someone want to kill her, her husband, or her son?

She re-entered the bedroom and walked to a large wall painting. She pulled on one side, and the painting swung open on its hinge, revealing a hidden wall safe. Her hands were trembling; the sensation of dread, and the feeling that she was somehow being watched, was increasing. She finally got the combination entered correctly, opened the safe, and pulled out the gun. Guns were illegal in 2030 for anyone not granted a license as a militia member; most States had passed laws stating that their official militias were exclusively formed of the members of local police departments and the National Guard. Somehow, Will had convinced someone that an exception should be made for him, and the gun and several clips of ammunition appeared in the safe one day. Hope knew that somewhere, a family was living much more comfortably today than they might otherwise, courtesy of a large cash contribution from her husband. She didn't mind. They had more money than they could ever spend in many lifetimes, and the peace of mind that came from owning the weapon was worth any price.

Whatever that price was, however, it wasn't enough to eliminate the sense she now had that she was being watched, a sensation so powerful that she believed someone unwelcome was in the house.

Hope heard a thump from down the hall. Josh's room. She heard the dog, Smokey, growl, and then bark. No. She would not let them hurt her son. Gun in hand, Hope sprinted for the boy's room. Drawing a deep breath, she flung the door open, dreading what she'd find inside, expecting to find a scene of horror.

What she found was a miracle.

Josh, her six-year-old son, was not lying down on his bed with his dog Smokey at his side, mortally wounded by the hand of the unseen intruder. Rather, he was sitting on the side of his bed, a baseball in his hand. Smokey, his four-year-old black Labrador retriever, stood several feet away, tail wagging furiously, eyes watching the baseball with great intensity. As Hope watched, the dog began to growl, and then barked twice at Josh. The boy smiled and tossed the baseball over the dog's head. The ball thudded into the wall and bounced to the ground, with Smokey following in hot pursuit. The dog finally retrieved the ball, tail high and wagging, and she trotted back to Josh with the treasure in her mouth. The boy held out his hand, and Smokey deposited the slobbery baseball in Josh's hand.

"Josh?" Hope's voice was barely above a whisper.

The boy and his dog both turned, having just then realized she was there. "I couldn't sleep, Mommy," he said. Josh spoke in a slow, measured pace, as if English were a second language he was learning and he had to first translate from his native tongue.

Hope set the gun on a shelf near the door and raced to her son, smothering him in a fierce hug, smoothing down his sandy-blond hair. Smokey, irritated at the temporary loss of her playmate, barked, and Josh dropped the ball on the ground, his throwing arm pinned to his side by his affectionate mother. "It's a miracle," Hope whispered, her eyes full of tears of joy. "A miracle." For the four words Josh had said as his mother entered his room were the first words the six-year-old had ever spoken.

She finally broke the embrace, moving back enough to see her son as he was now. The boy looked back at her, making eye contact, his deep blue eyes sparkling with an internal light, full of warmth and a wisdom beyond his years. Will had always said he could see that in the boy's eyes, even while most of the light had been deadened over the previous six years. Hope could see it, too. She'd always known her little boy was special, even without the miracle she'd just witnessed.

"I need to call Daddy," she said. She ran down the hall to get her phone, dialing it as she ran back to Josh's room, where the boy had resumed the game of fetch with Smokey, his face full of concentration and concern all at once. She was reminded that Josh's words spoke of having trouble sleeping, something he'd never struggled with before. As she dialed, however, she wondered: had Josh possibly had the same nightmare? Or sensed her feelings of dread and fear?

"I just left the office and I'm on my way home," Will said by way of greeting. She could hear the sound of the engine as he drove the car, which, quite sadly, featured armored exterior panels and bullet-proof glass. Hope smiled without humor; those features were to prevent all of those militia members from shooting at them successfully. "Did Josh say where he wanted to go to dinner?" The words, though spoken in a humorous cadence, carried with them the tone of a father saddened at the cruel hand life had dealt his beloved son.

"No, but if you ask him when you get home, you *will* get an answer." She wondered if Will would catch her hidden meaning.

There was a pause. "Are you trying to tell me something?" Will asked, his voice trembling with emotion.

"Four words. Full sentence." The tears were welling in her eyes once again, but the triumph in her voice was unmistakable.

She could hear Will breaking down as well. "My little boy is talking," he whispered. Then: "My little boy is talking!" he shouted.

"Whoa!" She heard the sound of tires squealing. "Sorry, lost control of the car for a second." Now she could hear the smile in his voice. "Can you put him on the phone? By the way, what in the world is the sound in the background?"

Hope laughed. "After you almost crashed the car by merely being *told* he's talking, I dare say you'll end up crashing into a tree if I let you talk to him right now. The sound you hear is your son playing fetch with Smokey, and they're both having a grand time."

"All right, all right, I can take a hint," Will said, trying to sound offended. "Guess I'll need to risk a few speeding tickets to get home more quickly."

"No, drive safely. We're not going anywhere until you get here."

"I love you, Hope," he said, his voice serious. "It's all the time you spent with him that's enabled him to finally break free. You're amazing."

"I love you, too," she replied. "And don't shortchange yourself. We both know you'd have spent as much time with him as I did if you'd been able. But it does take a bit of time and a singularly qualified individual to resurrect an economy of three hundred and fifty million people. Don't forget that you're setting a wonderful example for your son to follow. That's just as critical as reading and math and history. Besides, without you, how would he know how to throw the baseball so that Smokey can't catch it on the fly and break her teeth?"

He laughed. "And on that note, I must focus on my driving. See you in about a half hour."

"See you then."

They both hung up.

Hope watched the boy and his dog play for a few more minutes, and then addressed her son. "Josh?"

He turned toward her. That was unusual. Typically, Josh showed no reaction to spoken words. He looked at her, expectation on his face. He still wouldn't be accustomed to social customs, and would not necessarily recognize when he needed to respond to a spoken statement. That would come with time. "Do you know why you're able to talk with me now?"

"The voice said it was time," the boy replied.

That was... confusing. "What voice?"

"I do not know who. The voice said it was time for me to talk and be a little boy. And to protect you, Mommy."

Now she was disturbed. "Did the voice say what you needed to protect me from?"

"The bad men."

"What bad men?"

His face clouded with concern. "The men I saw in my sleep. They were hurting people. I woke up."

Her hands went to her face. "I had a bad dream too. Maybe the story I read before our naps was a bit too scary. For both of us." She tried to smile.

He shook his head. "They are real, Mommy. I know that they want to hurt you."

Now it was her turn to shake her head. "It was just a dream, sweetie. A very realistic dream, but just a dream."

"Why would two people have the same dream if it was not real, Mommy?"

She had no answer for that. Still, she felt the need to comfort him, as much as herself. "Look, I'll call the guards and they'll tell us that everything is fine. Will that help?" Without waiting for a reply, she searched through her contact list and found the number to the Guard Station. A crisp voice answered after the first ring. "De Gray Estates Guard Station. My name is Mark. How may I assist you, Mrs. Stark?"

She wondered how he knew it was her, and then realized her had caller ID. She was too spooked to think clearly at the moment. "Hi, Mark. I just had a question for you."

"Let me guess. You're holding a small costume party and need to add three or four people to the access list?" He gave a short laugh.

She laughed too. "Nothing quite so exciting, I'm afraid. It's just a concern I had. It's somewhat embarrassing, actually."

"Mrs. Stark, even if it kills me, I will help you ease your concern."

Hope thought that was rather dramatic. "I don't think it will come to that, Mark, but I do appreciate the sentiment. You see, my son and I both just woke up from realistic nightmares, and we both thought there might have been a break-in to the neighborhood."

"I totally understand, Mrs. Stark. I've had bad dreams before like that, where in your dream someone wants to kill you, and when you wake up you feel like the killer is sitting right there in the room with you."

Hope wondered why the guard speaking so strangely. She felt that it was almost as if...

She suddenly realized that the dream was real, and Mark was speaking under duress, bravely trying to give her information. There were three or four people involved, in some type of costume, and one of them was in the room with Mark. Probably forcing Mark to make sure she had no idea what was happening.

She needed to help him.

"That's *exactly* what this dream was like. Bad guys hurting people to come after me. It's almost as if I should call the police and ask them to come and take a look around."

"Oh, I don't think that's necessary, Mrs. Stark. We'd just be wasting their time."

She wondered about weapons. "It's at times like this that I really wish I had a gun. Even if a bunch of armed men charged into my house, I could shoot them."

"Yep, you could cut them down, all right. That would be much more enjoyable than them cutting *you* down, of course."

So it was too late to call the police now; they wouldn't be able to get here in time to make a difference. Additionally, she knew that those coming for her would have some kind of knife for weapons, but probably no guns. "Thanks so much for talking to me, Mark. My husband should be home soon, and he can tell me how silly I'm being."

"Not silly at all, Mrs. Stark. Take care of yourself."

"Thanks, Mark. You do the same." She paused for a brief moment, and then added, "Goodbye." She knew, somehow, that it was a literal goodbye. Regardless of what happened to her today, she wouldn't be talking to Mark again in this lifetime.

Hope did a mental recap. There were three or four people coming her way, armed with knives, but no guns. They had killed or would kill both guards at the entrance. She could call the police, but they couldn't be here in time. She could call Will and warn him, but he couldn't get here any faster, and she'd simply try to talk him out of coming. It wouldn't work; he'd come no matter what. She could try to run, but the men who had entered the community earlier in the dream would undoubtedly be making sure she couldn't run far, and having a six-year-old boy with her would slow her progress.

She was on her own. She needed to protect Josh at all costs, and defend herself as best she could.

One woman. One six-year-old boy. A dog. One semi-automatic pistol. Against four psychotic professional killers armed with knives. Or swords, if her dream was as accurate as it now seemed.

It just didn't seem fair.

• • •

Mark hung up the phone. "She's convinced everything is fine."

"I disagree." The words reminded Mark of the fear the man created in him, fear amplified by the mangled body of his friend and coworker lying only a few feet away.

"What are you talking about? I told her she was imagining things, that calling the police wasn't necessary..."

"You told her exactly the situation. She knows."

Thank God. "You have no way of knowing that."

"I know quite a lot. Mrs. Stark has a gun which she is retrieving now, and which she will attempt to fire at me. I thank you for uncovering that detail with your coded conversation."

Mark's head bowed. He'd tried. He prayed that somehow, Hope Stark could survive these monsters, perhaps even kill them first in self-defense. The killers' demise would certainly bode well for Gena. He had done the best he could for Mrs. Stark. He hoped he'd done all he could for his fiancée.

"I will not be the one to inflict Gena's punishment for your lack of cooperation."

Mark's head snapped back up. Was he actually saying...?

"I will leave that task to one of my colleagues. They are far less skilled than I. She will suffer more for it. Your lack of cooperation has made her suffering a necessity."

Sanity lost, Mark sprang to his feet to charge the man, but the killer moved his arm, and Mark felt something sting him. He glanced down, his anger replaced once again by terror. Somehow, his skin was on fire, literal flames burning through him. He opened his mouth to scream, but the killer's sword flashed. "I tire of your noise," he said. Mark fell to the ground, and the race was on to see whether the gaping wound in his neck or the flames would kill him first.

The Assassin sheathed his weapon without cleaning it, and he walked with supreme calm through the guard door on the inside of the property. He then turned and began his march to the Stark's home.

The death toll for the day was nearly complete. Two down. One to go.

It was time to visit Hope Stark.

III
DISCOVERY

Myra VanderPoole was fatigued.

She'd spent the entire day shopping, interrupted only by an early lunch and a light dinner. Years earlier, she'd spent time enjoying the night life as well, but that was before Jim had died twenty years ago. She still retained her old spending habits, though, enjoying the finer things in life with the money she'd received from the sale of the business she and Jim had built. Let the young Starks spread their wealth around like fools. She had earned hers, and she intended to spend every penny of it before she died, all on her own interests and pleasure.

The Starks, despite their propensity to lavish prosperity upon the unworthy, had proved useful. The plan they'd devised for this private, gated community was brilliant. It provided isolation from the general public and total privacy from neighbors. And they had an exterior security system for the community that was so advanced that even an elderly woman like her could walk about in the evening without concern for her well-being. It was as it should be. The annual dues for the community were excessive, used to pay for the upkeep of the fortress walls, security systems, and guards. Myra thought it was money well spent. After all, only the wealthiest members of society could dream of living here.

Myra felt vulnerable leaving these walls. Her driver made sure she stayed out of undesirable neighborhoods. He drove her only to the nicest shopping locations and restaurants in and around Pleasanton. She avoided the Dome, convinced that the structure would collapse one day, and she had no interest being inside when it did. Still, she'd grown accustomed to not worrying about anything while at home, and it was difficult to give up that sense of peace and venture out into society, exposed to the depravity of the mass of humanity. Tonight, after the day of shopping and dining, the driver would ensure that she returned home to the security found only within those massive walls, before he returned to his own home and family for the evening. He would get her inside, where a half-dozen covered golf carts were available for use by residents. She'd drive herself home tonight; usually, she had one of the two guards on duty assist her. Her shopping haul for the day was far smaller than usual.

Though it was barely early evening on the clock, the calendar dictated the early loss of daylight on this early winter day. Frank, the driver, pulled up to the De Gray Estates and off to the side of the entry driveway, near the Guard Tower. He stepped out and opened her door. Myra exited with her usual grace, holding the lone bag of purchases in her hand. Frank made as if to take her bag or arm to assist her across the driveway to the Guard Station for her brief security check-in. But she shooed him away. "Wait there, Frank, until the guard sees me inside." Frank sighed. He wished the old woman would let him drop her off closer to the scanner, but she insisted he keep the main driveway area clear in the event someone else wanted in or out. "Manners, Frank," she'd snapped at him more than once.

So Frank watched the old woman shuffle over to the outer man-trap door and enter the enclosed space, crouching slightly for the retinal scanner. After the outer door closed behind her, the light turned green, indicating that there was a match, and Myra tried to open the interior door. It didn't move. She shook the door, but no luck. "Confound it!" she snapped. "Guard, please open the door for me!" Frank realized that there was a problem.

"Mrs. VanderPoole? I don't see a guard inside the Station. Perhaps he's escorting a resident home?"

"An extended visit to the lavatory is more likely the case," Myra VanderPoole snorted, her tone biting as usual. She frowned. "And it appears that someone has left ice chunks all over the driveway. It's a wonder I didn't fall and kill myself. The neighbors will hear of this. Confound it, where *is* that guard?"

The old woman shuffled out of the man-trap and back toward the Guard Station window, where residents and guests could see and speak to the on-duty guard. She peered in the window as she approached, and then frowned. "Is the man actually *sleeping* on the job?" she said, her tone sharp. Then she looked in the window more closely.

"*Blood!*" she screamed, moving as quickly as her old legs could carry her. "Oh, dear God, there's so much blood, oh dear God, Frank, call the police, there's so much blood!" And she fainted, falling to the ground near the ice shards.

Frank, not sure what else to do, dug out his phone and called 911, telling them that Mrs. VanderPoole had suffered a fall on ice at the entrance to De Gray Estates and would need an ambulance. He let the dispatcher know that one of the guards normally on duty was not at his station. Frank hung up, called his wife to tell her he'd be late, and went to pick Mrs. VanderPoole up from the ground, wondering where the ice had come from.

They hadn't had snow or ice on the ground in a month.

• • •

Michael Baker received the call from dispatch about one of the rich old residents of the De Gray Estates falling near the entrance. He'd been a police officer long enough to realize that this was more a case of babysitting and paperwork than anything else. Sure, the dispatcher had said that the fall was apparently caused by ice, but it seemed unlikely that the woman had much of a case for pressing charges, as she'd fallen on her own property. The dispatcher noted that the caller had mentioned not seeing a guard on duty at the time of the call, which was unusual. They kept two guards on duty at all times, so that the gate was never without someone to attend it.

With a sigh, he pulled the car into the driveway of the De Gray Estates, commonly referred to as Rich Person Central by most of the residents of Pleasanton. He spotted old lady VanderPoole seated in the back seat of the rented limo with the door open, the driver waving a fan. The old woman's face was pale, but there was no indication of any injury. He was expecting something that looked more like a concussion, or perhaps some cuts or bruises caused by the fall. Frowning, Baker walked to the limo.

The driver saw him and stood up, coming to meet Baker. "Thanks for coming, Officer. I'm not sure what caused it, but I do know she hit the ground pretty hard."

Baker looked over and saw the shards of ice. "That's where she slipped?"

The driver nodded. "She was waiting for a guard to let her in, but nobody did. She went to the window there at the Station, started screaming, and, as much as an eighty-year-old woman can, *ran* toward me. That's when she hit the ice and fell. I think she may have fainted first, though, from the screaming, so that might have caused the fall as well."

Baker nodded, and glanced at the Guard Station. "I still don't see a guard there."

Surprise covered Frank's face. "That's very strange. They're incredibly insistent on having the ground level Station, at a minimum, covered at all times. When Mrs. VanderPoole needs an escort to her house after I drop her off, the guard in the Tower is the one who leaves. I've seen cases where the Tower guard will cover the Station so that guard can take a short break. With all of this noise and commotion, how could neither of them be there?"

Baker nodded, puzzled as well. He glanced up at the Tower... and gasped. The glass side of the Tower displayed a massive hole, as if something had crashed into the structure. His eyes trailed back to the ice, realization dawning. "That's not ice. That's glass." He pointed up at the Tower.

Frank saw it as well, and raised a hand to his face. "Maybe something crashed into the Tower, and the guard down here went to investigate?"

Baker shook his head. "They're pretty well required to ensure two people are on duty, and on watch, at all times. In a situation like that, the guard down on the street would call us first, and only then consider going to investigate. They're simply not allowed to leave the Station unguarded, and only leave the Tower unguarded to cover the Station."

As the two men spoke, a car pulled up into the driveway. Will Stark emerged, briefly silhouetted against the backdrop of the great glowing Dome he'd built, dressed in a dark gray suit and blue tie, and wearing an overcoat. His wire-rimmed glasses fogged briefly after leaving the warmth of his car for the chill of the wintry air. He frowned on seeing the police car lights flashing, and the limousine off to the side, clearly recognizing that something was amiss. He spotted his old friend Michael Baker and walked to the police officer.

"Hi, Michael," Stark said, shaking the officer's hand. He inclined his head toward Myra VanderPoole, still pale in the back seat of her car. "Is Myra all right?"

Baker smiled inwardly at the irony of that statement. Will Stark's first concern was Myra's condition. Had the situation been reversed, Baker knew, Myra would first wonder why Will was slowing down her entry into the neighborhood. "Not sure, Will," he admitted. "The call from dispatch stated that she'd fallen on a patch of ice, but there's more to it than that. Something has gone *very* wrong here."

Will, who had been scanning the entry while the conversation occurred, recognized the situation immediately. "Where did the Station guard go? And what happened up *there?*" His gaze shifted up to the Guard Tower with the gaping hole in the side, then down to glass. "That's not ice, is it?" His tone was ominous, and a frown formed on his face.

Baker shook his head. "We'd just hit that point when you arrived. Like I said, this is starting to look like something more serious than an old woman slipping and falling."

Will had turned his gaze back to the Guard Station, and his frown turned to a look of horror. "Michael," he said, trying to keep his voice calm, "why is there a giant hole in the ceiling of the Station?"

Baker's face sank as he saw the massive crater in the Guard Station roof. His eyes moved to the gaping hole in the Tower, the glass on the driveway, and back to the hole in the Station roof. He prayed those three weren't connected. Steeling himself, Baker walked over to the Station and peered inside.

Will heard Baker suck in his breath, and then the officer turned away from the window and retched. "Oh, dear God!" he screamed between heaves. He composed himself long enough to stumble to his cruiser, seize his radio, and call in. "Baker here. I'm at the entry to the De Gray Estates. Require backup, medical examiner, ambulance, and search unit relating to apparent double homicide, suspect is at large. Repeat: suspect or suspects at large." Baker's eyes seemed shattered, and his face made it clear that whatever he'd seen, he'd never be able to forget it.

Will saw and heard nothing else after hearing Baker's words. There had been a double homicide, and the suspect or suspects were at large... and it was hard not to assume the killer or killers had gotten into the community with other potential targets in mind. Why else would they murder the guards? Realizing that Hope and Josh were in mortal danger, he called Hope's phone, but she didn't answer. He left her a message, telling her to let no one in the house, to watch for intruders, and to get the gun out of the safe. He pocketed the phone, and had only one thought on his mind. He must get to his family, and protect them from whatever person or persons might mean to do them harm.

He raced to the man-trap outer door, letting the scanner identify him, but only when the inner door wouldn't open did he remember. No Station guard would be able to authorize his entrance. The system he'd designed to keep others out had failed to do so, and now was preventing him from getting in so that he could rush to his family's aid. He moved to the concrete gate, which stood ten feet high. He ran at it, trying to use his foot to propel himself high enough to get a grip on the top of the barrier, and then pull himself up. But he couldn't jump high enough.

"Michael!" he screamed, attracting the stunned police officer's attention. "Give me a boost!"

Baker seemed to regain his senses as Will's plan registered. "No way, Will. It's too dangerous. I am *not* going to help you run after those maniacs out of some noble idea of saving your family. Wait until backup gets here."

"Please," Will begged. "I *have* to go to them."

Baker shook his head. "I won't help you." A pause. "But I won't try to stop you. I know I'd be trying to do the same thing if my family was on the inside."

Will nodded, and scanned the area, trying to find the weakness in the system he'd designed, a weakness that might be there now that there were no guards on duty to prevent or observe his attempts at entry. Baker would not allow him to shatter the glass of the Guard Station and enter the community in that manner; the building was now a crime scene. Will glanced at the roof, an idea forming.

He couldn't go *through* the building. But he could certainly try to go *over* the building. The guards had defenses to prevent such attempts, but the guards wouldn't be stopping him from trying today.

Will saw the opening he needed in the form of a downspout running from the roof. He seized the pipe, and, with a surge of adrenaline, shimmied his way up the side of the building, relieved that the plastic was supporting his weight. He reached up and gripped the gutter, which was now two feet behind him, with one hand, keeping his legs and the other hand gripping the downspout for leverage. Once he had a secure one-handed grip, he let go with his legs and swung out, dangling, until he got his second hand fixed on the gutter. He built some momentum, swinging his body, until he built enough speed, and then with a heave threw his legs up onto the roof, pushing with his hands to ensure he stayed there. He took a deep breath, and then turned himself around, facing toward the peak of the steep roof.

Leaning forward, Will moved to the top. He passed the gaping hole and steeled himself not to look into the room below. He'd seen Baker's face, and he couldn't afford that kind of reaction himself right now, not when he needed to focus on getting to his house. Will reached the top, and shifted around so he was backing down the roof towards the inside of the community. When he reached the edge, he gripped the gutter, gently lowered himself down as far he could, and then dropped the remaining five feet to the ground. He knew that he needed to roll into the drop to avoid injuring himself, but the impact still staggered him, and he twisted his right ankle. Ignoring the pain, he took a deep breath, stood, and moved toward the fleet of golf carts, aware that a golf cart would get him to his house more quickly than he could on foot, with or without his injured ankle.

But the golf carts were all in flames. The situation was becoming more ominous by the moment. He'd have to go as fast as he could on foot, with his injured ankle, while wearing the worst possible running shoes. Will ran down the central driveway until it forked five ways. He took the fork to the far left and sprinted towards his house, which was a mile away.

He prayed he was in time to save his wife and son from the fate suffered by the two security guards.

IV
ASSASSIN

Hope Stark sat in her living room, watching and waiting.

It wasn't the ideal method of preparing for a potential invasion force of killers, but it would have to do. It was the best approach available to her to meet her ultimate goal of keeping Josh safe. They could try to run or drive out of here, but they'd certainly be seen or heard by the killers. If the killers had already beaten Will's security system at the gate, they'd be ready for one woman trying to run or drive away from a house while towing a young child. She silently thanked the security guard for sharing information about the killers. She feared he was dead, and hoped that if that were the case, that his death had been quick and painless. She was going to do everything she could to make sure it had not been in vain, and that meant making sure that her son survived whatever was out there. The gun was in her hand, loaded, safety off, a spare clip in her pocket.

Only time would tell if that would be enough.

• • •

The Assassin wove through the forest, staying off the main driveway. Thanks to the fool human guard, the Stark woman would know he was coming, and would apparently have a gun. He didn't like that. There was a chance she could get off a shot while he was still some distance away, and that meant she would have a chance to

34

hurt him. The Assassin didn't like fair fights. He needed to disarm her immediately. He would approach the house unseen, traveling through the thick tree cover of the forest enclosed within the massive walls circling the community. He would enter the house through the rear door, as the woman would no doubt be looking for him out the front. He had ways of defending himself and disarming her, but those methods worked best in close quarters.

He expected the Hunters would be lurking in these trees as well, and he soon spotted them. The men were, for reasons he'd never quite understood nor cared to consider, named after the characters in a human work of fiction known as *The Three Musketeers*. Supposedly the three characters worked together to defend their leader from attacks, which was reason enough for *their* Leader to appreciate the monikers one of their number had suggested. The Hunters enjoyed the names, and nobody seemed to remember what they'd been called before receiving the pseudonyms.

Athos was quite appealing to the ladies, with his handsome face, dark hair, and dark eyes, and the scar across his right cheek — ironically, a gift from Will Stark — only added to the appeal. Athos was the nominal leader of the trio, if only because he was the most sane and level-headed. His gift for knowing when others were telling the truth — even when those questioned did not know *themselves* if they were telling the truth — was incredibly useful as a tool for making decisions during the course of Hunts.

Aramis was the most peculiar in appearance. He'd seen a photograph of a human man wearing a top hat and monocle, and had become fascinated with the accessories, and now it was difficult to get the man to leave the hat off. Thankfully, he'd given up the monocle, at least during Hunts, after his fellow Hunters could no longer take him seriously. He'd compromised by wearing wire-rimmed glasses he didn't need. His wardrobe choices, combined with his white-blond hair, served to make the man look more like an aging professor than a young law enforcement officer. His demeanor, though, was more akin to a member of the Inquisition. Aramis knew every rule, law, and Oath of their organization, and the prescribed penalties for each, and he expected everyone else to know them and follow them with extreme strictness. Aramis tended to react with great emotion whenever someone slipped, as if he'd been personally violated in some fashion by their rule-breaking, no matter how minor the infraction. The mere mention of Will Stark's name could lead the man to convulsions — a fact that The Assassin enjoyed abusing on occasion.

The final member of the trio was the most bizarre in terms of behavior. Porthos wore his brown hair to his shoulders, often tying it back in a ponytail, and liked to wear a dark cloak with an oversized hood. The man believed that such garb gave him an air of ominous mystery when on Hunts. Porthos was the Hunter most at ease mingling in and exploiting human culture and technology, a useful skill for gathering key pieces of data used on Hunts, but a habit which led to the display of many odd human mannerisms, including a lack of filters or decorum when speaking to other Aliomenti. Porthos could find anyone who emanated any of the Energy their group cultivated, tracking it like a bloodhound following a scent. His primary personality quirk — an ease of mingling with humans — led him to often question humans in order to narrow the search area for a suspect, or find some obscure detail that made the Hunts easier to conclude. It was Porthos who had tracked Will Stark to the outskirts of this domed city in southeastern Ohio, and it was Porthos who had unearthed the detail about Stark that necessitated The Assassin's services.

Porthos spotted The Assassin and made his way to the killer. "Nobody's left the house since we got here, so the human woman should still be in there, and you can go blow her up or whatever it is you're planning to do. We'll take care of Stark when he arrives." The man seemed unsure of himself about the last part.

The Assassin glared at him with his blood-red eyes, showing no sign that anything Porthos had said was of any interest. Porthos took the hint and moved away. The Assassin took the opportunity to approach Athos, who was the only one of the three with whom he ever willingly conversed. Athos was a man of few words, at least around The Assassin, and the Hunter reached into his backpack and pulled out a large can that resembled an aerosol spray. He presented the item to The Assassin, and simply said, "Good luck."

The Assassin took the can and did not respond. He didn't need luck.

Hope Stark needed luck.

Actually, it was *Will* Stark who needed luck. Hope would simply die, quickly and painlessly. The rules said that Hunters were to conclude a Hunt with the least possible injury to the fugitive. Given the history between this trio and their Hunted target, it didn't take a genius to figure out that even Aramis was going to make this day one of pure agony for Will Stark. They'd ask for forgiveness later, and their request would be granted. Everyone wanted Will Stark apprehended.

Well, not everyone, not those in the Alliance. They didn't count, though, being Oath-breakers themselves.

The Assassin moved silently out of the small forest and into the Starks' back yard, heading for the back door. A small bit of Energy was sufficient to unlock the sliding glass door from the inside. He slid the door open, smiling in a manner that contorted his horribly scarred face, in anticipation of the final kill of the day. He pulled the sword from the sheath on his belt, in case the woman interrupted his preparations for the gift he was planning for Will Stark, and felt a slight sense of sadness.

It was a shame it all had to end so quickly. He was just getting warmed up.

• • •

Hope heard the back door open as the alarm chime sounded. She held the gun in her right hand, and moved toward the kitchen in silence. The killer would need to move through the kitchen to reach her, and she had no interest in waiting around for him to come to her with that horrible, bloodied sword. She intended to fight him as best she was able.

Hope heard the floor squeak and could verify where the killer was based on the noise. The noise was unnecessary, for the sensation of evil emanating from the man was so intense that she could orient on his location without using her senses of sight and hearing. Taking a deep breath, she leaped into the kitchen and started to pull the trigger.

An unseen force ripped the gun from her hands, leaving her without a weapon. The gun moved straight into the outstretched hand of the man she'd seen in her earlier nightmare. In her dream, his appearance had been terrifying. In person, that same look was incapacitating. The soulless blood-red eyes looked at her, hungry to see the light of life in *her* eyes extinguished in death. His heavily-scarred face showed the untold tale of horror the man had created with his life. The short sword held in his right hand was red with the dried blood of previous victims, most likely including Mark, the security guard.

The man glanced at the gun, and the clip of bullets dropped out of it, disarming the weapon. The killer threw the weapon to the ground. "You won't need that, Mrs. Stark." The man's voice was like ice, and Hope felt the temperature in the house drop as he spoke. The man glanced at the bullets lying on the ground, and Hope watched them shrivel into flattened pieces of metal. "You won't need those, either."

Hope found her voice, at least for the moment. "Who are you? Why are you in my house? I'm calling the police."

"You'll do nothing of the sort." It wasn't a suggestion; it was a command. Though she tried to reach the mobile phone clipped to her belt, the force previously used to pull the gun from her hands now kept her hands up and away from the device. The phone rang, startling her, and she recognized the ring tone for Will. The killer smirked, and the phone dissolved into dust, destroyed by an invisible, crushing force. The force controlling her arms now pulled on her, forcing her into a chair at the kitchen table, where her arms were pinned to her side as she was restrained in the seat.

The man smiled, which had the effect of exaggerating the scars on his face. "That's better. I have a bit of preparatory work to do, Mrs. Stark. I'll explain why I'm here, and then... you'll die." He said it without a hint of emotion, as if the concept of taking a human life had no emotional impact on him. Rather, if her dream had been accurate — and he was the living embodiment of the terror she had seen in her sleep — the man truly relished killing. And she was now unarmed, snared by some invisible force.

After sheathing his sword, the man pulled what looked like a large aerosol can from his pocket. He began to walk along the perimeter of the house, spraying a thin coating of the substance in the can on the exterior walls. Hope watched, confused, as the thin liquid expanded like foam, spreading to cover large portions of the wall surfaces. He exited the kitchen area and moved into the dining room, which sat on one side of the front of the house. As he left the kitchen, Hope felt the invisible force restraining her release, allowing her to move again. She glanced at the gun on the floor with the useless bullets next to it. She still had an extra clip in her pocket, but clearly the man had expected the gun attack. He was likely prepared for the possibility that she'd reload and try to shoot him... and her previous attempt suggested such an effort would be futile.

Her eyes fell on the rack of baseball bats Will kept next to the door, which were used in the batting cage he'd installed in the back yard. If the gun wasn't an option, perhaps another form of attack was in order.

After slipping off her shoes to help muffle her steps, Hope stood, silent on her feet, using her knowledge of the spots in the house which would creak and those which would stay solid and quiet underfoot. She selected one of the wood bats, and crept out of the kitchen in the opposite direction of the killer, still silent as a shadow. She stayed close to the inner wall of the room, out of sight, bat held at the ready. She could hear the killer moving out of the dining room, past the front door. He should be entering the room right about...

Now.

The man stepped into the room, his back to her, still spraying the foaming liquid on to the walls of her home. Subtlety no longer an option, Hope charged the man, swinging the bat with every bit of strength she could muster. The wooden bat shattered into splinters as it hit him full across the shoulders.

He paused briefly, grunted, and then continued his work, as if he'd merely been aware of a bead of sweat trickling down his back.

Hope's eyes widened, and she dropped the bat handle to the floor. She backed away from him, back into the kitchen, where she seized a large knife from the butcher block and returned to the chair she'd been in moments before. Perhaps it was a futile effort at self-defense. She could run now, but the other men from her nightmare were likely out there, waiting for her. If they were here to execute her, she meant to make them work for it. She would do whatever was necessary to prevent them from discovering her child. Running would never do, but delaying the killer from completing his mission might. If she held off dying long enough, Will might arrive at the house with the police in tow. That had the added advantage of her staying alive.

She wondered if the killer would be able to seize *their* guns in the same manner he had seized hers.

The killer came into the kitchen, having finished painting the walls of her home in the foaming substance. He pocketed the can once more, and turned to face her. The look on his face said that her attack with the bat had not gone unnoticed, and would not go unpunished. She made herself glare back at him with as much malice as she could muster.

"Mrs. Stark, the rules say that I am to explain the nature of the crimes committed, and then quickly and painlessly end your worthless *human* life. However, I believe there are exceptions in the rules for termination candidates who strike an Assassin. I shall have to ask for clarification on that point during our review of this mission."

Hope realized that meant he'd make her suffer before dying, regardless of what consequences he might face later.

The killer cleared his throat. "Will Stark has been charged with breaking innumerable Aliomenti laws and rules, though those are of no matter for us here today. Assassins are only summoned forth when rogue Aliomenti violate one or more of the Oaths all members must swear upon joining. The two minor Oaths include willful communication of the existence of the Aliomenti, or the sharing of our advances with the human race. Marriage to a human is considered to be an automatic admission of guilt to breaking those Oaths. For the guilty Aliomenti, the penalty is imprisonment. For the humans who knowingly or unknowingly aided and abetted the violation of these Oaths, the penalty is death."

Hope blinked, as she translated this into more practical terms. "What kind of nonsense is this? You're saying my husband is part of some group that sentences his wife to death? That's ridiculous. My husband loves me, and he'd never join a group like that or swear such a vow."

The Assassin laughed at her. "Your husband is not what he seems, Mrs. Stark. Not only did he swear to those Oaths, it was he who actually *instituted* them and the requisite penalties."

Hope shook her head. "No. That's not possible. You've got the *wrong man.*"

"I assure you, I do not. Will Stark's name and face are the most widely known in our entire organization, and he is the one man whose identity we could never confuse with another. His open use of his given name without disguise may suggest madness on his part, but it does not change who he is or what he has done. All criminals must meet their punishment in the end. Today is the day for Will Stark." He paused. "And for you."

"I'm telling you, you've got the *wrong man.* I've never heard of this alley-whatever group you're talking about. Will's not told me any type of secrets. Let me talk to him. You'll see. You've got the *wrong man.*"

The Assassin laughed at her again, this time with a mocking cruelty in the tone. "Silly *human* girl. Do you think your words carry any weight with us? Save your breath. You have so few remaining."

She considered her next move as he continued talking. "You see, your husband has been something of an embarrassment to our organization. One of our true leaders and innovators, leaving to lead a rebellion that strives to *help* humans? That is *not* acceptable."

Hope thought it *very* acceptable. "Now, see, *that* sounds like Will, always looking to help others improve their own lives. Where can I sign up for this rebellion you spoke of? I'd like to help him continue his noble work."

The Assassin ignored her cheek. "He has many times escaped our attempts at capture, and our Hunters have become quite disturbed. When they learned about you, well...it was as if they had been given a wonderful gift." His blood-red eyes glinted with malice. "*Bait.*"

She stared at him. "What... what do you mean, *bait?*"

"We have heard plenty of stories through our information gathering of Will's deep devotion to you. Even now, I am quite certain he is trying to work through the little obstacle I left at the entry to your neighborhood, as he has no doubt figured out that your life is in danger. And so I mean to show him a dramatic failure in this regard. Not only will you be dead, but your home will be in flames. In his emotional distress at losing you in this fire, he will be an easy target for our Hunters." He leaned closer, smiling. "They have not forgotten how he has shamed them and our group. I dare say the capture will not go well for him." At her look of horror, he laughed.

"And now, Mrs. Stark, we come to the manner of *your* death. Normally, I would simply run my sword through you, directly into your brain, and that would kill you instantly. No pain, for all that's worth. Yet you intended to shoot me with your little gun, and then you actually struck me with that piece of wood. That hurt my pride. Struck by a *human woman?* Such an embarrassment must be repaid. And so instead I believe I will let you die slowly in my beautiful fire, maimed so that you cannot escape. I am uncertain as to whether I should silence you as well, but I dare say it will be far more interesting to have Will hear you screaming as you burn to death, knowing he cannot save you." He moved toward her. "And now, we will see your legs and arms maimed."

Hope pulled the knife from behind her back, blade gripped in her fingers, and hurled it at The Assassin. He was stunned, and though he could move quickly, he could not get entirely out of the way. The blade caught him in the left shoulder, and he roared in pain. If she'd felt his presence and evil before, it was nothing to the malice she felt now, crackling like electricity around her.

He switched his sword to his left hand, and used the right hand to yank the knife from his shoulder. He stared at his own blood, shocked, and then turned on her again, screaming in rage more than pain. "Now you will suffer beyond comprehension!" He raised both blades now, ready to charge her, to... do what, she had no idea.

She caught the blur of white hurtling through the air as the baseball smashed into the man's face, shattering his nose, the already ugly face becoming even more so.

"You leave my Mommy alone, you bad man!" Josh shouted, shaking his fist at The Assassin, the picture of six-year-old fury.

The Assassin roared again and turned on the unknown assailant, and Hope was horrified that Josh had revealed himself. Now he could be hurt... or worse. She'd hidden the boy in his room, buried in his closet under clothes and stuffed animals, with the order to not make a sound or leave until he heard one of his parents calling for him. Clearly, the boy had heard the shouting and had come to protect his mother... just like the voice in his head had told him. Though she admired his bravery and devotion to her, she wished he'd chosen to remain in place. Now she had to prevent The Assassin from killing her son; she'd failed to make sure the man never discovered Josh's existence. She waited for the expected attack on the child.

But The Assassin stared at the six-year-old boy, rooted to the spot and unmoving.

"Go away, bad man!" Josh shouted.

The Assassin finally seemed to shake out of his fog. "Stark has a son." It wasn't a question, yet the tone suggested he wanted it to be. "It's impossible. No Aliomenti can have children. Yet here he is. It's not possible."

Hope took advantage of the distraction and hurled herself into the man, knocking him to the ground. She heard him grunt again as his damaged shoulder slammed into the wood floor. Then he brushed her aside, sending her five feet through the air. She landed with a thud, temporarily disoriented. She was somehow by that same kitchen chair again, with The Assassin getting to his feet near the opening between the kitchen and living room. Josh, who had been in the hallway entering the kitchen, ran to her. "Mommy!" he shrieked, his face shrouded in concern as he hugged her.

A few hours ago, a hug from her son would have been the greatest gift she could receive. Now, she just wanted to get him away from here. But instead, the evil mind of The Assassin formulated a new plan. "I've thought of the *perfect* punishment for you, Mrs. Stark. You'll watch the boy die in front of your eyes before you burn to death." He laughed, a cruel and triumphant sound that reminded Hope of fingernails on a chalkboard.

The laughter turned to a scream of pain.

Smokey had emerged from hiding, and her jaws were clamped around The Assassin's leg. The dog snarled and pulled, as if she were trying to amputate the leg with her teeth. At a minimum, she was causing The Assassin a great deal of pain. The man roared and slammed a huge fist down on the dog's head. Smokey yelped, but didn't let go of his leg. The Assassin raised his sword and jabbed it into the dog's side. Smokey yelped again and fell to the ground, whimpering.

"Smokey!" Josh screamed, and Hope's heart broke at the anguish in her son's voice. He tried to run to the dog, but Hope held him. The Assassin, noting the anguish as well, smiled at the boy and kicked the dog into the wall of the house. Smokey fell to the ground and lay completely still.

"You *monster!*" Hope screamed, while trying to comfort a sobbing Josh.

The boy broke free and sent a withering glance at The Assassin, who, to Hope's surprise, looked somewhat frightened. "I'll kill you for that," the little boy said, his tone the equal in malice to that of The Assassin. The voice was Josh's and yet not, as if from an unrepentant demon, and Hope was startled.

The Assassin took a step back, and then seemed to remember he was being threatened by an unarmed six-year-old boy. He laughed once, and then his face resumed its usual mask of venom. "Foolish boy," he hissed. "I'm tired of these games. This ends *now.*" He took a step towards Hope and Josh, the sword rising above his head, ready to finish them off.

They vanished from his sight.

He'd suffered insults to his pride as the two humans and the dog had fought him; while it was a rare human who could muster the courage to fight him at all, it wasn't without precedent, and some even landed blows that scarred his face before he overwhelmed them. This had been something different. He hadn't known about the boy or the dog, and between the broken nose, the stab wound in his shoulder, and the torn flesh of his leg, he'd taken the worst beating of his career. But he'd gotten through it and fully disarmed them, ready for the kill of not one but two humans — an extra treat — and now he'd been denied that reward.

There could be only one explanation, only one man who could have moved the human woman and child to safety, only one man who could have denied him his kills.

"STARK!" he screamed, so loudly he was certain the world could hear him. His anger and rage boiled up in the form of the flames he could expel from his body, normally at will, but the tongues of fire were beyond his control at this point, as great as the rage that consumed him.

The flames touched the foaming substance he'd sprayed on the walls earlier, concentrated on the rear wall of the house in the kitchen where he was facing. The foam, a flame accelerant he'd developed over the years as a way to enhance his natural pyromancy abilities, was intended to be lit with a tiny spark, the way the Hunters had used it to burn the golf carts at the community entrance. Instead, the substance was ignited with the heat equivalent of a small bomb. The foam exploded, blasting the rear wall of the house into the backyard. The somewhat weaker flames moving toward the front of the house blew out the glass in the front windows. The shrapnel sprayed Will Stark, who had just arrived at the front yard.

The remaining accelerant did what it was designed to do. Red-hot flames blasted into existence, engulfing the entire house in towering streams of fire nearly instantly, so that to an outside observer like Will Stark, it was as if the house had been erased and replaced by a giant bonfire.

The raging fires thirsted for oxygen, and while The Assassin's gift made him immune to the flames, he still needed to breathe. He gasped for air and tried to leave the house, but the loss of oxygen was so sudden and complete at his level that he only made it two steps before he lost consciousness. He fell to the ground, right next to the dog he'd kicked with extreme cruelty only a few moments earlier.

V

ABDUCTION

Will squinted at the wall of flame that was consuming his house, unable to fully open his eyes due to the intense brightness of the inferno. He could not fathom what force or power could engulf a five thousand square foot house in flames as though it were a scrap of paper thrown into a bonfire. What mattered most to him now was determining if either Hope or Josh had survived the initial explosion, and if they still lived amid the raging flames. The earlier news from Hope that Josh had finally started speaking now had a very practical benefit: his son had the ability to call out for help, assuming he still lived.

Will refused to think about any other possibility. He'd search for Hope and Josh until he found them, regardless of their condition or the pain and injury he might endure. He owed them that much for failing to protect them from the horror that stood before him.

He winced still at the pain from removing the overcoat, which had not only pulled pieces of glass from his skin, but had also aggravated his burns, burns that were only getting worse as he continued to stand so close to the burning building. He'd probably be advised to get plastic surgery for the burns after this. He didn't care.

Will tried to look into the house where he'd seen the man with the bloodied sword, the man who'd tried and possibly succeeded in killing his wife and son. The flames were too intense, but he imagined the killer had probably been badly injured or killed in the explosion, and if not, the flames couldn't be doing him any good. It was difficult to feel any sympathy for that monster, though. Will darted to the right side of his house, looking for any semblance of an opening in the flames or walls that would enable him to get inside. He saw nothing but towering sheets of fire. While he didn't particularly care if he suffered additional injuries, it wouldn't do Hope or Josh any good if he was so badly hurt when he got into the house that he couldn't help them get out. If they were already gone... he'd just stay in the house until he joined them.

For now, he'd search.

Will worked his way steadily around the side of the house, spotting nothing resembling an opening in the walls of flame, until he reached the back. It looked as if the explosion had been focused here, perhaps in the kitchen area, for it had taken a large section of the back of the house out. The flames were, if possible, even more intense near the gaping hole than around the front and sides of the house. Will suspected that it was because there was more oxygen here to feed the flames. He could feel the fire touching his scorched skin, and he inhaled a touch of smoke.

Gasping and choking, Will moved further into the back yard, falling to his knees and coughing as he worked to expel the smoke from his lungs. He knew what he needed to do now. He would plunge into his burning home through the now non-existent rear walls to continue his search. Fate would decide whether he emerged.

His lungs finally seemed clear, and Will took deep breaths, trying to flood his lungs with oxygen, and in so doing keep his body from shutting down due to the extreme burns. He stood up, faced the house, and started walking, a look of grim determination on his face.

Two sets of hands grabbed him from behind and hurled him twenty feet through the air towards the forest. Will landed in a heap, his glasses flying off his face well past him, and the just-inhaled air was expelled forcefully from his lungs. He tried to get to his feet, but his attackers began kicking him and punching him, the force doubly painful due to his burned skin. Forced to focus on his own survival, Will tried to pull himself into a fetal position, but the attackers seized his arms and legs and held him face down. The heavy blows continued, fists and boots smashing into him, and he heard loud cracks as bones snapped in his lower leg and rib cage. He lacked sufficient air in his lungs to cry out in pain.

"Stand him up," a voice rasped. Will was hauled to his feet, his shattered legs unable to bear his weight. He saw before him a man dressed in black, with wavy black hair and a handsome face featuring green eyes that glowed with hatred. The man's face was marred by a single scar across his right cheek. The man produced a large knife, more like a small sword, which glinted in the fading sunlight. "Let's see how *you* like this, Stark," the man snarled. Will felt the burnt skin of his face torn open as the attacker slashed him across both cheeks. One of his captors released him, and Will's battered body slumped to the ground; the second man maintained contact as Will collapsed.

Cold water was splashed on his face. "No sleeping now, Stark," the man with the scar announced. "You can't answer for your crimes if you're taking a nap." He laughed. "Aramis, it's your show."

The man maintaining contact shifted around so that Will could see him. The man had blonde hair so light it looked almost white, similar in color to Hope's. He wore wire-rimmed glasses and a top hat. He looked like a dull professor, which suited Will fine as he desperately wanted to sleep. Forever.

The man maintained contact with Will as he spoke. "I, Aramis, along with Athos—" he nodded at the scar-faced man, "and Porthos—" he nodded at a third man, who wore a dark cloak, "hereafter referred to as the Hunters, do hereby charge you, Will Stark, with many crimes, including, but not limited to, the following. That you did knowingly, and with extreme prejudice, provide to humans technological advances developed by and intended to be limited to use by the Aliomenti, and that in so doing you violated Aliomenti Oath number one. That to further this illegal activity you recruited others to your cause, and formed an organization known as the Alliance. And that you did marry the human woman known as Hope Stark, in violation of Aliomenti Oath number three, which carries the automatic penalty of fifty years imprisonment for you and the termination of the human woman, in order to ensure the ongoing privacy and secrecy of the existence of the Aliomenti from humans. How do you plead to these charges, for which we have amassed unassailable proof of guilt?"

The blond man finished his recitation and looked at Will. In his dazed state, Will was only vaguely aware that he was expected to respond.

Will answered truthfully. "What?"

He had to focus to avoid slurring his words, as his brain was working overtime trying to deal with the massive injuries he'd suffered in the past fifteen minutes.

Aramis frowned. "That is not an acceptable answer. How do you plead to the charges?"

Will coughed, spitting out blood. "I don't know what you mean." His voice slurred.

The man in the cloak snickered. "I think you kicked him too hard, Athos. He can't even answer a question now."

"Shut it, Porthos," Athos replied. "Acceptable answers to Aramis' question are guilty or not guilty, Stark. Answer!"

"I plead..." Will paused, and he noticed that the three men tensed at these words, as though expecting something disastrous to happen. But they continued looking at him, and Will completed his thoughts. "No understanding."

Aramis groaned. "Surely, Stark, you are quite aware that you've done every single thing I charged you with, no? Why are you stalling? Answer for what you've done, like a man!"

Will's voice continued to slur. "I don't remember any of the things you're talking about because I don't understand most of what you said."

Aramis slapped Will's face, and the pain nearly caused him to faint. "Wake up, Stark, and stop lying. You've never denied any of this before. Of course, usually you've managed to escape by now, too, but let's not go there. Answer the questions!"

"I am proud to be married to Hope. I don't know what that group is you spoke of, so I don't know what rules or oaths you're talking about. I haven't started any type of groups like what you described." Will wasn't sure how he managed to speak so many words at once in his condition.

Porthos groaned. "Athos, just Read him and get this over with. Screw the stupid rules that seem only to exist to keep us from capturing him. We all know he's guilty anyway."

Athos grabbed him, and Will thought he'd once again get throttled. But the man simply placed his palm on Will's forehead, closed his eyes, and concentrated. When he opened his eyes, Athos looked concerned. "He's not lying. He truly has no memory of anything."

Aramis turned on Porthos. "You *idiot*! Did you actually track the *wrong man?*"

Porthos shoved Aramis, dislodging the top hat, which Aramis stooped to retrieve. Athos and Porthos looked concerned until Aramis donned the hat and resumed his hold on Will.

Porthos glared at Aramis. "I tracked nothing wrong. The Energy reading was off the charts. There's only one registered fugitive with a reading like that, and that's Will Stark. The Energy scent was his. *Look at him*! How can you consider the idea that that man is *not* Will Stark?"

Athos spoke, his voice quiet and uncertain. "He has no memory in his mind of his past with the Aliomenti. That's not to say that the memories have not, somehow, been erased. But he does seem... taller, though."

"Impossible. Nobody has that type of technology." Porthos was adamant, but his face showed doubt.

"There's no way we can know that for certain," Aramis said. "We do not have information on what the Alliance does when it's not fleeing from us. It's not impossible to believe that they've developed just such a technology. We have no one inside the Alliance to report on such matters." His eyes narrowed. "Or *do* we?"

I wish I could move right now, Will thought. *I could get away and find Hope and Josh and escape while they bicker.*

Athos held up his hand, seeming to recognize this as well. "Gentlemen, this is not something we can settle here today. It is, indeed, our assessment that this man is Will Stark in the flesh, if not quite the mind, and that for his past crimes he is at the minimum subject to arrest. Are we in agreement?"

"Thoroughly," Porthos said. Aramis nodded.

"Then I would propose we detain the suspect and return him to Headquarters where he can be properly questioned to determine the extent of this apparent memory loss, and recommendation of final punishment," Athos stated. Then, in a lower voice: "Though I've never been unable to unravel even a cellular level indication of memory before. This is truly bizarre."

Aramis nodded. "I'm in agreement that we are within the rules to detain him. At this point, we've said enough that he's a danger to our anonymity even if by chance this is not *our* Will Stark."

Porthos snorted. "You basically just said that we broke Oath Number 1. Shall we have someone Hunt *us* down and bring *us* in for questioning?"

Aramis' face reddened. "The Oath specifically states that you must *knowingly* expose the Aliomenti. We had, and have, reasonable suspicion that this man is our main fugitive from justice, Will Stark. He knows more about the Aliomenti than anyone, no? It's impossible that we could expose our existence to *him*. He was Aliomenti before any of us!"

Porthos patted Aramis on the arm. "Ease up. I agree with you. But this is very strange. Very strange indeed. It's almost as if..." He paused, looking thoughtful.

"Out with it, man," Athos snapped. "What are you suggesting?"

"I'm wondering if this could be a trap set by the Alliance," Porthos said, frowning. "They know we're desperate to capture Will Stark. They erase or hide his memories and plant him here. Or they just find someone with a similar likeness. Then they sneak into this back yard, and shoot off Energy like fireworks. We show up, and while we're sitting here trying to figure out why Will Stark seems so, well, so *human*..."

"...the Alliance swoops in and captures us," Athos said. He glanced around. "I don't think that's true, but... any Energy readings *now*?"

Porthos closed his eyes, deep in concentration. When he opened them, he frowned. "You mean, outside of the three of us? There is *one* person." He turned toward the woods. "You can come out now, sir."

The Leader of the Aliomenti, a short man with thinning blond hair brushed straight back, emerged from the woods and walked toward the three Hunters and Will Stark. Will noted an odd symbol of gold stitched on the lapel of his expensive suit. The symbol seemed to show a dashed circle inside a solid one, with an upside-down V overshadowing both. There were other symbols, but Will's eyes weren't functioning well enough between the beating and his lost glasses to make them out. "What, precisely, is the delay here?" The Leader demanded. "Why are we not leaving with Stark immediately? Eventually, the human police and fire professionals will get through The Assassin's mess out there and come this way. We cannot risk exposure." He glared at the Hunters. "Well?"

"Sir, we have reason to believe that this may not be the true Will Stark," Athos admitted. "Porthos detected strong Energy here consistent with our favorite fugitive, but he has no memory of anything related to the Aliomenti... and no discernible Energy readings either. Aramis' Damper shouldn't completely eradicate any semblance of Energy from Will Stark, but it has." He took a deep breath. "I'm concerned that this man may be part of a trap set by the Alliance."

The Leader frowned, and turned to the man wearing the cloak. "I thought you could distinguish between Energy given off by different people, and thereby know who you were Tracking? Why did you not sense something different here?"

Porthos shrugged. "There are remnants of Stark's Energy here, and quite a bit of it. Perhaps he simply emptied himself of it, leaving himself without Energy or memories. But there is no Energy coming from him now, and I don't know for sure that that's not because of what happened during our last encounter." He glanced at Aramis and Athos. "He's given off no Energy since then, so his lack of Energy right now isn't a total surprise. I fully believe this is our man; whether he's faking humanness, or had his memory erased, or is employing some other deception, I can't say. But the readings I picked up from far away? Nobody else can crank out that much. This is our guy." He hesitated. "It *has* to be." His face betrayed his doubt, though.

Will's face seared with anger at this. Now, *after* they'd murdered his family and beaten him and burned down his house... *now* they think they might have the wrong person? "You *murderers*," he snarled, as best he could in his battered condition. "You killed them and beat me up because you thought I was somebody *else*?"

"Shut up, Stark," Athos said, kicking him in the ribs. He didn't put as much into it as before, but Will's body had suffered so much abuse that it was agony. "Nobody's going to lose sleep over a handful of human deaths."

"If you were concerned, you shouldn't have broken the rules and Oaths," Aramis said, as if this resolved all concerns. "You have only yourself to blame."

"I have *you* to blame!" Will said, raising his voice as much as he could. "You *think* I'm somebody that your group says broke some rules, and for that you beat me up, kill two good men, and murder my wife and son?"

"Look, I don't..." Athos froze. "*What did you just say?*"

"You killed those guards and my wife and son over a case of

mistaken identity, and you think that's *nothing?* What kind of monsters *are* you people?" His voice was breaking as he realized he was recognizing the obvious, that Hope and Josh were dead, and that he would die as well. He accepted his fate, and felt a strange sensation moving over his body, a sensation that was oddly ticklish. He wondered if that meant his body was giving up.

"*Oath-breaker!*" Aramis screamed. "*How could you?*" The others' faces had paled, though none had fallen to the ground in convulsions as had the odd man in the top hat, who was writhing on the ground several feet away from Will.

Athos looked at The Leader, and once more pulled out the long knife from the sheath on his belt. "Sir, you have heard the confession. Stark has somehow reversed the procedure and managed to father a child. Even Porthos knows the prescribed punishment for that Oath violation."

Porthos didn't even respond to the verbal jab. He simply nodded, and drew his own knife.

The Leader nodded as well. "I had always hoped to reclaim you to our cause, Will Stark." His voice was solemn. "You were the epitome of what our kind could be. But your misguided ideals have been your downfall. And now this. Fathering a child? Violation of the Fourth Oath? You know the penalty for that."

He glanced at Athos and Porthos, who stood ready with their knives, and nodded, turning back to face Will. He looked Stark squarely in the eye. "I, Leader of the Aliomenti, hereby sentence Will Stark to death for violating the Fourth Oath, the Oath forbidding having children. The child we can assume destroyed by our Assassin and his fire, which is the lawful punishment for the offspring."

The Leader breathed a deep sigh, and glanced at the Hunters. "Kill him."

Athos and Porthos, on opposite sides of Will's prone, battered body, plunged their knives straight down at Will's chest, aiming directly for his heart.

The knives clanged off an invisible barrier, sliding off Will's body, leaving him winded but otherwise free of further injury.

Both Hunters stood up instantly, looking around with suspicion.

"The Damper is off!" Porthos shouted, looking at Aramis' figure rocking on the ground.

"It's a trap!" Athos screamed. "Aramis, on your feet!"

The man did not stand; rather, he rolled back to Stark's still-prone figure, drew his knife and pounded it repeatedly at Will, shrieking, "Die, cretin!" His stabs were no more successful than the others, sliding off the invisible shield protecting Will.

"Where *are* they?" The Leader shouted. "Porthos, *where are they?*"

"I'm not detecting *anything,* sir! There's no indication that there's anybody using Energy nearby!"

Will felt the tickling sensations on his body suddenly solidify and grip him in a tight cocoon, and then the cocoon pulled him feet-first into the ground. His last vision before the dirt filled in overhead was the look of absolute shock on the faces of the four men left above.

VI
RESCUE

The silver-colored vehicle shimmered in the faint light of the Stark family's basement. The craft looked similar to a small car without wheels, suggesting an alternative form of transport. The top dissolved away, revealing occupants inside filling three of the four seats. All three moved from the vehicle without speaking, their faces showing determination and focus.

A young woman with shocking red hair and violet eyes, wearing a one piece body suit of deep green, walked several steps toward the back of the house, where Will Stark was being kicked and battered by three assailants. She stared at the finished wall, and a giant hole suddenly appeared, as if an invisible drill was being operated. Dirt, roots, and bits of rock flowed into the basement, covering the carpet with debris.

A man with short brown hair and brown eyes, wearing a similar bodysuit of pale green, examined the exterior of the craft, looking for any sign of damage. Satisfied that the craft was sound, he attached a small device to the ceiling above him; the device looked somewhat like a mobile phone. Once the device was planted, he climbed back into the vehicle and began adjusting a series of dials.

The third occupant, a man with jet-black hair, wore wraparound mirrored sunglasses, matching the color of his bodysuit. He grabbed a small backpack and sprinted for the stairs leading to the upper levels of the house, donning a device over his mouth and nose as he moved.

The man looked around for several items as he reached the first floor, breathing clean air purified by the device worn on his face. He retrieved the gun that The Assassin had taken from Hope Stark, as well as a clip of ammunition the woman had dropped during the altercation. He grabbed a spare set of eyeglasses worn by Will Stark. He also spotted the baseball Josh Stark had thrown at The Assassin. He hesitated, then added the baseball to the collection of items in the backpack and zipped the bag closed.

He walked to the unconscious form of The Assassin, and a look of pure rage contorted the visible parts of his face. He kicked the man's side, snarling "*That's* for my wife." He stomped on the man's chest, and the sound of ribs breaking could be heard over the crackling flames. "*That's* for my daughter." He spied the black Labrador only a few paces away, and kicked the killer in the face, watching his nose shatter in a spray of blood. "And *that's* for the dog." After donning the backpack, the man with the sunglasses knelt down, picked The Assassin up, and threw him over his shoulder.

As he stood, the man noticed that the dog was still breathing. A smile curled his lips. The animal seemed to sense the attention, and her tail twitched briefly.

He sprinted down the steps to the shimmering vehicle in the basement, and kicked the rear of the vehicle. A panel opened, revealing a large storage compartment. He threw The Assassin's unconscious form into the trunk, making no effort to prevent the man's head from slamming against the sides of the vehicle, and kicked him roughly into the compartment until The Assassin fit into the confined space. The trunk lid slid closed silently. He tossed the backpack in the front seat and turned around, racing back toward the steps.

The brown haired man noticed the movement. "Fil, where are you going? We need to be leaving, not sightseeing. It's too dangerous up there."

"One more trip, Adam. Can't leave any evidence behind."

"Why didn't you get it all on the first trip?"

"I had two hundred pounds of Assassin on my back. And this is a special bit of evidence."

He ran up the steps back to the first floor, the oxygen mask back over his mouth and nose, but not before he heard the woman shout out. "Adam! He needs a shield, *right now!*"

"On it, Angel!" Adam replied.

Fil reached the first floor, and sprinted to the gravely wounded dog, grateful to see that she was still breathing after his brief excursion to the basement. He gently picked her up in both arms, careful to avoid any excess pressure on the badly wounded and burned animal, and walked slowly down the steps, careful to avoid making any sudden movements that might disturb her. The dog's muzzle twitched, and a scratchy tongue reached out to the man's face in a silent, wet expression of canine thanks.

The dirt continued pouring into the basement from the hole Angel had created as Fil returned to the lower level. A moment later, the immobile form of Will Stark emerged through the hole in the basement wall of his home, floating through the air toward the vehicle. The woman named Angel moved her hand, and suddenly the dirt began moving back into the hole in the wall, filling it back up.

Fil sat down on the front seat, still holding the wounded dog, as Will was gently deposited in the back seat. Fil turned to face Angel, who sat in the back, her arms protectively shielding the battered man. A tear streamed down her face. "I wish we'd protected him sooner," she said, her voice choked with emotion.

"If we'd protected him sooner, the Hunters would have been alerted to our presence," Fil replied. "It was his unfortunate role to play in his own rescue."

Will, barely conscious, saw the dog lying on the lap of a young man wearing what looked like sunglasses. "Smokey," he whispered, his voice barely audible. "You saved Smokey. Thank you."

The dark-haired man merely nodded at him.

"My wife, my son... did you save them, too?"

The young man shook his head. "They were already gone."

Will wept, his burned face remaining dry. His body had lost all of its moisture, and he could no longer produce tears.

The dark-haired man turned toward the young woman. "Angel, he needs deep sleep, but he needs to remember this when he wakes up."

She nodded. "Got it, Fil." She reached into a bag near her feet, studied the contents, and removed a small vial of fluid. She looked at Will. "This will help you sleep, but you'll need to swallow all of it for it to work." Will nodded, opening his mouth, happy to be relieved of the pain for even a short time. He swallowed the fluid poured into his mouth, grateful for the promised sleep.

He would have swallowed it faster if she'd told him it was poison.

Fil looked at the man next to him. "We need to leave, Adam. Now. They'll figure out where we are soon enough."

Adam nodded, and as Will drifted into a deep sleep, a cover formed over the top of the vehicle, blocking out everything outside. The last thing he remembered seeing was the woman's right hand, raised to indicate something to the men. He was only vaguely aware of a golden tattoo on her palm, a tattoo with three intertwined dashed circles.

The incendiary device Adam had planted outside on the ceiling was started using a remote inside the vehicle. The readout showed five minutes, and started counting down.

• • •

Porthos looked around, trying to make sense of Will Stark's incredible disappearance. "It's the Alliance. It *has* to be them. Why can't I sense where they are? That... that... that vacuuming Stark into the ground trick, that was *not* minor Energy usage." He was frustrated, effectively rendered blind to a target he knew was out there.

"I don't know how they did that, but the fact that they pulled him into the ground suggests he must be nearby," Athos said, glancing around. "Perhaps they're in a secret chamber nearby? Or another house in the area?"

The Leader turned and looked at the burning building. "Or perhaps it was a means of getting him back into his *own* house?"

Athos started sprinting toward the building, followed closely by Porthos. "The basement!" Porthos said, catching on. "They're pulling him into the basement!" Aramis ran as well, and the Hunters vanished into the flames and smoke of what remained of the Starks' house.

The Leader walked closer to the house, but did not go in. He would leave the heat, smoke, and discomfort to his Hunters. He saw a scrap of paper on the ground, picked it up, and gasped in shock. He hid the paper in a pocket, fighting to control his emotions. The revelation from the paper, and its implications, would need to wait until later for processing.

Athos entered the burning house, stunned at the intense heat and low oxygen levels he encountered. The basement suggestion from

Porthos was sound; it would put Stark in the nearest structure to his departure point, and in the spot best protected from the flames. Upon spotting the steps, he sprinted to them and raced to the bottom, with Porthos close behind.

Athos looked around for some sign of Stark or members of the Alliance, suddenly aware that he'd be quite vulnerable to an attack right now. He looked around and then spotted something entirely different: a huge hole in the wall nearest to where they'd been standing outside. What truly caught his attention, though, was the dirt. The hole in the wall was strange enough, but at least it would explain dirt in a pile on the ground nearby. But in this case, the dirt was flowing back *into* the hole. Athos stared, wondering how that was possible.

Porthos reached him, his jaw agape at the sight of the dirt. "If we're right, Stark came in through that hole. The question is, now that they're filling it back up... where is Stark?"

Aramis reached them, likewise puzzled by the sight of the moving dirt. "No ambush by the Alliance down here, then?"

Athos shook his head. "No. They're gone, if they were ever here. Stark has escaped again. We need to get to The Leader and leave before the human police and firefighters spot us. We're in danger of exposure here."

The men paused for a moment, trying to determine if there was anything else to be done while inside the building. Athos noticed a strange noise. "What's that sound?"

The Hunters whirled around, searching for the faint beeping sound. Porthos found it. "It looks like a clock."

"What's a clock doing on the ceiling?" Aramis asked. "And why is it counting down from ten seconds?"

Athos sucked in a breath of air. "That's not a clock. That's a bomb!"

The three men teleported the short distance to the backyard, no longer concerned that the Energy usage would alert the Alliance to their presence.

The incendiary bomb detonated, exacerbating and reactivating The Assassin's accelerant. The remaining flames burned with renewed and increased vigor, and only moments later the spot in the basement where the Hunters had stood was covered in ash and dust, the only remains left of the entire Stark home.

● ● ●

Michael Baker had heard the explosion and had seen the flames. He shook his head. Will Stark had been a fool to run to his house after that killer. Now he was probably dead — given the timing of his entry into the neighborhood and the explosion — along with his wife and son. He couldn't imagine that any of them had survived.

When the fire trucks arrived, everything was in a state of chaos at the entry to the De Gray Estates. Crime scene investigators had photographed the Guard Tower and Guard Station from every angle, the shards of glass on the entry driveway, and the two dead bodies, and were diligently looking for any type of clue as to the identity of the killer. A fingerprint, a lock of hair, a strand of clothing. They'd finally released the bodies of the two guards to the coroner. When the fire trucks arrived they'd needed to wait to sweep the glass, and then realized that they needed a guard to open the gate, due to the biometric security features. They waited nearly twenty minutes until the man had arrived, pale and understandably jittery at the scene of chaos and word of his colleagues' deaths. The off-duty guard had seen the flames in the distance as well, and shook his head. "We lost good people today, didn't we?" Baker could only nod.

He rode behind the fire equipment in his cruiser, in no hurry to arrive at the home of a man he considered a good friend. Will and Hope were friends to many and friendly to everyone, their generosity and kindness legendary in the domed city and surrounding communities. He didn't want to rush to the house as he knew there was nothing he could do to help them now, and he had no great desire to locate their bodies... and he most certainly did not want to find the body of their six-year-old son, a boy the same age as his *own* son. The confirmation of their deaths would have a devastating effect not just on this isolated community or the domed city nearby, but the entire country as well. Will Stark was the symbol of the slowly emerging economic recovery. His death was not an omen they needed.

He rounded the final bend and pulled up at what remained of the Stark home. It was a scene of complete destruction. Nothing remained standing or intact except for the concrete foundation walls and floor. Every wall, every piece of furniture, every personal belonging, and every person — all had been reduced to nothing more than dust and ash. The only good news was that the fire had been confined to the house, and they'd avoided the chaos of a forest fire inside the massive walls of the community.

Baker shook his head, still too much in shock after the events of this day. Investigative teams would secure the area, but it was too dark to see anything, even if they could bring in portable lights. Clearly, there was nothing left to see. They'd all be back out here tomorrow morning, and he'd be here with them, trying to figure out what had happened.

He walked to the fire chief, who was staring at the destruction in disbelief. "Any chance of survivors?" He knew it was a ridiculous question, but felt he needed to ask.

The chief shook his head. "None, Michael. Not unless they got out before the fire started. We'll be lucky to recover any remains, let alone find survivors. If the explosion and flames happened as you described them... anybody inside would have been dead almost instantly, either from the blast or the heat. Given the level of destruction I'm seeing, this is clearly arson, and the arsonist used some type of chemical that made those flames spread rapidly, and burn at an incredibly high temperature. I'm guessing the explosion means that everything happened faster than the arsonist expected."

"Meaning...?"

"Meaning that our arsonist probably turned to ashes in there as well."

Baker nodded, and his expression was grim. That meant they'd never get answers as to why all of this had happened, why at least six people had died in this neighborhood today, counting the two security guards at the entry to the community, and the killer arsonist.

He shook his head at the tragedy of it all. "Call me if they find anything tonight," he told the chief and the lead crime scene investigator, without really meaning it. He climbed into his cruiser and headed back to the station, wishing he could go home to his wife and son instead, and hug them just a little tighter than usual.

VII
DEBRIEF

The Aliomenti Hunters and Leader watched the police cruiser leave the human community where Will Stark's home had once stood. They were safely hidden in the trees on the opposite side of the road near the entrance to that community, having exited without being seen by any humans, emergency personnel or otherwise. Like other advanced Aliomenti, they possessed many incredible skills, including short-range teleportation. Those skills enhanced their ability to exist in the human world without being discovered.

Athos wondered, in hindsight, if they should have used teleportation to enter the neighborhood. Having The Assassin kill the guards as planned did have a number of benefits, the most important being that they'd used no Energy getting inside. That meant Will Stark would have no idea where they were or if they were even involved. Since neither guard had been able to alert anyone to their presence, they'd significantly reduced the chance that anyone would see them. The fact that Stark's own security system had prevented the human authorities from entering the community to come to his aid — and potentially seeing the Hunters — was deliciously ironic. Stark had seemed truly stunned by the fire. Somehow, though, he'd contacted his Alliance friends and gotten his memory thoroughly erased, and everybody had gotten away.

Again.

He sighed, mentally reviewing the details of the plan as the

Hunters and Leader walked back to the hotel suite they shared. It had seemed the perfect plan, as flawless as a plan could be against a powerful, resourceful criminal like Will Stark. But The Leader would undoubtedly blame him for the failure, citing poor planning, or poor execution of the plan. Stark wasn't in custody, and thus the Hunt had failed.

The four men arrived at the outskirts of the hotel on foot, staying in the shadows, and then teleported into the suite. They couldn't travel far with teleportation. Teleportation was an Energy-intensive skill, with demands increasing exponentially as the travel distance grew. That was, in fact, another of the reasons he elected not to use teleportation to get into the neighborhood. The Hunters needed to be fully charged to deal with Stark. He hadn't wanted to use it to get back *out* of the neighborhood, either. They had a small transport craft, capable of near-invisibility, waiting outside the fortress. Once they'd subdued Stark, Athos had planned to summon the robotic craft to fly them all out, and they would board a private airplane back to Headquarters. The eventual use of teleportation was forced by circumstance; the sirens of the fire engines and police cars were getting too close, and they couldn't risk being spotted.

Athos spoke immediately. "Sir, I just wanted to say—"

"Silence," The Leader said, his face drawn. "I was *there*, Athos. The plan was sound. It was executed correctly. The Alliance clearly has some power unknown to us, and that is what they used to remove him from our clutches."

Athos was relieved. "Sir, I... thank you."

The Leader ignored him. "If you had told me the tale and I'd not been there, I'd likely have had you imprisoned for lying. But I saw it with my own eyes. We must deal with the reality of what this encounter with Stark means for our future."

The Hunters were tense, concerned about where The Leader might go with this.

"My first question is this: where is The Assassin?"

Porthos blinked. "He hasn't contacted you?"

"Clearly not, since I asked," The Leader replied, his tone one of scathing exasperation. "I am wondering if any of you saw him in Stark's house when you entered."

Athos opened his mouth to speak, and then closed it. He hadn't thought to look. "I saw no one in the house. That's concerning. We should have seen the bodies of the woman...and the alleged child. The fire was more intense on the exterior walls than on the inside; it was difficult to breathe, but it wasn't so hot that the bodies of the two humans would be burned to ashes."

"How much of the house did you search?"

"We were focused on looking for Stark on the way in, sir, and we teleported out before the fire bomb went off. We saw a large portion of the first floor and the entire lower level. There was no sign of anyone in the portions of the home we viewed."

"I was a bit slower to the lower level, where we'd surmised Stark had been taken," Aramis added. "As Athos said, there was no sign of any human or Aliomenti in the house. So the only possibility is that they were killed on the upper floor..."

"...or that The Assassin failed to kill them," The Leader finished. At the looks of incredulity on the faces of the Hunters, he continued. "I think we have to consider the possibility that an Alliance that could save Stark, in the manner we saw, would certainly be capable of saving his wife and child as well. If that is the case, The Assassin fled, or he was captured as well. This is a disturbing development."

Athos frowned. "They couldn't have gotten to the house that quickly; Porthos would have detected them. And the hole Stark used to enter the house—"

"And there's the issue, Athos," The Leader said. "We don't *know* if Stark ever entered that house after leaving our sight. We *assumed* it. Porthos," he turned to the man with the cloak, "did you detect any Energy readings inside?"

Porthos frowned. "No, I didn't. Well, let me correct that. I detected very *faint* traces of Energy, but they were fading, as if..."

"It was as if whoever left those traces had disappeared, wasn't it?"

Porthos shook his head. "Not possible. If they'd teleported away, even just a few hundred yards, the residual Energy left behind would have hit me harder than those flames. It was as if there were a few distinct Energy users, but they either left a long time ago, or they leaked so little Energy that they never *did* anything. They would have been neophytes, just learning to sense Energy, given the intensity I detected."

"I agree with your assessment, Porthos. It's another piece of evidence of what I believe happened." He paused, considering. "Let's move back in time a bit. Stark is distraught at the sight of his house ablaze, and is easily subdued, just as planned. Aramis Dampers him, and the three of you vent some frustrations on him." He scowled, and the Hunters quailed at the look, but The Leader merely continued. "Stark pleads ignorance, and drops the bombshell about having a child. Athos detects he is telling the truth. Porthos detects no Energy."

Porthos nodded. "He was dry as the desert."

"Yet, only moments later, he is rescued in what can only be considered a miraculous fashion. I've seen no telekinetic power strong enough to pull a man into the ground... and if it were, the result would likely crush the man... or suffocate him. Why did none of us detect any Energy during the time when our blades couldn't puncture the man and when he vanished into the ground? Surely such a feat would require an enormous amount of Energy. But none was detected."

Aramis nodded. "This goes back to the earlier point. There's no Energy in the basement of the house, which is where Stark most likely ended up after he was taken. But we see no one in the house, detect no Energy. This is very wrong indeed."

"On the contrary, it all points to two assumptions we're making, and one of those assumptions is clearly wrong. The first is that Stark's rescue, and the lack of any bodies in the house — living or dead — means that the Alliance is involved. I don't think we can disprove that this is the case; indeed, I rather think it *must* be the Alliance."

The Hunters nodded.

"But the second assumption is that the rescue could have happened solely through a massive expenditure of Energy. What if the Alliance had no need to use Energy to effect this rescue, and as such we only detected very trace amounts of leakage, rather than the massive spike we thought we should see?"

The Hunters considered this. "So, you're suggesting that the Alliance has developed technology that can do this?" Athos asked.

"Precisely. It fits, doesn't it? And because we had no awareness of this technological advance, we were chasing Energy bursts that didn't exist, and it gave them time to escape while we did so."

Porthos looked puzzled. "The concept seems to work, but I'm at a loss to explain what type of technology could do everything we've seen today. Is it possible rather that they've developed something that can mask Energy so it can't be detected?"

The Leader considered this concept. "Perhaps. In either case, the Alliance has clearly developed *something* advanced, and it is this *something* which enabled Stark's escape."

Aramis spoke up. "There's also the possibility that Stark manipulated us rather badly. And by us, I mean *me* primarily. When he made his... confession, I dropped my concentration levels, and as such my Damper was released. Stark may have regained sufficient Energy to do what we saw without help."

The Leader frowned. "Explain this in more depth, please."

"Consider: I have the Damper on. We have him trapped, and our focus is on finally subduing him and taking him back to Headquarters. Then he drops his bombshell. I lose my concentration and drop the Damper, Athos and Porthos lose their cool, and Stark quietly uses his Energy reserves to construct a shield against our blades and pulls himself away."

Athos shook his head. "Couple of issues there. First, you had the Damper on when I Read him. He couldn't have used Energy at the time, and as such he couldn't have used Energy to fool my Reading of him. He had no memory *anywhere* in him about his past dealings with us. Secondly, if your Energy is back, and you're Will Stark, why bother with deflecting knives and burrowing into the ground? Why not just teleport far away?"

"The man had been beaten pretty badly. His Energy reserves were undoubtedly being tapped for healing. He couldn't spare the Energy for something like a teleport at that point."

"And if he'd used Energy, even for healing, let alone his burrowing trick, I would have known immediately," Porthos snapped. "Nice try, Aramis. Your theory only works if Athos and I are both simultaneously unable to do our jobs while you're crying on the ground like a baby. Good cover."

"Shut up, Porthos!" Aramis snapped, turning red.

"Make me, tough guy. Oh look, Aramis, there's somebody saying they broke an Oath. Time to throw a fit!"

"Ahem," The Leader said, and the two Hunters were immediately silent, though they did glare at each other.

"We do need to consider Stark's claim of fathering a child," The Leader said. "Simply put, we have no direct, concrete evidence to prove or disprove the claim. There were no bodies seen in the house, and we'll need to monitor the local news reports for the next few days to see if any bodies are located, or if they at least reference a child as missing or deceased. The humans will know the truth of his claim of parentage. We may hear reports of five or more bodies found in the house by the human authorities."

"Five?" Porthos asked, arching an eyebrow.

"Stark. His wife. The alleged child. The Assassin. One or more Alliance members helping Stark." The Leader raised a finger as he listed each individual. "We could hear of five or more, or we could hear of four presumed deaths if the human authorities conclude that the Starks and their killer all perished in the fire and burned beyond recognition."

He paused. "But I doubt that any bodies will be found, regardless of the state of destruction of the house. You see, The Assassin cannot be harmed by fire. If they find *no* bodies, it means The Assassin wasn't in the house when you left right before that bomb went off. They'd find everything else in ashes, save for one man's body, dead or unconscious, and unmarked by fire. If we hear reports of something like that, my opinion will change, but until then, my conclusion is simply this: the Alliance has everyone that was in that house, living or dead. Stark was pulled from our grasp, The Assassin hasn't contacted us, and a body hasn't been found. He wouldn't hide from us, even if he thought he'd failed. No, the only explanation is that the Alliance has him. And they have Stark. More than likely, they have Stark's family as well, living or dead." He shook his head. "I've no idea yet of what technology or Energy skill the Alliance used to make Stark seem so *human*, but it's clear that everyone's abilities here are still working correctly."

He pounded his fist into the table. "I don't like this at all. It makes me feel so... *human*."

The Hunters shuddered.

"Sir?" Athos said. "With this new technology... what do we do now?"

"Continue to seek them out. You will need to travel more, move around frequently, and try to catch them unawares. There is no need for subtlety of action now. The order to avoid harm to fugitives is revoked; subdue first, harm to render unconscious as needed. We need our people to see these criminals return and admit to their wrongdoing, however it is that we get them back. We cannot sit back again and wait for them to make a mistake, or for our previous detection systems to work. We must seek them out, and stop them immediately. Their technological gains are troubling."

He glanced at the men, whose faces were full of determination, mixed with concern. "Go."

They vanished from his sight.

The Leader pulled out the scrap of paper he'd retrieved outside the Stark house and sat at the desk in the hotel suite. He glanced at the photo of Hope Stark in her wedding dress, her blue eyes radiant. Hope's joyful expression did not carry over to The Leader. The man looked sad, as if he might shed a tear. But then he slammed the photo down on the desk.

He'd verify later the news the photo seemed to convey, but the evidence seemed clear.

"You *lied* to me, Will Stark. *No one* gets away with lying to me."

VIII
CLEANUP

It had been a long day, and Gena Adams was exhausted.

Despite that, she was happy to have a job in this economy. It gave her the opportunity to earn her own way, no matter how meager those earnings might be. Still, working twelve hour shifts at The Diner had a negative impact on her feet and legs; she felt like an old woman instead of a twenty-year-old engaged to be married.

Gena limped into her apartment building on the outskirts of Pleasanton, outside the Dome, having walked the final mile here after the bus dropped her off. She was grateful that the bus ran as late as it did, and more so that the owner of The Diner always ensured that she caught the final bus, even if they were still in the midst of their final closing rounds. It was another reason she was happy to have a job; her boss took a personal interest in her, though thankfully not *too* personal. Mark wouldn't like that one bit. She smiled. Mark was possessive and protective of her in that way, and it was one of the many reasons she loved the man.

The apartment wasn't much, but they needed to save money for their wedding, and an eventual down payment on a house. They were willing to live more simply now so that they could reach those goals in the future. They had only one old car as well; Mark's job as a security guard required it as the bus lines didn't go near the private community where he worked. She supposed the rich people who lived there didn't want to see the poor folk go by on public transportation.

She walked to the second floor landing of the building and unlocked the door to their apartment. She was surprised to find that the lights were out, as Mark usually arrived home before she did. Only then did Gena realize that she hadn't seen his car in the parking lot. Perhaps he'd gotten stuck at work; he occasionally got some overtime when his shift replacement was running late, and she figured that was the situation here as well.

She flipped on the old television set, switched to the twenty-four hour news channel for background noise, and looked for something to eat. Most people found it odd that she worked at a restaurant and came home to eat, but after being around that particular cuisine for such a long period of time, Gena needed the variety.

"Our top story tonight: America's billionaire philanthropist, along with his wife and son, die in a massive fire at their home in southeastern Ohio. More details just ahead."

Gena froze. There was only one man who would be described that way, and that was Will Stark. Mark worked as a security guard in the neighborhood where the wealthy man lived with his family. Gena wasn't partial to rich people in general, but the Starks had been exceptionally kind and generous towards Mark, and she found herself tearing up a bit at the news of their deaths. She realized that this news explained Mark's absence; he'd likely be part of interviews to ascertain what had happened, and that's why he was running late. She checked her phone, but didn't see any texts. That was odd; usually if Mark knew he was running late he'd let her know.

"Authorities say that the home, located in an exclusive gated community outside the domed city of Pleasanton, Ohio, burned rapidly and trapped the occupants inside. Also killed in the fire was the suspected arsonist. Police aren't sure if arson was the primary motivation in the attack, or if the arsonist used the fire as a means of enforcing other demands, including potentially demands for a portion of the Stark family's massive wealth.

"Regardless of the motive, the nation has been deprived of one of its few true bright lights in recent years. Stark famously started his medical data mining company as a means of showing insurance companies where fraud and double billing were occurring, and provided true actual costs for medical services, devices, medications, and other supplies. After the insurance industry began using the data to reduce payments to medical practitioners, Stark made the data available to everyone, and the forced transparency of actual costs dramatically cut the price of

medical care in the country, making Stark a wealthy man in the process. He later invested in other businesses, including the building materials company which popularized creating panels of all sizes, shapes, and colors with nanomaterials, building components which are smaller than human cells.

"After several attempts on his life and aborted kidnapping attempts in his home town of Chicago, Stark relocated himself and his business headquarters to the small southeastern Ohio town of Pleasanton. Finding the city nearly deserted and bankrupt, Stark bought the town, razed and rebuilt its aging infrastructure with new technology, and enclosed the entire city in a dome created from nanotech components. The explosion of innovation, growth, and entrepreneurship in the once-bankrupt town has energized the entire nation.

"A well-known philanthropist, Stark is famous for giving away hundreds of millions of dollars in and around his local community, and he and his wife, Hope, have traveled the world seeking to aid and inspire others to success and prosperity.

"Will Stark was thirty-five years old. His wife, Hope, was twenty-eight. Their young son, who suffered from various developmental disabilities, was only six. Our thoughts and prayers go out to his grieving friends and community."

Gena allowed the tears to flow during the on-air eulogy. Stock video showed the massive walls encircling the community of mansions, and the buildings housing the two on-duty guards looked small in comparison. Live video, taken as darkness had fallen, showed still-glowing embers where the home of Will and Hope Stark once stood. Gena wondered how the arsonist could have gotten inside.

Unless... no, it couldn't be.

The phone rang.

Gena picked up the phone, her hand trembling. "Hello?"

"Is this Gena Adams?"

"Yes, it is. May I ask who is calling?"

"Ms. Adams, my name is Michael Baker, and I am with the Pleasanton police department."

Gena felt her heart drop in her chest. "Is something wrong, Officer Baker?" She tried to keep her voice steady, through some misguided notion that if she pretended nothing was wrong, then nothing *would* be wrong.

"Ms. Adams, have you by chance heard the news about the fire earlier today that took the lives of the Stark family?"

"I just got home from work and saw it on the news. It's awful, isn't it?"

"Unfortunately, Ms. Adams, they weren't the only ones who

71

perished today. I'm very sorry."

Her heart raced, and she began to breathe in gasps. "I... I don't understand. What are you saying?"

"I'm very sorry, Ms. Adams. The perpetrator killed both security guards on duty at the time in order to gain entry. One of them was Mark Arnold. I'm very sorry for your loss, Ms. Adams."

Gena choked back a sob. "No. It can't be him. We're getting married next month. He can't be gone! You've got the *wrong man*! I'll come down to the police station or the morgue or wherever and *tell you* you've got the wrong man! It's somebody else!" She was sobbing now, shouting in an attempt to hide the tears and shock and horror at the news she'd received.

The police officer let her finish, and then spoke in a calm, quiet voice. "I wish that were the case, Ms. Adams, but it is not. I'd strongly advise you not to come identify him; remember him as he was. There are others who can handle the official identification." He paused. "Goodbye, Ms. Adams. I truly am sorry for your loss." He hung up, leaving Gena with her tears and overwhelming sense of loneliness.

Mark was gone. She'd known it the moment the news story had ended. There was no way into that fortress of a community except through the gate, and that's what Mark guarded. He took his job seriously, and while he didn't care much for the other residents of the fortress community, she knew that Mark adored the Starks. He would do anything to protect them if they were in danger, even take a bullet if he thought it would protect them. In her grief, she experienced a brief sensation of pride at his bravery and heroism.

What possible motive could there be for killing Mark and then going after the Starks? The police had no leads in the matter, according to the story on the news. She figured it had to be money. Why else would they go into that community? Over the past fifteen years, with the Second Great Depression in full force, the inevitable envy and anger towards those not suffering through the miserable job markets had its most common expression in the form of armed kidnappings of members of wealthy families. It seemed from her perspective that about half of the kidnappings ended with the death of the victim, and the other half with the ransom being paid. From that perspective, she completely understood why Will Stark had built the massive walled community and developed such strict security. He didn't want anyone coming after his family.

Unfortunately, though, the walls had failed to protect them. Somebody had been willing to *kill* to get inside that fortress. But why? Surely it would be easier to get at the family *outside* the community, without the walls, gates, retinal scanners, and guards in the way. She didn't know if the Starks traveled with any type of bodyguards, but it still seemed to her that it would be easier to attempt a kidnapping-for-ransom in a location that didn't require entering a military-grade security system. Yet this criminal hadn't done anything of the sort. Perhaps the Starks had something on hand that the arsonist wanted, something valuable enough to risk the security gauntlet.

Her breath caught in her chest at that moment. For she remembered *him*, and suddenly she knew exactly who it was who'd gone after Will Stark.

The man had come into The Diner just a few days ago, ruggedly handsome, with his long brown hair pulled back. He'd been wearing a cloak like she'd commonly seen in old science fiction or fantasy movies, complete with an over-sized hood. The mystery of the man started with his name, a nickname which he said he'd been given by his boss. It was the name of a character from a well-known piece of literature. Something with a P. Pinocchio? No, that wasn't it. Poseidon? No. Gena snapped her fingers. Porthos. That had been the man's name.

They'd chatted, and he'd told her the story of a powerful amulet, a stone likely to explode with disastrous consequences in only a few days. It had been buried decades ago, and his team of explorers had positively identified the underground location as being just inside the walls of the Estates. His search was for a TV show, he told her; they were filming a pilot for a new series about professional treasure hunters, and she'd be on TV telling them about the current community situated on the ground covering this dangerous amulet. They'd talked about the need to dig this trinket up to prevent a disaster, though Gena didn't think the man truly believed that part of his research. He just wanted to dig the gemstone up because it would do wonders for the ratings of his fledgling program.

The conversation had shifted to the residents of the community, and naturally to the Starks. He'd seemed surprised to hear that there was a *Mrs.* Stark, actually. As they'd departed, he'd thanked her for her help and let her know he'd be talking to the Starks in a couple of days.

They had spoken two days ago. Which meant his "conversation" with the Starks would have been... today.

"He made it all up," she whispered. "The treasure... they were just after Stark the whole time. They just wanted to get to him."

"Very good, Gena."

His hand was over her mouth before she could scream. It was *him*, the man in the cloak. She hadn't heard him come in the door, hadn't heard him at all until he'd spoken. It was as if he'd just appeared out of the air right behind her.

"You may not believe this, Gena, but the man you and other humans revere, the man called Will Stark? He's broken his word, violated oaths he has sworn, and put the lives of many immensely powerful people at risk. And for what? So he can teach a little kid how to hit a baseball? You see, Gena, Stark *had* to be eliminated, before he became even more bold and brazen. He might reveal just how *talented* we actually are. And we can't have *that*."

The man she knew as Porthos was suddenly in front of her. Her hand went to her mouth in horror. He hadn't actually moved. He'd simply vanished behind her and reappeared in front of her.

"You killed Mark," she whispered. "You killed Mrs. Stark. You killed their little boy. Whatever you're doing or whoever you're protecting, is it truly worth it?"

"I personally killed none of them. The man responsible is missing in the chaos at the Stark house. I understand that he threatened to kill *you* if Mark didn't cooperate. Mark tried to fight him to protect you and the others, foolish though that was. So there are things worth fighting for, and things worth dying for, aren't there?"

Gena's eyes filled with tears. Mark had died fighting a killer, fighting to protect her and others. *That* was the man she loved.

Porthos looked right at her. "And just as there are things worth *dying* for, there are things worth *killing* for."

The blade was in his hand and slashing at her before she could scream, and he was gone before she hit the floor, never to rise again.

IX
TRUST

Millard Howe had been waiting for the hordes to descend.

When word got out that his client, the multi-billionaire Will Stark, had been killed in a fire at his home, and that his wife and son had died along with him, people made the expected polite noises of sadness and sorrow. A great humanitarian, they said. Impossible to replace in the business community. He was far too young. Terrible thing, the death of a child. The words were mere blather to Howe, because he knew what they *really* cared about.

What, exactly, would happen to the Stark family's vast wealth?

Howe knew how the game was played. He knew that those speaking with the most reverence about Stark — and especially those who used the misdirection of speaking more about his wife or son — were hoping to get the public behind the idea of a sizable portion of the estate in the hands of their particular organization. Advocacy groups and charitable foundations ramped up advertising efforts, as if such work would get Will or Hope to call and make a donation from the grave, as if some type of popularity contest would decide where the money would end up.

More practical types wondered what would be left to distribute. Many believed inheritance taxes would reduce the size of the estate to just exceptionally exorbitant, rather than the current mind-numbingly exorbitant. Others wondered about the fate of Stark's companies. Would the hundreds of thousands of people working for Will Stark in some fashion find themselves without jobs, the companies collapsing into failure without his insightful leadership? Would taxes and estate claims force the sale of those companies, leaving them under new management, and again risking jobs as new owners looked to slash costs to recoup their investments? The stock market dropped notably the first two days after Will's death was announced, as investors worried about these questions and the ripple effects that might follow.

Gossip web sites had a field day, speculating that one or more long-lost Stark relatives would emerge and claim the entire estate by right of genetic inheritance. More serious thinkers derided such theories. Both Will and Hope were well-known to be orphaned long before they even met, and any more distant relations had died out as well.

It all came down to the estate plan, and that meant eventually the media would find the Stark family's estate lawyer, Millard Howe. The emails started arriving in Howe's inbox less than thirty-six hours after news of the fire broke. Phone calls came shortly afterward. Howe found it impossible to get any work done that day, and even more impossible to leave his office and drive home through the throngs of reporters seeking answers.

Howe finally issued a press release, stating that the estate plan documents providing direction on the disbursement of the Stark estate had been stored in an ingenious fashion, so as to prevent any possibility of, or speculation about, tampering. Howe noted that he had urgent business to complete, but that he'd be traveling via plane three days later so as to retrieve the materials. Much to his surprise, the media left him alone. Apparently, watching an old lawyer work for three days prior to leaving for a trip to parts unknown wasn't seen as exhilarating for the average television viewer.

With media silence finally assured, Howe left his office early that afternoon so that he could leave on his journey as darkness began to fall. He'd be gone and back long before the three days were up, hopefully without being seen and without disclosing the secure hiding spot for the hidden documents. Howe crept out of his house in the early evening as darkness fell, glancing around to be certain he hadn't been followed, and made his way to a rickety old shed. He threw open the doors, revealing a workshop-style garage, where he'd been restoring a vintage 1998 Ferrari convertible. No one had ever seen him drive it. The license plates were from a different state. Stark had given him the car as a tool to use in this exact occurrence: Will's death coming after Hope and Josh both predeceased him. Will expected that such a scenario would be difficult for his attorney, and Will made sure people who worked for him had the fewest possible obstacles in achieving their goals. Thus, Millard Howe had a secret old automobile with a traveling bag and a map.

His first instruction from Stark had been quite simple: should the scenario occur, he should open the trunk, use the old fashioned paper map to drive to the location indicated, and use the key — also in the trunk — to enter the building he found there. At that point he would be able to retrieve the materials from their storage location, and carry out the terms of the Stark family's estate plan. He knew the specifics, of course, having written the document himself with the guidance and direction of Will and Hope. The actual document would be needed to ensure that he could carry out the plans without being questioned as to his own involvement in the process, which would be quite extensive.

Howe checked the map, avoiding the temptation to verify it using mapping software; no doubt some hacker out there was tapping any type of Internet activity or GPS searches from his home, just in case the crafty old lawyer decided to show his hand early. The map revealed a spot in West Virginia, roughly a four hour drive away. Naturally, he'd stored up gasoline over time — another suggestion from Will — so that he could make the trip to and from without needing to stop to pay for gasoline, refilling as needed with the fuel cans. After ensuring the thirty-year-old vehicle was topped off on all essential fluids and that tire pressure was optimal, Howe got in the car and drove, passing the domed city of Pleasanton and heading for the West Virginia border.

Four hours later, Howe pulled up to a building which looked abandoned, miles from the nearest highway or paved road. The locale was thoroughly isolated, showing that Will Stark liked privacy and security even in death. The lawyer got out of the car after pocketing the key, and looked around. He was reminded of old Western movies featuring abandoned towns, fully expecting to see a tumbleweed or two roll past him.

Instead, he heard a click and felt the muzzle of a gun at the back of his head. He hadn't heard anyone approach.

"State your name." The voice was stern without being threatening, enabling Howe to respond rather than stumble.

"Millard Howe."

"Why are you here?"

"My client directed me to come here in the event of his death."

"Who is your client?"

"Will Stark, and his wife, Hope, as well."

"Mr. Howe, what subject did Mr. and Mrs. Stark discuss first upon meeting each other?"

Howe smiled. "Architecture. Specifically, they talked about the plans for the house he wanted to build in Ohio."

The gun was lowered. "Thank you for your patience, Mr. Howe. We have had our instructions to follow here as well, and that started with ensuring that nobody arrived here that we did not expect. Please, follow me."

He followed the man into the building, noting that the door had no lock and would withstand little more than a gentle breeze anyway. Did that mean the key was useless? The man, who had brown hair and eyes, appeared to be in his late thirties or early forties. As Howe expected, the inside of the building looked much like the outside: run-down. The man turned and smiled. "Best way to avoid too much suspicion is to make people think there's nothing here worth hiding. Then they won't look." He walked to a wall, moved his hands over the surface as if trying to identify a specific location, then placed his palms on the wall. Howe heard a gentle tone, and the wall began sliding into the floor. Behind the wall was a door, which the man opened. He gestured for Howe to follow him inside, which the lawyer did with some reluctance. Howe was quite mindful of the fact that his host still possessed a gun. The fact that he was walking through a hidden doorway into a dark tunnel filled with some type of mist or fog was no less concerning than the weapon.

"What am I walking through?" he asked. "Is it mist, or fog? Have we somehow gone back outside?"

The man chuckled. "No." He didn't elaborate.

The tunnel was completely devoid of sound and light, and Howe was unable to see his host after several paces into the mist. Concerned he'd walked into a trap, the lawyer wondered if he should turn around and head back. Then he realized that with no visual aid to guide him, he had no guarantee he wouldn't spin himself in circles.

With no reasonable alternative, he continued moving forward, his hands balled into fists, anticipating a possible attack.

After a few minutes, Howe emerged out of the mist into a small room, light and sound returning with sudden abruptness. He blinked, acclimating to the light, and made note of his surroundings. Though minimal in square footage, the room was clearly of modern construction. The primary feature was a square table large enough to seat three people per side, polished to a glossy finish. The walls included numerous television screens. Tablet-style computers were available near each seat at the table. It looked to be a modern office conference room, though there was no sign of any type of projection device or speaker phone for outside calls.

Curious. And still quite concerning.

Howe looked at the man who'd guided him to this room. "I was told in my instructions that I'd be able to retrieve a copy of Mr. and Mrs. Stark's estate plan, including their last will and testament, once I arrived. May I have it, please?"

"I don't have it."

Howe's face paled. "Then why was I ordered to drive here?"

"I don't *have* it. I didn't say you couldn't *retrieve* it." He handed Howe a piece of paper.

When the Starks and Howe had sat down to draft up their plans, they were deeply concerned about theft and modification. Though kidnappings for ransom were the most common forms of attack against more prosperous citizens, forgeries of wills were gaining in popularity. Thieves would use an apparent robbery to hide their true purpose, which involved locating, altering, and replacing original copies of wills with alternates in which they'd be awarded with financial payoffs. The forgeries became sophisticated enough that several managed to succeed. The Starks wanted Howe to keep a copy of the final document, which was stored in a wall safe in his office. The Starks kept a copy in their own home. A third copy would be kept in a secured location, which Howe wouldn't learn about until after he actually needed it, the location stored on the map in the restored car. The intent was to retrieve all three copies, compare them, and ensure that there were no discrepancies. In this fashion, there could be no question as to whether the working copies were valid and true to the Starks' actual wishes.

Howe read the paper and noted the instructions. He was to send emails with specific subject headings from three of his email accounts: personal, business, and an account he used solely to communicate with the Starks. He was to order the text he received in reply in a specific order: the order of importance in life the Starks would place on the usage of the account. Once the text was assembled he was to decipher the text using the key.

Howe frowned. He sent the emails to the rather obscure addresses. He received two responses from each: one a message containing random jumbles of characters, and a second letting him know that the accounts had been locked and could never be accessed again. That meant he could never repeat the process and replace the messages if something happened to the originals.

He thought about the Starks, and where their priorities in life would be, and it was quite clear what the couple would consider the highest and lowest levels of importance. They considered one's family to be the first priority, and always considered themselves last. Howe used a word processing program to paste the text of the emails together, first the one sent to his personal mailbox, then the one sent to his work account, and finally the one sent to the account used only with the Starks.

Decipher the text using the key. Howe frowned. Typically, a key of this type meant a string of characters used to decode an encrypted message, but he didn't have anything like that. Or did he? Howe removed the key he'd brought from the trunk of the car and studied it more closely. He noted a random string of characters etched into the key, and smiled. Very clever. He brought up an Internet site that could encode and decode text using an encryption key. He pasted the encrypted message into the website and entered the key... and there was the official document.

He glanced at the brown-haired man. "Excuse me, sir. What is your name?"

"My name is Adam."

"Adam... what?"

"Just Adam, sir."

"Oh." Odd. "Adam, is there a means by which I can print out copies of this bit of text?"

Adam nodded, and showed the lawyer how to connect to a printer he hadn't previously noticed. Howe printed off several copies, in the event the original printout was damaged. While waiting, he turned back to Adam. "So, what is your connection to the Starks?"

"I manage the data center used to secure and store sensitive data processed in their businesses."

"What does that mean, exactly?"

"Some of the data processed by the Starks' companies is unusually sensitive, in particular those dealing with health and medical billing analysis. The company publishes sanitized and synthesized information — how many bone fractures occurred in Chicago in May, which zip codes show the most treatments for drug addiction, the actual number of hours spent performing an appendectomy across the country. That's the type of information that's useful in setting market prices, and letting different providers compete on cost, letting consumers shop around, and so on."

"OK, makes sense."

"To get that type of data, however, we need the raw, actual data. The data that says that Joe Smith, living at a specific address, with a specific birthday, had a very specific medical procedure performed at a specific location, by a certain specialist. That data cannot be seen by the public at large."

"Why not?"

"The most obvious answer is that there are privacy concerns if others can view your medical history. Think of it this way, Mr. Howe. Could you think of certain medical prescriptions other attorneys might be interested in learning that you took? Something they might use to suggest to prospective clients — indirectly, of course — that you might not be the best choice for them?"

Howe thought about that. "I see your point."

"That level of raw data is too raw for general use, even by our corporation. If the stakes were high enough, one of our analysts could be bribed to run reports seeking lists of medical procedures performed or prescriptions written for everyone who happened to have exactly the same characteristics that you have. A fishing expedition, if you will. They would be able to figure out that private information, or at least have a high degree of certainty that it applied to you. We store that very raw data in a top secret location, and use exceptionally robust security controls to make sure that only our systems can query that data, and even then the query must be of a certain level of generality. The servers here have been taught to recognize searches that are clearly trying to find data about a single individual. Those queries are denied unless specific protocols and procedures are followed that makes it clear that there is some appropriate use."

"Such as?"

"Generally, lawsuits that need a very fine sliver of data to prove or disprove a legal point. There was a case not long ago trying to prove that a company was generating an excessive amount of a specific chemical, and that it was disproportionately impacting residents who lived nearby, by greatly increasing their risk of a certain illness. To prove that point, their attorneys needed to show that there was, in fact, a disproportionate level of that specific illness near the plant. Those searches would look like someone trying to find one person in most localities, because the disease was so rare in most zip codes you'd only find one person at most meeting the description. But we were able to override and let the system provide the information."

"But that means there are still people within the company who could override the system and be subject to those bribes you mentioned earlier."

"The only person who has that authority is the CEO of the company. Until a few days ago, that was Will Stark. I don't think bribes would work on him."

Howe frowned. "No, but perhaps threats might..."

Adam arched an eyebrow. "You think the attack on his home was because he refused to cooperate with an illicit search?"

"Possibly." Howe decided he'd look at that angle later. "Since you manage secure data, it's probably advisable that I leave a copy of this with you." He handed Adam one of the printouts, which the man accepted. "No doubt there will be people who don't see the outcome they want from this. I'd hate to think my original copy of the document and this copy might be stolen or destroyed. We already lost the copy stored at the Starks' home. Is there a secure means of transferring a copy off-site electronically? So that I can print more copies if needed?"

Adam smiled. "Literally? No. Anything that can be transferred can always conceivably be stolen. But we can make a copy of the document which cannot be modified, and you can take that with you, along with the paper copies you've printed."

Adam provided him food and refreshments for his journey back, along with a small portable storage device with the promised read only copy of the will documentation. The supplies enabled him to make the journey home with minimal stops, and he pulled back into his own home at around three in the morning. Exhausted after the events of the day, he finally slept.

Howe woke only three hours later and went straight to his office, and was able to slip inside before members of the media arrived. He locked the electronic copy of the will in his desk, and the remaining printed copy in his wall safe, and went to take a shower and don a fresh set of clothing. Exiting the shower, he retrieved the copy of the will stored in his desk. Then he finally sat down and reread the will.

Essentially, all of the family's assets were held in a legal Trust, with control of the Trust being invested in a Trustee with the power to change the investment portfolio or spend available cash as desired. The Starks had stated publicly that they wanted to give a large portion of their accumulated wealth away to worthy endeavors over the course of their lives and beyond, with small amounts retained for future generations of Starks.

Due to the influence such a position would hold, there was a desire to keep that role within the family. Therefore, the Trustee position came with a documented line of succession with a level of complexity worthy of a constitution. In its simplest form, the role of Trustee had been held by Will Stark (which he'd legally shared with Hope as a co-Trustee), and was to pass to Hope in full upon his death, and to Josh upon the deaths of his parents. Each acting Trustee had the authority to modify the line of succession as they saw fit, which meant that Josh, upon taking the role, could name a future spouse or children as his successors. Each Trustee would control hundreds of billions of dollars' worth of cash and other assets, with the ability to influence those decisions from beyond the grave by their choice of successor, and as such each Trustee would wield enormous influence.

This familial line of succession concept had flaws, as monarchs throughout the history of humanity had discovered. The Trust and estate documents made some effort to recognize and address those flaws, but they didn't address everything. For example, the documents didn't provide guidance about what to do in the scenario that both Will and Hope died before Josh was old enough to assume control. That possibility was no longer of concern, though the thought that a six-year-old boy would be in charge of billions of dollars of cash and assets was frightening.

And though it addressed the circumstance of having no named successors remaining on the death of the current Trustee, the documents were still confusing to Howe in terms of what to do in such a circumstance. That was unfortunate, because he was in that circumstance today. The parts that he understood unnerved him. The parts that he *didn't* understand frightened him.

The estate documents stated that there would be two Advisors to any non-family Trustee forced to take the role in the event all family and named successors died before finding and naming replacements. One of those Advisors would be the family's current estate attorney. Him. He'd be responsible for guiding the decisions of the new Trustee, and could veto any he felt went against the documented points of guidance established by Will and Hope.

The second Advisor would operate in secret, and would only become involved in circumstances where the Trustee or primary Advisor had become challenged in their ability to make decisions unencumbered by personal circumstances.

In other words, the third person could freeze the checking account of the Trust if the Trustee or Advisor was being compelled to act by outside forces.

The thought that such an event might occur was troubling to Millard Howe. Just as troubling was the fact that he had no idea who was supposed to fill the role of this hidden Advisor. His documentation simply stated that this hidden Advisor would make themselves known to the Trustee in a fashion that only the Trustee would understand.

He sighed. He rather wished that the will had simply stated that all assets be sold and given to designated charities. The Starks wanted their fortune to be disbursed over time, and recognized that they could not define the best means to do so in a static document. They needed people they could count on to give that money away in a manner that would meet their approval. Howe leafed through other documents, and found the list of guiding principles for investing and granting funds. When word got out that they'd provide cash grants to people who met their criteria, they'd be flooded with requests. Thankfully, the Trust provided for ample salaries for Trustee and Advisors to ensure that they'd be able to dedicate themselves fully to the role.

There was nothing left to do but contact the new Trustee. Howe had always gotten the impression that the Starks were uncomfortable personally making the request to fill the role. They said that they feared their top choice would call himself unworthy and turn them down. Though they talked about getting over the fear and speaking to the man, the lawyer believed that he was going to be the one to break the news, and only after the Starks were gone. Suddenly, walking through a mist-filled tunnel with no sound or light seemed like a minor part of this job.

There was no time like the present. It was time to call the Trustee and give him the news. Good or bad news, Howe wasn't sure. But it would be a shock. He found the man's number and dialed.

"Pleasanton Police Department. This is Officer Baker."

"Officer Baker, my name is Millard Howe. I'm the legal counsel managing the estate of Will and Hope Stark."

There was a pause. "Hello, Mr. Howe. What can I do for you?"

"Mr. Baker, I am currently reading through the will the Starks prepared and filed with my assistance."

"I see. I've heard on the news that there's a lot of speculation and a lot of greed on that front. I don't envy you the job. Are you calling to request police protection while the estate is settled?"

"No, Mr. Baker. I'm calling to tell you that you are part of the settlement."

This time, there was a much longer pause. "I'm what?"

"I had understood that Mr. Stark had already spoken to you or was planning to do so, but it sounds as if he was unable to complete that step before... well, before it was necessary for me to do my job."

"What are you trying to say, Mr. Howe? I don't want anything from the Starks, other than to bring them back to us."

Howe realized the Starks had made an excellent choice for their Trustee. The best man for the job would be the one who didn't want it.

"I fully agree with your sentiment, Mr. Baker, but alas I lack the ability to make that particular dream a reality. However, you are named in the estate and I wanted to speak with you in person about what it says. Can we set up a time to meet as soon as possible?"

The officer sighed. "I'm off duty tomorrow. Can we meet first thing in the morning?"

"I'll make sure my calendar is cleared."

Two days later, Millard Howe did not depart to retrieve the estate documents as previously announced to the media. Rather, he held a brief press conference explaining the goals of the Trust as stipulated by the Starks, outlined the role of the new Trustee, and introduced a still-stunned Michael Baker as the man chosen by the Starks to fill that role. Howe identified the guiding principles the Starks had written for the use of the assets in the estate, and indicated that those who believed that they met those criteria could file a written request for funds.

Howe noted that the funds were secured in such a fashion as to make it impossible for either him or Baker to spend anything when under direct or indirect outside pressure. He noted that the Starks specifically wanted others to avoid the constant threats of kidnapping and violence they'd lived under, and as such wanted it made quite public that any efforts to compel them to act against the wishes of the Trust simply could not be met.

He intentionally left out the part about the third person in the group, the one who could freeze all assets. No sense exposing that person to the public, too. He couldn't reveal the person's identity even if he'd wanted to do so.

Neither Howe nor Baker had any idea of the person's identity.

X
SURVIVOR

Will felt the pain almost before consciousness returned.

It was intense, but tolerable, more of a dull headache than a raging migraine. He knew now that he would live and survive the injuries suffered from the events of last night. Had it been last night? He had no way of knowing how much time had passed since his world had faded into darkness, since he'd watched his house burn with his wife and son inside. His son had finally spoken his first words after over six years in complete silence, and he'd never hear the boy speak, never know the joy of his laughter.

He remembered the conversation of the men who had attacked him and prevented him from entering the burning house. His ironic laugh was internal. By hurling him away from the house and beating him, they'd probably saved his life from his foolish bravado and thoughts of rescuing the two most important people in his world.

More interesting about the conversation was the doubt expressed at the end. They'd called him by name, told him that this death and suffering were his fault. He'd protested his innocence, and they'd laughed at him, fully convinced of Will's guilt at whatever imagined crimes they'd charged him with. Then the doubts began. One of the men stated emphatically that Will had no memories of the crimes he'd been accused of, and his tone expressed uncertainty. What had changed his mind? A second man, who hadn't let go of Will until his convulsions over news of Josh's existence, stated that Will had no

Energy, a term spoken with special reverence. The third man, the one wearing the cloak, had agreed. This lack of energy or Energy added further doubts over his identity, and thus his guilt.

Was it possible? Were the deaths of his wife and son, the destruction of his home, the murders of two guards, and his own savage beating the result of a mistake? Was there truly another man out there with his name and likeness who had survived this encounter as Will and his family suffered?

The physical pain had lessened, but if anything, the emotional trauma had gotten worse.

The faces of Hope and Josh flashed before his eyes. The shining blue eyes of Hope, with a similar though faded glow appearing in her son's icy-blue eyes. What had his eyes looked like when he'd finally spoken? Had they started to twinkle as Hope's often did? He'd never know, now. Any chance of saving them from the fire had vanished. He cursed himself for accepting the sleeping potion from the young woman rather than insisting on being allowed to search his home, all the while recognizing that the effort, while noble, would have been futile.

He tried to convince himself that it had just been an awful nightmare, that the physical ache in his body was the result of an overzealous workout. He'd run a mile in unforgiving dress shoes, after all, in the chilly winter air. That might explain it. Yet the run had preceded the awful events that followed, and so if one had happened, so had the other.

He imagined playing baseball with his son, and tried to picture the smile spreading on his face as he hit a baseball for the first time. He saw his look of joy and pride as the two played catch in the backyard, just like millions of other fathers and sons. His dream was somewhat hollow, though. Josh should be laughing, talking to him in this dream. Yet he had no idea what his six-year-old son's voice sounded like. He'd never heard Josh laugh. The boy had never seemed to experience enough joy to laugh, nor enough pain to cry.

In the end, there was only one reality, one he'd carry for the rest of his life. He'd failed them. It was his responsibility to protect them from harm. And they were dead because of his failure, dead because of three crazed lunatics who'd beaten and detained him in his backyard, dead at the hands of another man who'd been dispatched to murder them and burn down their house. He could still see the bald man's head, the sword dripping with blood, presumably staring at the people whose lives he'd just ended. He wondered the purpose of the explosion and fire. Perhaps, in their twisted minds, they'd meant to send Will a message. After all, they seemed content to simply beat him before learning about Josh. Perhaps the fire was intended to be a message to stay away from them and their stupid rules.

That was their mistake. Will Stark was not a quitter. He'd regroup emotionally and physically and then he'd fight with everything he had, just as he had always done. He'd spent much of his life building his dream, finding his true love to share it with, and then they'd started a family to expand on the love they felt for each other. That part of him was gone. He'd never remarry, that much he knew, no matter how long he lived. Hope was the only one for him, and he'd never find anyone else like her, not if he looked for a thousand years. He'd failed Josh too, and therefore he'd never let himself have another child. That was his penance for his failure, to live the rest of his days alone, focused on a singular purpose.

That purpose was simple. He would find the men responsible for these crimes and ensure that they'd never hurt anyone again as they'd hurt him. No more innocents would die at their hands. They said they were part of some strange group, with a name he couldn't quite recall, and an odd symbol including a couple of circles. That was their mistake. He didn't need much information to get started, and he'd not rest until he'd destroyed them.

Resolved to the new purpose for his life, Will opened his eyes.

He was lying on his back, resting on a table in the middle of a room. The walls, floor, and ceiling were all the exact same shade of white. With no furniture other than his makeshift bed, and nothing on the walls, it was difficult to determine the actual size of the room. It didn't help that he'd never gotten his glasses back after the men had thrown him across his yard.

He blinked, trying to focus his eyes, but it didn't change what he could see, fuzzy though his vision might be. There was nothing on the walls. There was nothing *in* the walls either. There were no windows or doors. It was as if he'd been built into a box as he slept. Had he been rescued from harm from one group, only to be a prisoner to another? There was no indication that he was in danger just sitting here; the air was pure. Air? If there were no openings in the walls — no windows, no doors, no vents — how was he getting air to breathe?

The red-haired woman, whom he remembered was named Angel, walked through the walls as if stepping through a waterfall. No opening formed in front of her, and none was left behind her. She simply moved through the wall as if it was a mere illusion. Will relaxed just a bit. At least he knew he could get out of this building.

Wait. Did she just walk through the wall? It must be an illusion, something I'm seeing because I don't have my glasses anymore. There's really a door there that I just can't see.

Angel walked to him, a smile forming on her face. In spite of the events since his arrival at the gates of the Estates yesterday, despite being trapped in a room with no visible exits, despite watching a woman simply walk through a wall... somehow, Will felt complete calm in her presence, all sense of fear melting away. The loss of his fear, though, returned his attention to the physical pain in his body.

Angel sat on the edge of the table next to him. "Mr. Stark, I'm glad to see that you're awake. We gave you some fluids designed to help you achieve a deep sleep, and that's what you're waking up from now. The sleep enabled your body to do some healing, which is why the pain should be somewhat reduced from where it was when... well, when we picked you up." She rested a hand on his arm. "I do apologize, though. We could have given you something a bit more potent, and healed you of your injuries, but doing so might have led you to believe that what you experienced at your home was just a very bad dream. The pain was necessary to leave in place, at least somewhat, so that you could not deny the experience." She handed him a pair of glasses. "It would be helpful if you could see clearly, however."

Will accepted the pair of glasses, and breathed a sigh of relief as the world snapped back into focus. He winced at the effort. "Thank you. I don't think I can move well just yet. Are you a doctor? Is this a hospital room? And how is it that you just walked through that wall?"

She looked puzzled, and then nodded. "Of course, that would be something different for you. Let me answer your first two questions. I'm not a doctor, and this is not a hospital. But this is where you will recover from the wounds you suffered at the hands of the three Hunters. Not many human men—"

"Wait," he interrupted. "What are Hunters? And why did you refer to me as a *human* man? Isn't that redundant? Those men, the ones who did this to me, they kept referring to my wife as human, but acted like I wasn't. They said it like I knew what they meant." He took a deep breath. "I have no idea what they meant, or why they did what they did." He looked at her, and could read the sympathy on her face.

"I know you don't," she said. "I'll just say that they believed what they said to be true, and with that being the case, they acted according to the rules and laws of their organization." She frowned. "They acted on them despite the fact that those rules are wrong."

He frowned, and wished he hadn't. His face was still sore. "What about my other questions? The wall, the Hunters, the human this and that...?"

She smiled. "Mr. Stark, you have found yourself in the crosshairs of a great battle you had never been aware of until you arrived home and discovered that your family was in danger. There is much you need to learn, and you will have all the time you require in order to do so. But first, you must regain your health."

He shook his head, ignoring the pain. "I can't. I need to go after those men. I cannot sit back and let them walk free after what they've done. If you can help me to heal, I would certainly appreciate your assistance, and I can pay you. I need to get out of here. I need to go after those men. I can't let them... I can't let them do to someone else what they've done to me and my family."

The man with the wraparound mirrored sunglasses entered the room as Will finished speaking. Angel continued as if unaware he'd joined them. "Mr. Stark, I appreciate your passion and love for your family, but if you walk out of this room and try to go after those men, you will be captured and jailed and likely killed by them before the day is out. You must regain your health, and you must learn why it is that they came for you and your family. Do not throw your life away in a rash attempt at bravado."

Though he hated to admit it, he knew she was right. He needed to heal up. But that didn't mean it needed to be here. "I appreciate your advice, and I agree that I need to recover. I'd prefer to do that with my own doctor, where I can start my own hunt for these men. I'm happy to pay whatever you ask for the care you've provided and the rescue... wait, how did you get me away from them?"

The man, called Fil as Will remembered, spoke up. "Mr. Stark, I will be blunt. The world believes you to be dead, killed in the fire that took the lives of your wife and child. If you suddenly reappear, the world that believes you are a great hero will suddenly become suspicious, that perhaps you survived because you orchestrated the entire event. You would also advertise..."

"Now wait just one moment!" Will snapped. "How *dare* you suggest I had anything to do with what happened! I'd give my life right this second to give either of them a chance to live, and..."

Fil raised his hand, and Will noticed a strange, golden symbol tattooed on his palm. "Mr. Stark, I'm aware of your true and noble sentiments in that regard. The reality, though, is that public opinion is easily swayed, and usually in the manner that would see a shining star fall. People cheered you as you rose to great heights, but they will cheer louder as you fall. You are best served remaining with us, and getting your revenge from the shadows. The attacks those men perpetrated were so successful because of the element of surprise. What better element of surprise than the attack from one believed dead?"

Will opened his mouth to protest, then realized the man was correct. "Then I am dead, and I have no means of repaying you. I will work—"

"Mr. Stark, we have no need of money," Fil replied. "As for working, you are in no condition to do so. Your job at present is to heal, and to listen, and to learn. I ask only that you keep an open mind. What you hear will seem impossible, and you may think us liars in telling you what we do."

"I've just watched two people walk through walls," Will replied. "Unless my battered memory is wrong, three men tried to stab me and failed. I was pulled into and through the ground in my backyard. I don't believe any of that is possible. Yet I saw and experienced all of those things. I don't have much choice *but* to have an open mind."

Angel smiled. "A very practical philosophy, Mr. Stark."

"Please, call me Will."

"I feel more comfortable calling you Mr. Stark. Is that acceptable?"

Will shrugged. "Suit yourself."

The woman continued. "I also ask you for your patience as we move forward. You may want answers to questions, and find that we will not provide them immediately. This is not because we wish to keep you ignorant of the answers, but because some questions need more context before answering. Deal?"

Will nodded. "Deal."

"Mr. Stark, what we tell you will be told to you in confidence. In time, once you understand everything, you will have the opportunity to use those lessons to help others. Many, *many* others. But we must have your assurance, your oath, that you will not share what you do not fully understand, but not hoard forever for yourself what you *do* understand and believe could benefit others. Do I have your word?"

"I'm not sure I understand what you mean. I'd rather not involve myself in an oath... wait a minute." He frowned. "The men who attacked me, the Hunters, they said I'd broken an Oath or Oaths. What was that about? Is that what I'm doing now? Making an Oath that will make people kill me, or people that I care about?"

"The Oaths *they* spoke of fall into the 'be patient now' category," Angel replied. "We will explain them in due course, and how they came to be, but there are other lessons and goals to reach first. The Oath I am asking you to make is different. Think of it as the core Oath, if you will. Here's a simple analogy to explain what this core Oath means. Suppose that you were the first person to discover fire. Perhaps you were walking around after a thunderstorm one day, and you found a burning branch. If you were to pick up that branch and run into your village, and then into someone's home made of dried sticks, would that be helpful to them?"

Will frowned. "I suppose yes, it could be, but they'd be at risk, too."

"Why?"

"Because that burning branch might catch their house on fire." He winced, as the memory of his own house on fire, and what it meant, was still fresh in his mind.

"Exactly. Though you may have the best of intentions, it would eventually cause them great harm. Yet after some period of time when you truly understood fire — how to create it as needed, how to control where it burned, and so on — denying that knowledge to those in your village and hoarding it for yourself would be a selfish thing to do. I wouldn't do that, and I doubt you'd do that either. Rather, you'd share it so that others could stay warm, and cook food, and protect themselves from the wild."

Will waited for more, but Angel remained silent, simply watching him. "That's it? Teach people about fire, once I understand it well enough? Don't keep it to myself?"

"That's it."

"*That's* the Oath I was attacked over?"

"There are four Oaths that those who attacked you are concerned with. This is not one of those four, and in fact I doubt those who attacked you even know about this one. This is the Oath at the heart of our group; it sums up our philosophy and the distinctions between our group and theirs."

Angel paused, noted Will's look of understanding, and resumed. "To continue the analogy used before, we are a small portion of the population of the world, and our group is the only one that has figured out how to manipulate flames. The philosophical question for you, Mr. Stark, is this: do you wish to be part of the group that wants to keep that knowledge here? Or do you wish to be part of the group that gradually educates the rest of the world about fire and its safe usage?"

He smiled. "Call me Prometheus. Fire for everyone. I'll abide by that Oath."

"You swear it?"

"I do."

Fil nodded at Angel, and then turned and left the room, vanishing through the wall.

"Seriously, how are you doing that?" Will asked, his curiosity piqued despite his pain. "Is the wall an illusion?"

Angel laughed. "No, it's not an illusion. It will be explained to you. But right now..."

"Right, right, focus on getting healthy, I know." He sighed. "I just wish I could set it all right. Make it so that none of it ever happened."

"We can't change the past, Mr. Stark," Angel said. She rested a comforting hand on his shoulder. "If your roles were reversed, and it was Mrs. Stark here with me right now instead, what would you want to tell her? What would you want her to do?"

"I'd want her to be happy," Will said, without hesitation. "No more and no less. In whatever form that would take."

"Your wife loved you as you love her," Angel said, her voice quiet. "Perhaps she would want the same for you."

He considered that, and nodded. "I know," he said, with a deep sigh. "When I woke up, outside the pain and the sadness, the most overwhelming emotion was rage. I wanted to do nothing but track those men down and kill them, make them suffer. But I realize that's not going to make me happy, or bring my family back. There's a larger picture, though, and that's to make sure that others don't suffer the same fate that Hope and Josh suffered, and that other survivors don't have the type of emotional pain that I have. What I need to do is focus myself on anything that will stop those men from acting again. If that's through working with you and the others here, then that's what I need to do."

Angel smiled. "Well said, Prometheus. As I said earlier, we could have given you something to heal all of your physical wounds, but wanted to be sure at first that you didn't live in denial of what happened to you. You've passed that hurdle, and now we'll give you the true healing you need."

She pulled a vial out of her pocket and handed it to Will.

He accepted it, but couldn't keep a smirk off his face. "This vial is going to heal me of all of my injuries? I'm pretty sure I've got a broken leg and two broken ribs—"

"Three, actually."

"Three broken ribs. Lots of bruises. Burns of all degrees. And that vial is going to fix me?"

"And everything else you haven't mentioned. Remember, you promised to have an open mind." She chuckled. "Remember, I can walk through a wall. Why is it difficult to believe I can fix broken bones and bruises with some liquid?"

Will snorted, wincing at the sharp pain it produced in his broken ribs. "I can pretend the wall is a holographic illusion, rather than solid, while I'm lying on this table. My broken leg is much more tangible." He sighed, and glanced at the vial. "But I did promise that I would keep an open mind."

Angel nodded. "You'll need to drink all of it. And it will make you sleep until you're fully healed."

Still skeptical, Will drank the contents, and handed the vial back to Angel. "Tastes like mint."

"Peppermint, actually."

A wave of fatigue hit him, and he began to drift. "Already getting sleepy," he said, yawning. "See you in the morning."

"Sleep well, Mr. Stark." She walked through the wall as Will faded into a deep sleep.

• • •

Fil was waiting for her. "How are you holding up?"

"He's not what I had expected, but I think I'm more heavily biased by the myth of the man than you are."

"That's not what I meant."

"I know what you meant. Can I just say that I'm in shock, and leave it at that? I hadn't expected the injuries to be so extensive. He barely survived."

"You're still avoiding the real question."

"Short answer: I don't know. I'll tell you when I figure it out." She fixed him with a stare. "How are *you* holding up?"

"I'll live."

She snorted. "I see non-answers run in the family."

He shrugged. "My memories are a bit more vivid than yours."

"And that means...?"

"Like I said, I'll live."

She shrugged. "I guess we'll discuss the impact of having him here when we figure out the answers." Angel looked down at her feet.

Fil nodded. "Moving on...impressions of the man?"

"He's passionate. He wants to go after the Hunters; that's genuine. He's managed to gain control of his emotions very well, but he still wants them stopped." She looked up at Fil. "I have no idea if he'll still want to do that once he understands what he's truly up against. But I don't sense anything that tells me we should alter our plan."

"Agreed. I have no doubt he'll be the most demanding Energy student we've had, because he's incredibly motivated. And he's incredibly calibrated for Energy work. Adam is going to hate him, because he's going to want to train twenty-four hours a day, motivated by his sense of vengeance and his genuine talent."

Angel chuckled. "Not until he's done with the Purge. You do realize that he'll want to kill us after the Purge is done, right?"

"If he lives through it," Fil said. His face was grim. "That's why we'll teach him enough to kill us only after he's survived it."

XI
TRAPPED

The Assassin regained consciousness and found himself inside a coffin.

While he didn't believe he was dead, inside a wooden box, and buried underground, it was difficult to prove that wasn't the case. There was very minimal lighting within his confined space. He was lying on his back, and his head and feet were both touching the sides of whatever cell held him.

How had he gotten into this space?

He recapped the most recent events he could recall. He'd received a call from The Leader, which was always a good thing. Those calls meant he'd get to do his own form of Hunting, where he would rid the world of human scum. It was never a large group, however, just one or two at a time. The Assassin had never understood why the Aliomenti Leadership would not let him go on mass cleansing missions, rather than just tag along on a small number of Hunts.

The Leadership team was terrified of being discovered by the humans. The ten thousand Aliomenti were outnumbered by eight billion humans, and though any skilled Aliomenti could easily hold their own against a large number of humans, The Leadership remained concerned that discovery would lead to their gradual and eventual elimination.

He thought the humans were worthless, and The Leadership thought they were a grave threat to their existence. He was able and willing to eliminate the threat. He'd proposed campaigns of annihilation in certain key areas of the human world, which he assured his Leadership would result in the humans exterminating themselves. It had happened in their history before, though they'd managed to avoid mass extinction. With his plan, they'd finally be rid of the human threat and could rebuild the world as they saw fit, no longer hiding in plain sight, free to be themselves at all times. His suggestions had always been rejected.

He waited, patiently, for The Leadership team to make the right decision.

In the meantime, he availed himself of the opulent lifestyle the Aliomenti enjoyed. Immense wealth. Resort communities humans were unable to visit. Amazing abilities he once would have considered impossible. He wondered how traitors like Will Stark could walk away from all of it, renounce what he was and what he'd sworn an Oath to uphold, and openly flout Aliomenti tradition. How could they leave a beautiful existence for the stupid, untalented human scum who would never even know of, or thank him for, his efforts? He hated Stark for being a traitor, and even more for being an idiot.

Thoughts of Stark brought back memories of the moments before he'd lost consciousness, before he'd woken up here inside of some enclosure. The Leader had called, and told him that the Hunters had found Will Stark. That, in itself, was unusual. Stark knew how the Hunters searched for him, and was skilled at eluding detection and capture. Rumors of their last encounter suggested that the Hunters believed Stark might never be found again. Those rumors were apparently untrue.

The great joy of the call was the report that Stark had been shown to have violated Oath Number Three. Stark, married to a human woman? The Assassin's hate morphed into something worse: pity. The man had clearly lost his sanity. He wouldn't have believed it, but the Hunters didn't make mistakes, and if they'd reported this fact, then he knew it to be true. Nor did he care if it was true or not. Accusations of marriage to a human meant The Assassin got to work, because the humans married to an Aliomenti were always sentenced to death. They assumed any human married to an Aliomenti would know, or come to know, of their existence, and thus their secrecy was at risk. Risks were eliminated.

He remembered creating the plan of attack with the Hunters. Stark's house, where he lived with his wife, was heavily guarded. The Hunters' job was to grab Stark, which was not an easy task. They could teleport into Stark's house, grab him, and leave the wife to The Assassin, but their fear of Stark was potent. They fully expected the man to defeat them and escape. They needed to destroy him mentally first. When they'd learned the traitor was also a married Oath-breaker, they not only found a reason to bring in The Assassin, they'd found the bait they needed to distract Stark and mentally unbalance the man. The Assassin would kill his wife in spectacular fashion. If Stark loved her, as husbands were supposed to love their wives, he'd be so distraught he wouldn't be able to fight back. The Hunters could then bring him back to Headquarters to face the punishment the traitor so richly deserved.

He'd been delighted when the plans adjusted to allow him to kill two more humans. The Hunters said it was necessary to prevent the human authorities from entering the well-guarded community too quickly, and The Leader had approved. The Assassin didn't care about the reasons. He just needed targets.

Everything had gone well. He'd killed the two guards in a most artistic fashion, enabling the Hunters to enter the guarded community and wait for Stark to arrive. He'd gotten to the house without issue and entered with no problems. The woman was there, looking just like she'd looked in the picture.

The Assassin frowned. He knew he hadn't killed her, that he'd failed in his mission. He searched his memory, trying to remember why. What had gone wrong?

The boy. Her son. *Will Stark's* son.

He shivered at the realization. Stark had somehow overcome the sterilization protocols. Given the Oath against having children, most Aliomenti had opted in when the protocols were developed, and eventually it had become expected of all members of the organization. Stark had gone through it as well. Somehow, though, he'd overcome it. For there was no doubt the young boy was his son: same hair despite the different color, same face, eyes burning with a fiery intensity, and Energy that had been startling. He remembered now. The baseball the child had thrown at him had hurt, to be sure. But it was that resemblance to Stark, and that Energy, a brief flash of it so pure and intense, beyond what he'd ever sensed from anyone, that had frightened him. His astonishment, and the boy's burst of Energy, had both vanished when the mother, in a fit of insanity, had decided to tackle him. He seethed — a *human woman* tackled him, the Aliomenti Assassin. The boy's fury had turned to concern for his mother's well-being, and the Energy had vanished. The dog had attacked him, and he'd dealt with the stupid beast, and that had reminded him that he had at least one human yet to kill. The boy seemed uncertain as to what to do next, and the human woman had tried to put herself between him and the boy. He had them beaten now, could feel the fear of both of them, as his Energy worked its emotional magic and inflicted them with terror.

Then the two of them had vanished from his sight.

It was impossible. The boy was too undisciplined to manage it. The woman, of course, couldn't dream of performing it. Someone had teleported them away from him, denying him his assigned third kill, and the unexpected bonus of a fourth. It had to be Stark. No one else had that kind of Energy power. He'd lost control of his emotions, and his fire had burst forth in explosive fashion. The fire must have absorbed the oxygen in the house, creating an air vacuum sufficient to render him unconscious.

Still in his dark prison, The Assassin assessed his likely situation. If Stark had rescued the boy and his mother, he'd likely defeated the Hunters yet again. Stark and the Alliance had captured The Assassin, taking him prisoner. That's where he must be now, at the Alliance base of operations. He smiled. He could eliminate as many in the Alliance as he desired now. It would be self-defense for a captured prisoner.

He frowned, as another memory stirred. He must have stayed partially conscious for a time after the explosion of fire, for he remembered lying on the floor of the house, feeling the gentle touch of the flames warming him. Then there was a voice, one he'd never heard before.

This is for my wife. The Assassin winced, remembering the blow that followed those words. Was this an Aliomenti who'd broken the third Oath, like Stark? Perhaps a fresh recruit drafted directly into the Alliance? Reportedly, they didn't follow or take Oaths in the Alliance at all. He snorted. Ignorance of the law was no excuse. This man's wife had paid the appropriate price.

This is for my daughter. That made no sense. Had a member of the

Alliance fathered a child? He chilled at the thought. If the Alliance were so devoid of tradition, they'd think nothing of flouting the fourth Oath, avoiding the sterilization processes. The Alliance could be breeding children born with high Energy. Like Stark's son. The Assassin felt a chill. He wondered if The Leadership had considered that possibility. If not, they needed to know. Those children were a far greater threat than the traitors or the new direct recruits to the Alliance.

And that's for the dog. Instinctively, The Assassin moved his arm to block his face from the blow that had already struck him, though he felt no pain on his face at the moment. The man must have seen the dead dog near him, and drawing on his weak human roots felt sympathy for the animal. The Assassin's arm brushed the side and top of his dark cell, leading him to realize that it wasn't much larger than a coffin. When he touched the sides of this cell, he remembered being thrown into this prison by the man who had struck him, and remembered hearing muffled voices from outside that suggested that a woman and another man were part of the crew. It was convenient that his current cell was the size of a coffin. The man who had dared strike him would need one in short order. He was sure that he could find similar accommodations for the man's cohorts.

First, though, he needed to escape from this prison.

The minimal light in the space seemed to come from his right, and he twisted his head in that direction. There was a small seam and a faint glow. He had only faint memories of being thrown in here, but they ended with a door shutting on him. If he hadn't been moved, the light must be coming from the side that opened to the outside world. He decided he'd emerge in his own fashion.

He and the three Hunters had each developed a unique skill that enabled them to perform their duties with exceptional efficiency. Porthos had an incredible sensitivity to Energy, able to sense even trace amounts over great distances. His skill had evolved over time such that he could actually identify the person who had produced the Energy he sensed, and follow it to the original source. He served as the Tracker for the Hunters. Athos could touch anyone and know if they were telling the truth, and his skill was such that no matter how deep within them the truth might be buried, Athos could sense it. Aramis, though not as powerful as his cohorts in terms of Energy creation, possessed the Damper, the ability to suppress Energy in other Aliomenti. For most, his strength was sufficient to prevent one from using Energy at all. He essentially rendered other Aliomenti merely human. His strength increased the closer he was to a target, and so he was the first Hunter to lay hands on a fugitive tracked by Porthos. The suspect would be questioned, Athos would determine the veracity of the claims the fugitive made, and they'd return the criminal to Headquarters.

As an Assassin, he had no use for skills of such subtlety. The Assassin could generate fire from within, and the ability to shoot flames from his body added to his terrifying visage. He'd learned that he was immune from burns, though not from oxygen deprivation, as his experience in the Stark home had shown.

He would use those fiery skills to escape his prison. He shifted onto his right side, facing the seam, and touched his left hand to the crack. Then he shot forth a small amount of flame.

The material did not catch fire or burn. Frowning, The Assassin concentrated, and the flame from his hand burned with greater heat. The material still did not ignite. He extinguished the flame, conceding that this approach would not work, but in the process confirming something he'd suspected.

He was definitely a prisoner of the Alliance. No human could build something able to resist his flame.

He shifted his left leg back, over his right, bent the leg, and then used his knee as a battering ram, slamming it into the wall he'd just tried to burn. To his mild surprise, the entire side popped open immediately. He blinked rapidly, allowing his eyes to adjust, and then rolled through the opening.

He dropped three feet and landed on a clean white floor. The Assassin grunted in pain, his ribs still tender from the attack he'd suffered earlier. He rose to his hands and knees, getting his breathing under control, and then stood, taking in his surroundings.

He was in a small room. The floor, ceiling, and walls were completely white, and there were no windows or doors, and no visible sources of lighting or air. Yet he was breathing pure air and there was plenty of natural light filling the room. He was standing next to a strange vehicle, which looked something like a human automobile without tires. It was a shiny, silvery color, and did not have a top covering the seats in the passenger compartment. He'd clearly been in the rear compartment, and that annoyed him. They had thrown him in a trunk? Yes, those people would suffer greatly.

"I see that you're awake."

The Assassin whirled around. A man stood there. The Assassin hadn't seen him during his scan of the room, and assumed that the man had been hiding behind the front of the vehicle, out of his line of sight. The man looked to be older, with graying, thinning hair, and wore a one piece orange bodysuit.

The Assassin scowled at him, and amped up the Energy he projected at his victims, Energy designed to make the person feel frightened.

"I'm known as the Mechanic," the man said, seemingly oblivious to the burst of fear Energy sent his way. Stupid human. "I fix things around here. I'd appreciate it in the future if you would avoid trying to damage my handiwork." He nodded at the vehicle.

"What are you talking about?" The Assassin said, scowling with as much ferocity as he could muster. He was unaccustomed to people who didn't cower from him in fear.

"It won't burn," the Mechanic explained. "I noticed the smell of smoke when you emerged with such grace." The Mechanic paused. "Who are you?"

"I'm known as The Assassin." He smirked. "I kill people who annoy me."

The Mechanic shrugged. "OK, I'll keep that in mind." He squinted at The Assassin. "What happened to your face?"

"The scars come from those who tried to escape me. They scratched my face. I ended their lives. I consider them badges of honor."

"Not that. Your nose. What happened to your nose?"

"Someone kicked me in the face while I was unconscious, apparently concerned I had killed a dog. The fool will suffer greatly, all for the love of a furry bag of fleas."

The Mechanic laughed. "Impressive speech. I imagine the one upset about the dog was Fil. The man seems to have a soft spot for the creatures. I've told him it's going to get him killed one day, and it looks like you're interested in proving me correct." The Mechanic shrugged. "He never listens to me." He fixed The Assassin with a pointed look. "Would you like me to bring Fil here to you?"

Was he serious? "I'd love to meet this Fil of yours."

The man seemed to wince momentarily. "Then I'll go get him.

Before I leave, however, let me offer you a bit of advice. The terrifying killer routine won't work around here. Spare yourself the effort of trying."

"And where would we be?"

The Mechanic smiled. "You already know exactly where you are."

He walked toward one of the solid walls and went directly through it. The Assassin gaped at the spot in the wall where the man had just exited the room. There was no doorway, no opening in sight. Was it that easy? He walked to the spot in the wall and attempted to pass through. No, the wall was definitely a wall. His face collided with the very solid surface the other man had just melted through.

The Assassin roared, more out of frustration than pain, and tried hurtling his way through, ramming his shoulder into the wall. He tried other sections of the wall. He tried to burn the wall. He set his fire to every surface. Nothing worked.

Fifteen minutes later, he sat down, recalled his fire, and simply waited. He was trapped.

XII
ELITES

The absence of pain was so startling that it nearly caused Will to faint.

It wasn't the dead feeling caused by anesthesia, either. The pain simply didn't exist, and there was nothing to mask. He felt no pain near his broken leg, or his broken ribs. There was no pain on the vast portion of his body riddled with cuts and bruises, no general sensation of heat from his burning skin.

Will sat up, clenching his teeth at the expected pain. None came. His movement was smooth, without even any muscle stiffness. He touched his face, and then looked at his hands. The burns were gone, replaced by clean, unblemished skin. He tapped his rib cage, wincing on reflex, but found nothing there causing pain either.

He took a deep breath. The big test was the leg. He slid off the table, as if he were sliding into a cold swimming pool, until his bare feet touched the white floor of the room. With extreme caution, Will let his full weight come down on the leg. Nothing. He hopped up and down, and then took a few steps.

Nothing. Every injury was completely healed. No scars, no blisters, no pain. He couldn't remember ever feeling better than he felt right now.

Will sat back down on the small table he'd been using for a bed and lowered his head, feeling guilty. He was alive, his injuries completely healed, and feeling better than he'd ever felt before.

Meanwhile, his wife and son were being buried, mourners there to pay their last respects to the two people who'd been his whole world. They would mourn *his* loss, too, and Will wanted to go to the grave site and tell everyone there to waste no breath crying for him. He was alive and his wife and son were dead through his failure. He'd vowed to Hope on their wedding day to always protect her, and vowed the same to his newborn son. He'd failed, and now a box with his name would be in the ground, empty like his heart, lower than dirt like the man he was.

He was still brooding when Angel entered the room, so mellowed at the thought of his family that he barely noticed her miraculous entry through the wall of the room. Whether it was his mental funk or the human mind's rapid adaptability, he simply accepted the oddity and treated it as his new reality. Angel had the effect of brightening his mood, however, and his mild depression ceased as she walked toward him, smiling. Perhaps one day she'd tell him how she accomplished that feat.

"You're sitting up!" she exclaimed. "I take it you've found your injuries are adequately healed?" She arched an eyebrow, combining that with a knowing smile.

He grinned sheepishly, finding it difficult to remain remorseful against her irrepressible cheer. "Consider this doubting Thomas an official convert. I'll try to be somewhat less skeptical in the future."

"I'm glad to hear that, because everything you learn from this point forward will test your skepticism like never before." She pulled two chairs from around the other side of the table-like bed. They were a deep burgundy red, and appeared solid, with no visible cushioning. How had he missed them as he was standing up and walking around? The color alone should be noticeable in this room of nothing but white. He moved to one of the chairs and sat down, and Angel joined him.

He looked at her a bit more closely. Her hair was shoulder-length, a vibrant red that was shocking. Her face was round and cherubic, highlighted by friendly violet eyes that seemed to possess an eternal twinkle. Her skin was smooth and unlined. She was tall, nearly matching Will's own six foot stature. She wore a deep green body suit that reminded him vaguely of those worn by ship crews on TV shows he'd watched as a child, shows about future missions into space. He glanced down at himself, and noticed that his attire was similar in style, though it was a pale white instead of the deep green Angel wore.

"Are you a witch?" he asked.

She blinked, startled. "What?"

"Are. You. A. Witch?"

She frowned. "What on earth would make you think that I'm a witch?" Then she burst out laughing. "Sorry for that, but your question is very amusing to me. I'm curious, though. Why do you ask if I'm a witch?"

His face reddened. "I'm not trying to offend you, trust me. All of you have done more for me than I deserve, or can ever repay. But it's not just you, it's Fil and... I don't think I caught the other man's name...?"

"Adam."

"Right, Adam, too. All three of you. Everything I've seen and experienced, right since I was about to be killed by those men... it's beyond my understanding how everything happened. I know I promised to keep an open mind, but I keep thinking about it, and I can't explain *any* of it. The only explanation I can come up with is magic, and I don't *believe* in magic."

Angel grinned. "I thought you were going to keep an open mind? What if I *am* a witch?"

He smiled, unable to resist. "Are you a good witch, or a bad witch?"

Angel chuckled. "Neither, actually. I'm so accustomed to everything in our community that it's difficult for me to see it from another perspective. I imagine many things seemed quite magical to you. Giving you a vial of liquid to drink that cured all of your injuries didn't help matters, did it?"

"It would have been worse if steam was coming off of it, or I'd seen you stirring it up in a cauldron."

She laughed. "Good point. But no, to answer your question, none of what you've seen is magic. There are a couple of things we've learned how to do — our group, that is — that are highly advanced. Our friends in the other group think it makes them almost a new species of superhuman. In fact... didn't you mention that the Hunters used the word *human* as a sort of put-down?"

He frowned. "I think so."

Angel nodded. "To them, that's exactly what it is. We are super humans, the Aliomenti, and everyone else is just human. We're better, they're lesser life forms. That type of attitude. If you call a Hunter a human, he's likely to forget his vow not to kill you, because they perceive it as so great an insult." She paused. "They didn't think you were human though, did they? But they did think your wife was."

He nodded. "They were really shocked about my having a son, too. Why is that?"

"The Aliomenti swear four Oaths before being admitted, before receiving the knowledge we're going to share with you. I'll tell you more about them later, but the fourth says that you will not have any children, and it's tradition that new members undergo various routines to make sure the Oath can't be violated." She sighed. "The real reason most of them do it is because the penalty for violating that Oath... well, that's why they stopped trying to capture you alive and openly tried to kill you."

Will felt his jaw drop, and he stared at her in disbelief. "They *kill* you if you have a child?"

She nodded, somber. "There's a story behind it, and as you learn more you'll probably get an understanding of why the Oath was implemented, but... I agree, it's quite a stupid rule."

"My wife, my son...they were killed because of that Oath as well, weren't they?"

Angel's face turned grim. "You're getting me off topic, but yes, a violation of one of the Oaths was the reason why they were targeted. To them, you violated the Oath against having children, and so you and your son had to die. To them, you violated the Oath against marrying a human woman, and so *she* had to die. Had they not discovered your son, they would merely have arrested and detained you for many decades."

Will slammed a fist into his chair. "This is *stupid!* Four people are dead, and I was beaten and nearly killed, by a group that makes people swear an Oath not to get married and have children?"

Angel grasped his hand. "Mr. Stark, I agree with you. The Oaths have been horribly modified since they were first created, and those Elites who enforce them today do so out of a sense of fear and a desire to retain and enhance their own power in the world. That's why our group was formed."

Will stared at her intently. "You seek to destroy these people?"

"We seek to *change* them, and defend those they would harm. We do not seek to destroy. The vast majority of those who are part of the original group do not care for these methods, but are content with their own lives and do not wish to see that change, so they say nothing. They are cowards, not evil people. We actively recruit them to our point of view, and we have made a great deal of progress, but we are still greatly outnumbered, and the Hunters are extremely proficient at finding those we have converted to our way of thinking, and then returning them to their original group against their will."

"How many have been caught?

"Our numbers are only as high as they are because we directly recruit humans to our side, and the Hunters don't know who they are. As for Aliomenti who've switched to our side... well, they've gotten every single one they've gone after. Except one."

Will looked at the floor. Him. They'd gotten everyone they'd ever gone after except for him. Or, more to the point, the man they *thought* they were attacking that night, a man with the same name.

He looked back at Angel. "Teach me. Tell me what I can do to fight those people, to stop them."

Angel nodded. "Let me give you some basics. Our core organization began over a thousand years ago, started by a land baron who wanted to figure out why the serfs working his land were so often sick and died so young. He recruited a group of younger people from his land, and charged them with figuring this out. They went one step further, and figured out how to become quite healthy, avoiding most sicknesses, and generally being better able to live a longer, happier life, to grow as a person. They merged together a few Latin words that loosely translate as *personal growth* and coined the phrase Aliomenti."

"And they're still around a thousand years later. I think I've seen this on late night infomercials."

Angel laughed. "Not quite the same thing. The land baron thanked them and tried to send them back to their farms, but they revolted, ran away, and made camp in the wilds of England. Over time, they developed many unique abilities, based around the ability to create and manipulate what we call Energy, and that helped them to become very rich and very powerful, and that wealth and power has grown to this very day."

"Sounds intriguing. Where do we get to the part about killing children?"

Angel frowned. "Let's just say that there were events in their history which caused huge devastation to the group, and they overreacted by banning anyone from engaging in the activities they thought were the root cause, through the Oaths. And yes, some of those events evolved around a marriage and a child, and the trauma that came from it nearly destroyed the entire group and all of the members."

Will scowled. "Still, killing children? Banning people in love from getting married? Wouldn't they have learned their lesson over time and figured out something new?"

Angel sighed. "Memories last a long time in this group."

Will just shook his head. He couldn't conceive of anything happening that could possibly justify such a response.

"Over time, members of the group began to rebel against the harsher aspects of the Oaths. They left the Aliomenti community, which over the years evolved into a massive series of hidden estates in some of the most beautiful lands on Earth, and they instead lived in small groups of isolated cells, bound together by a common mission. We would live in and around human communities, using our skills to influence them subtly. The idea was to help them develop the skills and technologies we had already developed, at a pace that was reasonable and safe, while avoiding the attention of the core group of Aliomenti. These people referred to themselves as the Alliance, and current members include the three people who brought you here. It's tricky work, and we must be careful about revealing too much, too quickly. If we showed them everything we're capable of immediately, they'd burn us at the stake if they could catch us."

Will laughed. "I thought you said you weren't a witch? What could you possibly show them that would cause that reaction?"

Angel smiled at him. "I'm not a witch."

She vanished.

What the...? Where in the world did she go?

"I'm right behind you."

He spun. *But she was...*

"...right in front of you and then I vanished. Yes. About ten percent of Aliomenti develop enough Energy to perform teleportation, and a smaller percentage can travel for long distances in that manner. I happen to be one of them."

Will's face was frozen in shock. *She lied to me. She's a witch. I'm getting turned into a toad for sure.*

"Heavens no, you'd look dreadful as a toad. And I couldn't do that anyway. As I said, I'm not a witch, and this isn't magic. But do you understand now why we're rather cautious about such displays of Energy manipulation around those who aren't aware of our existence?"

Will couldn't think. She could read his mind. He was completely terrified of her.

"I'll take that as a yes. You don't have to be terrified of me, though. The men you want to destroy or slow down can do this too, Mr. Stark. You'll learn to do the same in time. But you must trust us, as difficult as it can be in the face of the unknown. Now, are you still mostly concerned about my walking through that wall?"

Suddenly, he could do nothing but laugh. He fell out of the chair and onto the clear floor, rolling around, laughing with such intensity that tears formed in his eyes. The absurdity of everything that was happening to him had finally burst forth. He finished a few moments later, but remained on the floor, unwilling — or possibly unable, he wasn't sure which — to bother to climb back into the chair.

"Mr. Stark, as I've noted we use something called Energy. It is a force, something like fire, something like electricity, generated by the human body, within every human cell. The Aliomenti learn to sense and grow and control this Energy, sometimes to a phenomenal degree. It is what enables me to do things like read your thoughts and emotions, and even influence them. Do you notice that you're calm around me? I send Energy to you with calming thoughts, and you feel that. My mind is able to hear thoughts and sense emotions from others. I've developed quite a bit of Energy capacity and creation capability over time, and that's why I can teleport. And there's another thing I can do."

Will felt pleasant warmth surrounding him as he lay on the floor, listening to her speak. She was telling him it was science, the basic electrical signals the body used to fire synapses in its cells, but to a massively larger degree, enabling powers he'd only suspect to see in one who practiced magic. Yet magic didn't exist. And this warmth... it was solidifying around him, surrounding him like a warm glove, and he was gently raised off the floor, rotated slowly in the air, and deposited back into his chair. The warmth left him.

"I can do that as well. And we can teach you to do the same, Mr.

Stark. The Hunters can do these things. There are many other Aliomenti who would like to see our group eliminated, and those men and women can do these things as well. Will you allow us to help you achieve your potential?"

Will took several deep breaths. He'd promised to keep an open mind, and he'd clearly need one to deal with this new reality. He needed to learn these skills if he was going to face the people who'd killed Hope and Josh. He'd need to learn them to fight those who would seek to harm others in a similar fashion. It was his duty. And he had to admit it was tempting outside of a sense of duty as well. What would it be like to do what Angel had just done?

He looked to Angel. "Will I feel that warmth again if I follow your training and teaching?"

Angel looked surprised. "You felt that?"

"When you moved me? Yes. It felt like a warm glove surrounded me and picked me up. Was that... was that your Energy that moved me?"

She nodded. "It was, but I'm surprised. Usually humans can't sense Energy at all. You have a tremendous sensitivity."

Will scowled. "I thought *human* was a bad word around here. And what does it mean, I have a tremendous sensitivity?"

Angel smiled. "Relax, Mr. Stark. In the Alliance, *human* simply means one untrained in our practices, one who cannot yet sense or use Energy. Consider it a synonym for a potential apprentice. And the sensitivity means that you'll likely progress at a much faster rate than most."

"So I learn to sense and manipulate this warmth. That's it?"

She nodded.

"*That's* the big secret the Aliomenti want to hide? *That's* why my wife and son were murdered?" He managed to keep his tone conversational. Angel had done nothing to them, after all.

She understood. "Perhaps electricity is a better analogy than the fire example from before. Many years ago, a few people were aware of electricity, but the implications and usages were unknown. Most people, if they'd even heard of it, might see it as nothing more than the output of an experiment performed by Benjamin Franklin. He invented lightning rods, but the building block of electricity wasn't of any use. Why? Because nobody knew what to do with it at that point."

Will shrugged.

"But think about electricity two centuries later. It's used to power lights and air conditioners and furnaces. It allows people to use refrigerators and microwave ovens. Without electricity, we would not have seen the advances that led to radio, television, computers, or the Internet. If you went back to Franklin's era with that knowledge, you'd be rather wealthy and powerful in a short period of time. Energy is like that. It's limited by how much you can generate and your own creativity, much as electricity seems to be. Would people kill to have and retain exclusivity about such a technology decades or centuries before others? You know the answer to that, Mr. Stark."

He nodded.

"Understand, Mr. Stark. The advances you have seen are rather extreme, and you haven't seen everything. We're too far advanced to simply drop everything on the world at once. We agree with our Aliomenti brethren on that concept, though not on punishment for so-called violations. We believe in sharing that knowledge, tempered with patience. That's what our symbol represents." She held up her right hand, palm facing him.

The symbol was tattooed on her palm with gold ink. Three dashed circles merging in the center around what looked like a letter A. Each circle contained an object: a scroll, a tongue of fire, and a bird.

"Our group — the letter A — is at our core, and enables us to make our advances. But our circles are open. We want our knowledge — the scroll — and our technical and Energy advances — the fire — to go out to the whole world. We also seek peace and prosperity and work to achieve that as well, hence the dove. They are tattooed onto our palms, always with us yet out of sight, and our unity is shown when we shake hands and our symbols come together. Our new recruits must wait a year before they receive the tattoo on their palms. We make them wait as a precaution, to make sure loyalty is proven before too much is revealed. We don't like doing it; unfortunately, we can't take the risk at this point of doing otherwise."

Will nodded. "I saw something similar on the man at my house. I don't think he was one of the Hunters, though. I thought he was their boss."

Angel looked interested. "The Leader was there?" She nodded. "That makes sense, if they thought they were capturing a dangerous fugitive like you." Will opened his mouth to protest, and then realized she was teasing him. "Yes, the Aliomenti have a symbol as well. They also have a scroll and a tongue of fire, along with a sword, representative of power. The symbols are within a dashed circle, indicating that sharing is encouraged, but only within the group. The outside world is off limits. That's why there's a solid outer circle surrounding it. And the giant A... well, that's their way of reminding themselves of the importance of the Aliomenti organization, the first and most important part of their life. They are the Elites of this world, and they are focused on making sure it stays that way. The four items in their symbol — the scroll, the fire, the sword, and the letter A — also symbolize the four Oaths. They wear their symbols on clothing except when they go into human communities; they don't usually like to draw attention to themselves if they can avoid it. If you are human and see the Aliomenti symbol, there's a good chance it's the last thing you'll ever see."

Will glanced at the symbol on her palm again. "I prefer yours. How do I get started so I can begin fighting the Aliomenti?"

"Mr. Stark, we don't *fight* the Aliomenti in the traditional sense of the word. We are not an army, and they have the same skills we have. They also outnumber us about a hundred to one, and thus any offensive would probably end with all of us being eliminated. Please understand, the Aliomenti are estranged family to us. We prefer reunion, not war. The dove is part of our symbol for a reason. Most of our efforts involve recruiting from their numbers in secret, winning over the silent majority. We know that men like the Hunters are beyond reach and reason, but many others simply need to be told that there's a different way."

"I can respect that," Will said with grudging acceptance. "I can't say with certainty that I'll act with restraint if the opportunity arises, but I will do my best to follow your guidelines and earn the right to wear your symbol. Now, how do I begin?"

"You'll need Energy training, where you'll learn how to sense, manipulate, and grow Energy, and how to use it to perform various tasks. For any of that to work, however, you'll have to undergo the Purge first."

"That sounds... ominous."

She sighed. "It is, unfortunately. Right now, a great deal of what's inside you is preventing you from sensing and using your Energy. It's there; I can feel it. You probably can't. The Purge will change that.

But it won't be a pleasant experience."

"How bad?"

"You might have fond memories of your injuries from the night of the fire, and how minor all of those broken bones and burns were."

He fixed her with a pointed stare. "Could it be fatal?"

"I don't know. I don't think it's possible, but I don't know."

Will considered his options. "It sounds like this is what I need to do, though. I'm ready when you are."

Angel looked at him with deep sympathy. "Fil and Adam can prepare the Purge. I'd advise you to rest up until then. You'll need it." She patted him on the arm. "Good luck, Mr. Stark." And she walked through the wall and out of the room.

Will climbed out of the red chair and moved back to his bed, left with that sobering message.

He'd been burned, cut, kicked, punched, beaten, suffered broken bones, and had likely been within a few moments of being killed.

What might this Purge be, that Angel thought it might be worse than *that*?

XIII
GREED

Will Stark had routinely made the impossible look easy, Michael Baker decided. Baker had once thought that developing a company which created building walls out of cell-sized materials was complicated. The true challenge, he decided, was not in how Will made his money. It was how he gave it away. That simple task was proving to be a greater stress and workload for Baker than attempting to protect the domed city of Pleasanton and its surroundings from crime.

Baker had had no idea why Will Stark's lawyer would be calling him, but if he had tried to guess it certainly wouldn't have been to take on this role. He'd worked with Stark in establishing and running a youth baseball program, and the two had become good friends in the process. Baker had suspected that Stark's will had designated funds to keep the program running in the event of his death, and when he visited with the lawyer suspected he'd be asked to ensure those funds were spent appropriately. Will Stark and his wife, Hope, had a larger role in mind for him. He'd been named the Trustee, not of a small amount of money designed to fund the youth baseball program in perpetuity, but of their entire estate.

The shock of his new role paled in comparison to the amazing memorial service the city held in the Starks' memory. They'd built a small dome on the center square of Pleasanton, inside the larger dome covering the entire city. The three caskets were of identical size and design, because the fire had cremated the Starks' bodies inside their home. Holographic projections of photographs and movies had told their life stories, tracking Will's meteoric rise to business success, his purchase of Pleasanton out of bankruptcy to operate as a business under his rules, the construction of the dome and reconstruction of the city infrastructure. People were reminded of the simple wedding ceremony of Will and Hope, a couple genuinely in love, who radiated those feelings even in the still photos from the ceremony. There were photographs of the beautiful baby boy born to them a few years later. Comments from business and political leaders were displayed around the city. And the testimonials from people the Starks had helped over the years, ranging from angel investments in fledgling businesses to people whose homes had been saved from foreclosure, were incredibly powerful. Baker wasn't the only grown man who'd cried without shame for the first time in memory that day.

Baker had resigned from police duty the following morning. It would take time to be able to walk away completely, but he was able to devote more time each day to his Trustee work. The idea of being wealthy and giving away money had appealed to him in the beginning, but he now realized the seriousness of his charge.

In the meetings over the first few days, Millard Howe, the Starks' estate lawyer, went over quite a few different documents with him, all with various processes and guidelines to follow, and others explaining what they were trying to accomplish. Baker thought it was all excessive. He expected they'd hear about various causes, discuss the merits, and, if they so decided, transfer funds to the recipient. The endless forms, processes, and decision trees the Starks left behind seemed superfluous. The charts were pasted up on the walls of Howe's modest one-story office building outside the Dome, covering most of the surfaces other than the windows overlooking the small parking lot outside.

When Howe told him how much he'd be paid for serving in the role, Baker had been thunderstruck, and thought he'd misheard. Making as much in a month as you had in a year was surely overkill. Given that Howe told reporters that Baker would be compensated so as to ensure he could maintain his previous standard of living, he thought he'd earn the same in this role that he had as a police officer. Howe noted that Stark knew the pressure Baker would face in the role, and the statement was designed to prevent people from thinking that Baker was suddenly wealthy and worthy of the type of threats Stark had faced on a daily basis.

They'd issued a press release early on. Will and Hope wanted to give the vast majority of their estate away, ideally while still living, and the Trust was established to continue their quest. The Trust had rules noting that money must be given away at the discretion of the Trustee after consultation with the Advisor, and only after passing many criteria to ensure the funds met the Starks' values. The basic tenets were published with a web address enabling people to print out the detailed request forms if they met the criteria. Baker and Howe would review the forms, verify that the request in fact met the Starks' guidelines, and then respond with their decision, also in writing. Papers would give them a trail with necessary signatures, something which appealed to Howe's legal nature. Baker expected it to be a smooth, simple process.

The reality had left his faith in humanity shattered. And that came from a man who'd spent years in law enforcement.

The office was flooded in a deluge of paper mail. Of the thousands of letters, only a few dozen met the guidelines the Starks had established and which had been printed clearly on every press release published, and on the web site available for downloading forms. While there were a handful which were close, the vast majority were people who simply wanted money, and expected to receive it, despite meeting none of the criteria the Starks had established. And they had no qualms about employing whatever means necessary to achieve those ends.

Dozens of letters arrived claiming to be blood relatives of one of the Starks, typically a previously unknown child of Will's. Several claimed to be a missing aunt, uncle, or cousin, and demanded a "proper share for a member of the family," even threatening legal action if the Trust did not immediately grant them their demands. The most disgusting were the handful of letters from those claiming that Josh had been their father. Baker was sickened that anyone would be so lazy as to not check facts before claiming to be the young adult child of a dead six-year-old boy. The tamer versions tried to sound formal by incorrectly lengthening "Will" to "William" or "Wilson," assuming that the use of a full formal name gave credibility to their claims. Both Howe and Baker knew that the man's full given name was, in fact, just Will.

The second type of scam involved the verbal promise. These claimed that one of the Starks (again, in some cases, including Josh, who'd never spoken a word in his six short years of life) had promised funds for varying purposes. Both men knew that the Starks made a habit of never walking away from an encounter where they expected to give someone money without actually completing the transaction on the spot. Baker recalled Will talking to a parent during a youth baseball game, and the man had made enough of an impression about a business idea that Will decided to provide an angel investment. Stark had gone home, gotten his checkbook, and written the check on the spot. But Stark hadn't told the man of his decision until he'd returned with the ability to make the investment. He had a difficult time thinking the Starks had made many "check in the mail" promises. They made the decision early on to reply with a candid response that neither man had been informed of any verbal promises, but to invite such requesters to go through the defined request process. Only a few did, and the two men were left with the likely explanation that no actual promises had ever been made.

Others actually went so far as to submit written letters – reputedly signed by one or both of the Starks – promising funds. The vast majority had the kind of typographical errors that the Starks simply wouldn't make, including managing to misspell Will, Hope, or Stark, or simply left out the actual signature in the designated spot. The few that passed these basic criteria contained signatures that were so obviously forgeries that Millard Howe's legal team went after the requesters for mail fraud.

Of the tens of thousands of letters received, fewer than five percent used the forms required. Of the five percent that followed the process, only a handful met even a majority of the guidelines the Starks set down.

Baker found himself rereading the letter Will had sent him. It helped keep him sane. The letter, in its simplest sense, talked about Will's experience in dealing with his philanthropic image. Many people asked him for money; some demanded it; others attempted to compel him for it. He most preferred to direct his money where it would multiply in its effect, providing gifts or grants to promising business startups likely to employ dozens or hundreds or even more down the road. He'd provide charitable gifts to those who had experienced true misfortune and for whom the funds would provide a chance to restart their lives. He donated money to research organizations that sought cures to common diseases and illnesses, especially those impacting children. He did not, as he stated, prefer to give money to people who had experienced no specific misfortune and for whom the money would be used just to fund their own lifestyle. To Will, that was the true definition of greed: to hoard resources to oneself, for the sole benefit of oneself, regardless of the level of fortune the person possessed; a poor person could be greedy, and a wealthy person generous. Both Will and Hope, wealthy as they were, met the definition of generosity better than anyone he'd ever known.

Will also noted that he'd heard stories of Baker, by no means a wealthy man, displaying generosity of this sort in helping the victims of crimes he was working as a police officer, and saw a similar generosity of spirit in the work the two men did in establishing and running the baseball program for children in and around Pleasanton. Hope was moved by the stories Will shared about Michael Baker, and she stated emphatically that Baker was the man she wanted as Trustee. Will had agreed. And so Michael Baker found himself in this role, reading thousands of letters, most of which so clearly went against the publicly stated purposes of this Trust.

He felt a sense of relief when his phone rang, interrupting his read of yet another forgery. He listened to the voice on the other end. Millard Howe looked up, having noticed that Baker had said nothing on the call, and watched as Baker's face went ashen. The former police officer hung up the phone and sprinted from the room. Howe trailed after him.

"Michael!" Howe shouted. "Michael! What's wrong? Where are you going?"

Baker didn't answer. He emerged into the parking lot, jumped into his car, and drove away at high speed, oblivious to the fact that there were other cars in the vicinity. Howe stood, watching him, wondering what to do. He finally realized that he'd never track Baker down at the speed the man was driving, and that he'd simply have to wait for Baker to contact him.

Howe moved back into the office and shut the door, then walked to his desk. He heard the door click shut behind him as expected. Then he heard the sound of the deadbolt lock being turned, which was unexpected. Howe whirled around, tensing for an attack.

Then he relaxed, recognizing the man now standing inside his office. "Adam? What are you doing here?"

"We need to talk, Mr. Howe." The man looked somber, and Howe found himself concerned.

"How did you get into my office? I didn't see you outside."

"I move quietly, Mr. Howe. Please, let's sit down and talk."

Howe didn't move, suddenly wary.

Adam shrugged and sat down at the table Howe and Baker had used, in the seat Baker had only recently vacated in such rapid fashion. "Mr. Howe, I wanted to let you know that I am the secret Advisor to the Trust, the one named in the will."

Howe blinked. He hadn't even thought of the other Advisor in the past two weeks, given that the Starks for some reason had not seen fit to let him or Baker in on the person's identity. "What 'secret Advisor' are you referring to, Adam?"

"The one mentioned in the will you helped the Starks draft," Adam said, repeating his earlier words.

Ah, that cleared it up. "So you read the will I asked you to store securely, gleaned that there was a role for a 'secret Advisor'—" he flashed air quotes "— and decided you'd volunteer for the job?"

Adam smiled. "I'm not volunteering. I was volunteered, much as you and Mr. Baker were volunteered. And as was the case with the two of you, I accepted my role."

"And what proof do I have that what you're saying is true? The Starks left me instructions to name Mr. Baker as Trustee in the event of their deaths. They never told me the identity of another person who would be involved."

"Mr. Howe, you are an intelligent man. If the Starks defined a role within the will for a secret Advisor, it would make sense that they went to the trouble to actually find one, correct?"

Howe shrugged.

Adam laughed. "Ever the lawyer, aren't you? I'll keep talking then. If they named such a person, then someone would need to know about it and be able to verify it was true. If I showed up shortly after the Starks' deaths and said I was the Trustee, would you believe me?"

"I have documentation from the Starks stating explicitly that the role was Michael Baker's. I would not have provided you the necessary means to expend funds on behalf of the Trust."

"Precisely. I couldn't be the Trustee, because they'd told someone

— you — that someone else had been given that role. You were the estate attorney for the Starks, so you would be involved as well. Mr. Stark liked to split responsibility, which is why he had you craft everything so it wasn't just one person making decisions in a vacuum, and he didn't want two people because he didn't want to have 'ties' in determining what to do. Three was the smallest number that could meet those challenges, and so he had three people in mind. Everyone knew about you. You knew about Baker. So who would, logically, know about the secret Advisor?"

Howe's eyes widened. "Michael knows you?"

"Indirectly. Let's just say that he and I share a common secret, which was Stark's way of making sure we'd be able to confirm each other's identity. I don't need to confirm Michael's, because you've already done that, but he'll be able to confirm mine."

Now Howe was curious. "What secret?"

Adam laughed. "Mr. Howe, what good are secrets if too many people know them? I knew that my information from Stark had been shared with only one other person, and when Mr. Baker was named Trustee, I finally knew who that was. I've made arrangements to have my previous role significantly filled by others, and can thus devote a good deal of time to my new position. I'll make contact with Mr. Baker, so that he can confirm that Mr. Stark chose me for the position."

Howe scowled. "How do I know you won't coerce Michael into agreeing to your claim?"

Adam shrugged. "You've undoubtedly set up code words. Words you use to communicate with each other if something goes wrong, without alerting others. Mr. Stark had us establish a similar system in the secure data center, and I imagine he recommended that the two of you develop something along those lines. So if I coerce Mr. Baker in any way, you'll know." He glanced around. "Where is Michael, by the way? I'd like to talk to him."

Howe shrugged. "I have no idea. He ran out of here just before you materialized in my office, looking upset and driving off quickly."

Adam furrowed his brow, and then his brown eyes widened. "He's not on the police force anymore, so he's not receiving dispatch calls. That means there's only one thing likely to make him react like that." He headed to the door, just as Howe reached the same conclusion. Adam raced out of the office into the parking lot, leaped onto a motorcycle, and sped off, with no helmet on his head. After locking the office, Howe jumped into his car and drove after him.

Moments later the men arrived at the hospital serving residents outside the Dome. "I hope it's nothing serious," Howe muttered. Adam only grunted his assent. They entered the building, found signs indicating the direction of the trauma wing, and rode the elevator to the fourth floor.

Howe tried to get the room number of Baker's young son, but the woman on duty merely pushed her glasses further up on her nose and shook her head, murmuring something about patient privacy laws. Adam approached, and asked for Mrs. Baker's room number. Adam leaned in, smiling, but the desk worker ignored him, instead pretending to work on her computer screen, obviously sensing that the two men at the desk were working together. Adam thanked her for her time and walked away, grabbing Howe's arm. "Let's go."

He marched down a side hallway, and Howe grabbed his arm, pulling Adam to a stop. "What are you *doing*?" he whispered.

"I saw the room number reflected in the glasses that woman wore," Adam replied. "Mrs. Baker is here. Let's go." Howe reluctantly followed, wondering if they were breaking some kind of hospital rule.

Adam led the way to the room and knocked on the door, stepping aside so that Howe would be the first person Michael Baker would see. A moment later, the ashen-faced former police officer opened the door a crack, a small hint of relief appearing at the sight of the familiar face. "Millard. Thank you for coming. I should have called and told you, but..."

"Don't worry about it, Michael," Howe replied. "We figured it out."

Baker noticed Adam. He looked at the man intently, frowned, and said, "I don't believe I know you, do I?"

"Not directly," Adam replied. "We do have a common friend, though."

"Millard?"

"Will Stark."

Baker glanced at Howe. "Should I know this man?"

Howe shrugged. "He's a colleague. May we come in?"

Baker hesitated, and then opened the door with some reluctance, closing it immediately after the two men had entered the room.

Katherine Baker was lying on an elevated bed, and it was unclear if she was sleeping or unconscious. She had numerous tubes running into her body, the familiar beeping sound tracking her pulse the only consistent noise in the room. Bandages covered her face, which was clearly bruised heavily. A small boy was on the bed with the woman, curled around one of her legs, his face positioned to watch her. The boy could be no more than six or seven years old.

"Your son?" Adam asked.

Baker nodded. "His name is William. We named him after one of the best men we'd ever known."

Adam nodded. "A wonderful choice. What happened to her?"

"Witnesses said she and William headed out to do some grocery shopping. When they got home, there were people waiting for her. They pulled the two of them out of the car, and threatened my wife if she didn't give them money, money they said Stark owed them. They... they picked up a rock and hit her in the head, meaning to scare her, but got carried away and kept at it until my son's screaming and tears finally made them run. She's got a lot of facial lacerations and bruises, and a severe concussion as well. The doctors say she'll be OK, eventually, but she's going to need to stay in here for several days, probably a week. William was there and saw the whole thing, and he's quite traumatized by it. He refuses to leave her side, because he's convinced she'll die if he does. I'd love to get him to go home or to a friend's house, but I can't get him to leave."

Howe was conflicted. He glanced at Adam, but the man's face was terrible, the look of someone who'd experienced a most horrifying event. Adam put his hand on Baker's shoulder. "I promise you, Michael, that the people who did this will be punished."

Baker smiled weakly. "Thanks. Unfortunately, it won't take away my son's memories of what happened, or stop the nightmares both of them will have."

Adam was quiet for a bit, and Howe felt awkward silence surrounding them.

Adam went over to the sleeping woman and held her hand, apparently deep in thought or prayer, and then he leaned over and gave her a gentle kiss on the forehead, releasing her hand. He crouched down and looked in the eye of the tiny boy huddled at his mother's feet. "Hi there, William. I'm a bit hungry and would love to get a candy bar. Do you know anyone who could show me where I might buy one?"

The little boy, his eyes red from draining out all the tears his tiny body could produce, tried to look brave. "I know where," he whispered.

Adam smiled, and glanced at Baker. "If it's OK with your dad, can you show me? I get lost all the time."

To Baker's shock, and Howe's as well, the little boy glanced at his dad. "Can I, Daddy?"

Baker only nodded, and the little boy crawled out of the bed, and led Adam by the hand from the room.

Baker glanced at Howe. "You do know that man, right? He's not going to run off with my son, is he?"

Howe shook his head. "I've met him before; he runs parts of the Starks' businesses. He told me he's the secret Advisor just before we figured out you might be here." He paused, glancing at the doorway. "I get the feeling your son is safer with him than just about anyone."

Baker nodded. "Oddly, I get the same feeling."

"He said you'd know he was the secret Advisor, because of something Will would have told both of you." Howe gave Baker a pointed look. "Any idea what that might be?"

Baker shook his head. "Not a clue. But I have a feeling he'll tell me in due time."

XIV
PURGE

Will woke to the sound of Angel and Fil entering the room, not because of a door opening or closing — such devices simply didn't exist in this room — but because the two were having an animated discussion in whispers, unaware that Will could hear them.

"—brought him here, what were you thinking—"

"—plan, the...change him—"

"—if he's wrong?"

Then they seemed aware that they had an audience, and ceased whispering. Angel had the decency to look guilty. Fil looked at Will as though offended the man had dared to be right where they'd left him.

Will arched an eyebrow. "Anything I should know about?"

"No," Fil said.

"That's it? Just no?"

"Just no."

"You know, you're reportedly going to give me something that will make me feel worse than I did shortly after receiving what were probably second-degree burns, getting shards of glass blasted into my body, being thrown through the air, and having three men I've since learned have what I would consider to be supernatural powers kick me with so much force that bones broke. I'm putting a lot of trust in you. Keeping secrets from me isn't exactly going to help our relationship."

"We have no relationship," Fil said, his voice cold. "We're doing each other favors. My life and my business are none of yours."

Will glanced at Angel. She shrugged. "It *was* a private conversation and it has nothing to do with you. If there's something you need to know, you'll know."

He sighed, but calmed noticeably as the young woman approached. He knew she was sending calming Energy his way, and wondered if the technique worked on everyone. He glanced back at Fil, and the man's face was still cold.

Apparently not.

"OK. Then can you at least give me some explanation of what this Purge is, exactly?"

Fil pulled a bottle out of his pocket. It was larger than the mere vials that Angel usually provided him. "This is it." He handed the bottle to Will. It was a dark, reddish color, and looked a lot like....

"Is that *blood?*" Will gasped. "Seriously, you told me you aren't witches, but I guess I should have asked if you're some other type of supernatural creature. I have no interest in becoming a vampire."

Fil scowled, and opened his mouth to hurl an insult Will's way. Angel placed a hand on the man's shoulder, and he closed his mouth, still seeming to look daggers at Will through the ever-present mirrored sunglasses. "Mr. Stark, it's not blood. That's just the color that the various components create when mixed together. We are very much human, just operating with a higher degree of the potential we can reach compared to most of our fellow humans. None of us drink blood." She glanced at Fil, who still looked annoyed at the suggestion, and gave him a friendly elbow. "Well, Fil thinks about it sometimes."

Will sighed. "It does look like blood, but I appear to have no choice. What does it do, exactly?"

Fil answered. "It's a mixture of selected food substances chosen for their individual and collaborative impacts, as well as special additives of our creation, designed to extract and expel harmful substances from the body and enable true health and Energy development."

Will blinked. "What?"

Fil scowled. "What do you mean, *what?* I just answered your question. Weren't you listening?"

"I don't want a scientific explanation. Just the facts. In English. With specifics on what it's going to do to me. I'd like to mentally prepare myself for the tortuous pain I'm supposed to endure from swallowing the blood stuff."

Fil's face curled into a snarl. Angel spoke up. "What we've found over time is that most humans have large quantities of what could best be called contaminants in their bodies. These contaminants have two primary effects, though sometimes they're subtle. First, they prevent your body from operating at optimum efficiency. For example, you might eat something that lessens the ability of your stomach to fully digest the next food you eat, or slow your recovery from an injury. Over time, these contaminants can add up, and it means your body operates at less than peak efficiency, sometimes *dramatically* less. You'll see various aging markers, lower muscle tone, and so on."

Will glanced down at himself through his glasses and patted his stomach. "I think I can relate to that point."

Angel nodded. It was quite clear that she and Fil did *not* relate. Both were extremely lean with excellent muscle tone. Will thought they both looked like the gymnasts he'd watched during the Olympic games when he was younger, before the worldwide economic depression caused the event to be canceled starting in 2020.

"The second thing they do is mask the Energy that your body naturally produces. Everyone produces some, but few can actually sense it, and if you can't sense it, you can't manipulate it to perform various tasks, like those I demonstrated to you before. Once those contaminants are gone, you'll feel better than you've ever felt before. You'll sense the Energy. Your body will be able to produce more Energy, and attract more from nature.

"Contaminants are impossible to avoid, so most of us will do a Purge several times per year, and it's unpleasant for us, like having a really bad cold. But with thirty-five years and no Purges...I can't imagine it will be pleasant."

"I've had colds before, Angel. I can deal with that."

Fil shook his head. "The various agents in the formula will seek out and bind to the contaminants, wherever they are. In muscle, in bone, in organs, in your brain, in tissues and ligaments. They will then seek an exit from the body, taking the contaminants with them. When there's not much contamination to remove, it's sweating and a runny nose. You, on the other hand, may literally bleed out your eyes. We simply don't know; we've not had anyone Purge before with such a buildup."

Will winced. "Your bedside manner needs work, but I appreciate the warning. Still, if this is what I need to do to prevent others from going through what my family and I went through, it's a price I'm willing to pay."

Fil glanced at the bottle. "Angel will stay and be prepared to take action if needed. When the effects of the Purge hit, please *try* not to kill her."

"Wait," Will said. "If I'm going to be dangerous, why are *you* leaving?"

"You're far more likely to try to kill *me*. My presence would exaggerate your desire for violence."

Good point. Will watched as the man walked through the wall of the room. He wondered when *he'd* leave this place. He hadn't actually tried yet, but wondered if he needed this Energy to get through the wall.

"Can I ask you something?" Angel asked, and Will nodded.

"What were they like?"

"Who?"

"Your family. Your wife and your son."

Will sighed. "They were my whole world. A lot of people thought my world was business, or making money, but those were just things that I did. My life was pretty lousy until I was about twenty years old, because before that all of my family was dead and I was completely broke. It wasn't much fun before that. I had an older brother, but he died when I was only about four or five years old, and it destroyed my parents. They were the type who thought the oldest child was always the best, but they tolerated me while he was around. After that? Let's just say I didn't get many examples of love from them. When they died, I didn't even care, and I doubt that fact would have bothered them because they didn't think I was worthy of having an opinion on anything."

"That's awful. You're not exaggerating just a bit though, are you?"

"They said those exact words to my face on more than one occasion, starting right after my brother died."

Angel's hand went to her mouth.

"They never had money. We were living in an economic depression, so that wasn't unusual. They showed no sign of love for me at all, or to each other, and I promised myself that I was going to fall in love, and live my life for that love. I promised myself I'd be rich, too, but it was more important to be accepted and loved just for being me. Hope gave me that. She was the first person who ever simply accepted me for who I am, and loved me for it unconditionally. If I hadn't met her, I don't know where I'd be. I guess I'd still be pretty rich, but there'd be no purpose in having it, or guidance on what to do with all the money I would have had. I never had that issue with Hope. She accepted me and let me be who I needed to be, and gave me a moral center and heart. And she made me laugh. We laughed all the time. It was such a happy home."

Angel wiped a tear away from her eye. "She sounds wonderful." Will could only nod. "What about your son?

"We wanted so desperately to have children, but we couldn't, and I found out that the fault was mine. I visited doctors in secret, and nothing helped. I finally found a private researcher who had some different theories and techniques, and after I went to him, Hope was expecting not long after. Josh being born was the happiest moment of our lives, and we were very happy people, total opposite of what I grew up with."

Will smiled as he thought of Josh. "He had the most incredible eyes. They were this amazing blue color, like ice reflecting a clear sky, and they had an amazing intensity to them. I'd watch him for hours, because I'd look into that little boy's eyes and feel like I was looking at a truly amazing soul, one with wisdom and intelligence and knowledge. For some reason, though, he was never able to talk. Our doctors gave up trying to figure out why, because there was nothing physically wrong with him. Hope and I would spend a lot of time with him every day, especially Hope, and we'd read him stories and try to teach him things. We joked that if he ever started talking he'd be the best educated child in history. I'd teach him how to throw different pitches and hit, because I loved baseball and wanted to share that with him. I have no idea if he knew what I was doing or if he'd like baseball if he could play.

"He never spoke or laughed or cried. Never made a sound. I always wondered why, if maybe it was something I'd done by accident, or if there was something I *hadn't* done. I wondered if I'd failed him somehow, failed some parenting test and because of that, he couldn't speak. That's one of the things those attacks took from me. I never heard my son's voice in any form. I wish I could have heard him laugh just once. You know, Hope called me while I was heading home that day, and told me he'd started talking, and I was so emotional about it that she wouldn't put him on the phone because she feared I'd lose control and crash the car. Maybe I should have insisted, and talked to my son even that one time, and told him I loved him and was proud of him."

Angel's face was damp with tears. "That was beautiful. I think they both knew how you felt about them. Including your son."

Will nodded. "I hope so. Do you understand now why I need to do this? I don't care if it's painful. It's a way to honor their memory by making sure those monsters never hurt anyone else. They denied me my chance to connect with my own child, and I can't let that happen again." He glanced at the bottle. "I guess I need to drink this."

He took the top off the bottle and started drinking. The liquid was smooth and cool, and tasted minty, not at all what he imagined blood would taste like. He drank the entire bottle, and sat it down.

After a few minutes, he glanced at Angel. "Will I start to notice everything working?"

Angel nodded, tears forming. "Sadly, I think you will. And very soon."

Will nodded. Then it started.

A sensation of heat — not a soothing heat, but scorching heat, hot enough to boil water — started in his core and arced out to his extremities, followed by what felt like a razor carving his insides up. He tried to scream in pain, but couldn't gather the requisite air, his body seeming to shut down in pure shock. The razor sensation seemed to be scraping against every internal inch of his body, caring not what it cut or shredded. His limbs moved crazily, as if seeking something to strike as if it would calm the pain, and he understood Fil's request to try to not to kill Angel.

There was a brief respite, and he was able to breathe for a moment. He noticed the moisture on his skin as he sweated with the strain of the experience, and felt the moisture around his eyes. And he noticed that Fil had returned, laying a comforting hand on Angel's shoulder, a hand she grasped and held with great firmness. Apparently, he wasn't always cold and heartless after all.

Then the next wave hit.

The materials in the Purge formula found every possible exit from the inside of his body. The sweating was of incredible ferocity, gallons of moisture pouring from his pores. He just had time to smell the foul aromas before material poured from his nose, ending his sense of smell. Fluid seeped out his ears. He retched, if it could be called that; there were no heaves, just a mass exodus of putrescence exiting his mouth. His mind reeled, unable to comprehend what was happening, shrieking for oxygen, unaware that his excretory organs were participating in the expulsion efforts. His limbs lost all control as muscles and tendons spasmed, and he slumped to the ground as if made of jelly, his limbs contorting out of his control.

He had no idea how long the torture lasted, only that he was suddenly breathing pure, sweet air again, gasping in huge gulps to feed his screaming cells with their fuel. He could not open his eyes out of pure exhaustion, but his ears worked well enough to hear Angel crying, the sobs seeming to come from miles away.

He sensed footsteps. "We'll need to clean him," he heard Fil say, his voice tight.

"He can't walk," Angel said, choking the words out between sobs as she sought to calm herself.

"I know," Fil replied. He bent down and picked Will up with ease, and started walking.

"He looks *awful*," Angel whispered. "He *smells* awful."

"I know," Fil said again, his voice strained, yet patient.

"Will he ever forgive us? I didn't know it would be that bad. I tried to warn him, but I still had no idea it would be that bad."

"I didn't either."

Will managed to crack his eyes open for just a moment, before the bright sunlight of the outdoors blinded him. His body thoroughly exhausted from the horrific intensity of the Purge, he finally crashed into unconsciousness.

But not before he'd noticed the single tear sliding down Fil's cheek.

• • •

The fire still burned in Will as he woke up, but he found it to be a pleasant sensation. It was more akin to a hot washcloth on his face, rather than the burning embers he'd been subjected to, internally and externally, in the past several days.

He wondered how long he'd actually been here. He'd been asleep a lot, and given the traumas or medications he'd been subjected to prior to each round of sleep, he imagined he could easily have slept twelve hours or longer each session. He'd also been inside the entire time, which meant he had no ability to observe the daylight or the nighttime. He vaguely remembered being carried outside after the Purge had completed, carried somewhere by Fil with Angel following, apparently to clean him from the mess of everything that had come out of him. When it had all ended, he'd caught a brief whiff of the stench and gagged, but there was nothing left in him to vomit up.

His strangest memory was the sight of the tear on Fil's cheek. Did the man actually have compassion for his suffering? Overall, he seemed cold and distant, and while he wasn't specifically seeking friendship, he sensed a deep resentment from Fil, something that was uncomfortable with Will's presence in their community. Perhaps he believed Will to be a threat in some fashion.

Regardless of Fil's opinion of him, Will had work to do, and right now that meant recovering from the trauma of the Purge. His initial assessment was that he definitely felt better. *Much* better. He felt lighter. His muscles had no knots of tension and moved with greater smoothness. He thought he was seeing with a lot more clarity as well. He moved his hands to adjust his glasses, only to note that they weren't there. He blinked with surprise, but reminded himself that one of Angel's magic potions had healed broken bones; there was no reason at this point not to believe Fil could create something that could perfect his eyesight. His eyesight was now strong enough that he realized, with shock, that his all-white bodysuit actually had streaks of pink in it. He figured that must be Fil having fun with him.

The warmth he'd noticed inside was still there; what was odd was that it seemed to move and be more intense wherever his concentration focused. When he thought of his eyes, the warmth seemed strongest there. He concentrated on his feet, and his toes tingled. He looked at his hands, and felt them warming, almost seeing something sparking off of them. He cupped his hands together, and felt the warmth grow until he seemed to be holding a ball of fire. Smiling, he went into his pitching windup, turned, and threw the ball of fire at the chair that was standing in for the catcher in his little daydream.

The chair flew backward and slammed against the white wall.

What the...?

"I see you've already started experimenting with Energy," a new voice said. "That's excellent. You'll be a fine pupil."

Will turned and saw the brown-haired man from the escape vehicle, wearing a pale green bodysuit. The man was grinning at him.

"That's the Energy? That warmth?"

"Indeed it is. Most of my pupils take quite some time to notice the Energy at all, dismissing it as a post-Purge fever or some other form of fantasy. Most of them also possess very little Energy, so it's not difficult to understand why they can't sense it or manipulate it. You already possess a decent quantity, which suggests that you're predisposed to this type of skill, even with absolutely no training." He chuckled.

"What's so funny?"

"Those Hunters were looking for a man named Will Stark, the man who possessed the greatest ability to produce, acquire, and manipulate Energy of any Aliomenti in history. New as you are to Energy work, I dare say that at some point, the Aliomenti will wish they'd kept you captive when they found you. It looks like they may have found the right man after all. And they helped deliver him straight into the hands of their enemies." Adam smiled.

Will smiled too.

XV
DUEL

The Assassin sat on the floor in the room with his back against the solid wall, waiting for someone to come for him. He was trapped here in this room of uniform color with no windows or doors, and he was enraged, so much so that he was prepared to litter the room with bodies.

Everything about this place was strange. Since he'd awakened from his capture and crawled from the trunk of the vehicle, he'd detected no sense of Energy. He was accustomed to being bombarded with Energy in the Aliomenti communities he frequented, most notably the Aliomenti regions of Headquarters. Here, there was nothing. His experiences and inability to escape led him to conclude that he was in the hands of the Alliance, but if that was the case, he should sense at least some Energy. Was the Alliance now devoid of Energy? And if so, how were they restraining him?

He stood and faced the wall behind him. There was something very strange about these walls. He had seen the man who had called himself the Mechanic walk straight through the wall, yet there was no sign of an opening. He leaned close, his eye nearly touching the surface, trying to identify the materials used in its construction. He noted two details of interest. The surface of the wall gave off a soft glow, and he felt a gentle breeze coming from the wall, noticeable only when he was this close to the surface.

The Assassin moved back from the wall and began pacing. The wall was built of some type of permeable material. It kept him in, yet somehow allowed in exterior light and air. He detected no sounds from the outside, and had felt no moisture from outside precipitation. Was this room a standalone building? Did it have one or more walls or the ceiling facing the elements? Or was it part of a larger structure, perhaps a fully isolated room? That would explain some of his puzzling observations. They could control the amount of light, air, moisture, and noise available from the outside, and allow only what was desired through the permeable walls. Such permeability apparently allowed an Alliance member through, but kept him from leaving. He allowed himself a brief, grudging moment of respect for the Alliance; they'd created an exceptionally useful bit of Energy work here, one that mysteriously gave off no sense of Energy in its operation.

The brief feeling of commendation ended. He needed to leave this building. Though he was in no danger of suffocation or otherwise succumbing to the elements, he was still trapped in here by unnatural means. He would leave, exact his revenge, and return to Headquarters where he belonged.

The Assassin slapped himself on the head. He was thinking like a stupid human, who would need to walk through a door or crawl through a window to leave a room. He could teleport, albeit only a few feet at a time. But that should be enough.

He marched back to the wall until he stood only a few feet away. One typically needed to have a firm picture of the target location in mind to teleport successfully, and unfortunately he had no idea what the outside of this building looked like. He had no idea of landmarks, or even the exterior shape, size, and coloring of the building housing him. So how should he do this? Could he just say "go forward five feet" and have it work? He'd need to test the approach.

He moved back several paces, and then spun around in circles until he had no idea which way he was facing. Once the disorientation was complete, he dropped his short sword straight down as a marker of his starting spot. He concentrated on simply moving himself forward two feet, without opening his eyes, and felt the familiar sense of displacement indicating he had actually moved. He opened his eyes and turned around, and found the blade marking his original spot two feet behind him.

Perfect. It worked. Not something he'd typically need to use, but in a situation like this, it was a critical nuance to his skill. And it would be the downfall of the Alliance, especially the man named Fil.

After retrieving and sheathing his weapon, The Assassin marched back to the wall, stood two feet away, and closed his eyes. He performed the same exercise, projecting himself forward four feet this time.

He felt the familiar sensation of displacement during the teleportation, but his body was jarred immediately after. When he opened his eyes, he found himself pressed flat against the permeable, but solid-to-him, wall.

Frowning, he moved back just a few inches, so that he was nearly touching the wall surface, and repeated the process. Once again, his teleportation effort only succeeded in smashing his face against the very solid surface of the wall. He grabbed his sword and stabbed at the wall in frustration, but the weapon merely bounced off the surface, without leaving even a small mark.

"You need to develop better learning comprehension."

The Assassin whirled toward the voice, short sword instantly in his hand, assuming a defensive stance.

A young man sat in a chair he hadn't previously noticed, lounging casually. He had short, jet-black hair, and wore wraparound mirrored sunglasses, a human fashion item that aggravated The Assassin greatly.

"Who are you?"

"I was told you were looking for me."

The Assassin scowled. "You're the one who threw me in... in there." He gestured toward the vehicle sitting in the center of the room.

"Guilty."

The Assassin stared at the man. He emitted no Energy, yet showed absolutely no fear in the face of a scar-faced man wielding a sword. "Do you know who I am?"

"Yes. You're The Leader's lapdog, sent to perform the noble, brave work of killing unarmed human women and children. A true model of bravery for all to emulate." The man clapped in a slow, mocking fashion.

"Humans aren't worth the space they take up. I'm doing us — and them — a service by ending their miserable existence. The only shame is that I'm not allowed to be more thorough." He moved toward the man, slowly, his blood-red eyes never leaving the face of this man who seemed unafraid of him.

"You judge an entire species based upon the acts of a tiny few, acting irrationally. Tell me, did you ever bother to follow up on that mob? Learn about the fact that every single one of them was ashamed of their actions, and sought you out to seek forgiveness? Or did you cede all control of your emotions to your hatred and anger, lumping the innocent with the guilty, forgetting that you yourself are committing the very crime you suffered?"

The Assassin stiffened. How could he possibly know? "You have no idea what you're talking about."

"No? An Assassin, very much like you, decided that two people very dear to me needed to die, because it had been learned that at least one of them could do things she shouldn't be able to do. The two people killed were my wife and my young daughter. Does that sound familiar?"

The Assassin's breathing caught in his chest.

"They notified me of what was going to happen. But they didn't tell me where, just gave me a link to set up a two way video feed, so I could watch them be slaughtered, and they could see me helpless to defend them. I did watch. I would not abandon them. I met their gaze, told them I loved them, and that I'd avenge them."

The man rose to his feet, nearly a head taller than The Assassin. "I should hate all Assassins, shouldn't I? I should kill you on the spot, right here, right now, simply because of what you are. Yet when given the chance, I kicked you a few times, and then I gave you medicine that healed your wounds. Why? Because I won't give in to the animal nature like you have. I won't become what I detest."

The Assassin laughed. "Lovely speech. A morality plea? How comic. And the arrogance, too. *You*, able to kill *me*? *No one* kills *me*. Least of all a coward too weak to avenge those he claims to have loved. I avenge my own with each bit of blood I spill. You spit on the existence of yours with each life, like mine, that you spare." The Assassin stepped forward, blood-red eyes glinting, the malice so intense that the temperature in the room seemed to rise.

The man in the sunglasses stood still. The Assassin was nearly upon him, and laughed again. "Foolish human. You should have killed me when you had the chance." He raised his sword.

The man smiled back at him. "Oh, I'm not foolish."

The Assassin felt an invisible glove surround him, pinning him still, and there was a look of shock upon his ugly, scarred face. He still felt no Energy from the man.

"I am, though, quite human, just as you are at your core. You deny it as something shameful, but without that starting point you have no way of measuring how much you've developed yourself. Or, in your case, how far you've fallen."

The Assassin's scowl deepened.

"I refuse to deny what I am. The humanity in me prevents me from killing you now, even though I could do so with ease." The Assassin felt the glove start to tighten, ever so slowly, until he couldn't breathe. Then the glove released, just enough to enable him to breathe again. "But I won't. I will not, however, deny others their opportunity to act on their own nature. You see, Assassin, when I rescued you from that burning house, I brought someone else with me as well. Like you, I healed her of her wounds. And now, she'd like to reveal her own inner animal to you."

The Assassin blinked. Was this man talking about the human woman married to Will Stark? Was this young man, not Will Stark, the one to make the woman and child vanish? How could he do that, with no detectable Energy?

"But before I let the two of you get reacquainted, I feel you must do so on an even footing. She comes to you unarmed. And you must meet her unarmed as well." The sword was torn from The Assassin's grasp, and he watched as it moved through the wall and outside the room, safely beyond his reach.

"She also comes to you not enhanced by Energy, so we will even things up in that area as well." The Assassin felt something surround his Energy stores, shutting off all access to them, and he felt helpless and human as he experienced the same sensation those meeting Aramis' Damper felt. He fell to the floor, surprised, as the invisible, restraining glove released him, but quickly scrambled to his feet. Instinct screamed at him to charge the man, but he controlled himself.

"Now that the two of you are on a more even footing, Assassin, I'd like to present an old friend." The man licked his lips, and then whistled.

A dog, a black Labrador retriever, trotted in through the wall, attracted by the sound of the whistle. The dog seemed cheerful, tail high, panting in the manner of her kind. She trotted to the man with the sunglasses, who patted the dog on the head. "Assassin, meet Smokey. Smokey, meet The Assassin."

The dog paused, sniffed the air, and turned to face The Assassin. The dog's hackles rose, and a deep, rumbling growl sounded. The hairs on the back of The Assassin's neck stood on end. He knew true fear, his first experience of the emotion — on the receiving end — in a very long time.

"Smokey remembers what happened the last time you met, you see. She knows that you attacked two humans she cared for. She remembers that you hurt her as well." He smiled, and there was no mirth to the expression, even without being able to see his eyes. "I believe she'd like to discuss the matter with you, in her own fashion."

He patted the dog on the head. "Sic 'em, girl."

Growling, the dog charged The Assassin. The man threw an arm up to defend himself and fell in the process. The dog seized the limb in her jaws and bit down with every bit of savagery a canine could muster, tearing skin and muscle. The Assassin screamed as the sharp pain overwhelmed him. He tried to position himself to kick her, but with four legs planted firmly on the ground, she easily maneuvered around the attempted blows. Survival instinct kicked in for him, and he moved his torso closer to her, rolling off his backside on to his knees, with the dog hanging on to his shredded arm. The Assassin raised his elbow and slammed it into the dog's head, but Smokey didn't react. He tried again, and this time she saw the blow coming. She released her jaws and sprang away, and The Assassin howled anew as he struck his own mangled arm. The nerve endings and muscles were torn and blood flowed freely. The arm was effectively dead.

While The Assassin stared at his injury, the dog pounced again, paws hitting him firmly in the chest, knocking him onto his back. The force of it slammed his head onto the ground, and he saw stars. His instinct kicked in, and he threw his injured arm in front of his face while swinging his good arm in an arc. The good arm made contact, and Smokey was knocked away from him, hitting the ground on her side. Smokey rolled twice, scrambled up on all four paws, and charged the man again. The Assassin had been trying to get to his feet, his good arm under him as he tried to press himself up to his knees, and the weight of the dog landing on his back unbalanced him. He landed face-first on the floor in a pool of his own blood, and felt the dog's teeth sink into the skin of his neck, the snarling rage filled with blood lust, and The Assassin was very aware that he was going to die.

"To me, Smokey." The man's voice carried to The Assassin's ears, faint. But he felt the teeth release him, was aware that the animal had left him, and was suddenly quite grateful to be alive. He spent several minutes face down on the ground, breathing rapidly at first, then more deeply, until his heart rate stabilized. He was still weak from the blood loss in his arm, but he was alive and would survive. With agonizing effort, he used his functioning arm to push himself up onto his knees, resting back on his haunches.

The man with the sunglasses sat in the same chair, watching him with interest. At his side sat the dog, Smokey, the latter sporting a look of extreme contentment as the man scratched her behind the ears. There was no sign in the dog's current demeanor of the vicious beast that had attacked and nearly killed him, save for a small amount of his blood on her snout.

"You see," the man said, "we all have our moments of violence, when our inner animal comes out, including cases when we are actually animals." He nodded at the dog. "And yet here you see Smokey in a state that would be her most normal, a pleasant and friendly companion, happy with the simplest gestures. When she felt threatened, however, she reacted with violence, though perhaps if she'd taken the time to assess the situation she would have realized that you are currently no threat to either of us, and thus the attack was unnecessary."

He patted the dog, and Smokey trotted back toward The Assassin. The man lurched backward away from the animal, terrified that she would attack again. He crashed into the wall, that wall that allowed everyone and everything in and out but him, and he was trapped. His legs kept moving, trying to push his body through the wall, desperate to get away from the vicious beast before she attacked him. He threw his good arm up in front of his face. Smokey moved closer, cautious, and sniffed. He could feel her hot breath on his face, see his own blood still on her snout.

The Assassin's will broke. She was too close, he was too frail, and he had none of his usual tools of violence available to defend himself. He let his legs go limp, and dropped his arm from its defensive position. The dog had defeated him, and she would kill him.

Smokey watched him, panting. Then she moved up next to him and licked The Assassin's face. She sat down on her haunches next to him, tail wagging.

The Assassin was stunned. Wasn't this animal the same one that had attacked him without remorse only a few moments earlier? What was this behavior?

"She likes to be scratched behind the ears," the man with the sunglasses offered.

"You have *got* to be kidding me," The Assassin muttered. But the dog hadn't attacked him again. Yet. And so, with a great deal of anxiety, he reached his good hand over, resting it on the dog's fur, and started to scratch. The dog's eyes closed, and she seemed to be very content.

"I think she likes you."

"She has no need or reason to like me," The Assassin said. "I fully expect her to finish me off at any second."

"She reacts as instinct demands to defend herself and those she cares for," the man replied. "If you are no threat, then she's quite happy to be friends. If you move to attack her, however, or threaten me... well, you know what she can do when provoked."

Fil stood. "Come, Smokey," he called, and the dog trotted away from The Assassin, back to his side. Fil faced The Assassin. "I will send someone in to provide medication that will heal those wounds and help you sleep, at which point we will discuss your future options."

"You can't trust me," The Assassin snapped. "I'll kill every single one of you when I get the chance. You should execute me now, not restore my health."

"A man who pats the head of a dog that just mauled him is one who can learn to trust and be trusted. I dare say you are more capable of change than you realize." Fil and the dog left the room, melting through the walls, and the Mechanic reappeared. He pulled out a potion and gave it to The Assassin.

"What's this?" the injured man asked.

"It's the medication Fil mentioned," the Mechanic replied. "It will help you sleep and heal the wounds you got in your little duel."

The Assassin smirked, the action sending a shooting pain through him. "More like it will kill me," he muttered.

The Mechanic shrugged. "We've had every opportunity to kill you.

I could do that right now."

The Assassin nodded, though it nearly killed him to acknowledge the fact. "I know." He opened the bottle and drank the contents. He started to feel the effects of the sleeping potion almost immediately, and as his eyes started to flutter shut and the adrenaline of the fight wore off, he truly felt the pain.

He was vaguely aware of the Mechanic carrying him to a bed that hadn't been in the room moments ago. Perhaps the chair the man with the glasses had used could be changed into one? The Mechanic placed something on the bed next to The Assassin. "I have a feeling you'll need this again. Use it with greater wisdom in the future." He turned and left.

The Assassin's good arm moved to the object, his hand grazing the surface, and he felt the familiar texture of his sword just as sleep claimed him.

XVI
ENERGY

Will had settled into a routine that had become his new normal, reflective of the incredible ability of human beings to adapt to new circumstances.

A few weeks earlier, his life revolved around his wife and son, his philanthropic work, and his businesses, in that order. Today, he could no longer spend time on any of them, outside the happy memories he had to dig to find. More frequent were the flashbacks of the last minutes before his rescue. Michael Baker's look of horror at seeing the two dead guards. The killer standing in his house, the blood dripping from the sword the man carried. The explosion and fire that destroyed his house. The maniacal frenzy of anger and rage in the faces of the three Hunters as they kicked and beat him, as Athos slit his cheeks to match the scar on the Hunter's face, of Aramis' look of righteous fury as the man tried to stab him to death along with his fellow Hunters.

What truly told him that his life was different was waking up each day in that empty white room, where he'd roll to his side and not see Hope's sleeping form beside him. There was no daily walk down the hall to see Josh and his faithful companion, Smokey, wondering and ever hopeful that that day would be the one the boy would finally speak. That day would never come now, and he'd go to his grave having never heard his son's voice or laughter.

But his new normal now dominated his thoughts, and he kept

pushing the flashbacks deep into his mind for later, a brief moment when their recollection would serve as a form of penance and self-condemnation. At the moment, he was focused, at Adam's direction, on making sure that he remained floating three feet off the ground, levitating himself with his own Energy. The marvel of human adaptability was that this seeming wizardry was as normal to him now as driving a car had been then.

Progress had been steady. Adam worked with him for a few hours at a time, mostly teaching him how to sense and grow his Energy levels. Will, with nothing else to do, spent every waking moment before and after his sessions figuring things out for himself.

He had also finally left the room he'd been living in, walking through the walls like the others did. Adam noted he was not a prisoner and never had been, and the other buildings in the community were built with a similar technology; he was free to attempt to enter any he liked. The buildings were, in essence, intelligent; if he wasn't permitted in a building, he wouldn't be able to get in.

Will tried to think of the various Energy skills he'd heard mentioned. He mastered empathy fairly quickly, able to read emotions with startling accuracy, and telepathy shortly after. His education included ethics around the use of his skills; deep empathic or telepathic work was considered rude to perform without permission. He recalled the feeling of invasion when Angel had demonstrated the skills several weeks earlier, and understood that logic quickly and easily. The Empathic reading skills could, with practice, become a "push" technique — you could project Energy with a specific emotional charge and create that emotional change in your target. Angel's calming influence on him was his most obvious example of this. He kept those skills in check, though he knew he'd use them if needed if he ever came up against the Elites of the Aliomenti — the man called The Leader, his council, the Hunters, and The Assassin. Those were the men and women whose drive to global Aliomenti elitism had led to the overzealous enforcement of Oaths, and apparently included authorization for the murders of those like Hope and Josh who simply were in the way. There'd be no restraint around those people.

His latest skill under development was telekinesis. This was the ability to project and control his Energy outside his body, most often used to move objects that could not be reached with the hands. He found that Energy seemed immune to weight, and that it was more difficult to lift something with a large surface area than a large weight. During his self-study he'd applied the approach to his own body, and managed a crude form of flying that took so much mental control that it exhausted him. When he mentioned this to Adam, the man noted that there were better ways to fly; they'd practice those at a later date. For now, Will simply accepted the fact that he could prevent himself from falling to his death, but he wouldn't be emulating an airplane any time soon.

Adam told him that many of the Aliomenti perfected a special skill, typically tied to their personality. Angel had very strong empathy skills, which Will had already deduced. Each of the Hunters for the Aliomenti had a skill which, when combined, made them incredibly effective at capturing someone. Porthos had extreme sensitivity to Energy, able to locate even tiny bursts from great distances. He could reportedly even sense *who* had generated the Energy he detected. His Tracking skills enabled the Hunters to find their targets rapidly. Aramis had developed an incredible Energy Dampering ability. The man could essentially wrap insulation around a person's Energy and stifle it, in some cases eliminating their access to it entirely. Athos combined telepathic and empathic skills to be a human truth detector, so powerful that even when those queried didn't know the truth, Athos did.

Will tried his hand at each of the abilities, and found that he could "hear" Energy if he focused. Each member of the Alliance produced a different tone, and Will made mental notes matching tones to people. He used the technique to track Adam once in an effort to practice the skill. It took an incredible effort, though, and he filed the capability away to revisit. Likewise, he was able to damper Adam's Energy a bit, but it was a skill that didn't come to him easily. He wasn't sure how to test Athos' skill, however, and let it go.

He made himself walk around the camp each day, taking breaks from his self-imposed, rigorous Energy training. The camp was comprised of small buildings, all of a similar size, shape, and color to the one he had been using. He didn't see many people, which was at times reassuring — the Alliance probably preferred to keep their numbers spread out — and at other times concerning. Were they just widely dispersed, or were the numbers of the Alliance simply that small? Nobody would give him answers.

He enjoyed sitting on the outskirts of the camp, his back against one of the massive trees circling his new home, trees reminiscent of the community at De Gray Estates. The weather was tropical and pleasant: bright sunshine, fresh air, and a sense of serenity his high-paced lifestyle had never afforded him. If only he could have brought Hope and Josh here...

Will had asked where in the world they were, and was told that it wasn't important for him to know. He was treated well, was given nourishing and delicious food, had been healed of wounds that should have killed him, and was able to do things he never thought possible. Yet he often felt like a prisoner, one not trusted to keep the secrets of the Alliance, doing his penance to earn the right to wear the golden tattoo on his palm.

He stood and made his way into the forest. He had a few secrets of his own.

Will had found the tree during his first solo journey outside the building nearly a week ago. While he walked among the majestic trees in the forest, as he'd felt a tremendous sense of peace, he'd seen the small tree nestled among the giants. The leaves were a paler green than those of its neighbors. Will sat down and watched the tree, entranced at the sight. And then he'd seen it, a slight twitch in the tree, and one of the limbs moved, ever so slightly, so that it caught one of the few rays of sunlight that managed to sneak through the canopy above. The tree was fighting for every nutrient it needed to survive, including sunlight.

Will was inspired, for it couldn't be easy for a tree to move, and he wanted to help. This tree was every young entrepreneur he'd ever assisted, trying to make it in a difficult world, fighting for every bit that they could get to press on towards their goals, seeking to make themselves better, not to drag others down. Will had no money to give in this case, and money would do the tree no good. But he had Energy now, and he wondered if that would help the tree.

He stood and walked to the tree, moving to avoid interrupting that vital bit of sunlight. Touching a branch of the tree, he projected his Energy forth into the limb, hoping that it would help the tree find and process the nutrients it needed to grow. Instead, the tree seemed to straighten under his touch, growing taller. The color of the leaves deepened, and more buds began to sprout. It was exhilarating for

Will to see the tree succeed. He put both hands to the trunk, as a means of more rapidly passing his Energy into the tree, wondering if it might further enhance the tree's growth.

The tree's rate of growth did accelerate, but what Will didn't expect was the feedback effect he got. Will felt Energy coming back to him, somehow purer and richer and in greater quantity than what had been in his body previously. In some strange form of symbiosis, Will was getting stronger as he helped the tree grow stronger.

His encounter with the tree was like a timeless meditation, and it was only with great reluctance that he allowed the connection to end. He passed Adam on his way back into the camp; Adam shot him a strange look, but said nothing. Will glanced down and was surprised to see that his white bodysuit seemed more pink than white. That must have been what caused Adam's reaction. Will wondered how the clothing had managed to change color; he didn't remember it being so pink when he'd donned it earlier that day. He pushed the thought aside, focusing on visiting the tree again each day as time permitted.

When he visited the tree this day he was amazed. His visits had occurred for just over a week, and during that time the tree had shown remarkable growth. Today, his tree — *his* tree — had reached a height sufficient to push its tallest branches up above the canopy into the direct sunlight. It was a moment of extreme pride for Will, as if his own child had achieved some remarkable accomplishment. His face fell at the thought of Josh. His own son never had the chance to reach for the sunlight. Will added yet more pressure to himself to learn and get stronger; no other children's lives should be cut short for lack of defense against the evil elements of the Aliomenti.

The feedback effect had grown each day, as both man and tree had strengthened and increased the amount of Energy they could share and provide to each other. Will had seen the obvious effects in his work with Adam; he didn't need telepathy or empathy to know that he was progressing at a rate that astounded and even frightened his trainer.

Will put his hands to the tree trunk. The tree was now strong and sturdy, and though he once could wrap his hands around the trunk, he now struggled to wrap both arms around the same section. The Energy flow today was incredible; Will wondered if the tree's ability to directly tap into the sunlight overhead had something to do with it.

He found his senses strangely magnified, his awareness of his surroundings intensified. And he sensed something else when he closed his eyes.

He could see Adam and Fil talking, both men animated in their gestures, and with looks of concern crossing their faces. He became gradually aware that he could hear them, faintly at first, but as he focused their voices became clear.

Fil: *"...Shielding, his Energy levels are getting far too strong to be missed."*

Adam: *"I know, the growth is beyond explanation. He's already hinted at red. In less than four weeks. He's going to be teleporting soon, whether he intends to or not. I need to make him aware of it before he finds himself three miles away with no idea how he got there, or worse, drops unannounced into an Aliomenti community."*

Fil: *"No. Shielding first. We cannot allow him to be a danger to this community, Adam. Our numbers are low enough as it is without inviting an attack. His Energy level is going to attract Porthos' attention soon."*

Adam: *"I'll work on both in the next session. We meet up again tomorrow."*

Fil: *"If you wait that long, you'll likely be meeting the Hunters, not Stark. You need to find him now. He should be rather easy to locate."*

Will pulled his hands from the tree, and the eavesdropping session ended. He made them worried, fearful that his rapid Energy growth would attract the Hunters to their camp. At the moment, he was more concerned about anyone finding him near this tree. He sprinted through the forest toward camp, focusing on tracking Adam as he ran. As he edged past the tree line into the clearing, he slowed to a walk, normalized his breathing, and sat down at the edge of the forest, his back against a tree as usual. He knew Adam was looking for him, and would follow his Energy trail. It was best to stop him here, before he moved deeper into the forest.

He closed his eyes, tracking Adam's Energy sound. It seemed to move in a straight path, and then suddenly shifted. Will opened his eyes, frowning and turned in the direction of the sound. It was almost as if Adam had...

He stood up and walked back towards his tree. The men had talked about teleportation. Will knew what that was, vanishing in one location and appearing in another, instantly. Angel had demonstrated the ability to him in his first days here, and Adam had made allusions to the skill, saying it took enormous amounts of Energy to be able to move even a few yards. If Will's judgment was correct, Adam had just teleported several hundred yards, which meant that the man was exceptionally powerful, more than Will had originally thought. It wasn't the skill that concerned Will, however. It was the destination.

As he expected, Adam was there in the clearing, staring at the tree. His tree. The man's face was a mask, as if he were deep in thought. Will couldn't imagine what he was doing, but he wanted to get Adam away from here.

"There you are!" Will's words startled Adam, who spun, his face bearing a look of genuine surprise. "I had a question for you, but couldn't find you."

"It appears that's no longer the case," Adam replied, a thin smile on his face. "Practicing your tracking skills on me? I thought you'd given up on developing that particular skill."

"It appears that's no longer the case," Will said, smiling, expecting a like response from Adam. Instead, the man turned back toward the tree.

Will frowned. "Something bothering you, Adam?"

Adam sighed. "There's something very strange about this tree. It seems to have an Energy vibration very much like yours; I tracked you here because of the strength of the Energy in this area. Yet I found the Energy I tracked in the tree and its surroundings. No sign of you." He turned to face Will. "Most unusual."

"Trees can have Energy, too?" Will asked, surprised.

"In theory, anything alive can have some, though most have rather minute traces. Humans in general have the most, but even there, the vast majority have what little Energy they possess suppressed. This tree has Energy levels I'd expect more from a reasonably adept human trained in the Aliomenti sciences, perhaps even a pink. I've not sensed such readings in a non-human organism before."

"A pink?" Will asked. "What does that mean?"

"Ah, yes, we haven't discussed that yet," Adam said, chuckling. "Our clothing in this camp changes color based upon our Energy levels. The colors roughly correspond to the wavelength of the visible light spectrum; the longer the wavelength, the greater the Energy. Each color progression represents an order of magnitude increase in accumulated Energy levels. White, pink, and red are the first few levels. Most people peak in the yellow range, though many don't get that far."

Will glanced down at his clothing. It was definitely pink, and the color seemed to have deepened even in the past few moments, to more of a pale red color. "What does my coloring mean?"

"It means you've accomplished a great deal, and if you keep progressing at this pace you'll hit orange and be able to practice teleportation."

Will thought about Fil's jet-black clothing. "What does Fil's color mean?"

Adam considered. "Fil's a very special case. A very *advanced* case."

A mental case, Will thought. "Listen, I wanted to talk more about teleportation, maybe practice it..."

"Not yet, Will. We need to work on another skill. Your Energy development is moving at a very rapid pace, and as your Energy levels increase you'll be more easily detected by someone like the Hunter Porthos. We've developed a skill called Shielding, which is something unknown outside the Alliance. It basically lets you hide your Energy and make it difficult or impossible to detect."

Then what I saw was real, Will thought, though he'd never thought to question his visions. *I'm becoming a risk.* "I don't want to put anyone at risk. I *can't* put anybody at risk. When can we start?"

"Let's start now."

Adam taught him that those with large stores of Energy naturally leaked a small portion of that Energy out into their surroundings, even when not doing Energy work. It was equivalent to the leaking of heat from the body, or electricity from wires. Unfortunately, if the individual was powerful enough, even minor leaks amounted to large amounts of Energy, and could be sensed by others. This was not something that the majority of Aliomenti concerned themselves with, for they were not Hunted; for the Alliance, the skill was essential to survival. All of them had learned to Shield to avoid detection from a distance.

Will practiced the technique, which amounted to building a mental barrier of insulation around his Energy, forcing it to remain inside him. The trick, as Adam noted repeatedly, was awareness; he would only Shield when he made the conscious effort. Over time, it would become a skill like driving, able to be done with less conscious effort, but in these early days he needed to be quite diligent. They were essentially copying Aramis' Damper skill, voluntarily using the technique on themselves.

They were just finishing up and starting back to the camp when they heard loud, rumbling noises overhead. Adam's face tightened.

"Thunder?" Will asked.

"No," Adam replied. "Hunters. They've found us."

Will's face fell. "No. They've found *me*."

XVII
MACHINES

Adam sprinted back to camp, bursting through a haze inside the tree line that Will hadn't noticed before. Will trailed closely behind. Nearly all of the buildings in the clearing had vanished, leaving not even a trace of a foundation or imprints in the grass. Only three remained, one of which was the building Will used for lodging. Adam headed that way now. Will noticed a similar haze overhead, as if a cloud had formed over their clearing, level with the tree canopy above. Fil and Angel burst from another of the remaining buildings. Angel's face was fearful, but Fil's face showed nothing but mangled fury. "*You*!" he screamed, sprinting at Will. "This is entirely *your* fault!"

Fil was on him faster than Will believed possible, and the two fell to the ground, with Will landing on his back. Fil threw fists and elbows at the pinned man, and it was all Will could do to get his arms up and defend himself. The blows came at a rate which eliminated the possibility of fighting back, and Will felt his skin bruising, his arms becoming numb. Angel looked like she wanted to say something, but opted against speaking. Both spectators looked nervous and antsy at the sounds of the nearby Hunters, glancing in the direction of the noise, watching as the hundred or more craft in the original convoy split up, presumably chasing after fleeing Alliance members they'd detected.

The attack by Fil finally stopped, and Will lowered his arms. Fil's face was one of pure fury, obvious despite the sunglasses that masked his eyes. Will didn't need his empathy training to know what fueled it. Will's growing Energy, and the leakages he'd never Shielded until moments before, had drawn the attention of the Hunters and brought them here. Will hadn't fought back because he believed he deserved each and every blow.

Adam pulled Fil off of Will. "We need to get moving *now*. Deal with this later."

Will glanced up. Aircraft of the approximate size of bicycles were visible over the nearby forest, the spot Adam and Will had just vacated. Had they zeroed in on the tree? A burst of flame erupted from one of the aircraft, igniting the trees in the distance. *His* tree. Will felt his own fury mount, and he started toward the attack zone.

Adam grabbed him. "No, Will. There are too many of them, and too few of us. There were at least a hundred craft initially, and most of them are chasing others of our group who have already fled. We need to escape." Adam pulled him along until Will moved of his own volition. Out of the corner of his eye, Will saw Fil and Angel vanish inside one of the remaining buildings, just as he and Adam entered Will's room. "Stand still," Adam ordered. Will, not sure what to expect, did as he was told, standing still directly behind Adam.

The bed and chairs in the room melted into the floor, and the walls, floor, and ceiling collapsed inward toward the two men. Will felt a moment of panic; perhaps he was being executed for his role in leading the Hunters to camp. Adam looked calm, watching as the modest-sized room reformed around them and shaped into what looked like a flying bobsled with a clear top.

"Sit," Adam said, and Will sat without thinking, surprised — though he wasn't sure why — to find a seat had formed under him. The chair molded itself to him, and restraining bands serving as a seat belt held him in place. Will looked out of the clear, seamless top, and saw another vehicle where Fil and Angel's building had stood. Shape-shifting buildings? He wondered what type of Energy enabled *that*. The third building remained in place and unaltered.

Things had definitely changed over the past month or so. Now, a building that stayed in one place and maintained its shape was the oddity.

The building — now a vehicle — lifted silently off the ground and followed Fil and Angel's vehicle into the forest, away from his tree.

Will glanced behind them, back toward what was left of their camp. "What's that last building?"

"That's where the Mechanic works. He's usually the last one to leave. I hadn't thought that would be your first question, though." Adam steered the craft expertly through the trees. Will turned around, and noticed that there were no controls. Adam was somehow piloting the craft with his mind.

Will considered the comment. "What was I supposed to ask?"

Adam risked a quick glance back at him, before returning his focus to the flying vehicle in front of him. "Perhaps why Angel and I stood back while Fil... well, while Fil vented some frustration. Given that you didn't try to fight back, though, I imagine you figured that one out on your own."

"He's mad at me for drawing the Hunters here. I don't fault him for that."

"You should be faulting *me*, though. As your trainer I should have recognized that your Energy levels were going to make this inevitable, and taught you to Shield sooner. I really should have told you to stay in camp; we have a technology that Shields all of us while we're in the clearing, so if I'd told you then you could have stayed where it was safe and nothing would have happened. Fil really should have come after me, but he chose you instead."

"Lucky me," Will muttered. "Why?"

"We go back a long way together. I helped him during a rather difficult time of his life, and so I think he feels a sense of obligation to give me a break when I don't deserve it. In the circumstance just now, he was simply too angry to let it all go, and you were the second best candidate." He shook his head. "I thank you for your patience with him there, and with me now."

"So since I wasn't going to ask you *that* question," Will said, "what was I *supposed* to ask?"

"You already know. Ask now."

Will shrugged. "How is it that my room is now a flying bobsled?"

Adam laughed. "I hadn't expected quite that wording. This is your introduction to our most prized technology, the one that the Elites don't have. They can match us for Energy easily — well, except for Angel, and especially Fil — but this... this technology gives us the edge we need to survive." He made a sharp left turn to avoid a tight cluster of trees, and then straightened back out to track behind Fil and Angel. "And the reason that they don't have this is that we borrowed this technology from humans, then enhanced it in our fashion. What you are seeing is our version of nanomachines."

Will was stunned. The stuff he'd used to build the Dome over Pleasanton was a material that could shape-shift from stationary building to flying vehicle? "I own a company that makes nanos, and we're not building any that can... do all of this. And we're the only ones, too. Other than my company, everyone's pretty much abandoned the technology."

Adam sighed. "For decades, nanotechnology was hailed in human circles as the next great leap in technology. Microscopic machines were going to heal our wounds, cure us of diseases, and make materials stronger and lighter than anything seen before. And then the advancement stopped. Why?"

Will shrugged. "A lot of research stopped during the depression. Nanotechnology is expensive to research. It was a pretty easy thing to cut. That's why I had the only company left. Nobody else wanted to throw the necessary capital at it. I do remember hearing of some failed trials for the medical applications, though."

Adam nodded. "Exactly. The Elites got wind of it. Humans becoming healthier and stronger runs counter to what they stand for. Though it's not technically a violation of the First Oath, because the technology initiated with humans rather than Aliomenti, it was still seen as a threat to the Elites' power. And so, they used their wealth and influence to sabotage research, and encouraged businesses to pull investments. That included those medical trials, by the way; the Elites sabotaged the samples so that patients died, rather than getting healthier. They weren't worried about a mere construction company like yours, so you were left alone. With their mission accomplished, the Elites forgot about the technology, because after all, no human idea could have enough merit to warrant further research by the Aliomenti." Adam laughed. "The Alliance thought otherwise. We picked up the scraps, bought the research and prototypes, and even brought in the top researchers, who were now without jobs. Those men and women became full Alliance Aliomenti and focused on the research they had thought lost to them forever. That's where we got the Mechanic, by the way. He was the best, and his theories were among those supposedly disproved by the sabotage. The Mechanic, along with a few brilliant youngsters, made nano-machines far beyond any they thought possible before, making huge amounts of progress in only a few years."

Will smiled. Served the Elites right. "So this flying ship is made of a few thousand tiny machines, then?"

"A few *trillion*, actually, maybe more." He chuckled. "When you're dealing with machines smaller than cells, the numbers get very huge very quickly. A thousand machines are a number you'd use for internal work, inside the body. For anything tangible...you'd need far more."

"Inside the body... there are nanos that are part of The Purge, aren't there?" Will asked. Fil had mentioned "special additives of our creation" as being part of the formula.

"Correct," Adam said, as he swerved to avoid another tree. Just how large was this forest? They'd been traveling at a high rate of speed for quite a while. "There are foods and other natural substances which will accomplish the same thing, but at a much slower pace. Less trauma as well. That's how our earliest members achieved what they did. With nanos, however, we could rapidly accelerate the timetable of advancement. That's why all of us go through the Purge a few times a year, and why we had you go through it right away. We couldn't afford to have you wait twenty years to clear your system and start sensing Energy."

Will shook his head. "No, definitely not. It was horribly unpleasant, but now that it's over with I'm glad you went that route with me. So what else can these machines do?"

"Well, we've built some to protect our camps. There are always a few set up overhead that reflect the image of trees so no clearing can be seen; another type actually blocks Energy, and keeps it inside; so we put a thin layer around the whole perimeter of camp. If the Hunters are spotted, we put a lot more of those up." Adam smiled. "And we have a few folks doing research on how they can affect the human brain."

• • •

"I will *not* get in there." The Assassin glared at the Mechanic, arms folded across his chest in a show of defiance. Everything in him screamed at The Assassin to draw his sword and execute the man. But he knew he'd be stopped.

"We've discussed this. The Hunters are arriving even now. If they find you here, they will assume you've gone rogue. If they see you fleeing with me, they will assume you've gone rogue. If they see you with me and you then go back to Headquarters, they will take you for a traitor. You must flee with me, and you must not be seen."

"Then leave me here."

The Mechanic laughed. "Not an option. You've been gone a long time. You'll be seen in the empty enemy camp. You can't think that they'd trust you since you've never reported to them about your intentions to spy, now can you? Nor have you returned after your little outing chasing down Will Stark's wife and child. No, if they find you right now, you'll be taken for a traitor and executed."

"You will *not* put me back in there."

"I'm giving you the chance to climb in on your own. You have five seconds."

"I really will kill you...."

"One..."

"...as soon as I get out..."

"...two..."

"...of this. The..."

"...three..."

"...indignity has been..."

"...four..."

"...uncalled for, and..."

The glove snapped around The Assassin, and he was hurled into the trunk of the vehicle, and the lid snapped shut behind him. He screamed and shouted the vilest curses he could fathom at the Mechanic, though he doubted the man could hear a word he said. The Mechanic climbed into the front of the vehicle as the building evaporated around him, and he spotted the fire and heard the Hunters' craft nearby. He glanced over at Smokey and whistled. The dog trotted over and jumped into the vehicle with him.

"Too late to run now, girl," he muttered, giving the dog a friendly pat on the head. "I'll need to try some trickery on these guys."

He concentrated, and the vehicle shimmered... then vanished. The craft hosting the Aliomenti flew overhead and saw nothing but an empty clearing.

● ● ●

"So that's why they couldn't stab me? How you pulled me through the ground into the house?"

"Yes," Adam said, still trailing Fil and Angel as the flying craft maneuvered through a seemingly endless forest. "Angel dug a tunnel with nanos to make the passage a bit smoother for you, but we ran out of time when you mentioned your son. I got the nano shield around you just in time. We could have used Energy and teleported you, but that would have told them where we were and we might not have escaped. That's the nice part about nanos — we can do many things with them that you could also do with Energy, but the Aliomenti can't detect them."

"I still don't understand how they work. Not at this level of sophistication, at least."

Adam thought for a moment. "Each of the machines has several components: a generator, a small camera and microphone, a small panel capable of showing color, some computation circuits, communication circuits, anti-gravity magnets—"

"Whoa. What? Anti-gravity magnets?"

"We don't have much to do here outside performing research. We've had the individual components for a while. We just miniaturized them down and taught them how to communicate and problem-solve together. Form a wall. Form a room. And so on."

"Or form a flying car?"

"Of course. Might as well take advantage of the anti-gravity capability."

"Of course," Will said, wondering if Adam noted his sarcasm. The machines sounded more like magic than all of the Energy abilities he'd seen.

"Each of us in the Alliance has a sizable number of nanos inside them. Some fight illness as a supplement to our immune system. Some repair wounds. And some interpret signals from our brains and communicate those to our nanos."

"Wait, so you just think something and the machines do... whatever it is you ask them to do?"

"So long as they can figure out how to do it. There are some limitations. They aren't allowed to do anything to kill another person, for example, though they don't know how to think of everything that might cause a death."

Will shook his head. "This sounds impossible. Yet I have no reason to doubt it. A few weeks ago, I'd have considered a flying car to be an impossibility, and yet here I am, chased by people who want to kill me because I have enough Energy to destroy a small apartment building."

Adam laughed. "You've adapted well. We'll need to get you some nanos for use. You have the health ones in you already..."

"What?"

"The ones that patched you up from your last encounter with the Hunters... you didn't think we took them back, did you?"

"Well, I hadn't thought much about it at the time since I'm just now learning about these machines, but..."

"No, they're still inside you, making sure nothing bad happens. They'll patch up the bruises you got from Fil pretty soon, if they haven't already. We'll need to get the communication nanos inside you, and then gift you a few to get started. I'll ask the Mechanic to build you a batch of a few trillion when we stop running again."

"So how often does this happen?" Will waved around. "How often do you have to pack up and move?"

"It's probably been about twenty years since the last one, I'd wager. We've gotten pretty good at evading their traps since we know what they are. They don't innovate much anymore, which helps. We build out of the nanos exclusively. We don't have a lot of possessions because we don't really want any. It's easy to move when your home becomes your transport vehicle."

"I can see why Fil is so upset about this, then. He must've been extremely young when you last moved. Known mostly a stable home location most of his life."

Adam chuckled. "Fil's life has been anything *but* stable. And he's old enough to remember the last move."

"When do we stop flying?"

They'd been weaving through forests now for about thirty minutes; Will could hear no sound of the Hunters chasing them in their flying cars, but he had to consider the possibility that the pursuit teams could travel in silence as well.

"Angel scouted out the next location a few years back; we change it about every three years just to make sure there aren't any other Aliomenti in the area. This one is about a hundred miles from the last location. Should be there in about a half hour. We like to move enough that they can't find us again by simply flying circles around our last base, but don't want to move too far."

Will glanced around. "Where are we, anyway? I've not seen any cities, or rivers, or anything else that gives me an idea where on the globe I am."

Adam turned a bit, partially glancing at Will over his shoulder. "Is it really important to know?"

Will frowned. "Why is it such a difficult question to answer?"

Adam grimaced. "I knew this would come up eventually. You see, there's something you need to understand. It's—"

The craft lurched, thrown violently to the side. As the craft stabilized, Will saw the craft with Fil and Angel smash into one of the giant trees, then plummet to the ground. Adam righted their craft, and then leveled up and over the tree canopy, banking sharply to the right, away from Angel and Fil. "So much for hiding in the trees," he muttered. "We need to distract the bad guys so the good guys can lick their wounds."

Will glanced out the side of the craft. He counted six different vehicles chasing them, and spotted the three Hunters piloting half of the squadron. They were dismally outnumbered.

"Angel's hurt," Adam muttered. "Pretty bad, too."

A lump formed in Will's throat. Angel had been his introduction to this new world, and had always treated him with kindness. If something happened to her because of his stupidity...

"We need to go to her, then, and help!"

"And do what, exactly? Fil's there with her, and that's the best we could hope for. It will do her no good if we get shot down as well."

Will shifted backward to watch the Aliomenti aircraft. "What are they made of?"

"What?"

"What are their aircraft made of? Ours are made of the nanos... what about theirs?"

"Not sure. Some type of metal or plastic, I'd assume. Glass. Electricity for their various control systems. Not sure what the fuel is. Why?"

"We need to get them heading away from Angel. I have an idea."

Adam shrugged. "I thought that's what I *was* doing."

"I know. Can you go faster? And a bit lower? Just skim the tops of the trees."

Adam nodded, not questioning his pupil's plan, and the craft shot forward and banked down. "What are you doing?"

Will grinned. "Playing a video game."

He turned around and faced the rear of the vehicle, spotting all six of the Aliomenti craft following. *They've assumed the other craft is destroyed and the occupants gone*, he thought, and then grimaced. *I hope they're wrong on that point.*

Will channeled Energy into his hands, forming it into a large ball, roughly the size of a bowling ball. He maneuvered it out of the craft, suspending it in the air, adding more and more Energy until it was the size of a small house. He then froze it in one place, rather than letting it move with the craft carrying him and Adam. Then he watched.

The lead craft hit the Energy field and lost control, spinning wildly down into the trees. Two others crashed immediately after, following so closely that they could not react, and followed the rapid descent of the first craft. The Hunters veered wildly around the invisible barrier, but did not stop to check on their companions. *Nice guys, real team players*, Will thought. "Looks like Energy and their electrical systems don't mesh very well."

Adam snickered. "Old-fashioned punks getting what they deserve, if you ask me. Are the Hunters still coming our way?"

"Unfortunately. I'm thinking we may need to take the attack to them."

Adam nodded, and swung the craft around until he was facing the Hunters, then accelerated at them. Will shot bursts of Energy at the three aircraft, managing to strike Porthos and Athos. Both men gave looks of surprise as their aircraft plummeted down into the tree line. Aramis stared at Will as the Hunter flew by, his face a look of shock and fury. Will smiled, and flashed a taunting wave the Hunter's way. Aramis decided against staying to fight, and flew his craft down to check on his colleagues.

"That should keep them busy for a while," Adam remarked. "By the way, you're leaking Energy. Get your Shield up."

Will's hand shot to his mouth. "How long?"

"I just noticed it in all the commotion, but... I suppose it's possible that your Shield has been down since we left camp."

"No," Will whispered. He'd led the Hunters to them originally. Had he set a trail for them to follow as well? He set up his Shield, and Adam confirmed that the Energy leak was stopped. Adam took a circuitous route back to the downed aircraft belonging to Fil and

Angel, making sure that there was no actual Energy trail or direct path for the Hunters to pick up again.

Fil held Angel in his arms, tears streaming down his face from behind his sunglasses. Angel looked horribly pale, her deep green bodysuit stained red. Will and Adam sprang from their aircraft and raced toward them.

Fil looked up at them. "She's lost blood. I used machines to stitch her wounds and internal damage, but I can't replace blood."

"I have type O-negative blood," Will said. "That's the universal donor type." He pushed up his sleeve, and looked at Adam, somehow sensing the man could actually do something as obscure as a blood transfusion in the middle of a jungle. "Take mine. She needs it more. This is all my fault anyway. Take it all if you need to, but save her."

Adam nodded. He fashioned the necessary needles and tubes from nanos and fashioned a crude blood transfer link between Will and Angel. Will watched the young woman's face, desperate to see her pale features gain more color. And gradually, they did; Angel began to breathe more easily. Adam stopped the transfusion and began bandaging the wounds.

Will insisted that Adam take more, as much blood as he needed. Adam shook his head. "She has enough. You've saved her."

"I owed her that much. She's the closest thing to family I have any more. I won't let someone else suffer for my mistakes again."

He was weak from the blood loss, and started to drift to sleep, but he caught the emotion from Fil without needing to focus on it. The emotion was powerful. And unlike the previous emotional bombs directed at him by the man in the sunglasses, this emotion wasn't one of fury, or rage, or anger, or even sadness.

It was admiration.

XVIII
REPROGRAMMING

As had been the case for most of the unplanned relocations in his time with the Alliance, the Mechanic was the final member of the community to leave the original campsite, and also one of the last to arrive at the new. As his craft circled the clearing for the new camp, the Mechanic scanned the community and noted the familiar patterns. Many of the buildings had reformed in their usual layout, and people began to explore the environment around the clearing to locate sources of water and the foodstuffs they consumed. This was what the Alliance referred to as unpacking. There were a few minor injuries, but the healing nanos in each member of the Alliance could be seen working, knitting the various scrapes and scratches closed.

As he descended, the Mechanic had a vision of something happening several miles away. It involved a small cluster of people, including Fil and Angel. Fil held Angel, who looked extremely pale and bloodied, while Adam and a third man stood nearby. He frowned, as he was uncertain who this other man was. He watched as Adam ran a tube between the stranger and Angel, and watched as the clear tube turned a deep red. The Mechanic nodded. Angel had been hurt and lost blood, and the stranger was providing a transfusion. She would be fine, and that made him happy.

The craft landed, and the nanos surrounding the vehicle separated and formed into a building around him. The vehicle he flew was unique, as it was one of the few structures in the entire Alliance camp that wasn't constructed of nanos; rather, this craft was formed entirely of "normal" materials. It needed to be, for it was a craft unique in the entire Aliomenti universe, and only a very few people knew its true purpose. The Mechanic needed to work on a few modifications he had planned over the next week or two, and was pleased to see that the craft had come through the escape and relocation without suffering any damage.

The Mechanic opened the hatch and allowed the dog to run loose. He left a patch of grass open through the floor of the building, a feat made simpler by the fact that the entire structure was built from intelligent machines. He also adjusted the building to allow in more sunlight, and Smokey indulged herself, sleeping on the grass as the rays warmed her dark fur. Pets weren't officially disallowed in the community, but were avoided as a common practice, so the Mechanic made do for Smokey as best he could under the circumstances.

His other house guest would not be quite so pleasant. He would need to prepare the appropriate materials before releasing the man from the trunk.

In the rear seat of the craft were two cylinders, each about two feet tall and roughly a foot in diameter. These machines, like the vehicle they were in, were not composed of nanos, and as such were irreplaceable. He moved to the first of the machines, which was used to generate new nanos, and adjusted the settings to create a small, highly specialized batch of fifty million of the tiny devices. This batch of machines was unique, as he'd need to override a key portion of the standard code operating all of the other nanos, in order for them to perform the task he required.

Most of the nanos he generated with his device were general purpose machines used to perform various tasks by Alliance members who owned them — such as shaping the buildings they lived in and the clothing they wore — and used the standard operating system coding image. That image could be modified to provide machines with more specialized, internal functions. There were images to create Purge nanos, immune system supplements, injury repair, sleep enhancers, and more. To date, the most challenging code image he'd built had been for the internal nanos that served as the communication channel between the brain and the general purpose nanos. The challenge there was ensuring that no one could use or control nanos not owned by them. Alliance members could "gift" each other nanos if it was necessary, but most simply came to him to produce more if there was a true need. The gifting process worked well for temporary projects, and since the Alliance worked to avoid waste, he only rarely created new batches, outside the standard batch for new members and regular batches for the Purges each member performed.

This set would be the most unique of the unique, building on the internal communication nanos code set. He only expected to create one batch of this type. Ever.

It had taken time to get the code change just right, and he'd been working on it almost without interruption since The Assassin had been captured. He hadn't gotten a lot of support for his idea since it was so unique and high risk, but he intended to press on and go through with it, knowing that it was a critical piece of the future. He was so close he could almost taste it. He used his general purpose nanos to form a small drinking glass to hold the custom nanos created just for The Assassin.

It was time to get the test subject.

The Mechanic marched to the rear of the vehicle and kicked the panel, which opened to reveal The Assassin, a highly-trained and now highly-irritated killing machine, who had seen better days. The Mechanic winced at the smell of the vomit inside the compartment; apparently, all of the changes of direction during the flight hadn't been pleasant for his guest.

The Assassin groaned and rolled out of the trunk, so disoriented that he forgot that it was several feet off the ground. Perhaps, given his nausea, he didn't care. The Assassin hit the white surface with a resounding thud, and groaned again. The Mechanic chuckled. If he hadn't known better, he would have interpreted the man's actions as those of a drunk.

On hearing the chuckle, The Assassin snapped off an intense stream of profanity.

"Your language suggests to me that you may not like my accommodations," the Mechanic stated, unable to resist adding an air of emotional trauma to his tone.

"The current accommodations are reasonably spacious, if a bit restrictive on freedom," The Assassin replied, his voice strengthening as his equilibrium returned. "The accommodations just now ended resembled a coffin."

"I bow to your expertise on that front," the Mechanic said, bowing.

"What do you want from me?" The Assassin snapped, his frustration boiling over. "Why do you injure me and then heal me? If you want me dead, why not execute me and be done with it? Surely you realize that the instant I'm free of these restraints, free of this room, I'll seek all of you out and kill you, right? So what do you want from me that you keep me alive, knowing that doing so means risking *your* lives?"

"I want you to be my spy at Aliomenti Headquarters," the Mechanic said, his voice quiet.

The Assassin gaped at him for a moment, and then enjoyed a loud laugh at the Mechanic's expense. "You can't seriously believe I'd do that, do you? Or are you that big a fool? I admit that is a possibility, since you were the one foolish enough to leave me with my weapon. I promise that should your concentration wane for even a moment, long enough to crack that Energy shield you use on me, I will put you to the sword, you and that dog. Yes, Mechanic, you may come back here one day and find your smelly canine butchered in your home. I won't soon forget, and will never forgive, the shoddy treatment I've been given here."

"Your complaints evoke little sympathy in me, as you've just expressed an earnest desire to kill me. You may recall that you were seized and brought here following your attempt on the lives of the family of one of our Alliance members here, and I dare say you won't win sympathy there either."

The Assassin stared at him. "Stark is *here*? But the Hunters were after him."

"They, like you, failed in their mission. Will Stark was our extraction target that night, and *we* were successful. You were a nice bonus."

The Assassin glared at him. "How do you know I failed to kill them?"

"You talk in your sleep. Nasty habit you should work on."

"What happened to them?"

"What?"

"What. Happened. To. Them." He paused, and upon receiving no answer, continued. "The woman. The boy. How did they escape?"

"How would you expect me to know that? I wasn't part of the rescue team. I choose to believe that the woman and the boy — and our friend Smokey here — beat up the famed Assassin, and fled the house he'd set on fire, laughing all the way."

The Assassin snorted. "Hardly. Some powerful Aliomenti teleported them. I assume Stark did it before the Hunters trapped him; if Stark is here, I'm even more convinced that's the case."

The Mechanic shrugged. "You have your story; I have mine."

The Assassin rolled his eyes and palmed his sword. "I repeat myself: what do you want from me?"

"I have already answered that question. You are to become my spy — my eyes, my ears, my hands — inside the Aliomenti Headquarters. You will provide me with the information I need, and as I direct you, you will act. You will betray nothing you may have learned here to those at the Headquarters."

"On the contrary. I know that Will Stark is here. That's useful information for The Leader, sufficient to earn pardon for my failures that night."

"The Leader already knows. Why else do you suppose we were attacked?"

"It's a moot point regardless. I will not do as you wish. You have no hold over me strong enough that you can compel me."

"I rather disagree," the Mechanic replied. He directed his general nanos to form an Energy-dampering exoskeleton around The Assassin, rendering the man immobile. The hatred in The Assassin's gaze was haunting; even though the Mechanic knew he could not be harmed, the malevolence in those blood-red eyes startled him. He did not doubt that, at this very moment, The Assassin would strike him dead if the opportunity presented itself.

The Mechanic picked up the concoction of specialty nanos and moved to The Assassin. "Bottoms up!" he said, giving The Assassin an evil look that mirrored the one the captive had leveled at him a moment earlier. He directed the exoskeleton to open the man's mouth and hold his tongue down, which would force the man to swallow. The Mechanic poured the solution down the man's throat, watching The Assassin's glare change from one of hatred to one of fear. He'd seen what these potions could do already in terms of healing injuries, and no doubt understood that the Alliance could create something far more damaging if they chose. Once the fluid reached the man's throat, the Mechanic forced his mouth closed to ensure that the man swallowed the fluid, preventing him from coughing it back up.

It was a cosmetic gesture to ensure that The Assassin believed it was a liquid formula. In reality, the machines had made their way to his brain upon entering his mouth, and he needn't have waited that long. The customized nanos could have entered The Assassin's body without any liquid at all. He released The Assassin's mouth, and said mouth began spouting profanities at him once more.

The Mechanic closed his eyes, and waited for the feedback signal. The Assassin's flow of verbal abuse continued unabated, which was to be expected. After a few moments, however, the Mechanic could see something via the nanos he'd inserted into The Assassin's brain: himself. The communications nanos were embedded and in place.

The machines were in. That was the easy part. The behavioral modification test would be somewhat more unnerving. The Mechanic released the exoskeleton from The Assassin and reformed it around himself as a protective measure. He then walked over to The Assassin, who was just beginning to stretch his muscles after the latest confinement. The Assassin looked at him, puzzled, as the Mechanic punched the killer in the face.

The Assassin roared in pain. "I'll kill you!" he screamed. He drew his sword, but did not strike. The man stared at his arm as if it were no longer part of him. His arm was strong, and he'd swung that sword thousands of times before. Yet he could not move his arm to strike the Mechanic. He turned to face the Mechanic. "What did you do to me?" he whispered, his eyes fearful.

"I told you: you are to be my spy inside Aliomenti Headquarters. I've simply made sure that you'll behave and perform well in the role. It would hardly do for you to kill me, now, would it?" He chuckled, primarily because he knew The Assassin hated the sound being directed at him.

The Assassin's face was a mask of confusion. "What was the punch about?"

"There were two reasons. First, it was the best way to ensure you'd instinctively want to attack me, and I needed that to make sure that your reprogramming is working correctly."

"And the second?"

"You've ruined the lives of a lot of people dear to me. Consider it a small payback for what you've done to me and my extended family."

The Assassin sneered. "You're *pathetic*. Your emotional attachments will get you killed, and your effort to ensure it won't be me who does it simply means someone else will do the job. Truly, now, are these long lost dead people really worth losing your life over?"

"They're my reason for living, and if it takes my life to save theirs, I will gladly pay that price. That said, I'd just as soon *not* pay that price if I can avoid it. Therefore, now I can use *you*."

The Assassin looked modestly confused. "And what is the plan on that front?"

"You will return to Aliomenti headquarters. I will teleport with you to get you close enough to be detected and walk; at present it is quite a significant distance. They believe you died in the fire you set the night you and the Hunters attempted your various assaults on the Stark family. You will tell them the truth, to a degree; that you were so excited at the prospect of the deaths of the Stark woman and the boy that your pyrokinesis erupted, igniting an explosion that knocked you unconscious and, you suspect, also killed the family of Will Stark. You were kidnapped by the Alliance, which fed you various drugs to keep you in a state of deep sleep."

"And why would they believe that?" The Assassin asked.

"They know that there was an explosion because the Hunters were camped out in the Starks' back yard when it happened. They have not seen you since. They most likely assume you dead, and reasonably so. We have given you drugs, but our true intent in doing so has been to heal the injuries you sustained in the fire and your encounter with the Starks. Your story is consistent with both what they know, and what you experienced, and as such they'll detect no lies from you."

"If I was drugged, how did I escape?"

"You had enough lucid time to understand that you were being given the drugs. You figured out how to stop swallowing the drugs and as such your alertness returned. There came a day when you were out of your cell, and the bindings securing you to your table were removed to allow for a change of clothes and washing. You feigned still being addled until that point of freedom, and then rose to the occasion, killing several of the Alliance with their medical knives and instruments.

"In the chaos that followed, you found your sword and escaped the camp, gradually working your way back to Headquarters. You'll note to them that the camp is fairly small and basic and easy to move, and so given the time it took you to escape and arrive at Headquarters, it is probable that the Alliance moved again following your escape, figuring out that your next step would be to report to The Leader all that you learned."

"And what have I learned, *Master*?" The last word was said with a sneer. The Mechanic smiled. The Assassin couldn't fight him, or what he said, but it certainly hadn't altered his charming personality.

"You have learned that Will Stark has been in this camp."

The Assassin glared at him. "Clearly they know this, as you already indicated. How is this useful to me? I need something showing that my time spent here was not wasted." He frowned. "Drugged or not."

"Will Stark is still working his way through the ailments that plagued him during their Hunt for him at his home. His Energy is quite low and he has forgotten how to do much of what he once did. He is better than he was at the house; however, he is unlikely to be able to withstand a well-planned and executed Hunt at this time. This is the time to strike to get Stark if that is still something they wish to accomplish."

"Of course it is something we wish to accomplish. Will Stark is the worst example of a traitor to his Aliomenti Oaths. He must be captured and tried for these crimes. Nothing has changed that."

The Mechanic smiled. "Perhaps. I dare say much has changed at Aliomenti Headquarters since you left to execute Will Stark's family. But that is part of what you are going to find out for me. What are the priorities with The Leadership, with the membership as a whole? Who are they tracking for possible Hunts, and why? Once I have that type of information — which *you* will gather for me — then I will determine how you will act."

"Act?" Concern showed in The Assassin's blood-red eyes.

"Yes. You see, I am giving you this order today: you are never to kill another human. Nor may you kill an Alliance member. You may be asked to kill a member of The Leadership, by me, but I am issuing no such order at this time. You may not directly refuse an order by The Leadership to violate any of these rules, but you must use your cunning to fail to successfully complete these orders in manners that seem plausible. You are not to mention or even give hints that you are operating under my instruction and control, or the control or instruction of anyone else." He looked The Assassin straight in the eye. "Is that clear?"

The Assassin winced. Every fiber of his being rebelled against the order, for he lived to kill humans in particular, and yet whatever magic this man had performed was overwhelming that desire. He had no doubt that he would perform as ordered because he was incapable of choosing to do otherwise. "Clear."

The Mechanic smiled and slapped The Assassin on the back. "Wonderful! We'll need to arrange for your escape, gather some supplies, and provide you a map to help you return."

He paused. "Ah, yes. There's one more very important detail you need to be aware of."

The Assassin's eyes widened as the Mechanic related the story. It was impossible. It had to be. But he had no choice but to believe.

He'd been given his orders.

XIX
INITIATION

Michael Baker pulled his car into the parking lot at The Diner, enjoying the sight of the giant Pleasanton Dome in the background. It had been six weeks since he'd last been here. That visit had been far more ominous, for it involved an investigation into yet another murder the night of the fire. A young woman had been found dead in her apartment, a young woman Baker had called to tell of her fiancé's death in the murder and arson assault on De Gray Estates. Her time of death suggested she'd lived with that horror only a short while. The woman had worked here, at The Diner, and they'd needed to come and interview employees and guests about enemies and possible motives.

Today, though, Baker was at The Diner to enjoy the cuisine and to meet with someone who had no relation to those murders and deaths. He walked in and glanced around. He spotted his lunch companion in a booth in the far corner, walked over, and sat down.

"Thanks for joining me," Adam said. "How's your wife doing?"

"Remarkably well," Baker replied. "Her doctors are genuinely surprised at how quickly her wounds healed. It'll take a long time for her to get over the emotional aspects, but physically she's back to normal."

"And your son?"

"You'd never know he'd seen his mother attacked. He's back to being a regular boy." Baker glanced at the man. "It seemed to start when you took him for a walk that day in the hospital. What did you say to him?"

"If memory serves, I asked if he preferred his candy bar with or without nuts."

Baker laughed. "I guess that's exactly what he needed to hear, then. Thank you." Adam nodded in acknowledgment.

The waitress came over, and both men placed their orders. After she returned with their drinks, Baker resumed the conversation. "Millard told me that you're claiming to be a third member of our little group, and that the two of us share some unique piece of knowledge about the Starks that will convince me of this." He took a sip of his drink. "Can you elaborate?"

Adam nodded. "I appreciate your skepticism. I probably would have avoided even having this meeting without some type of proof ahead of time, especially given the nature of the claim. I will tell you something that Millard knows. The Starks kept their will on file with me because it is my job to protect the most sensitive data that their companies deal with. Millard came to my site to retrieve the will after their deaths."

"Why come to your site if he had a copy of his own in his office?" Baker asked.

"Will liked to have multiple copies of anything important to help ensure nothing was changed without his approval. With each official change, Millard kept a copy on file in his office and gave two copies to the Starks. One was kept in a safe in their home. The other came to me and was stored in a secure manner, as a check copy. Obviously, the fire prevented a comparison with the copy stored by the Starks. Thankfully, the two copies in existence matched, and as such prevented a rather nasty dispute resolution process."

Baker nodded. That level of foresight didn't surprise him. He'd heard tales of other wealthy people storing their wills in a very insecure manner, enabling unscrupulous individuals to modify the documents to their liking and helping themselves to portions of an estate they were never intended to inherit. It was another manner in which those who survived through the economic depression in a prosperous manner were attacked, a more subtle approach than the kidnappings, blackmail, and extortion that were now commonplace. Will Stark, of course, would know this, and invent a means to prevent those types of criminals from succeeding.

"Okay, I'm convinced that you were part of the process of storing the will. But that doesn't mean that the Starks intended for you to be part of the decision-making process for disbursing funds."

Adam chuckled. "Of course not. But Will told me something at one point that leads me to believe he wanted me to be involved. Not directly, day-to-day, mind you, or deciding who gets what. Given the nature of my role with his companies, he probably wanted me to be involved in ensuring the security of the process, theft and extortion prevention, and so on. Or perhaps another voice to weigh in on some of the more difficult cases, to help ensure the guidelines the Starks set are followed."

Baker rolled his eyes. "Neither Millard nor I would go against their wishes."

"I'm not saying that you would. But this Trust is large enough that it's likely to outlive all of us. Having a hidden third party, not subject to outside pressure as you might be, is a shrewd maneuver. Will and Hope picked three people they knew they could trust to continue their work. What happens when we're gone? Who replaces us? We will do our best to replace ourselves with others true to the beliefs and tenets the Starks set out. With each replacement, though, you run the new risk of finding someone who will be overcome with greed, or who lets others pressure them. This structure helps."

Baker shrugged. "I'm not concerned about that part of your story, Adam. What interests me is understanding why you think there needs to be a third wheel on this bicycle, and why that third wheel is meant to be *you*. Do you have some way to convince me?"

Adam leaned in closer. "Tell me this, Michael. Were there ever times you talked with Will when he seemed... *different?*"

Baker blinked, his breath catching in his throat. He recovered quickly. "Different? What do you mean?"

"Like he was a different person. Much more direct, more forceful. His face seeming... I don't know, harder. Different like that. As if he were some type of undercover agent, putting on his alternate career face, as opposed to the easy-going, jovial family man the world knows."

Baker stared at Adam.

How could he know?

Baker knew Will mostly as the world knew him... driven, to be sure, but with a gentle spirit, full of laughs and good cheer, generous with a smile or a story or a large amount of money for a good cause. But on a few occasions, always in one-on-one circumstances, Will seemed different, older and wiser. A man who had been through hell and back. In those circumstances, Will steered conversations away from the usual fodder, such as the odd crime scene Baker investigated, or the best way to coach a troubled youngster. Instead, Will spoke of the life-altering changes cutting-edge technology could bring, about the ability to truly unleash human potential. That he'd personally and secretly spent much time researching those types of technologies. And he spoke of the lengths to which those controlling such capabilities might go to prevent those concepts and ideas and technologies from reaching the general public.

Even murder.

He'd thought of those conversations on the night Will had died, wondered if Will had truly discovered what he'd spoken of, and run afoul of those who would do him harm. If so, his gamble on that research had cost him, his family, and two or three others their lives.

"Will spoke to me in that... *different* way," Adam said, his voice quiet. "Talked about life-altering technology he was secretly working on, things we can't even imagine. Evil forces who would stop at nothing to suppress it. But he told me his philosophy on dealing with that, and really about life in general, that he summed up in a short Latin phrase. *Exsisto change vos volo obvius universitas.* To him, it meant that you work on the important things, things you believe in, regardless of what others think, without fear."

"*Be the change you want in the world.*" Baker translated the phrase he, too, had heard Will Stark proclaim during these alternate personality episodes. He looked Adam directly in the eye. "I know that wasn't something he spoke about on a regular basis. I truly felt when he spoke to me that he meant those musings and messages to be for my ears only. If he told you the same thing... I can only suspect that he meant for you to be part of the team." He held out his hand. "Welcome aboard."

Adam clasped the offered hand and shook. "Many thanks." He sat back as the waitress delivered meals to the two men, and then resumed the conversation. "What's strange for me is that while I'm convinced Will wanted me *in* this role, I'm not exactly sure what he wanted me to *do*. Clearly I'm supposed to be the hidden voice in the shadows; everyone knows who you are, and can figure out rather easily that Millard is, and would be, involved as well. Yet I don't have a job description."

Baker chuckled. "I rather wish I did at times. I seem to be inventing the job as I go along."

Adam raised his glass of water. "To poorly-defined problems, then?" He smiled.

Baker laughed, raising his glass as well. "Indeed."

"So, since I don't have a role description, but I'm supposed to help, let me ask you a question." Adam paused a moment, considered, and then continued. "What is the biggest issue or concern that you have? Perhaps I'm supposed to get rid of the obstacles, move them into my world of hidden and secret data and documents, and make everything work more simply."

Baker thought about this question. "Decision-making isn't a large burden for me. There are two basic concerns I have. First, processing everything simply takes a lot of time. The amount of mail we get — paper and electronic — is pretty staggering. Millard and I spend hours each day just tossing out the communications from the obvious panderers. Then we have to weed through what's left and figure out which requests mesh best with the guidance the Starks provided. Once that happens, there's the laborious task of actually responding back to everyone, either explaining our rationale for denying their request for funds from the Trust, or congratulating them and sending a check, which Millard and I both have to sign. Very cumbersome."

Adam frowned. "I thought paper checks disappeared twenty years ago?"

Baker sighed. "Sadly, no. The Trust has a checkbook and a checking account with a *very* large balance. We have to keep a record of all funds disbursed and both authorize and record each payment. It's time consuming, to be sure, but..."

"Why don't you set up electronic payments? Most everyone has the ability to receive funds electronically, and surely whatever bank is holding funds of such magnitude for the Trust can send payments out at your direction, or provide any reports on payments that you'd need. Just make sure that people know that if they send in a request, they'll need to send in a canceled check or bank account numbers as well. Better yet, make sending that type of information something done after they've been approved. Tell those who are receiving money now, for example, that they will get the funds but that we are moving to an electronic system to help us with our tracking of payments."

Baker shook his head. "Our current system is working okay. Besides, we don't know how to set that up. Yes, I know it's pretty old school by now, but the paper check approach has been working."

Adam shrugged, and paused for a moment, as if in deep thought. "It's something I can do if you're interested. Think about it, and let me know. Now, on the communication front, we should look to automate that as well. We can establish a website—"

"But..." Baker interrupted, seeming to have second thoughts. "Come to think of it, I do find writing those checks tiresome, and I dare say that the amount of paperwork is only going to grow over time. We really do need to figure out a better system. If you know how to do this, perhaps we should consider it. The paper we get is wasteful. I'd rather set something up that could pre-screen everything, and then have those requests that pass the initial automated screening come to us. Perhaps we could tie in payments to that as well..."

"Well, you'd need a website with a form for the entry, some coding on the logic to use, and then workflow management to make sure that nothing gets paid out until the two of you formally approve. Once that happens, you can have the people who are approved log back in and provide electronic funds transfer information and we can execute the payment."

"That sounds perfect," Baker said, and he was sure Adam could sense the relief in his voice. "How long would it take to get that established?"

"We'd need to figure out what pieces of information the two of you would need, some logic on the initial screening, how to detect people trying to game the system by answering in a way they think you want them to answer, and so on. We're not doing month end processing right now, so I can probably mock something up in a few days for you and Millard to review. I can test the transfer approach after setting the system up. Wait, you're probably getting a salary or a stipend, correct? For running the Trust?"

"Yes," Baker said, electing not to elaborate on the exorbitant amount.

"So we test it out. If you have the information for your account and the Trust account, I can do a quick mock-up site just for you. You pick the amount, it sends that to your account, and you can verify that it came through. Typically it's just a few pennies at a time for tests like that, but it will show us if it works and how long it takes the funds to clear. You'll need to tell people receiving grants from the Trust how long it will be until their money is accessible."

Baker nodded. "Let's go back to Millard's office after lunch. The account information is there."

The two men returned to Millard Howe's law office after the meal was over, as the office served as the acting headquarters for the Stark family's Trust. Baker explained that, as Howe suspected, Will had given Adam a unique bit of information that had also been shared with Baker, and that information was such that Baker knew Adam was meant to be the third party in their group. With that question resolved, Baker explained to Howe Adam's idea of automating the request and payment process for those petitioning the Trust for funds. Howe, who was so buried with processing paperwork for the Starks that he was losing other clients, readily agreed. They provided Adam with the necessary information to test out electronic transfers, and over the next several hours the trio sketched out the interface and logic flows for the website. Adam stored photos of the sketches on a secured tablet computer, and the men destroyed the original pieces of paper courtesy of the shredder/incinerator in the law office; they didn't want anyone stealing the papers and deciphering the logic flows. Adam then headed out to begin his development work.

Baker and Howe shared a look, and both breathed a sigh of relief. A huge burden had been lifted from their shoulders.

• • •

Adam drove a rental car to the outskirts of Pleasanton, returned it, and walked away. Once he was outside the town and into more sparsely populated areas, he pulled out a small phone and dialed a number from memory. "It's me," he said without preamble to the person on the other end. "I have the information. I should have the transfers starting in the next few days." He listened to a brief flurry of words. "Yes, I'll track them down when I complete my official duties. I don't want to leave them with too many problems to deal with in the future." The voice on the other end of the call spoke again, and Adam nodded. "Yes, I know it's the only way to handle this, but I don't like what it will do to those men. They're good people." And finally, Adam finished the conversation, simply stating, "I'll make it as painless as possible."

After hanging up the phone, Adam triggered a minor Energy burst which disintegrated the device, eliminating the ability to track the call. He then teleported to the abandoned house Millard Howe had visited a few weeks earlier.

Despite what the Starks' lawyer believed, the abandoned house wasn't disguising a hidden data center. It truly *was* an abandoned house, accentuated with the general purpose army of nanos controlled by Adam to make it appear that it housed a hidden entrance to a private office and, presumably, a hidden data center of computers and storage equipment. The secret entryway, the mysterious fog causing sensory deprivation, the tables and chairs — all of those were temporary nano-based creations. Only the handful of current technologies like the computers, printers, and portable storage were real.

Adam was a student of computing technology, earning a living in the human world during the Second Great Depression by offering data storage and security services to those firms still in business. He'd eventually come to the attention of a successful businessman named Will Stark, who heard reports of the innovative young man with a tremendous gift of not just analyzing data, but securing it from the prying eyes of hackers. Adam had remotely taught Will Stark much of the general philosophy Stark used for operating the technology departments in his many business interests, especially the idea of eliminating single points of failure in both technical and process designs. If one person or technology component could fail, and thus bring down an entire business function, it needed some type of backup or failsafe to ensure no loss of operational ability. Data stored in only one place, for example, could be lost or tampered with, and thus multiple copies were constantly created and checked against each other. Stark learned well from these lessons and applied them in other areas, from the design of his highly secure community and home, to inventing the elaborate method of verifying and executing his will, to the operation of his philanthropic Trust after his death.

He had come to trust Adam in all things.

Adam, however, was about to rob Will Stark and his Trust of every cent of cash they possessed.

Patience was in order, however.

Adam had already created a mock-up of the site requested by Michael Baker, because Adam had used various persuasive Energy techniques to impress on the former police officer the correctness of Adam's own existing approach and design. And while Adam focused that conversation on the benefits of paper reduction and freeing up time for both Baker and Howe, the reality was that the entire conversation had one purpose: obtaining the information needed to access the Trust's checking account electronically. Though it had taken a while, his mission had been a success.

Adam would be long gone, along with the money, before they realized what had happened. He activated the website as promised, and ran a couple of small transfers to Michael Baker's personal account. Once he'd confirmed the process worked, he set up a script, which would transfer relatively modest amounts of cash at irregular intervals to dozens of accounts he'd established around the world. Each of those accounts automatically forwarded electronic deposits to other accounts, and eventually all of the money would end up in a small handful of hidden accounts in the most secure human banks on the planet. Adam's script would run, and his website would work as promised, until one day, a petitioner to the Trust would find that a promised transfer never arrived. Baker and Howe would check the balance and discover, too late, that there was nothing left.

More than likely, both men would go to jail for embezzlement, for crimes that Adam had committed. The public would scoff at their stories of the mysterious man named Adam, a man who had no last name or address, who supposedly worked for Will Stark but for whom no payroll information would ever be found. After all, if you controlled the most secure data in the company, you could vanish from existence rather easily.

The stories of his existence, told by Baker and Howe, would be considered the desperate lies of thieves caught in the act. That part of the plan was the one that bothered him the most. The larger plan required that he pilfer all of those funds from the Starks' account, but the historical record would show that two good, decent, innocent men had committed a terrible crime of greed, and the funds would never be found. The two men and their families would be forever shamed. Adam had an idea to make right that injustice while still accomplishing his primary goal; the two men deserved a better fate than that currently awaiting them. He'd figured out the problem two years earlier, after everything was set in motion and it was too late to stop. He needed to finish this side project to preserve the reputations of Baker and Howe.

But Adam also had a job to do. He launched his script, and watched the lifetime fortune of the Starks gradually become his own.

XX
SACRIFICE

Will stopped training with Adam after the attack.

He was convinced that he'd progressed too quickly, and that as a result he'd not taken the time to assimilate his new abilities; his singular focus on advancement meant that he'd not learned to focus on the basics like Shielding at critical times. As a result, Angel had nearly died. He needed to slow down, truly understand what he was doing, what he *could* do, and what he needed to focus on. And he needed to stop making stupid mistakes before somebody actually *did* get killed.

Angel made a full recovery over the next day or so, and thanked Will for the blood he'd donated. She said she felt stronger than ever because of the gift. Will felt it was the least he could do, and said so.

Angel simply sighed. "Stop blaming yourself. All of us noticed the leak and we waited too long to correct it. There's no way you could have known about it."

"But I did," Will protested. "Adam showed me how to Shield that day. I stopped doing it once the lesson ended, and I didn't even think about it when they showed up and chased us, right before they... hurt you. I was taught what I needed to know, and didn't do what needed to be done. I hope one day you'll forgive me."

"There's nothing to forgive, but if it makes you feel better, I will say the words. *I forgive you.* They found us long before the lesson occurred, and showed up after it was over. Whether you remembered or not is irrelevant to whether they found us. Stop worrying about it."

Will opened his mouth to protest, but Angel held up a hand. "No more. Get back to work." She winked at him and walked away.

Will sighed. Women were confusing. He wondered if she'd been difficult as a teenager.

He did allow Adam to give him the communication nanos, and he was gifted a few hundred billion general-purpose nanos to work with. He managed to get his machines to form body armor around him after some practice, but the new toy wasn't nearly as exciting as it would have been a few weeks earlier, before he'd nearly destroyed them all at the old camp site.

Their new camp looked similar to the old; the structures used for dwellings built of nanos, the large wooded enclosure, the clearing used as a common area for communication. Will moved to the edge of the clearing and sat up against a tree, watching the interactions of those in the camp, wondering what these people did with all of their time. He got the impression that the 16-20 hours per day he'd spent practicing Energy work wasn't the norm, and that most of them spent no more than an hour on Energy work each day. He learned that the nanos were used to perform much of the manual labor: gathering food, processing waste, and generating electricity. Adam had, in his typical vague fashion, indicated that most of their time was spent on self-directed research... whatever *that* meant. Will asked what research Adam was doing, and Adam stated that Will *was* his research at the moment.

Will stood and headed into the forest, thinking about the impact of the Energy work he'd done with the tree. Clearly, both he and the tree had benefited from the symbiotic relationship. The tree had grown dramatically during the time he'd worked with it, growing from being one of the smaller and weaker trees in its grove to one fighting for dominance with other trees that had been much longer established. Likewise, Will had gone from a relative weakling in terms of Energy capacity to one fairly strong in the community; the glances he received as he walked through the common areas in his bodysuit with the yellowish-orange tint said that others recognized this. Thankfully, no one seemed to feel threatened by his accelerated achievements, at least not until the hundred or more Aliomenti fighter craft, including the three piloted by the Hunters, showed up and started shooting. Rather, they seemed pleased and encouraged by his growth, proud of him for the effort he'd put forth and the results he'd gotten. It didn't take much in a small community of telepaths for word of his relentless pursuit of Energy growth to reach the entire population.

Will found a small tree amid the giants in this forest grove as well. He sat down on the soft earth and watched the tree, the leaves rustling in the light breeze, the branches swaying. The canopy wasn't as developed here; this tree managed to receive significantly more sunshine than did his tree back at the previous camp. He smiled at the possessive thought. The tree belonged to no one; it merely did what it was born to do, grow to its greatest possible height, competing against other entities for sunlight and air and nutrients in the soil. To fail was to perish; to succeed was to live. The tree did not care what other trees did; it simply made whatever effort necessary to get sufficient resources to grow. Will smiled. Sometimes, though, an extra helping hand could make all the difference.

He wondered about the tree. Had it continued to grow, stretching high above the others to reach greater quantities of sunlight and air? Or had it stagnated without his efforts? Or worse, had the attack by the Hunters damaged it, perhaps beyond repair? He wished he were there. Will pictured the tree, seeing himself standing near it, hands on the tree's trunk. In his reverie, his focus lapsed and he felt a surge of Energy. There was a flash... and then he was there, with his hands on the burned-out trunk of the tree he'd nurtured and been nurtured by, a simple link and a reminder of the basics of life. He felt the warm rush of Energy from the tree, though weaker than he'd remembered due to the attacks. He instinctively fed his own Energy back, feeling the synergy and symbiosis as each living thing reprocessed the gifted Energy and fed it back, better and more powerful than before. The tree was healing, and Will's Energy was growing. It was like old times, before the Hunters found them, before...

Will backed away, moving a dozen yards from his tree. The surge in Energy was noticeable, even for him, new to the experience. It was like a powerful, sweet smell, overwhelming all else. He was worried now. Had he triggered the Hunters' warning signals again with that burst? It was with some relief that he realized that the camp was some distance away; if they came here now, they'd find no one to capture or kill besides Will. Still, he slapped on his Shield, hoping it wasn't too late. Again.

He heard a soft popping noise. A man had materialized where

Will had stood only a moment earlier. The man had long, brown hair and wore a dark cloak. It was Porthos, the Tracker Hunter, and the man had found him yet again. Porthos turned around, searching, and finally faced Will.

A sneer curled on Porthos' face. "Well, Stark, you managed to escape and hide for some time. But you're getting a bit sloppy in your old age. You let us find you twice now in, what, a week? A rather poor showing. What's the matter, lonely from hanging out with all of those losers that call themselves the Alliance? At least you've got your Energy levels back to more Stark-like levels." He chuckled at his own joke.

Will folded his arms. "Why are you here?"

Porthos blinked. "Is that a trick question? I'm here to capture you, you fool, or at least slow you down until my friends arrive. Fear not, they're a bit out of range right now, and they'll need a few more teleportation hops to get here. But they'll be here soon enough. I'm sure Aramis would love to see you again. Probably invented a few more crimes to charge you with at this point." He took a step toward Will. "Or you could just come quietly, and save me and the rest of your old friends the trouble of subduing you."

Will frowned. "My old friends? I think not. My friends are the members of the Alliance. Not Athos, Not Aramis. And certainly not you."

Porthos put a hand over his heart, covering up the golden Aliomenti symbol, in mock pain. "Truly, my feelings shatter at your harsh words. But I must confess, I don't understand you, Stark. You lure us to your home. You escape. You hide for a very long time. Now you're luring us again. Tell me, what's the purpose of this game of cat and mouse? Has your life lost its meaning, and you've become bored enough to risk us killing you? Or is there truly some Will Stark master plan you're building toward?"

Will snorted. "Life is never dull. But I prefer to live it under my own terms, without the threat of someone taking my freedom away. I can't rest, because while you operate under those rules, the threat is there."

"As you said, Stark, life is never dull. Perhaps it is the threat of loss of any type that motivates you. Tell me, how motivated were you after we destroyed your home?" The man's eyes glinted, and a sinister grin covered his face.

Will took two steps toward Porthos, and then stopped. "My motivations are of my own choosing, not driven by someone else's actions. But I'll never forget that moment, or forgive you for your part in it."

Porthos chuckled. "Again, my feelings are truly crushed." He paused, and then smiled. "Ah, I see the rest of the guests have arrived for our little party." He glanced behind Will, who suddenly felt the presence of another man. Aramis. The shadow with the top hat gave away the identity, and before Will could react, Aramis grabbed him by the arm. He felt as if the wind had been knocked out of him, as if someone had started crushing his lungs and prevented him from breathing. It was Aramis' unique gift, known as the Damper, and it was erasing his Energy. The power it provided the Hunter in thwarting those Hunted was immense, and Will knew he needed to free himself and escape. He rammed his elbow into the Hunter's stomach, and Aramis let go, gasping, trying to refill his suddenly-empty lungs.

Will darted away, trying to distance himself from both Hunters, glancing behind him as he ran. He sensed that a third man had appeared, directly in the path he was racing along, and Will bounced into him. Athos reached around and put Will into a bear hug, and Aramis and Porthos both advanced, with the former ready to slap on the Damper, and the latter prepared to help escort Will back to the Aliomenti prison. Will stomped down on Athos' foot and slammed his head back in to Athos' face, snapping a bone in the Hunter's foot and breaking the man's nose. Athos let go, screaming, his hands flying to his face and the gushing blood. Will dipped under Porthos' arms and darted from the tree. He'd wanted so desperately to get to the tree; now, he wanted to get back to the camp, safely, without the Hunters. He remembered the new tree he'd been looking at earlier, and...

Will reached his tree, which was still healing from the blasts of the Aliomenti fighting craft, and he felt a huge surge of Energy into him. The Energy pulsed, and Will felt a sense of displacement. Then he was back at the tree outside the new camp. He immediately Shielded his Energy and sprinted back to the clearing. He found Fil and Adam having a hushed conversation, but both of their faces relaxed upon seeing Will.

"Where have you been?" Adam asked. "I was going to restart your lessons, because Angel said you were probably ready, but I couldn't sense your Energy at all. I'm sure that your Shielding skills have improved, but I should be able to find you in camp at this short distance regardless."

"I teleported. Back to the old camp. Listen, though—"

"You did *what?*" Fil asked, his voice venomous. "Who taught you how to teleport? And how did you travel so far in your first effort?"

"Nobody taught me, it just happened, and I don't know how. There was a spot in the forest there where I liked to go, and I pictured it and thought about how nice it would be to be there again, and there I was."

Fil was shaking his head. "You're out of control. You must learn to discipline your use of Energy."

"Right, I know, but understand this. I think... I think I surged some Energy while I was there, because... well..."

"Because one of the Hunters showed up?" Adam asked. Will nodded. "I noticed the intensity of the Energy there right before they discovered our previous campsite. We'll get back to that point, but right now, it's more urgent that we understand what happened with the Hunters. Tell us."

"Porthos showed up first." Based on the facial reactions, this was no surprise. "He taunted me about losing my touch and him finding me again so quickly. Aramis showed up and put his hands on me, and I felt my Energy waning rapidly, but I elbowed him hard in the stomach and got away. Then Athos showed up and tried to restrain me so Aramis could get me again; I head-butted him, broke loose, wished I was back, and here I stand. My Shield went up the instant I arrived."

"You *idiot!*" Fil seethed. "If you only Shielded when you arrived here, they may be able to track you here because your Energy signal was so strong. We're going to need to move camp *again!* And so help me, if Angel or anyone else suffers an injury again due to your carelessness, I will knock you out cold and deliver you to the Hunters myself!"

Adam glared at Fil, and Will was taken aback. "I... I don't know what to say. I'm sorry. I'm trying to learn everything, but... maybe it's all happening too fast."

"No excuses," Fil snapped. "You've been putting us in jeopardy since you got here, not to mention the massive risk we took in rescuing you to begin with. I..."

"Why rescue me, then?" Will asked, fuming. "I've always wondered that. The Hunters thought I was somebody I wasn't; maybe I'm better able to pull off the act of being that man now with the Energy training I've had. But they seem to think I'm some super criminal, breaking all of their rules. I'm not that guy. I'm *nobody*. Why rescue *me*?"

Fil's teeth clenched. "Everybody makes mistakes." He turned and left.

Adam watched him leave. "You must understand. In our world, Will Stark is basically a god. He was exceptionally powerful, drove many of our innovations, and in many ways formed us into what we are today. Others abused his ideas; the concept of not marrying wasn't one done as an excuse to murder innocent humans, for example. It was meant to ensure that such an important commitment wasn't made without ensuring that the new spouse was capable of handling the truth of what we are, and integrating in some fashion with our society without exposing our existence, and possibly endangering our lives. Think of the men and women you consider heroes, Will. If you thought they were in danger... wouldn't you go rescue them if you had the ability to do so?"

Will let out a deep breath. "I wish I knew what that guy has against me."

"Who? Fil?"

"Yes. You seem friendly enough. Angel treats me far better than I — or anyone else, for that matter — actually deserve. Fil seems to feel a genuine hatred for me. Is it because I'm not this superhero legend, and he's blaming me for only being who I truly am?"

"He doesn't hate you, Will. Your presence, though, reminds him of several of the most painful experiences in his life, and he'll need to be the one to explain. I will tell you, though, that he, too, lost a wife and young child — a daughter — to an Aliomenti Assassin. He had to watch them die, Will. Your experience... well, it was a bit too close to *his* experience, and triggered memories he's tried to bury."

Will lowered his head. "I had no idea. It certainly proves those men are evil, though."

Adam raised a hand. "You didn't know, and I request that you seem astonished anew when Fil decides to let you know about that painful part of his life, even though I doubt he ever will. As you might imagine, he doesn't like to think about it or discuss it."

Will glanced up. "Did they somehow damage his eyes?"

Adam frowned. "His eyes? No, I don't think they did. Why do you ask?"

"I was wondering why he always wears those sunglasses."

Adam smiled. "He'll tell you that particular story when he's ready. But it's something that only he can choose to share." He turned to leave. "I was thinking of doing a lesson, but it was to be about teleportation and it would appear you've got the basics down. Perhaps we can pick it up in the morning?"

Will nodded. Adam walked away.

Will moved away from the buildings and headed into the woods. His foolishness and lack of concentration had nearly gotten Angel killed and uprooted the community once, and might well do so again. His presence caused Fil great pain. Adam was uncomfortable working with him, a fact Will had pieced together with his telepathic and empathic skills during several of their lessons. Adam simply was not certain how to deal with someone like Will, who tried to cram years of training and growth into days or hours, and who spontaneously started practicing new and different skills without guidance or consultation.

And he might bring the Hunters down on them again. He wouldn't let that happen, and risk the possibility that this time, someone like Angel would be hurt — and not survive the injuries.

He'd fought the Hunters to regain his freedom, but he wouldn't keep it if it meant others would lose theirs. The Alliance members — Angel, Adam, and even Fil, surly though the man could be — were his family now. He'd lost one family through his own failure, and he wasn't about to have another be lost for the same reason.

Will made it back to his spot in the woods, and once again pictured his tree with its burned-out limbs, struggling to work its way back to health. He pictured himself being by his tree, and unlocked his Shield enough to power the teleportation effort. He was not surprised this time to find himself back outside their old camp. Nor was he much surprised to see Porthos still there, trying to piece together the Energy patterns that would tell him where Will had gone after teleporting away.

"Miss me?"

Porthos whirled. "No, you aren't around long enough for me to miss. And I expect you to stay in our prison for a very long time when I finally capture you; I won't miss you then, either. I don't really like you running off like that, however, because it makes it so difficult to track you effectively when you keep moving so quickly."

Will nodded. "I agree. I'm giving myself up."

Porthos' eyes widened and he stared at Will. "Stark, you can't possibly expect me to believe you."

Will walked toward him. "Here I am. Take me to your Leader. Bring Aramis to subdue me if you want. I'm not going anywhere and I won't resist."

Porthos felt an incredible sense of elation, and a smile formed on his face.

After all of the years, all of the Hunts, all of the failures... he would finally see Will Stark brought to justice.

XXI
HEADQUARTERS

Adam stretched as he woke after a restful night's sleep. The argument between Will and Fil yesterday was still on his mind, and he sensed that it had broken Will's spirit a bit, more than anything had since his arrival in camp following his rescue from the Hunters. The two men had argued before, but Will had been more assertive, more combative in the previous encounters. The man was now so concerned that he was a threat to the safety of the others in the Alliance camp that he had no desire to further develop his Energy abilities. That was a problem. As a member of the Alliance, he needed to have those abilities well-developed should he ever encounter the Hunters or other Aliomenti who might find him and try to subdue him. Will had escaped yesterday, probably because the Hunters were so surprised to see him. There was no guarantee he'd be so lucky again.

On the positive side, Will had been eager the day before to practice teleportation, and Adam had been impressed that he'd so quickly developed the Energy stores needed for that skill. He knew many long-term Aliomenti who could barely teleport a few hundred yards, and Will had managed a greater distance in just over a month.

He needed to figure out how, exactly, Will was building his Energy so quickly. It was simply unnatural.

To be sure, the Aliomenti all knew that there was some type of genetic component that could predict how quickly someone would develop. In the early days, before they had the ability to supplement their development with nanos — most notably through the Purge — their group had politely expelled slower-developing members, but that was before the Oaths had been written and penalties defined and enforced. Today, the Alliance could focus on recruiting people of high character and motivation first, and supplement their genetic potential.

In this case, perhaps they had supplemented somebody who already had a powerful genetic potential and capability; after all, they didn't scan for that anymore. Was that the explanation for Will's rapid growth? Adam rather doubted it. Still, whatever it was, it had caught them all completely off guard. They shouldn't have needed to worry about Shielding or accidental teleportation or anything of the sort for years. He knew Will blamed himself, but the rest of the Alliance, men and women with far more experience in such matters, had been blind to the implications of his growth as well. They needed to be more cautious and patient with his training, and make him more aware of the implications of his progress. Lesson learned.

Speaking of lessons, he needed to find Will.

He mulled over how best to handle the teleportation lesson. The odd thing with teleportation was that once you'd done it, doing it when intended wasn't a huge issue, outside learning techniques for going somewhere you hadn't been previously or how to plan for the Energy drain from an exceptionally long trip. The challenge was preventing the kind of unintended "hop" Will Stark had experienced the day before, brought on by lack of focus and control over the Energy required to move. Keeping Energy tightly bound, as would happen when Shielding, tended to prevent the issue, but emotional situations would crack that focus, release the Energy, and put the person at risk. They'd need to review those concepts.

Adam approached Will's building. He should probably gift Will the nanos comprising what had become Will's home, and request a new batch from the Mechanic as a replacement. Will had a small number of nanos already, but was probably ready for a more standard allocation. That would be another lesson for another day, however, so he elected not to make the gift until they'd done more work with the machines.

Adam frowned as he neared the building. Will should be inside, but he detected no Energy there. Even if Will was Shielding, he should be able to sense the presence of at least *some* Energy in the room. Adam smiled. Perhaps their prodigy had taken Shielding to a new level. He should raise the idea to the Alliance of letting the Aliomenti Elites know about their Shielding skills. The thought of those tyrants thinking they could walk right past someone from the Alliance without knowing it was priceless.

Adam walked into the building. There was no sign of Will.

Perhaps he'd gone for a walk in the woods. Will seemed to enjoy the tranquility to be found among the dense forests surrounding their clearings. Adam remembered that Will had lived in a wooded community, and that his home had been surrounded by large, old trees. It made sense that he'd experience a sense of home in the forest.

Adam walked into the woods, circling farther and farther from camp. He detected some Energy readings, fairly strong, and while he found a clearing with a few smaller trees, he found no sign of Will Stark.

Very curious.

Adam walked back to the camp and approached the building Fil and Angel shared. He walked in; the interior of their building was a bit more elaborate than most, and featured two private rooms along with a public area anyone could enter. He found Fil there, deep in thought.

"Have you seen Will?" Adam asked without preamble.

Fil laughed. "I truly doubt Will Stark would willingly associate with me at this point. On that note, no, I haven't seen him since last night, when he nearly put everyone in camp at risk once again. I haven't forgiven him yet for so nearly killing my sister the last time he failed to focus."

"Duly noted. We'll make sure in the future that we handle Shielding a month into training, though few need such skills until they've been at it for five years... if they're lucky."

"Save the sarcasm, Adam. *Your* sister wasn't the one who nearly bled to death."

"Speaking of Angel, has *she* seen Will?"

"I haven't," she answered, emerging from her room. "I thought he'd be having a lesson with you."

"That was the plan. I checked his building, and looked for him in the forest. There's a spot with a bit of an Energy buildup — not enough to attract any attention." Adam added the last bit quickly when Fil looked ready to explode again. "But that's the closest thing to a sign of him. Do either of you have any sense of where he might be?"

Both Fil and Angel closed their eyes in concentration. Adam watched Fil. Though the man hid it well, his Energy levels were exceptionally high, and he was more likely to find something than anyone else. Angel's Energy levels were extraordinary as well, though nowhere near the levels of Fil. She was more empathic than her older brother, and more likely to sense what Will was thinking even without actually invading his thoughts.

Angel opened her eyes. "I'm not getting anything besides a faint Energy marker in the woods outside the camp. That's probably what you found, Adam." Adam nodded. "My concern, though, is the mental state he was in. He seemed very depressed, and his conversations with me... I got the sense that he feared he was a danger to us and he didn't like that." She took a deep breath. "That, combined with the fact that we can't find him... I'm concerned he's essentially run off on his own. That he left the camp so he can't risk any harm to any of us anymore."

Adam's eyes widened. "I hope you're wrong."

"So do I. But his pain and his fear were genuine. I heard him blaming himself for the situation at his house while he was sleeping in those first few days. He kept saying it was his fault, that he'd let them be killed... and his greatest fear is doing that again. If I'm wrong, we need to impress upon him that we'll work with him, but we don't want him running off." She looked straight at Fil, but her brother was still in deep concentration.

A few moments later, Fil opened his eyes and cursed.

"That *idiot!*" he seethed. He turned to Angel. "I think you're too late on that idea. He's run off, all right." He looked at Adam. "He teleported from that spot in the woods near here. That was the Energy burst you detected. He showed up back in the woods by our previous camp, again, where he'd met the Hunters before. Unfortunately, one of them was there."

"Porthos," Adam said. It wasn't a question.

"I get no Energy sense of either of them now. Porthos is powerful enough that I could pick him up in that location from here if I concentrate, and he's never learned to Shield, or bothered if he knows how. But he's gone. And so is Will."

Angel's eyes widened. "What are you saying?"

"I'm saying that we can go check that spot, but all signs point to that stubborn idiot either being captured... or turning himself in to the Hunters."

• • •

This time, nobody beat him up or tried to kill him. At least, not yet.

A craft arrived in the clearing, driven by Athos. He stared at Will Stark, his face a mix of emotions. It was one part triumphant, one part fear of sudden and tremendous disappointment.

Will had not put up a fight at all. He sat in the craft, which was clearly not as well-built as the Alliance nano-based vehicles, nor as gentle on takeoff and landing. Will looked out the window as the craft rose into the air. He saw massive forests behind him, and eventually a huge body of water appeared on the horizon in front. Will realized he still had no idea where on the planet he'd been living for the past two months. Right now, he didn't much care.

The craft flew out over the body of water, and soon there was nothing to see but gentle rolling waves. Athos and Porthos both tried questioning him, but Will ignored them, focusing on nothing but the motion of the water below. Eventually, the Hunters gave up and left him alone.

After they'd traveled over water for several hours, Will finally saw land. It was an island, fairly large, with beautiful beaches around the perimeter. The buildings were glass and metal, and looked remarkably new and clean, as did the streets forming a patchwork as they moved inland from the beaches.

The craft flew over those beaches and buildings and roads, and Will noticed in an offhand manner that, despite it being midday with clear skies, there were very few people out on the beaches, or even out on the streets of the island. Odd.

The craft was heading for the middle of the island, and Will noticed a much taller building, one that appeared to be formed of a black marble exterior, polished and gleaming in the sunlight. But it was the name emblazoned across the top that got his attention more than all else.

ALIOMENTI.

This must be the Headquarters of the organization, though it certainly piqued Will's interest. For an organization willing to kill to protect its anonymity, a large modern building on what seemed a private island with the group's name on the front seemed remarkably out of character. The giant, golden Aliomenti symbols flanking the name on the building also seemed out of place.

Athos landed the craft on a landing strip near the building, and taxied the vehicle into an open hangar at the base. The structure was massive, easily thirty stories tall, and with a footprint that would cover several standard-sized city blocks.

The Aliomenti were definitely not keeping a low profile. So why did they want to abduct him for supposedly talking? Why were they so intent on killing his wife and son because they might know about it, if they were willing to broadcast the name and symbols in such an obvious fashion?

Will's determination shifted again. He'd come here to eliminate the risk he posed to his new family. Now he was ready to fight again to avenge the deceased one. Apparently, they'd made up a different set of rules for him, for this other Will Stark, and now his family was dead, and his new family — Angel, Adam, and even Fil — were at risk as well. He couldn't stand the hypocrisy.

He kept his face stony, however, and ensured his Energy Shield was up. No sense letting on what he was up to until the time was right. Especially since he hadn't planned on trying to fight and, if he survived, escape. Right now, he had to improvise every step of the way.

He followed Athos through the hangar and into the main portion of the building, which was as opulent as the outside. White marble floors, columns, and gold trim were to be found almost everywhere. Will noticed three other strange details.

First, there were dozens of screens of information flush with all of those marble walls, all displaying financial information. Prices of commodities. Exchange rates for currencies. Active stock market data. The numbers looked wildly different than Will remembered, but then, the world was still in a delicate state economically, and he'd not seen such data for nearly two months. A lot could change in those circumstances.

Second, he felt his Energy being crushed within him as he walked, as if Aramis' Damper was settling on him. Yet Aramis was nowhere to be seen. He still had some Energy left, but not enough to teleport.

The final strange detail: other than Will and the two Hunters, every other person he encountered in the building was clearly human. Will had enough of his Energy and enhanced senses to recognize that none of these people would know what Energy was if he asked them.

The Aliomenti were broadcasting their name and interacting with humans. Inwardly, Will seethed at the hypocrisy.

Athos and Porthos were clearly well-known among the humans. Everyone smiled and bowed slightly as the two men passed, and Will could sense their obvious fear of the Hunters due to his empathic skills. Will figured that the two of them probably loved generating that fear. Will himself received curious looks as they worked through the lobby to an elevator bank, and thought he saw one woman whisper "must be a new client" to her friend. Will found that conclusion amusing.

They reached a bank of elevators, but moved to a separate elevator clearly set off from others. Athos held up a card, but Will detected the short trickle of Energy that went into the security device. It was indeed a handy mechanism. It guaranteed that none of the many humans working in the building could ever enter this particular elevator car, even if they should come into possession of one of the cards.

As the doors closed, Athos fixed Will with a stare. "Why'd you do it?"

"Do what?"

"You put up a fight not too long ago. Now you stand there and let us take you away without so much as a contrary word. That's not like you at all, which makes me think you're up to something."

"I don't want to put my friends at risk anymore." Sometimes the truth was the best answer, even if his true answer might change in the near future.

Athos laughed. "And why is this suddenly a concern after so long? It's not as if those risks didn't exist before."

Will shrugged. "Perhaps I'm just getting old."

Porthos snorted. "Now *that* I'll give you."

Will gestured in a circular motion. "What is this place? Humans everywhere? As I recall, at one of our more recent get-togethers, you were quite upset to find that I'd been involved with a human. Why are so many here?"

Athos stared at him. "Have you lost your mind? Or just your

memories?"

"At least one of those. I'll let you decide which."

"This is our business front, which we use to develop significant wealth in human currency so that we can live in luxury when we must interact with their world. We've essentially set up the world's largest bank with a very select clientele. All Aliomenti, of course." He smiled. "Given our abilities, the holdings are rather extensive. We own the whole island, and it's primarily populated by the humans who live here and work the hotels, shops, restaurants, and beaches. Officially, the island is a nation unto itself, and as such we limit travel here. Only the human workers and Aliomenti coming in for visits are allowed on the island. So it serves as our financial stronghold and our primary playground in this world. The humans who work here in the bank handle the chore of investing our surplus cash, exchanging currencies, and so on."

"And the name?"

"It's our business name. It just so happens that it's more than that. We can talk Aliomenti *business*, as in banking activities, in public all we want, and we do. In the event the term is used with its other meaning and overheard, everyone simply assumes we're talking about the bank."

A thousand-year-old secret society of incredibly gifted, telepathic people who lived in perfect health would certainly seem capable of developing an immense presence in any global industry over time. The financial statements of this company — if they had to issue any — would be incredible.

"Where are we going now?" Will asked, as the elevator doors opened. He saw Aramis standing there, the man's face greedy with expectation. The Hunter grasped Will's arm, and he felt the Damper working.

"We're going to meet with The Leader," Porthos replied. "He has questions for you, and he'd like to get answers to them before you're gone."

"Gone?" Will asked.

Aramis chuckled. "Mr. Stark, despite your long absence, you remain an Oath-breaker and your sentence has been pronounced. The fact that you turned yourself in and appear to be devoid of much of your memory and Energy is irrelevant." He rubbed his hands together.

"You see, you will, with our prodding, provide The Leader with answers to his questions. When that is done, I will have the honor of taking you to our Assassin. And then, Will Stark, you will die."

XXII
TURNCOAT

The level of the building where The Leader resided was straight from the Gilded Age, the purest example of sheer extravagance that Will had ever seen.

It was a single open space, save for the elevator shaft in the center. The entire floor was built of pure marble, polished so brightly that Will had to squint to allow his eyes to adjust. The columns here were silver throughout, and Will was quite certain that the silver wasn't simply plated on the outside.

The columns changed to gold as they approached The Leader. The man had styled this section of the floor as if he was a monarch holding court. In addition to the golden columns leading his way, thick rugs and carpets lined the floor, and heaping piles of gemstones of all shapes, sizes, and colors ringed the carpets, forming an aisle leading to The Leader's chair. The chair itself appeared to be made of solid gold, the exterior lined with sparkling diamonds, inlaid with a red velvet cushion.

The Leader stood from his chair as Will and the Hunters approached. He looked to be in his mid-forties, with slightly thinning blond hair brushed straight back. His smirk was suggestive of a child who had just gotten away with swiping a cookie without getting caught, and the smirk reached his eyes.

"Mr. Stark, so good to see you again! It has certainly been a long time."

Will said nothing.

"Come now, my old friend, you mustn't be upset about the circumstances. All of our rules and laws and Oaths were created for the protection of our community and ideas. What is the term you used in the human business world you so excelled at all those years ago? Intellectual property? Thieves who steal intellectual property, I believe, are committing the crime of industrial espionage. Sadly, Will, you elected to become the greatest purveyor of industrial espionage in our history, among the other broken Oaths. Even *you* are not above our laws."

Will blinked. Something was out of place. "What do you mean... 'all those years ago'? My businesses still exist."

The Leader laughed. "Come now, Mr. Stark. You mustn't be so fond of your little enterprises that you pretend they still exist. You are well aware that they ceased to exist mere decades after your alleged death, torn to shreds by the hands of all of those humans you loved to support, each trying to extract what they could for their own ends. And in the end, they destroyed the engine that you built for them, as humans always do."

Will shook his head. "But my business can't have been gone *decades* after my alleged death. I haven't been *gone* that long."

The Hunters looked at each other, and started laughing. The Leader joined in as well, the intensity growing as the look on Will's face grew more and more confused. Athos, still laughing, stepped forward and rested a hand on Will's shoulder, pausing in his chuckling long enough to concentrate. He frowned. "This is fascinating," he commented. "To the best of his knowledge we are, oh, two *months* beyond that little event where The Assassin burned his house down. I see your friends have kept you in the dark, and likely in some type of hibernation or stasis, for quite some time."

Will threw up his hands, exasperated. "What are you *talking* about?"

The Leader smiled at him. "What year is it, Will Stark?"

"2030, of course."

The Leader shook his head. "Hibernation indeed! No, Will, it appears your so-called friends, the people you sacrificed yourself to protect, have been less than forthcoming about your own current reality. You see, Will, you've apparently been asleep for nearly two *centuries*. It's currently the year 2219, *not* 2030."

Will staggered backward as if punched, and felt the air leave him. It was impossible. Completely impossible. He'd only counted two months or so since the Hunters had assaulted him in his own back yard. This man was claiming that somehow, what he'd seen as two months had in fact been 189 years. Twice as long as people actually lived. Had the drugs he'd received put him to sleep for decades at a time? But there was still a flaw in that logic.

"That's not possible. None of you have aged. None of the people who rescued me have aged. I'd think 189 years would make anyone look ancient, regardless of how young they were when the count started."

The Leader and the Hunters burst out laughing again. At *him*. Will seethed quietly.

"You really don't remember *anything*, do you? When you went through everything all of those years ago, all of those exercises, all of the foods and medicines, you helped your body remember how to stop aging. Your cells don't die off; they reproduce completely and cleanly every single time. Therefore, you don't age. You learn more, retain more, understand more. You build substantial wealth. Do you remember any of this?"

They'd learned to become immortal?

And it all clicked into place. Immortality. That was their true discovery: the fountain of youth. That was something they were willing to protect at all costs, something they were willing to kill over. It wasn't the ability to sense and control Energy that truly guided them; it was the reality that, after the people working in the building below were gone, they'd live on in eternal youth and health, growing their wealth, expanding their control over the world. Over the course of a century, two centuries...the amount of wealth a person could amass was mind-boggling. What if they lived even longer than that? In fact...the man they thought he was, that man must have been centuries old as well, in order for him to have acquired as much power as they all claimed. No wonder the Hunters seemed so familiar with him, seemed to take capturing him so personally. In their memories, they might have been after Will Stark for decades or centuries, and even if they'd gone twenty or thirty years between attempts, they still could have made those attempts at capture dozens of times. He could start to understand why they'd been so violent; he imagined that failing at something for centuries might well trigger that type of reaction in someone.

Still, it changed his perspective quite a bit. And he wanted to know why, if he was supposed to be so critical to the Alliance, that Adam and Fil and yes, even Angel, had elected to simply put him into hibernation rather than rehabilitate him or help him recover his memories. He had no doubt they could do either, after having seen the potions and nano-based "medicines." Or perhaps that was it. They needed the time to develop the technology to fix him, so they'd put him in hibernation until then. That seemed more comforting. Fil, in all his cantankerous moods, was recalling the literal centuries of work to revive him to what he once was, and was understandably furious when the man he'd restored was putting his family and community at risk, rather than simply remembering who he was and how to truly be a member of the Alliance.

The problem with this scenario is that it meant that, somehow, his entire life had been a lie.

Somehow, his memories of his long life had been erased, replaced with those of another, and while he had retained his name, he had no recollection of the skills and knowledge he'd gained over his previous decades, or even centuries, of life. He'd lost his Energy stores and skills. It certainly explained why, after he woke up, that he'd regained the skills so quickly. His body probably remembered everything; it was his mind that needed to catch up.

The Leader had stated this to further demoralize him, of course, to break down his mental defenses and gather information, undoubtedly about the Alliance and their locations. He needed to survive, to get back there himself. To thank them for what they'd done in rebuilding him, but also to question them in depth about why he'd been altered in the first place, why they'd never told him the truth. He knew it was the truth; the ramifications of what he'd seen with the Purge and the nanos and everything else meant that these two factions could undoubtedly live forever. He needed to reclaim his place with the Alliance, now that he had a truer sense of what that was, and not give himself up to this loathsome bunch.

And that meant he needed to end this interview *now*, and escape.

Will looked back at The Leader. "As a matter of fact, I do seem to remember a few things. For example, I remember that you always did have a terrible inferiority complex, always needing to compensate with external possessions to make everyone forget just how weak you truly are." Will glanced around the room at the jewels, and rugs, and precious metals on display, then turned his gaze fully back on The Leader. "I see that particular problem has gotten worse. Or is there a *new* problem that's come up in the past few decades that's driving this?" Will arched an eyebrow.

The fake smile on The Leader's face darkened. Aramis looked scandalized, an expression he seemed to have mastered. Athos clapped his hand to his mouth, whether to cover a gasp of shock or a laugh, Will did not know. Porthos had no such insecurities. He snickered openly, and then snapped his mouth shut and stayed silent when The Leader glared at him.

"I see you've remembered your lack of tact and decorum, Stark. You never did appreciate all the benefits our group had to offer, never did play by the rules, and you certainly never treated your betters with appropriate respect. Perhaps I was wrong to hold this sentimental little meeting to enjoy a laugh about the good old days." He looked at Aramis. "I have no need of this man anymore, seeing as how my own spy has taken the time to update me fully on the situation with the Alliance." Seeing Will's look of horror, he laughed. "Oh, did I forget to mention that? You see, on the night you vanished from the annals of history, someone else vanished as well. Someone *else* your Alliance friends drugged into hibernation for two centuries. Thankfully, he escaped the clutches of the evil that is the Alliance, not long after your little arranged meeting with Porthos. In the process of escaping, he apparently took one or two lives, for he *is* an Assassin, after all. *The Assassin*, in fact. He, too, was surprised to learn how long he'd been away. We had to appoint another Assassin in the interim, so now I have *two* of them to keep busy. You see, they abducted and drugged the man I sent to kill your wife and child. Now he has returned to me, and this very day he will end your life. Isn't that simply *perfect*? Oh, and Will?" His smile turned to an evil glare. "They drugged one of their greatest enemies, The Assassin, just like they drugged you. What does betrayal to that degree feel like?" The Hunters all laughed, as The Leader looked at him, triumphant.

Will fumed. He added another short-term goal. He'd planned to use his Energy to escape, assuming he could overcome Aramis again, and failing that, he'd use his nanos to help out. He didn't have a lot, just a very basic allocation, but it should be enough to do what he needed done. Now, though, he would avenge Hope and Josh first.

He'd simply have to wait a while longer. And after 189 years, a few more minutes or hours were no big deal.

Aramis came forward, grasping Will by the arm, and he could feel the Hunter's Damper ability coming to play. The dampering effect in this building negated the impact Aramis had, since there was little Energy left to suppress. But Will played the part, acting a bit more unsteady on his feet and lightheaded, and allowed Aramis to lead him away from the throne of The Leader and back to the elevator.

Once inside, Aramis spoke. "You really lost your memory? Wow. It must be horrible to be executed for crimes you don't remember committing." The Hunter snickered.

"You told me that my death sentence was for being the father of my son, Aramis. I very much remember him, and I remember his mother as well, and every single moment I spent with both of them. They were the two most amazing people I've ever met. If my relationship with them is considered a crime by this group, then I am proudly guilty as charged."

Aramis snorted. "Humans are unstable, though. Given enough time, both of them would have lost interest in you, or betrayed you in some fashion. Sounds like they would have been perfect fits with your Alliance, wouldn't they?"

"If living forever makes you such a cynic, Aramis, I'm rather pleased that you're taking me somewhere to die. I'd hate to be a miserable old coot like you, bored out of my mind, with no one to love or to love me."

Aramis was silent after that.

The elevator did not stop in the lobby, but continued to a floor labeled Lower Level 7. Will assumed it was underground, and Aramis confirmed it. "The building that's visible is where the humans do their work. Other than the penthouse suite The Leader commands, we work underground, out of sight of the humans, and they can't get in without Energy. We're discouraged from doing Energy stuff in the main building; it has decent dampering capabilities in the walls, not so much to stop anything, but to remind us where we are. No such restrictions on the Lower Levels, though. Usually we just teleport down here, but I figure using the human-invented elevator to escort their champion to his final end is more fitting." He smiled in triumph.

The doors opened. "Seventh level of hell, right this way," Will muttered.

They headed down a long hallway, and reached a door with a name in a language Will could not understand. A separate plaque hung on the wall near the door, simply reading: "The Assassin." Will noted to himself that this was the first time in two months he'd actually entered a room via a door. Or perhaps it was the first time in two centuries.

Aramis knocked on the door with the hand not used to control Will. "Enter," an icy voice said from inside. Will felt a chill inside him. This was the voice of the man who had killed his wife, and who had silenced the voice of Josh before Will had ever heard his son speak. Yet even without knowing that, he could detect a sense of pure evil in the man.

Aramis opened the door and they walked in. A man sat in a simple chair, dressed entirely in black, sharpening the blade of a familiar-looking short sword, the edge visibly razor-thin and glinting. So this was how they planned to kill him, then? With a giant knife? Will had been hoping for something less painful. Then again, he was hoping not to die at all, so the method chosen for his execution was moot.

"Today, I finish what was started so long ago, Will Stark," the man said, his voice a whisper. He glanced at the blade, checking the sharpness on the tip of his finger. Will could see the blood drip down onto the floor, despite the very light pressure he'd used. Will focused on the blade, directing half of his small batch of nanos to cover its surface, and he made ready to direct the machines to alter the attempt at mortally wounding him. He directed the other half onto his skin to act as a shield; he'd need to both alter the trajectory of the blade, and bounce it off of his skin, to avoid serious injury. Adam had told him that this was the approach he'd used to save Will from the sword attacks in his backyard that night so long ago, though Adam undoubtedly had more nanos to work with. His allotment would need to be enough.

The Assassin stood up, facing Will. The man's head was shaved clean, marred by dozens of deep gashes that had scarred over. His eyes — irises and pupils alike — were a deep blood-red. The image, the voice, the aura of pure evil — Will knew this man was a gifted killer.

Aramis remained behind his prisoner, with his right hand firmly planted on Will's left shoulder. The Assassin glared at the Hunter.

"Aramis, I don't want to hear any complaints about blood on your outfit."

Aramis shook his head. "If I let go of Stark, he teleports out of here. The dampers don't work down here like they do above ground. So, I'll stay put. Just try to be careful. Oh, and one more thing?"

The blood-red eyes remained unblinking.

"Right. Like you said, at least *try* to keep the blood away from me. Carry on, then." Seeming to be concerned about this, Aramis moved so that he wasn't directly behind Will, and formed closer to a 45 degree angle with him, believing it would put him farther away from Will's splattered blood.

The Assassin tossed the sword handle back and forth in his hands, as if deciding which should have the honor. He settled on his right, and advanced to within two feet of Will.

Everything after that was a blur.

The Assassin pulled his blade back and jabbed it forward with tremendous force and speed, attempting to run it through Will.

Will moved his nano-shield down to the targeted area of his body and condensed the shield, forming an impenetrable barrier. At the same time, he had the nanos on the blade force the trajectory away from his body.

The blade, initially on target for Will's abdomen, slid to Will's left, striking the nano-shield on Will's oblique muscle area, and bouncing off to The Assassin's right.

Sensing that he was safe on this pass, Will pulled the nanos off the sword and onto his back, to prevent The Assassin from trying to stab or slash him as he pulled the blade back for another attempt.

The combination of the redirection and the bounce off the shield turned the blade, still at full speed, at a 45 degree angle to Will's body, directly at the Hunter.

The blade had barely slowed down when it entered Aramis' body, and did not stop until the tip exited through the man's back and clothing.

All three men were in shock. Aramis looked down at the growing red stain on his clothing, and realized it was a fatal wound. He dropped down to his knees, looked up at The Assassin, and said, "I told you not to get any blood on me." He fell forward into The Assassin's legs, before the man could release the hilt. The Assassin tried to pull the blade out of the dying man's body, all the while keeping his eyes on Will.

With the Damper of Aramis released, Will suddenly had full use of his Energy. He could teleport out now, but there was work to be done, and deaths to avenge. He hurled himself at The Assassin, knocking the man to the floor, separating the killer from his sword. Aramis' body crumbled to the ground.

Stark, listen to me. Will blinked, continuing to wrestle The Assassin, trying to get his hands on the man's throat. *I'm on your side now, Stark. Listen carefully inside your head, but keep fighting. They're watching us.*

Will threw a forearm at The Assassin's head. *That hurt. They're watching. We must make this convincing.* The Assassin suddenly shifted his weight, and Will found himself on his back, staring up into a face lined with deep lacerations hardened into scars.

Why should I believe you? Will projected.

The Assassin punched Will in the head, and Will felt a bit woozy. *One of the Alliance people gave me a potion. Makes me have to do what he wants. He wanted me to get you out of here, but in a way that lets me keep working here, spying on the Elites.* The Assassin threw another punch, and Will shifted away at the last instant, causing The Assassin to curse out loud as his fist hit the hard floor.

I'm listening. Will tried to roll into The Assassin and take advantage of the man being off balance, but the man shifted his own weight, and Will was driven back into the floor.

Here's an area outside our building you can teleport to in a few moments. Will saw an image of a small copse of trees near the Aliomenti building, and saw where the sidewalk was. *I need you to block this punch.* The Assassin threw a punch at Will, who blocked it with his arm. *Now throw me, and the gun will fall out.*

Gun? Will whipped his body, and The Assassin flew off him, landing hard several feet away. In the process, a small gun fell out of a holster hidden under the man's belt, landing between Will and The Assassin. Will didn't need to be told the next step. He snatched the gun before The Assassin could recover and sprang to his feet, aiming the gun at The Assassin while flipping the safety off, his look of fury not faked. *You killed my family. I think you expect me to be merciful here. Merciful would be shooting you in the head and killing you with no pain.* Will aimed the gun at the man's head.

No! You must say that out loud, but shoot me in the shoulder, the leg... somewhere it won't be fatal. Tell me it's a crueler fate to suffer. And Will realized that he was correct on that point. Living with your failures was punishment; death was mercy.

"You expect mercy from me, don't you?" Will asked. "You think I'm going to take this gun, which looks a lot like *my* gun, and that I'm going to shoot you in the head so that you die quickly. That I'll kill you to avenge my family." Will aimed lower, at the man's groin, and The Assassin winced. "I think I'd rather you suffer, though." Will shifted to point at the man's leg.

The Assassin laughed out loud. "You fool! What makes you think the gun is actually loaded?" *It's loaded. Shoot me. Gloat.*

Will pulled the trigger, and The Assassin screamed in pain as muscle was shredded and bone was shattered, blood spouting from the wound. *Good shot, oh that HURTS! You may shoot me again if you see fit, but know this, Will Stark. Oh that HURTS! Know this... I failed to complete my mission that night. Go! They'll be coming for you!*

Will froze temporarily, and then recovered. "It appears to be loaded. I'll check again, just to be sure." He pointed at the other leg and shot The Assassin again. The screaming began anew, even more agonizing. "Suffer long," Will said, glaring at the man. After recalling all of his nanos, he pictured the area outside, and teleported out of the building. *Good job, Will Stark.* Will could hear the agony in the man's thoughts. *Tell my boss I did well.*

"But I don't know who that *is*," Will said, to no one in particular. He flipped the safety on and took in his surroundings.

He was outside the massive building, and near the sidewalk. There was no sign of any life, human or Aliomenti, on that sidewalk. Will moved to it and began walking, at a casual pace, away from the building. He needed to get off this island, and get back to his new family in the Alliance. To Angel, to Adam, and yes, even to Fil, who was likely rejoicing that Will was gone for good.

It was too far to teleport, though.

He saw a figure emerge up ahead, wearing a dark cloak, with a thick hood covering the head. Will couldn't tell if the person was a man or a woman, but he distinctly saw a hand emerge from the sleeve, wearing a thick glove, and motion for Will to follow. Will did so. Thus far, his instinct on who to trust had been quite good — at least for staying alive, though not for learning the truth — and he sensed this person was there to help. This cloak was definitely *not* being worn by Porthos.

The figure in the cloak led him down the sidewalk, back into the trees, and on a circuitous route through the small park. He emerged on the runway where the small aircraft carrying him and the Hunters had landed. The cloaked figure glanced about, and then darted into the hangar. Will followed. There, he found the same craft Athos and Porthos had used to bring him here. The figure pointed to what appeared to be a navigation system, showing his path. He'd been living on the northeastern edge of South America, and the island he was on was...inside the Bermuda Triangle.

Creepy.

With the hood still hiding their face, the guide pointed into the vehicle. "I should fly this back where I came from?" Will asked. A nod. "Will I be able to fly it? I've never flown anything before." Another nod, but no words. "OK. Thank you." He tried to duck down to get a glance under the hood, but his guide turned quickly and walked back out of the hangar. Will shrugged and climbed into the craft.

As he sat, the top closed automatically. "*Select destination,*" said a soothing female voice. Will shrugged, and tried zeroing in on his old camp location on the screen. Once he found it, he tapped. "*Destination selected,*" the voice confirmed. With no further direction from Will, the craft backed out of the hangar, turned, and raced down the runway, gradually lifting into the air. Autopilot. Of course.

Will settled in for the journey, soon drifting off to sleep.

In the trees along the runway he'd just left, the hooded guide watched the vehicle soar into the air and out of sight. The hood came down, and the woman underneath gave a gentle wave into the distance.

"Good luck, Will," she whispered.

XXIII
REUNION

Will woke, feeling as if he'd had a full night's sleep. He had answers to many of the mysteries of his past two months, and the basis for better questions. Like who had wiped his memory two centuries earlier, and why. Like how they'd kept him in suspended animation all that time, and why.

The craft had landed in the same clearing where the Hunters had found him earlier, showing that the autopilot feature in the vehicle was quite well-developed. He was back in the thick forests that were so familiar to him now, and it seemed that the trees remembered him as well. He could feel their Energy flowing to him, and he responded in kind, feeling the now familiar intensification of the Energy flowing back to him. Perhaps trees had developed this capability in the past two centuries. Then again, he wouldn't have known two centuries ago for purposes of comparison. He noted his clothing was yellowish-orange, and wondered if he'd start mutating at some point in the color progression.

Will thought through his actions carefully; acting impulsively in the past had caused problems. Will's part in the stabbing of Aramis, and then his shooting of The Assassin, would be analyzed and discussed by the Aliomenti Elites. He expected that they'd provide whatever form of medical care existed in this future time to stabilize the injured man. He wasn't sure if Aramis could be saved, though he couldn't get himself to be upset about that. The man had been quite pleased to take Will somewhere to die, and tried to directly kill him in the distant past. Will had defended himself, without meaning for Aramis to be hurt. He didn't feel the same way about The Assassin, though he doubted that the gunshot wounds would be fatal. He hadn't made the shots with the intent of killing the man. If someone had told him he'd be less upset about the impending death of a man who'd tried to capture him, rather than one who had tried to kill Hope and Josh, he would have questioned their sanity.

Had The Assassin been telling the truth? Was he truly now a spy on behalf of the Alliance? And who was the master he'd spoken of? That would be another detail he'd need to learn. He ruled Angel out immediately. He'd been with Adam quite a bit, and the man seemed too stable to try something so rash and bold as to turn an Aliomenti Assassin to their cause. Fil seemed the type, or at least the most likely of the three he'd met. Of course, there were dozens of others in the camp, and every possibility that one of those men or women were responsible. Will simply didn't know any of them well enough to make an assessment.

He needed to get back to them, his closest friends and confidants in the Alliance camp, if for no other reason than to warn them. But the last thing he wanted to do was to bring a wrathful team of Elites on them. If he was one of the Elites, he'd expect Will to go right back to the Alliance; then he'd follow Will Stark there with a truly massive attack force. Will had hurt two of their number badly, and now he needed to protect his closest friends in this future time, even if they'd been incredibly deceptive. Revenge was a powerful motivator, as Will well knew, and he couldn't believe that his attack and escape would be forgotten. Focusing on all of this helped keep his mind off the *other* revelation from The Assassin; he needed to compartmentalize and deal with *that* information later.

He decided that he would not return to camp. He figured he was quite safe here, actually; the Elites would not be likely to come here and only get *him*. His best move all around was to stay here. Or move away from here, but to a site away from the camp. Perhaps he could mislead the Aliomenti into chasing him all over the planet. That would protect his core group, but what if he unintentionally led the Aliomenti to a *different* Alliance camp? He had no idea where those camps were located, or how many there were.

He needed to communicate with Angel, and Adam, and Fil. But how?

Then he realized that he had a rather untapped ability, the first he'd mastered here in this future world of people with nanos, personal flying craft, and incredible mental Energy abilities. Telepathy. And the person who'd taught him was Angel, the one he trusted above all others. It was a very low Energy ability, which meant that even Porthos shouldn't be able to track it. And it was a risk that Will needed to take.

He directed his Energy in the direction of the camp, very low level, and thought of Angel. He hoped Angel would sense the Energy and contact him.

He didn't have to wait long. *Mr. Stark? Is that you?* Angel's voice projected into his mind.

Yes. I escaped from the Headquarters. A few of them got hurt in the process, including one of the Hunters, and he's hurt very badly. I have a feeling they aren't going to like that. I'm not risking coming back to camp and bringing all of them after you.

There was a pause. *Where are you?*

I'm back in the forest near our old camp, right where they took me. I—

Angel, Adam, and Fil appeared in the clearing. "Drop your Shield. You need to flood this place with Energy," Fil said.

"What?" It was the last thing Will ever expected to hear from Fil.

"Do it," Adam said. Will did, and Adam explained the logic as the Energy flowed from his pupil. "We're pretty well Shielded, outside the Energy remnants left from teleporting here. If you're right, they already know *you're* here. Our best bet is for you to kick off lots of Energy, which should mask ours, and make them think any surges they've detected are just you."

That made sense. Will spread his Energy around, especially into the trees, and felt the strengthening of the return Energy. The trio watched him with great interest. "How are you getting stronger while you're doing that?" Adam asked.

"What do you mean?"

"I'm seeing the Energy all around us, so clearly you're sending quite a bit out. Yet your Energy levels are actually rising *faster* than that. They should be dipping, at least for a short while, until your body can regenerate its stores." Adam seemed genuinely baffled at the phenomenon.

Will shrugged. "I don't know how to explain it, either." He told the story of seeing the young tree here, and feeling compelled to send it Energy, and that somehow this helped the tree grow rapidly and resulted in more Energy coming back to Will than he was sending. "I guess it's like it is in nature. We breathe out carbon dioxide used by plants, and they send back oxygen we breathe in. Why it's stronger than before, though, I can't explain."

Fil nodded. "As interesting as that is, we do need to focus on the problem at hand. Angel said that you escaped Headquarters in a manner likely to draw a violent response. True?"

"Correct. Aramis took me to The Assassin, but I was able to use my nanos to deflect the blow and Aramis was stabbed instead. I fought with The Assassin, and in the skirmish his gun fell free. I retrieved it, shot him, and teleported out." Will frowned. "But I think I had help."

"What do you mean?" Angel asked.

"The Assassin was talking to me in my head. Telling me what to do, how to beat him as we were fighting after Aramis was stabbed. Told me to throw him and the gun would fall; I didn't know he carried a gun. Told me to shoot him non-fatally and make it seem like I was interested in him suffering more than killing him. He gave me an image of a place to teleport to in order to get out of the building." Will looked at the men and woman standing with him. "He said to tell his master that he did as ordered. Any of you know what that means?"

"I have a hunch," Fil said. "One of our members has a knack for creating specialized nanos. It sounds like something he would try."

"But how did he get them into The Assassin?" Will asked. "When would they have met?"

"We picked up more than just you at the house that night," Angel said. "The Assassin, the man sent to murder your family... we captured him and brought him back to hold as a captive."

"It was a risky plan," Fil said. "Like you, he brought inherent trouble, perhaps even more. You would only cause harm through inaction but without intent; The Assassin would willingly inflict great harm. If the devices meant to contain him didn't hold, or the reprogramming didn't work... it could have been a problem for all of us."

"But it appears that it *did* work," Adam noted. "We may be down to only two Hunters, and The Assassin will be unable to go on any official missions for a time if you shot him."

Will pulled out the gun. "This looks familiar. Something else you pulled out of my house?"

Fil simply nodded.

"Anything else about that night you want to tell me?" Will asked, fixing a pointed stare at the trio.

Angel fidgeted. "Your dog survived. She's back in camp right now."

Will blinked, and a foggy memory of seeing the injured animal on Fil's lap in the escape vehicle appeared in his mind. "Why didn't you let me see her? What would be the harm in letting me see Smokey?"

"You would have wondered why we were able to save Smokey, and not... others." Angel looked quite unhappy at saying this.

"Seems a fair question, though," Will noted. "You rescued me from a beating, found my dog and the man sent to kill my family. Why could you not save my wife and son?"

"They were already gone when I got there," Fil said. "I could get The Assassin and the dog. But not them."

Will stared at the man. "With the technology I've seen here since I arrived, I dare say you could have saved them. Why not try?" The Energy coming from Will now was powerful enough that the air was sizzling, and it was doubtful to all present that the intensity was due solely to the interaction with the trees.

"They were *gone*." Fil fixed him with what was likely a deadly stare through those sunglasses, as if offended at being challenged. "As in, they were not there. I could not find them. Therefore, I could not rescue them."

"I thought you said that they were dead?" Will snarled, advancing on Fil.

"No. I've said they were *gone* every time you've asked. I cannot help you to comprehend what the word means."

"You used a word commonly meant to indicate death, especially in the context of a raging house fire and an Assassin sent after those people. Any sane, decent person would know that and avoid using the expression." Will jabbed a finger at Fil. "Unless you *wanted* me to think them dead."

Fil shoved Will with both hands. "Take that back! There's no reason whatsoever I'd want to deceive you!"

Angel jumped between them. "Both of you need to stop it! Right now!" The two men continued to glare at each other, but backed away. "Fil wasn't clear, but there's no reason to think he'd want to deceive you. I would know if he'd tried."

"Shut up, sis," Fil muttered.

Will's eyes widened. "She's your sister?" he asked Fil.

Fil nodded, and Angel elbowed Fil gently. "My overprotective big brother. Always playing the alpha male lest anyone try anything to hurt me." Will was shocked to see a slight smile form on Fil's face.

Will shook his head. "You people are full of surprises," he said. He glanced at Adam. "What about you? You their cousin or something?"

Adam chuckled. "Thanks for not asking if I'm their uncle." All four laughed.

"So, about that night you pulled me and others away from my burning house," Will said. "Anybody care to tell me exactly *when* that was? Relative to, say, today?" He arched an eyebrow.

Three heads dropped. "Oh," Angel said. "That."

"Yes. That." Will glanced among the faces. "Why on earth would you find me and drug me into a sleep for almost two centuries?"

Adam frowned. "But you weren't drugged. Who told you that? The Leader or one of the Hunters?"

Will nodded. "They figured out pretty quickly that I think it's about two months after the events at my house. They corrected that *minor* oversight. I'm sure it just slipped your minds to mention it. Needless to say, not having anyone tell me that rather critical piece of information tends to make me less than trusting about anything any of you say from this point forward." He fixed a glare at Fil. "And question the motivation for what I *am* told."

"They were half right," Adam said. "Yes, it's far into your future. But we didn't drug you into some kind of suspended animation all this time." He glanced at Fil, then at Angel, and both of them nodded at him. "When we rescued you from the yard and the house that night, the craft that we used... it was a time machine."

Will blinked. Then he laughed. "Right. I know, at this point I'm supposed to believe anything. But a *time machine*? No. That part I cannot believe. I will not believe."

Angel walked to Will, and put a hand on his arm, and he could feel the calming Energy she was sending his way. "It's a lot to take, I'm sure. But you *know* we're telling the truth."

"I don't know *anything*!" Will screamed. "Do you understand just how much every part of my life has been completely turned upside-down? I'd like to think I've handled everything really well, truly I do. But right now I don't even know *who I am*! Am I some amazing Energy-wielding warrior traitor who had his memory wiped clean and became a business tycoon only to sleep for two centuries and wake up not remembering anything? Or was I truly born in the year 1995 and brought forward in time after my family was killed by some crazed murderer? Something else entirely? Oh wait, the killer said he failed in his mission to kill my family, which means that *they were still alive* at some point, and *nobody* saw them. Then this same man, the man who wanted to kill my wife, and then my son when he learned of Josh's existence, this trained *Assassin* suddenly helps me escape from captivity, because somebody put some tiny robots in his brain. And on top of it all I seem to attract trouble wherever I go. I'd like to go home, back to being that businessman, and just go out to that nice dinner with my family. And I'd like to see my son. Do you know he never talked? I never heard his voice. All I want is to go home and hear his voice, and tell him I love him. Is that too much to ask?"

Will felt his knees sag, and he let himself fall to the ground. "I just want to go home, to my family," he whispered. "I don't want to do this anymore."

Angel went to him, tears in her eyes as she knelt down and put a comforting arm around him. Fil's face was its usual mask, yet there were tremors there of some unspeakable emotion. Adam looked at the siblings, and then at Will. He knelt down in front of the man.

"Will," he said, "I think we can make that happen."

XXIV
QUESTION

They gave Will time to regain control following his emotional outburst, and then the group made its next moves.

Will put a very tight Shield up, hiding his Energy so well that none of the trio could sense anything, even standing next to him. Each of the trio did a thorough search of Will and his clothing, to ensure that the Elites had not placed any type of tracking device on Will, and found nothing. Fil generated a flying craft of nanos, and the four climbed in. No one spoke as Fil carefully piloted the craft through the trees; he avoided breaking through the top canopy so that the Elites couldn't search for them with satellites. Nobody wanted to speak and break concentration on the Shield Will had established.

They landed at camp an hour later. Will climbed out of the craft, still rather numb from the revelations of the past twenty-four hours. He walked to the edge of the camp and sat with his back against one of the large trees encircling the clearing, pulling his knees to his chest and wrapping his arms around them. His mind was in shambles as he tried to make sense of everything. The emotion he'd kept bottled up for two months, as he absorbed and accepted with calm the massive paradigm shifts he'd undergone, had finally burst forth and taken its toll.

Fil walked over to him a short while later, the sunlight reflecting off his ever-present mirrored sunglasses, his face softer than Will had ever seen it. He gave a faint smile when Will glanced up at him. "I thought you might want to visit with someone." Fil turned and whistled, and Will saw a black Labrador Retriever come trotting out from behind one of the buildings.

Will stared at the dog, and the dog stared back, frozen.

"Smokey?" Will whispered. The dog's tail began to twitch, shuddering with the effort, as if overcome by a powerful emotion she couldn't otherwise express. "C'mere, girl!" Will said, louder, and patted the ground next to him, stretching his legs out. The dog started toward him, slowly at first, then at a full sprint, eventually slowing down only because her tail was wagging with such force that she couldn't walk straight. She darted to Will with a joy that only a dog can express, licking his face as he wrapped his arms around her neck, hugging the only family member he still had with him, his face moist for reasons other than the dog's wet kisses. Smokey curled up next to him, then crawled into his lap, and Will laughed as he watched the dog try to fit her too-large frame onto his too-small lap. She settled for nestling next to him, her chin rested on his leg, her tail still twitching with joy. Will was content to scratch the dog's head, and remember the times he'd seen her nestled up against Josh in the same manner.

Will realized Fil was still standing a few paces away, watching the interaction between Will and Smokey. While the shade of the trees in the area made it difficult to tell, it looked as though Fil's cheek was a bit moist. "Thank you," Will said, his voice quiet. "I needed that."

Fil nodded. "She did as well." He turned and walked away, giving man and dog time alone.

I must be losing my mind. A trained assassin helps me escape death, I'm two centuries into my own future, I've been reunited with my dog, and a man who's acted as if he'd rather have that Assassin here over me brought me my dog back. He chuckled. It was odd how Fil's act of kindness seemed stranger than teleporting himself dozens of miles away.

The trio headed his way, each bearing a purposeful look.

Will glanced down at the dog. He was tempted to sic her on them to avoid whatever new fate they had devised for him, but decided he liked her right where she was.

"Don't get up," Adam said, smiling faintly. He sat on the grass near Will, and the siblings joined him.

"Have you accepted the part about the time machine yet?" Angel asked, her eyes worried.

"Right now, I find it hard to accept anything," Will replied. "And yet nothing else that seemed impossible so far has turned out to be impossible. I'm willing to entertain the idea that it's true, with a heavy dose of skepticism."

Fil nodded. "A fair approach. We have a proposal for you, however, and for you to accept that proposal you must accept the premise that the machine we've mentioned does, in fact, work."

Will shrugged. "Continue."

"From what we know first-hand, combined with what we've been able to ascertain from your recounting of your time at Headquarters, it would appear that your wife and son exited the house before The Assassin was able to kill them." Fil said this without emotion, but Will shook at the word *kill*. "I did not see them in the house, so clearly their escape was accomplished before my arrival. It's also likely that it happened before the house caught fire, for The Assassin himself was knocked unconscious from the oxygen loss with the flames. The Assassin can translate his Energy — which is not terribly strong, by the way — into fire, and he can control and move fire as well. He also seems to be immune to fire, which means you could throw him into a bonfire and he wouldn't suffer any burns. Point being, if he's unconscious from the fire, they would be too, and still in the house. Unless they escaped *first*."

Will nodded. "That makes sense. He told me that *he* had failed. If they weren't there, I'm fairly certain he would have considered it a failure of others who had told them where they should be. So he at least saw them."

"Right. He sees them, they escape, the fire starts, you're injured, the Hunters get you. Somewhere in there we show up, get you, Smokey, and The Assassin, and leave. The Hunters leave. No sign of Hope and Josh Stark. But this makes no sense. If you're dealing with a human woman and a small child, and they are caught in their house by a trained Assassin who has Aliomenti abilities, how could they escape? He had a sword, and he'd already used it to kill two trained security professionals only moments earlier. He's stronger and faster than they are. They might have been armed, but The Assassin could easily have gotten the gun from them, and in addition, The Assassin did not have any gunshot wounds when we returned. Yet they weren't there. I ask again: how could this be?" Fil's right eyebrow appeared at the top of his sunglasses, which seemed to mean that he was arching the brow. Will found this oddly amusing.

Yet the question itself was not. How indeed? He'd not been at this long, but he knew that no untrained person — or human, as the term was used in present company — could possibly escape him now. He could fly, teleport, or use telekinesis to grab them.

And then he had the answer. "Somebody helped them. Somebody Aliomenti-trained."

Fil nodded. "So the new question is: who? And more importantly: *why*?"

Will looked back at him. "On that note: why rescue *me*?"

Adam spoke up. "You must understand the importance of the Will Stark that the Hunters know and remember. He was the most powerful and influential member of the Aliomenti for many years, and directed many of its innovations and much of its progress. Yet he reached a point of fundamental disagreement over the swearing of the Oaths, and more critically, with the penalties imposed for breaking them. And so he left, letting others know they were welcome to join him as part of an alliance of like-minded Aliomenti who believed it their role to *help* humanity, rather than thwart its efforts to improve. People left the various Aliomenti communities around the world and rallied to Stark, and started integrating into human society, using their abilities to nudge the most receptive minds in the direction of progress. A few married humans, but none of those had children. With the numbers of Aliomenti dropping and their progress slowing down, The Leader had to make a decision. He found three uniquely-skilled Aliomenti and called them Hunters, sent to hunt down these so-called rogues and bring them back. His scientists were fascinated by Aramis' Damper ability, and figured out how to repeat it in small rooms, specifically jail cells. The Hunters' skills improved, and it reached the point that they never failed to get their man, and quickly. But they couldn't catch Will Stark, no matter how many times they found him. To be blunt, Will Stark is our hero, our George Washington if you will. We didn't have any reason to believe you weren't the same man, any more than the Hunters of the time did. And none of us here regrets getting you away from them.

"Our records show that there is no mention of Will Stark following the fire at your house. You didn't suddenly appear a few days later. We knew the Aliomenti hadn't gotten you, because that news would be broadcast. Nobody in the Alliance heard from you either. As we finished the research on the time machine and wondered what our first test would be, we made the rather startling conclusion that you'd disappeared forever during the fire because we'd gone back in time and retrieved you. To us, we were saving our greatest hero from the death the Hunters surely would have visited upon you. We needed to ensure that the fire was seen as having burned everyone in the house, and all evidence of the actions that happened there, from existence. That meant we needed to bring back everyone and everything that would have been found, including the gun."

"But what if Hope and Josh had been there?"

"Then Fil would have gotten them as well, of course. But they weren't."

"Because somebody else had already helped them?"

Adam paused. "Somebody got them out of the house. We aren't *exactly* sure of whom, or their motivations. We just know that the two of them were never spotted again after that fire."

Will's blood chilled. "Who else could it have been, though?"

"We don't know," Adam replied. "But... we have an idea."

"Who?"

"You."

Will blinked. "What are you talking about? I was getting beat up in the back yard, remember?"

"No, not *then*-Will. *Now*-Will."

Will realized he'd stopped patting Smokey, for the dog nudged him, and he resumed scratching behind her ears, trying to process this concept. "So, you're saying... I go back in time... and rescue Josh and Hope?"

Adam nodded.

Will slid out from under Smokey's chin and rose to his feet. "When do I leave?"

Fil's jaw tightened. "You may wish to think this over and consider the ramifications."

"What ramifications? I have the chance to save my wife and son from certain death at the hands of a horrific assassin. There are no ramifications to consider."

"You could die in the process."

Will waved him off. "It's a price I'm willing to pay."

Adam raised a hand. "Let's consider this in more depth, Will. I think we're all fully aware that you're willing to pay whatever price necessary to save your family, but there are historical facts to consider. It's not just that Hope and Josh don't appear after that night. You don't either."

"Which means I die while saving them, or I succeed and bring them back here."

"Which means you might die in a failed attempt, or not make it there to begin with. This time machine is not a heavily-tested device. Its first and only round trip was that very evening. We have no way of knowing if you'd make it *there*, let alone make it *back*."

Will swallowed hard. That meant that the three of them had risked their own lives coming after him, or at least after the man they thought he was. Adam was pointing out that he might die during the journey, or simply not make it there at all. He'd be lost, and for nothing. That was far less appealing. He took a deep breath. "I understand that. It doesn't change my mind, though. The opportunity is there. I have to take advantage of it, despite the possibilities of negative outcomes."

"There is also another point to consider. Our present means that the past has already happened as it is supposed to happen. That is, The Assassin fails and Fil finds no trace of Hope and Josh. He does find The Assassin alive. That means that no one — including you — killed The Assassin before he could attack Hope and Josh. The Hunters survived to this day. That means no one went after them. The Hunters successfully attacked and assaulted you. That means no one interfered. That means, Will, that if the trip is successful in getting you back there, you mustn't interfere with any of that. Do you have the ability to refrain from blasting Aramis or Athos or Porthos, from killing The Leader, or anyone else who might cause you or them pain? Will you stick just to your mission as defined, or will it be too tempting to teleport to get your gun and shoot The Assassin on the spot? Will it be enough to get there, let The Assassin see them, and then rescue them to bring them back to this time, where they'll be safe?"

Will hadn't considered that possibility. He wouldn't mind a shot at Athos and Porthos. Aramis might be dead by now, and The Assassin had helped him escape Headquarters, so there was less animosity there. But he understood: he couldn't alter history. "No blasting of the bad guys. Understood. Are we ready yet?"

"No," Adam said. "Because there is one more scenario to

consider. You make it back to 2030 safely. You rescue Hope and Josh from the house, getting them away from The Assassin. But the time machine fails. You cannot return here. History says that Will, Hope, and Josh Stark do not exist after that fire. How will you make that stay true if you cannot leave that time?"

"We'll go into hiding, we'll change our names and our appearance, we'll..."

"You, personally, would have a massive target on your head courtesy of the Hunters, and your skills aren't strong enough yet to continually escape their clutches or hide from them. They wouldn't know that Hope and Josh survived, and as such would have no reason to look for them, with or without new names or faces. After all, The Assassin wouldn't fail to kill a couple of *humans*, right? You, on the other hand, they *do* know about. They would know that you survived. They likely suspect that the Alliance, as it existed at the time, was responsible. They will throw everything they had into finding you. And if they find *you*..."

"...they find Hope and Josh," Will whispered. "I can't let that happen. I can't save them and then lose them again."

"If they had captured you, we would have some record of it; the Elites would trumpet the news everywhere. If you escaped them as you did here, they would chase you with ever-greater intensity. And eventually, they'd figure out who you were protecting."

Will was shaking his head. "No, I won't let that happen."

"But there's only one way for it not to happen in this scenario, where the time machine fails for the return journey." Adam took a deep breath. "It means that you must actually die in that fire."

Will stared at him, jaw agape. Fil's jaw twitched, which for him was quite expressive. Angel gasped in horror, and burst into tears.

Will felt like crying as well. Though it seemed unlikely to matter — the ship had worked for one round-trip, and if he made it to the past there was no reason to think it wouldn't work to return him — he had to consider the possibility. Adam's message was clear: he could not live in that time frame after freeing Hope and Josh. They could mask their identities and forge new lives there, but Will could not. He must return after their rescue to 2219, or perish in 2030.

"If that were the case," Will said, his voice trembling, "it would mean I would get to hold my family one last time, to hear my son speak, to tell them how much I love them, and that I would need to leave them to keep the evil people away from them, from trying to hurt them again."

He paused, unable to continue.

"You see the concern, then," Adam said. "That is why I must raise this scenario. The question of you, Will, is this: are you willing not just to *sacrifice* your own life, but to *take* your own life, if the situation you find calls for it, in order to protect your family and leave history unaltered?"

Will took a deep breath. "Yes. I am."

Adam nodded. Fil drew in a sharp breath, turned, and walked away, followed closely by Angel, who was crying with even greater intensity.

Will watched after them. "Do they always get so emotional?"

Adam watched them as well. "Few people ever see such a pure example of altruism or heroism, and certainly not to that degree." He glanced at Will. "I don't think they expected to be among the few who do. They went back in time to find their hero, and have watched you become the man they sought. Today, you truly are the Will Stark of legend."

XXV
DEPARTURE

The preparation for the departure in the time machine was quite extensive.

Will had assumed that he'd simply jump in, go back in time, rescue his family from The Assassin, and come back to this point. Thankfully, Fil, Angel, and Adam had completed a similar journey recently, and were able to walk him through the level of planning required for such an "easy" trip. He came to the conclusion that time travel was far too complicated to handle on a regular basis, and was happy he'd only have to go through it once.

It was assumed that the Hunters had been lying in wait for him for quite some time. Given the sequence of events, they likely had camped out in the forest behind the house before The Assassin entered. They were expecting the historical Will Stark, and knew that teleporting in would alert Stark and allow him to defend himself. Everything that happened that night had likely been scripted to ensure that Will Stark, member of the Aliomenti and founder of the Alliance, would arrive at his home in shock, lose his concentration, and fall into a state of despair sufficient for the Hunters to subdue him.

Therefore, Will could not simply arrive in the time machine and walk into his house. The Hunters would see him there — twice — and that would cause quite a bit of confusion. They'd attack the "current" Will and the original Will, still in 2030, would not be attacked and rescued by the Alliance trio. He needed to land somewhere away from them, out of sight of the community's security cameras, but close enough that he could see when The Assassin entered the house. More than likely, that meant that he'd need to land the craft in the forest outside his nearest neighbor's house, teleport into his house, wait until The Assassin began his attack, and then rescue Hope and Josh.

Adam had spoken with the Mechanic, whom Will had heard mentioned before. The Mechanic, as it turned out, had been the one controlling The Assassin since the killer had arrived in the future. The Mechanic noted that under his questioning, The Assassin stated that he had been unaware that Josh and Smokey existed. The boy had attacked him to stop The Assassin from killing Hope, Hope had attacked the man to prevent him from hurting Josh, and Smokey had bitten the man with great fervor after The Assassin had thwarted his human combatants. After The Assassin had managed to stop the attacks, the mother and child had vanished from his sight. That suggested remote teleportation, which was an incredibly advanced Aliomenti skill. It meant he'd need to surround both of them with Energy and then picture them moving to a new location, presumably the forest where the time machine would be sitting. That effort would drain most Aliomenti of Energy completely.

He needed to stay out of the basement of the house, as that was where the trio had arrived for their rescue mission. It sounded as if Hope had initially hidden Josh and Smokey upstairs, probably in the boy's room. That meant that Will would need to observe The Assassin enter the house, teleport to his bedroom, and wait until sounds indicated that The Assassin had thwarted the attacks of Hope, Josh, and Smokey. He would then need to teleport back to the time machine and remotely teleport Hope and Josh to him. He'd need to convince them to get into the craft to escape very quickly, because the Energy depletion would likely exhaust him to the point of needing sleep. Fil suggested that his tree recharger technique might help, which Adam and Angel both agreed was a good idea. The plan, if executed correctly, would not alter the recorded events of history, nor the memories of the Hunters, the trio, The Assassin, or Will himself.

He was provided with a full allotment of general-purpose nanos, in the event that something went wrong and he'd need to shield the three of them after depleting his Energy with the remote teleportation effort. They'd not gotten any indication of the Hunters' experience of the events of that night, but it was certainly possible that Porthos might detect the remote teleportation Energy surge coming from nearby, and move to investigate that after Will disappeared from sight. No doubt the Hunters would be immediately on the alert for any Energy readings and suspect the Alliance of masterminding Will's rescue. Thus, Will needed to move very quickly in terms of getting his passengers into the craft. The most efficient approach would be to teleport them directly into the machine.

The craft was simple to operate. It had the calculated date, time, and position coordinates locked in so that he'd arrive at the designated area of his own community with time to observe the arrivals. They'd coded the machine so that it would return to the year 2219 roughly five minutes after it was expected to depart. The Mechanic set the machine up so he'd simply hit one of two buttons. The Depart button would seal the vehicle for the trip, warm up the engine, and then depart for the past. He'd have about thirty to sixty seconds between hitting the button and the machine moving to the new time. The Return button would work in the same fashion, so he'd need to be prepared to defend the craft from the inside if the Hunters found him before the craft jumped forward in time.

Adam quietly asked Will if he had the gun. Will nodded. He knew the circumstance under which he'd need to use the weapon. He preferred to take the positive viewpoint that it would be unnecessary.

And finally, it was time to go.

Will climbed into the vehicle. He was about to become a time traveler. If all went well, he'd be sitting in this exact spot in less than ten clock minutes, springing the hatch and watching his son jump out to reunite with his dog. Smokey had shown tremendous emotion at seeing Will after so many weeks. He couldn't imagine how the dog would react upon seeing her greatest friend.

Adam walked up to him. "Will, I just wanted to wish you luck on this journey." He held out his hand, and Will shook it. "I want this mission to succeed, and I wish I could go with you. But unfortunately... well, you know." Will nodded. They'd discussed the logic of having someone go with Will, but realized that two people would generate more Energy and attract the notice of the Hunters more quickly. And he certainly couldn't take more than one anyway, as the craft only held four people. Will had argued that the risk was his alone to take, and that had ended the discussion.

Adam released the handshake. "I greatly admire you, Will. I always have. Few men have the courage to face the unknown, and immense danger, with no thought to their own safety. Your family... they have to be the most fortunate people who ever lived. I hope I'll get to be counted among their number in the future." He smiled, and stepped away.

Angel came next. She looked at Will, and the tears started. "I'm sorry, I shouldn't be crying. Simple thing to do, right? We did the same thing not that long ago. The machine worked, we got our man here safely. It will work out the same for you as well." She wiped her face dry with a sleeve, and then leaned over and hugged him.

Will was truly touched at the affection the young woman had shown him during the time he'd known her. "You're a wonderful young woman, Angel," he said. "I'm glad you've become part of my life. You've been the family I've thought lost all this time, and I can't thank you enough for that." He smiled. "I'm looking forward to introducing you to my wife and son shortly." Angel smiled at him. "Oh, and Angel? Tell your brother to relax a little bit." He smiled, and Angel laughed, stepping aside.

Fil stepped forward. As always, his face was a mask, his eyes hidden behind those mirrored sunglasses. The man opened his mouth to say something, thought better of it, and closed it again. He simply held out his hand, and Will clasped it.

"So... looks like you'll get your wish for a while." Will looked the man directly in the eyes, his expression neutral.

Fil frowned. "What wish is that?"

"You've considered me to be a great risk to this community since you brought me back here. I've not helped to change that thinking, I'm sure. Now I'm heading into the past, and there's a very real chance that I won't ever return." Will tapped the gun. "So you'll have your safety, and I may be dead and gone."

Fil's face reddened. "I have *never* wished for your death," he snarled. "You've been a risk to our community, to be sure, but if we'd thought the risk not worth it, we never would have used an untested time machine to go back to save you, would we? No, we would have left well enough alone, and left you to the Hunters. They would have finished you off. You're completely wrong about me."

"Am I?" Will asked. "Then why is it that other people have tried to teach me and train me so that I can learn how not to *be* such a risk? Why do they try to make me feel at home? Why is it that you, and *only* you, seemed to only find my faults and see only the risk? I never asked for *any* of this, Fil. All I ever wanted to do was go home to my family. Until yesterday, though, this had become my home, and the people here my family. You're the only one who has consistently pushed me away. And before I go risking my life on multiple levels to save the people in the world who mean the most to me, I'd really like to know what it is I've done to you that makes me deserve such treatment."

Fil's face tightened, and his teeth were clenched, as if responding was the greatest effort of his life. "It's different with me," he said, his voice quiet. "My view of Will Stark was not the same as the rest of the people you've met here. The rest of them, they know the legend, the greatest practitioner of the Aliomenti arts, defender of humanity, the man who fights the Elites for true freedom for our people. But for me, Will Stark was the most selfish man who ever lived."

Will's face fell. "What? Why?"

Fil ignored him. "When we had to risk our lives with the time machine to rescue you, it was a kick to the gut. Why was I risking my life to save this man, this selfish man so heavily glorified by others? It was wrong. And it seemed I was proved right. You figured out how to grow your Energy faster than anyone has ever done. Yet you never told any of us how. You were careless and caught the attention of the Hunters, and my sister nearly died because of it. Yet Adam says that we're supposed to blame ourselves for failing to train you adequately. To me, the extra training wasn't what was relevant; for you, selfish man that you are, no amount of training would make you apply what you'd learned, because you wouldn't think to do something for the benefit of others."

Will started to protest, but Fil held up a hand. "Why did I think that? Because I knew that, if our mission to rescue you was successful, a good man would want to go back in time and rescue his family. Not just rescue them, but *be* with them. With his wife, a wonderful woman who deserved the best husband the history of the planet could offer. He should have been there spending time with his son, as it always seemed he wanted to do, to help that little boy discover himself and grow into a man. Yet you didn't do that, did you? The technology was there, and you didn't do a *thing* with it. The only explanation I had was that you were selfish, that you didn't want to waste your new abilities for those people, and especially not for that little boy, the one who never spoke, the one who wanted to be able to tell his father that he was his hero and that he loved him. But you weren't there."

"I don't need to listen to this!" Will shouted. "Here I am, ready to risk my life to go do *exactly that!* Why on earth would you prejudge me like that?" He shook his head. "I'm going to go take care of the people who need me most." He punched the Depart button, and the top closed. He could hear the engine warming up.

"What I've been trying to explain to you is what I have always thought of you in the past, and why." Fil spoke to him telepathically, and Will busied himself looking at the simple controls. *"What I've learned, though, is that you truly are the hero I always believed you were when I was young. You've proved it beyond any possible doubt. Understand as you go back in time that the person who needs rescuing is your wife, though. Your son made it through just fine. With any luck, one day I'll become the man you are."*

Will looked up sharply at Fil. The man reached for those ever-present sunglasses and pulled them off, revealing a pair of shockingly blue eyes, eyes that revealed an incredible depth of intelligence and wisdom beyond their apparent years. Eyes that literally sparkled with Energy. Eyes that looked at him with admiration.

Eyes that belonged to his son.

"Josh?" he whispered, and for the first time, the man he knew as Fil smiled, a huge, joyful smile, the smile of a man who has finally figured out who he is, and that his beliefs as a boy of a heroic father were fully justified. It was a smile that reached his eyes, the eyes he'd waited so long to see just like this.

"Save Mom, Dad. She's the one who needs you."

Dad. It was true, then. But that also meant...

He looked at Angel, and she too was smiling at him, tears of joy on her cheeks this time. "Love you, Daddy," she mouthed, and blew him a kiss.

The top of the time machine snapped opaque, blocking his children from view, and then he no longer felt their presence, losing them again in time just as he'd finally found them.

XXVI
RETRACE

2030 A.D.

The Leader sat at the head of a large table in an opulent conference room at Aliomenti Headquarters, joined there by the three Hunters. It was the first meeting at this location since they'd failed to capture the outlaw Will Stark at his home. The news continued to be disturbing, suggesting that Stark, wherever he was, was cleaning up anything that could be used to trace him.

There had been no sign of him. Porthos had spent nearly every waking hour in deep concentration, trying to detect even the slightest hint of the fugitive, but there were no Energy trails of Stark's to be found. That wasn't unusual; Stark had amply demonstrated to the Hunters over many decades that he could go years or decades without detection, somehow becoming invisible to Porthos' skills. More concerning was the fact that the Energy of others the Hunters were charged with finding was also impossible to sense, as if the entirety of the Alliance had vanished. They couldn't simply hope that the scourge was wiped out, however; they needed proof that the criminals had been destroyed. An Alliance that managed to hide its existence was far more dangerous, because it had the chance to grow and recruit new members without detection, without the true Aliomenti thinning their ranks.

The news from the humans on Will Stark was also ominous. It seemed that the large sums of money that Stark had earned had vanished as well. The man had established accounts and processes through which his fortune would be disbursed upon his death, and yet the money had run out far too quickly. The two men charged with performing the distribution had accused their national government of stealing the money, and had various means of proving it to be true. Porthos found the story entertaining; then again, he'd been the one who had so enjoyed a book by a human that he'd insisted the Hunters adopt the names of the characters. Athos believed that Stark had simply taken his own money back — since he was not actually dead — and had not bothered to tell anyone. With the sums of money in question, he could engage in his favorite form of recruitment — directly from the humans themselves. On the positive side, Aramis noted, it meant he wasn't poaching anyone from the core group of Aliomenti, or worse, those working at Headquarters with The Leadership team.

Outside his usual fatigue concerning the never-ending negative news about Will Stark, The Leader was distressed by two points after the mission had ended, both of which had been hinted at in their meeting immediately after Stark had escaped.

First, The Assassin had not returned to Headquarters. Nor had he contacted them. Nor had the human or Aliomenti investigative teams on the scene of the fire located any suggestion of a male victim of the fire matching his description. That most assuredly meant, as they'd speculated previously, that the Alliance had gotten him, and it wasn't simply a case of him trying to continue his mission until he was finished.

"Gentlemen, with The Assassin's capture, we must fill the role of official Assassin for The Leadership team. Thankfully, we were able to locate another bloodthirsty human-hater within our organization. While he's not quite as skilled or creative as The Assassin we have recently lost, he will more than make up for the deficiency with sheer cruelty and hatred." Porthos clapped quietly, stopping only after a glare from Athos.

The Leader resumed. "The Assassin was no lover of humans, as you well know. Yet he recognized that, despite his most fervent wish, he could not simply eliminate them with impunity. We strive for secrecy above all else, and massive numbers of deaths would lead to investigations we simply cannot risk. My greatest fear with our new Assassin is that he will lose control and carry out the type of rampage that could lead to questions that would be... uncomfortable.

However, he is the best candidate we have." He nodded to the door. "Come in, Abaddon."

The man entered. Like The Assassin, Abaddon was dressed in black. He had multiple tattoos left exposed by his clothing, each of which depicted gratuitous killing and torture. The Hunters each winced at the twisted nature of the images.

It was his eyes that would give potential victims the greatest degree of concern, however. They were a deep brown, almost black, but there were streaks of different shades of red in each eye, as if the bloodshed he sought had reached the very windows of his soul. The eyes told of a man who was pure evil and chaos and a lack of self-control. The random nature of the streaks made the man look cross-eyed, as if to give an idea of the instability at his core.

"Abaddon, please meet my Hunters, the men charged with finding and bringing to justice within these walls those who would violate our laws and Oaths. In the circumstances in which they find compelling evidence of interaction with humans, to the degree that the human or humans may be reasonably assumed to know of our existence or our advances, they will inform me. And in those cases, and *only* those cases, you will be authorized to fulfill your blood lust, limited just to the offending humans. This role does not provide you sanction or backing to execute humans for any other reason, and if you are found to be doing so, you, too, will be considered in violation of your Oath to not enable humans to learn of our existence. In front of the Hunters as witnesses, do you solemnly swear to carry out this role and abide by its rules and limitations?"

Abaddon's lip curled up, and it was apparent that his twisted mind was already trying to find loopholes. He nodded, a sharp, crisp movement that was barely noticeable.

"Abaddon," The Leader said, "we must hear you state your agreement. A nod is not sufficient."

"Agreed," Abaddon said. His voice was reminiscent of nails scraping a chalkboard, and the Hunters glanced at each other, each to confirm he was not the only one frightened of this man.

"Then you are hereby and officially the new Assassin for the Aliomenti Leadership. You will report to me. I expect that I will not hear accounts of any unauthorized activities. Am I perfectly clear?"

Abaddon's glare put a chill in the room. "Crystal."

"Phenomenal. Now leave us."

Abaddon left. Porthos waited until the door shut, and turned to The Leader. "While I'm not in the habit of questioning the mental stability of one of my Aliomenti brethren... that guy is a terrifying and insane monster. I'm quite fearful he is going to do something... imprudent."

The Leader shot a lethal glance his way, and Porthos lowered his head.

"I do not appreciate the skepticism, Porthos. I am well aware of Abaddon's instability. Sadly, most of my other candidates are far too soft. I am concerned that should the need arise, they would hesitate to execute humans, and would perhaps not even make the effort. Therefore, I had to appoint one of the opposite mindset lest the role lose its deterrence effect."

Aramis nodded, while Athos stroked his chin. "We need that. If word gets out that Stark was married and fathered a child, without being captured or executed...well, I fear that the wrong message may be sent to those who are less than fervent. The understanding that someone like Abaddon is hiding in the shadows to enforce Oaths... well, I for one would think twice." At The Leader's narrowed glance, Athos amended his statement. "Figuratively speaking, of course."

"And now, gentlemen, we must once more address the Stark problem. I have reason to believe that any child born to one Aliomenti-trained parent will be born with abnormally strong Energy stores and Energy control, and likely would be able to perform our most challenging tasks with ease, and perhaps perform others we can't even fathom. Thus, Stark's child is an inherent danger to us; he may spontaneously and publicly do things humans — or Aliomenti — should not be able to do. That will raise questions. However, it is worse than that." He paused. "I have reason to suspect that Stark's wife is an ancient Aliomenti woman long thought dead." He glanced at the Hunters, who looked startled at this revelation. "The Energy ability enhancement mentioned with *one* parent is likely enhanced by orders of magnitude with *two* such parents. This child is not just a risk to expose us; he may well be able to destroy us. *Alone.* We must locate him. If necessary, we may resort to bringing Abaddon into play."

He glanced at the man wearing the cloak. "Porthos, you must begin traveling again. Interact with and travel around in the human communities as you have in the past. *We must find the Starks.* If you find the boy, the parents are sure to make an appearance, but be warned, the boy will be quite powerful. Should the boy become fearful, he may unleash enough Energy to kill you and destroy a human city block. Do not treat him lightly because he is a boy; he will be just as difficult to capture as his father, if not more so. Focus on him."

He turned to Athos and Aramis. "The two of you will travel as well, but stay separated from Porthos. They will be able to sense three of you coming far more readily than one or two. In fact, I recommend that the three of you stay separated from each other to the greatest degree possible." He paused, gathering his thoughts. "It seems impossible that anything other than technology or newly-discovered Energy skills by the Alliance was responsible for the escape of Will Stark. Thus, he may be with them on at least a periodic basis. The two of you are to spend your time solely focused on finding the hidden Alliance base of operations. We seem unlikely to find them with traditional methods of Energy tracing; thus, use alternative means."

Athos nodded, and Aramis raised his hand. "Sir, what do you mean by 'alternative'?"

"Given the Alliance love of humans, we must look there. They wish to edge humans forward in terms of technological development, and as such I suggest that you look for reports of unique advances and search for Alliance influence there."

Aramis nodded. "Understood, sir. I'll begin immediately."

The other Hunters affirmed this statement, and left the conference room.

Alone, The Leader reached into his pocket and pulled out the photo he'd picked up at Will Stark's home, during the time when the Hunters had gone to check for Stark inside the burning house. He looked at the picture there, the picture of a woman known as Hope Stark.

The eyes told him that she had once been known by another name, in the far distant past. And that was the second thing that had him so distressed after the events at Stark's home.

That woman had died young, or so he'd long believed, the victim of horrific abuse that others had performed and that he had allowed. Her death had shattered him, and the guilt at failing to stand up for the young woman was a feeling he'd never forgotten.

He had failed as her father.

Now, though, he was looking at a current photograph. This woman was alive and vibrant. She looked older than he remembered, of course; she'd been only a teenager when she died, and Hope Stark was in her late twenties. But there was no denying it was the same woman.

That meant that the man who had pronounced her dead so long ago had lied to him.

It was yet another reason to hate Will Stark.

He wouldn't believe it until there was strong evidence to support it, stronger than a mere photograph. He must go to the source and verify. The Leader rose from his chair, entered the elevator, and rode down to the ground level where the flying craft were kept. The guard on duty saw that it was him, and waved to him to take his choice of vehicle. The craft was a long-range variety and completely fueled. He'd need the entire capacity of the tanks to make it to his locale and back. He was powerful, to be sure, but he had never taken to teleportation, living in fear that he'd somehow miss his target and stay in the realm between locations forever. So he used the crude, almost human-like private personal aircraft on his journey instead.

He kept his mind blank during the hours-long trip; such mental quietude was beneficial, and the craft would handle navigational matters better without his interference. He eventually descended into a thick forest, well away from the large cities dotting England, and the craft came to rest in a small clearing.

The Leader emerged from the craft, and memories flooded over him. He remembered the somber procession as he and the others had come to bury his daughter. Ironically, if they had held a trial for her murder there, everyone present at the grave weeping her demise would have been found guilty, save for one. The box had been lowered and covered with dirt, and a small wooden cross served as the only marker and reminder that she'd ever existed.

The Leader opened the rear compartment of the craft, where various tools were stored, and located a sturdy shovel. He could generate sufficient Energy to simply blast the dirt away, but he felt it appropriate to handle the excavation with a simple tool, a testament to where they'd been when the fledgling Aliomenti group had formed. And so he spent the better part of an hour, pushing the blade through the coarse soil, his arms and back aching from the unfamiliar form of exercise.

At last, the shovel struck something solid. It was the wooden box, still there after so many years. He moved with great purpose and precision, clearing the dirt completely off the box, then used Energy to raise the coffin from the hole in the ground to rest on the grass near his craft.

He raised the lid.

He knew it would be empty, of course, but the shock was still powerful. There was no sign that any person, alive or dead, had ever spent time in this box stored in the ground.

He spotted a pouch, however, and lifted it. Reaching inside, he removed a short handwritten note.

If you are reading this note, you have finally come to the conclusion that Elizabeth did not die of the trauma she received at the hands of those she considered her extended family.

Know this: I will never allow you to hurt her again, no matter how long either of us walk this earth. If I so much as sense that you are looking for her, your walk will come to a swift and certain end.

Men such as you should never be permitted the title of father. May your guilt and suffering be eternal.

WS

The Leader crumpled the note, a surge of Energy and anger turning the ancient paper to dust.

Will Stark had issued him a warning and a declaration of war from the distant past.

He would get his wish. The Hunters would no longer be out to simply capture Will Stark for a formal sentence of death. They would be under orders to kill the man on sight.

•••

2219 A.D.

The Leader sat in his office at Aliomenti Headquarters, remembering his discovery about Hope Stark, reminded of his journey to her grave site in the aftermath of the failed attempt to capture Will Stark at his home. They'd never managed to trace Will after that day, and had not seen him again until he suddenly reappeared in what must have been the Alliance camp, surging massive amounts of Energy. He smiled at the memory of the stunned look on Porthos' face when the man had rushed in to report that he'd just detected Will Stark for the first time in nearly two centuries, despite the searches his best Hunters had carried on during the interim.

They'd bungled the operation, however. So fearful that the man would harm them, they'd tried to subdue him first, rather than simply kill him as they'd been ordered, and they'd failed. Stark had escaped them yet again. Then he'd given himself up, and Porthos, displaying what later turned out to be foolish thinking, had thought to bring the man in to see him before the execution. Porthos knew The Leader had many questions about Will Stark from years ago, not the least of which was why Stark had never bothered to tell the man his own daughter was still alive. And he had definitely wanted to know. But it became quite clear, only a few moments into the questioning, that the man would answer nothing, and so they'd gone ahead with the execution order.

He should have gone with Aramis to Will's execution, not because the man needed help, or even in hindsight so that he could have stopped Will from overpowering The Assassin and escaping. No, he should have gone because he'd personally vowed to see Will Stark dead, and he should have been there to witness the event.

Nothing could be done about it now, though. You couldn't change the past.

He was tired, though. He was tired of the waiting, tired of the failure and the excuses, tired of being outsmarted and outfought. This battle with the Alliance, with Will Stark, was distracting them from their mission. Humans throve like never before, a mere century or so after the Cataclysm, and their numbers were growing. Commerce was growing. Prosperity and advancement were accelerating at a rate never before seen in human society.

That could not continue. Not if the Aliomenti were going to continue to be the dominant force on the planet, as they had been for over a thousand years.

They'd done everything they could to keep humans docile and subservient, all in a subtle fashion. The Alliance opposed them. He remembered a human discovery or two that were supposed to lead humans to infinite life spans a few centuries ago. They'd threatened the companies working on those technologies with loss of funding, threatened the researchers making breakthroughs. They'd even managed to sabotage one experiment in which they ensured that every person in the group receiving the treatments had died within six months. That scared people away to the degree that they gave up on their own; nobody wanted to die *sooner*, after all. Those days were gone; they'd wasted time on Stark and his family that would have been better served keeping their boot on the neck of humanity. It was time to reassert Aliomenti supremacy, and that meant there would be no more subtle, hidden tactics.

The Leader sent a communication out to every one of the Aliomenti throughout the world. They were all Hunters now, he said. They were all Assassins. They were to find anyone who was part of the Alliance. They could be brought to Headquarters for re-education if the capturing parties thought it best; if not, they were to be executed. On the spot. Without questioning.

He added an addendum, however. If anyone found a woman who looked like Hope Stark, famous for marrying the notorious outlaw years ago, she was to be brought to Headquarters unharmed.

It was what any father would do, of course.

XXVII
EMBEZZLED

2030 A.D.

It had been about three weeks since Adam had created the website for requests, and Baker and Howe found that their time had been greatly freed up. The site did exactly as requested, centralizing all requests and eliminating piles of paper mail and teeming masses of email and phone calls. They'd put out a press release stating that they were recycling any requests not already processed, and if people hadn't heard back yet, they needed to resubmit on the website. New requests received in any other manner would simply be discarded.

The website pruned down about 90% of requests immediately. The percentage of discards dropped slightly each week, meaning they had to fully review a greater percentage of requests as time went on. Baker wondered if the miscreants trying to scam the system had gotten better at giving the answers they wanted — rather than the truth — after getting immediate rejections, or if they'd simply stopped trying. Howe did a bit of searching and actually found two web sites where people shared strategies for gaming the site and getting money. One of those sites even charged a membership fee. Both Baker and Howe found that to be quite entertaining.

Howe put one of his paralegals to work scanning both sites to identify the techniques used, and the three of them discussed the techniques the sites recommended. Were there signals that could be found to determine if these "loopholes" were being used? In other words, could they figure out a way to make the system know if the user was gaming it?

The paralegal suggested mapping the IP addresses used by people posting on those sites, and then blocking them from entering requests. While it was easy to defeat and would certainly miss some people trying to game the system and likely find a lot of "false positives," it was another step to let the public know that they took their roles as caretakers seriously. The paralegal wrote up a document explaining the concept for Adam, and they planned to batch it up with other such enhancement requests and send everything to Adam at once.

The two men also loved the ability to send payments via electronic transfers to those whose requests had been approved. Though it seemed this should have been done before, given the advanced stages of currency technology, neither man had any idea how to implement it, and both were loath to bring in an outsider to get into the accounts. Since Adam knew what he was doing and was an insider, they resolved both issues. The men approved requests now and got reports the next morning regarding the funds that had been disbursed the previous day.

The first sign of trouble came when the email sent to Adam with the requested enhancements bounced.

Baker stared at it. How could the email address not exist? He'd been using it to communicate with Adam, several times a day, for the past three weeks, and had gotten responses from the address. He rechecked the address, and it looked correct. He sent the list again, copying the address from a reply he'd gotten from Adam. Once again, he got a reply indicating an invalid email address.

He called Adam's mobile phone. It was out of service.

Now quite anxious, he called Howe, and the attorney met him in the office a short while later.

It was Howe who answered the phone call from the reporter. "Sir, can you comment on the rumor that started circulating overnight regarding the Trust?"

"I'm afraid I can't comment on rumors, especially those that I've not heard."

"The rumor is that the Trust is out of money."

Howe stared at Baker, in shock. How could that be possible? There were tens of billions of dollars in cash in the Trust account, and awards were rarely for more than a hundred thousand dollars. At the rate they were awarding money, they should have funds for the next few decades. It was a preposterous rumor.

"I have no comment on that rumor."

"So you aren't denying, then, that the Trust is out of money?"

"I've found that anonymous sources are rarely correct."

"On the contrary, I've found that anonymous sources are rarely *incorrect*, sir. Does this mean you are denying that the Trust is out of money?"

"I'm saying our policy is that we do not respond to rumors. Good day to you." Howe hung up the phone.

"It's not actually possible, is it?" asked Baker, who'd been listening to the call on speaker phone.

"I can't see how it could be."

The computer in front of Howe made a tone indicating receipt of an email, and then another and another, until the sounds were quite constant. Howe refreshed the email screen, and both men stared in shock.

Nearly all of the subject headings were the same. *Insufficient funds to complete the electronic transfer request. Request incomplete. Please deposit additional funds and retry the transfer.*

The few differing subject headings were clearly from news organizations who heard the same rumor. Unfortunately, it appeared that the rumor was, in this case, true. Or at least had the *appearance* of being true; perhaps someone was spamming their email inbox with the error messages in the hopes they'd call and offer up key account details.

"I think our system has been hacked," said Millard Howe.

Michael Baker looked at the screen, and remembered the canceled email address and deactivated mobile phone number. "No, Millard," he said at last. "I think we gave the keys to the thief." He looked up. "I think this is Adam's doing."

Howe's face said he'd drawn the same conclusion. "We'll need to alert our bank to stop processing any outgoing payments effective immediately, and take the website down."

"How? Adam's the only one with the passwords to do so."

"Then we'll need to issue a press release indicating that our accounts have been compromised and that no further requests will be processed, and no further disbursements will be forthcoming, until such time as the apparent compromise is resolved."

Baker looked at him. "Do you think that will work?"

"I don't know. I don't know what else to do, though." He looked at Baker, and his expression was pained. "You do realize what will happen, right? Public opinion will say it was us."

Baker blinked. "What?"

Howe nodded. "We were the only two people known to have access to that account. We were the only two people known to be able to authorize payments. The account has apparently been drained. Who else could it have been? The two men they can see, or the phantom without a last name or address we will claim masterminded it all without our knowledge?"

Baker opened his mouth to speak, and then closed it. He knew Millard was right. Adam had not only vanished with all of the money, he'd left them holding the empty bag, and no judge or jury would find a non-existent person the culprit.

Baker turned to Howe, feeling helpless. "What do we do now?"

Howe looked at him. "You're young. You have a wife and child. If memory serves, you're taking a vacation starting in a couple of days, correct?"

Baker nodded.

"Take your vacation. Your funds are well-diversified. Extend the vacation. Travel to a foreign country you love. And then stay there. You didn't do anything wrong, but if you think people were out to get you — and your family — when you had access to money... wait until you see what happens when you suddenly have nothing."

Baker felt a chill. "So you're telling me to run? Hide? Won't that make me look guilty?"

Howe fixed him with a stare, suddenly looking quite old. "Leave that to me. Stay away. Watch the news. You'll know when it's safe for you to return."

Baker didn't like the look on Howe's face, but he stood up, and started to leave. He stopped, turned around, and walked back to the attorney. Holding out his hand, he said, "It's been a pleasure working with you, Millard. I wish it hadn't ended this way."

Howe shook his hand. "Likewise, Michael. On both points."

Baker left, and Howe waited to hear the sounds of the car pulling away before he started to carry out the plan he'd come up with while they'd been talking. Having Baker run would make him look guilty, but less so if there were alternative stories to consider. No one would believe an invisible man had stolen off into the night with billions of dollars, never to be seen or heard from again. But they might believe that an attorney, out of greed, and perhaps a sense of being underpaid over the years by his wealthiest client, had attempted to siphon money away into his own private accounts. Nor would they doubt that the old man might fail, literally losing the money in an effort to steal it.

And they'd fully believe what steps the man might take next in an effort to avoid punishment, whether in the courts for his crime, or in the court of public opinion for his stupidity and greed.

He pulled out a clean piece of paper and started writing out his confession, trying to make it sound plausible despite making the scenario up as he wrote. He became engrossed in the level of detail he could invent, including his (imagined) slights at the hands of the Starks, his decision to abuse the power of the purse he'd been given for the Trust, and how he'd failed.

"You should consider writing fiction."

Howe, bent over his desk, sat upright so quickly that he nearly toppled his chair. Adam stood behind him, peering over his shoulder at the writing. He clapped the attorney on the back. "High quality. I imagine some of your legal papers over the years have taught you well in the art of writing fiction." He smiled, as if this comment should be treated as banter between friends.

"How *dare* you show yourself here!" Howe pushed the chair back from his desk, and stood so that he could look Adam in the eye. "Why? Why would you do such a thing? Why would you leave a good, decent young man like Michael Baker in such a position? I realize attorneys aren't always considered the most honorable people around, but I'd like to think I've run an honest practice. Why me? And how could you do that to the *Starks*?" He put his hands on the desk behind him, leaning into it as if out of breath, and one hand slid out of sight toward an upper drawer.

Adam looked him in the eye. "The bullets have been removed from the gun, so there's no sense going to the effort of trying to retrieve it." Howe froze, and then slowly stood back up. "As difficult as it will be for you to accept, I am doing *exactly* what Will Stark told me to do. He knew you'd never go along with it, so unfortunately I had to act in secret."

Millard Howe shook his head. "I'm supposed to believe that Will

Stark told you to steal all of his money and frame me, and Michael, for your crime?"

"Yes on the first part, but no on the second. We'd not thought of that difficulty when we set this plan in motion, and were horrified when we realized what would happen, but the money needed to be moved. I've been working on a means to blame a third party, so as to shift blame away from you and Michael, precisely because I know Will would not want your good names tarnished like that. The crime will be pinned on someone else."

Millard Howe folded his arms across his chest. Despite his advanced years, he still towered above the younger man. He hoped he looked imposing. "Would you like to fill me in?"

"Naturally. Were you aware that the federal government secretly enacted an electronic funds transfer tax?"

"No."

"They did. No one was told. In fact, the Treasury Secretary and the Chairman of the Fed did it entirely on their own. No Congressional discussion, no notification of the President, nothing. They just did it. Basically, it's supposed to slap a surcharge on electronic transfers above a certain size. But you see, there appears to have been a bug in the code." He arched an eyebrow.

"And what would that *bug* be, Adam?"

"Rather than taking a *small* percentage of *large* transfers, it took an excessively *large* percentage of *all* transfers. Unfortunately, that percentage for our transfers was well above 100%; apparently, their programmer recorded the multiplier for the percentage as a whole number, rather than a decimal, and the bug hasn't yet been formally acknowledged. How can they? It's an illegal 'tax' and such a terribly obvious mistake that they'd look like fools as well as criminals. But in the end, the result was that for every dollar transferred, they exacted that fee as a surcharge from the same source account, a fee that was *multiples* of the amount transferred. It was enough to drain the massive checking account of the Trust." He arched an eyebrow. "I'm not sure that type of bug can be satisfied with a mere apology. Are you?"

Howe knew what he thought: this man was lying through his teeth. But the story was compelling. "I think you're lying to me, Adam."

"I have documentation to prove that it happened, that shows the division within the Federal Reserve which processes that stealth tax. I can even provide documentation showing bank balances and approved amounts of transfers, along with the amounts that actually left our accounts."

Interesting. "And what exactly is to be done about this, then?"

"This will be your show, Millard. You will first shred your little suicide note; you need to stick around." Millard winced; he hadn't expected that note to be seen by anyone until... well, that was past now. Adam handed him a digital, read-only disk. "You then will write an article with full sources, including archived web site pages people can review, which explain the rumors, the transactions, and the stealth tax taken, all of which is on this disk. You will note that this tax was imposed without the required approvals of the various legislative and executive layers of government. And that this clandestine maneuver has resulted in the Fed illegally seizing the cash assets of the Stark family's charitable Trust and foundation, to the tune of approximately thirty-eight *billion* dollars. You will demand that the Fed and Treasury provide full reimbursement — plus your legal fees, of course — for the funds seized, and immediately cease collecting this tax surcharge unless it is approved by appropriate measures. And then you will come with me."

"Where are you going?"

"Right now? I'm going to go tell Michael to enjoy his vacation."

"And when I'm done? When you're done talking with Michael?"

Adam smiled. "I have a new opportunity for you. One that will make life a lot more interesting." He clasped the lawyer's shoulder. "Tell me, Millard, have you ever heard of nanotechnology?"

●●●

The meeting with Howe had gone as expected. It had taken Adam several years to create the fictitious documentation, exaggerating the statements about the merits of such a tax, limiting the edited conversations to just the right number of individuals to make it appear a conspiracy. The programmer alleged to have performed the transfer surcharge, including the mathematical blunder, was a relatively new member of the Alliance, one who had, indeed, worked in the IT department with the Federal Reserve, and who had 'vanished' from society a year earlier. Since the man's family had predeceased him, he was agreeable to Adam using his name as one of the perpetrators of the fraud.

The entire story was an intricately woven fake, one that would take years to uncover. The upcoming disappearances of Millard Howe, who had uncovered the conspiracy, and Michael Baker, who had unwittingly played a part in exposing it, would add to public speculation that it was true, and that the powerful men behind it were trying to silence witnesses. Adam chose not to feel guilt over the public condemnation that *those* two men would face for several years. They hadn't committed *this* crime, but Adam had found enough evidence in his email hacking efforts that he could certainly have convicted them of many others. Justice, imperfect though it was, would still be done.

And the money would go where it rightfully belonged.

XXVIII
FOUND

2030 A.D.

The investigations around the fire at the home of Will and Hope Stark had finally died down.

The fire itself had burned with such intensity that everything within the walls of the house had been turned to ash. The exterior walls had likewise been completely consumed by the inferno, and the only things remaining were the bricks forming the chimney and the concrete foundation walls and floor of the basement. The pile of ashen debris in the lower level was extensive, and it was impossible for the investigation team to determine if anyone once living was buried there in cremated form. News sites noted that, given the nature of the destruction, it was almost as if a small-scale, space-confined nuclear weapon had been detonated within the walls of the Starks' home, as only a device such as that could generate the heat required to create the destruction they'd observed.

After over a month of waiting, none of the Starks had come forward. A reluctant coroner had no choice but to officially rule all three members of the family dead, despite the lack of bodies to prove it. After all, he reasoned, even if the family had taken an impromptu vacation, they'd likely hear about what happened and speak up after so much time had passed if they were alive to do so. Police likewise reported that they'd found no evidence suggesting that the arsonist had escaped the raging fire he'd started. With no living victims to press charges and no criminal to charge with a crime, the case was closed.

Tabloids enjoyed teasing readers with conspiracy theories about the nature of, and the purpose of, the holes in the basement and backyard. Had the Starks expected an attack and started building an escape tunnel? Had the arsonist tunneled his way in? Were they building a secret vault under their backyard, with entrances from the surface and the basement?

Eventually, the conspiracy chatter was replaced with a more serious question. Will Stark, with both his own phenomenal success and investments in many fledgling businesses, was both the face and the engine of the country's nascent recovery from economic turmoil. What did it say for that recovery when someone was clearly willing to murder the man? And who would take his place?

While such questions continued to be discussed in public, the nation's watchful eye turned away from the burned-out shell of the Stark's home. News channels no longer demanded access to film the scene for the alternating depressing and scandalous stories of the day. The site became a less dramatic visual as cleanup crews removed the ash and rubble, leaving nothing but the smooth concrete poured to form the foundation floors and walls. Quiet and silence returned to the site the Starks had once called home.

Late one night, there was movement at the house.

A fine line formed in the concrete floor, working its way around, until it formed a square measuring eight feet per side. The square began to rise slowly into the air, a solid slab of concrete a foot thick. The square cleared the floor and a gap opened up, revealing that the slab was supported by four large steel columns. After several minutes, the original slab was over seven feet above the floor of the basement, and another slab appeared, the entire structure rising out of the ground like the elevator car it was.

Hope Stark stood in the elevator car, holding the hand of her son, Josh.

Mother and son took deep breaths, the first bit of fresh, outdoor air that the two of them had breathed in nearly two months. The underground bunker Hope had built was designed to withstand another economic calamity in which food, water, or air quality might be compromised, or in which their personal safety was threatened. Nobody else knew it existed, and nobody else knew how to get in.

Not even Will.

Hope had found a use for her long-dormant Aliomenti abilities when the house had first been built. She had remotely teleported small amounts of dirt out from under the house, and scattered it around the property, until she'd cleared out sufficient space for the bunker. Using scuba gear for breathing, and a flashlight to enable her to see, she was able to teleport herself into the underground bunker and gradually reinforce the walls, create the hydraulics for the elevator car, build connections into underground electric, water, and sewage lines separate from those going to her house, and added an air filtration system. She gradually stocked food supplies, water, and materials for entertainment in the bunker. Over a period of several years, she completed the underground hideout, which would enable them to live in moderate comfort for several months without needing to leave.

Hope was troubled, though. She was the only person who knew that the bunker existed. Yet someone *else* had teleported her and Josh from the kitchen to the bunker just as The Assassin was preparing to strike the death blows. It was unnerving to know that somebody out there knew her true identity, and had the ability and desire to save her, and more importantly, save Josh. More frightening to her, though, was that she'd been intending to do it herself, but the very real threat of Josh being injured had frozen her at the moment she'd needed to act. Someone had bailed her out.

Hope had technology that kept Energy inside the bunker. She could relax and be at ease, and it enabled Josh to learn of the gifts he'd been born with, without having to worry about being detected. She glanced at her son. Josh had grown tremendously in all facets of his life during their self-imposed exile. She found that he'd absorbed most of what she'd taught him over the past six years, and the few things that were fuzzy were quickly corrected. She taught him about Energy and about how to Shield that Energy to make sure that nobody unfriendly could find him once they left the safety of the bunker. She explained her own life story, how she came to meet Will, and the reason that Will must now stay far away from them.

The little boy nodded during this last part without really meaning it, for he wanted his father there with him. She knew what he was thinking, even without using telepathy or empathy. Josh was hurt that Will was staying away. Though she explained that his father's only goal was to keep the boy safe, Josh believed the truth was something else entirely, that Will had *chosen* to stay away to avoid dealing with him anymore, dealing with his issues. Her efforts to convince him otherwise had proved futile for now; she hoped things would improve soon. She didn't want Josh to poison his sibling's understanding of Will. Her hand instinctively went to her belly, and she felt the movement. She knew the baby was a girl, her little angel, a future reminder of Will as he moved around and drew the Aliomenti away.

Josh also missed his dog, Smokey; she was the closest thing to a friend he'd ever had. Hope feared that the dog had died in the fire, but elected not to say that to the boy. Josh had enough issues to deal with already.

Hope knelt on the concrete and looked Josh in the eye. "It's a very dangerous time for us, Josh," she said. "We must pretend we are different people. And we must avoid seeming different, and that means we have to avoid using our Energy unless absolutely necessary, and even then we need to use the least amount possible. You are very, very powerful, and the people who did all of this would sense that and find us both. Do you understand?"

The little boy nodded. He was trying to look brave, but he was clearly scared.

"We'll need to use different names." She thought for a moment. "Stark can be rearranged to spell Trask, so that will be our new last name. You... you should use your middle name. So you can go by Phillip or Phil."

"That's spelled F-I-L, right Mommy?" Josh asked.

Hope didn't correct him. "That's very good. I will be... Phoebe. The first four letters can be rearranged to spell Hope." She patted him on the head. "Nice to meet you, Fil Trask."

The little boy grinned at the new name. "Nice to meet you too, Mommy Trask."

"Those are fine choices for names," a man's voice said. "You'll also need some money for your journey." He walked out of the trees toward them. Hope pushed Josh behind her, but he poked his head out to watch.

"Your secret is safe with me... Phoebe." He smiled. "I'm one of you, and I'm on your side." The man held his left hand palm-side up, and light erupted from his palm, partially illuminating his face and his short brown hair.

Hope was able to recognize the man, and sense that he was trustworthy. "It looks like we carried everything out successfully, then. The Assassin got in. The fire started. We got away." She shook her head. "It took a great deal of effort to play my part and not blast that man into oblivion. He's simply too terrible to be allowed to walk free. It was difficult enough working to suppress Josh's Energy all of those years, even more so when I realized that one of the side effects turned out to be his permanent silence."

Adam looked at her with sympathy. "I don't envy you that part of these past seven years at all, Phoebe. I assume he knows what happened on that front?" He glanced at the boy, and the mother nodded. "He may have issues with it later, but very young children are extremely adaptable and resilient. As to The Assassin... he's terrible, all right. But we must be careful what we ask for. Sometimes, we get just that. And it's worse than what we already know." He smiled at Phoebe. "You did well. I know Will is quite proud of you, wherever he might be at the moment. He'll always be keeping an eye out for both of you in his own fashion. Never forget that." He looked at Fil. "Your father loves you, young Fil. More than you'll ever know. Don't confuse his lack of presence with a lack of love." The little boy stared at the man, and then looked away. It would take time for him to truly understand.

Adam turned back to Phoebe. "Will told me that my sole job after this happened was very simple: it was to make sure that both of you are taken care of. How are the two of you doing?"

"Mommy's been puking!" Fil sang. He mimicked the act and sounds in case there was some confusion about the meaning of the term.

The man looked at her with concern. "Are you ill?"

She shook her head, a hand resting on her belly. "Just a bit of morning sickness."

He nodded. "My congratulations. My charge extends to your newborn as well, of course, in terms of safety." He cocked his head, and then smiled. "Your child loves the stories you tell of your husband. Do you want to know if Fil is getting a brother or sister?"

Hope shook her head. "I already know. Right now, I just need to get us out of here."

Adam nodded. "Here's a credit card, checkbook, and debit card for you, along with a folder containing other key documents. There's a house for rent in the new neighborhood I've scouted out for you, which will be a good place for you to live. The checking account is already nicely funded, and the rest of your money — *all* of it — is accessible as well when you need it. We'd rather not open a new checking account with several billion dollars in place, for obvious reasons." He smiled. "You need not get a job because of financial concerns, Mrs. Trask."

He walked closer, and handed her the materials. Her name — her *new* name — was on the checks and debit card, with an address in a small town in Oregon. The forms included birth certificates for both of them as well. "You'll be able to start fresh there, with your new names, but we need to work on your appearances. You in particular, Phoebe, are fairly easily recognized, and a single mother arriving in a new community with a sizable amount of money, and an appearance much like a very famous dead woman, is going to raise a lot of eyebrows."

Phoebe smirked. "You worked out the names ahead of time and pushed them to me, didn't you?"

Adam's feigned look of innocence was the only answer she got.

Hope shrugged. "In terms of altering appearance... well, I haven't tried that in a while, but I think I remember the process. I'll need to teach Fil, however. I think we can both go with the dark hair, since we're better known for the other end. Especially me, the platinum blonde."

"Agreed. Both of you have rather round faces, so I'd recommend a narrower facial structure."

Hope nodded. "I can work on my changes; would you be able to walk Jo—er, Fil, through the process?"

Adam smiled. "I'd be delighted." He glanced at Josh, now known as Fil. "Fil, has your mom been teaching you how to use your Energy?"

The boy took a moment to realize that *he* was Fil. "Yes. I can move things around without touching them now!" He grinned.

"You'll be able to do much more than that when necessary. For now, though, that will suffice. You need to concentrate your Energy on your hair, and see the Energy changing the color to black."

Mother and child did as he suggested, and Adam watched as the hair on their heads gradually darkened until it was pitch black. Adam applauded lightly. Phoebe and Fil looked at each other, and both gasped at their new hair color and the remarkable difference it made in their appearance.

"You'll need to use the same approach to narrow your face, Fil. Please realize that this ability is more cosmetic than structural. You can narrow your face a bit, but you can't make yourself a foot taller. Just be careful that you don't narrow your faces too dramatically." Mother and son repeated the process, and when they were finished they were nearly unrecognizable as the "dead" Hope and Josh Stark. The widow Phoebe Trask and her son, Fil, had been born.

Adam took the driver's license back from Phoebe, and held it up so that it faced the dark-haired, narrow-faced woman. The empty section for her picture gradually filled in with her new face, one that would take time to get used to seeing.

"I will take the two of you to the outskirts of your new town, to a hotel there with a reservation in your name, Phoebe. There will be a package there waiting for you, which will have some cash in it, and the keys to a minivan with your remaining possessions. Your story is, in essence, a true one. Your husband perished in a fire which destroyed your home and possessions, leaving you a widow at a young age, with a young son and another child on the way. You have a modest amount of money from a life insurance policy, and wanted to move away to start fresh and erase the sights that would remind you of your loss. You've come into some possessions from donations, which will be in the minivan, but you will need to do some shopping." He glanced at Fil. "You will need to go to school, and you will make friends there and learn in a classroom. School and learning will be very easy for you, Fil, because your mom and dad have taught you so much. But it is very important that you avoid using your Energy unless it's *exceptionally* important. Do you understand?"

"Yes." Fil said. His mother told him this on a regular basis. Time would tell how well a six-year-old boy truly understood such words.

"Remember, if you use a lot of Energy — either of you — the people who did this to your house will find out, and they will come after you. They are not happy that they failed. And Phoebe... I think you are wise to assume that they'll figure out who you *truly* are as well, if they haven't already." The woman merely nodded.

He looked at the two of them. "Since I've been asked to keep an eye on you, I'm going to move into your house. I will age myself and become your father-in-law, Phoebe. Adam Trask, at your service."

He bowed low, and despite the seriousness of the situation, Hope found herself laughing. "I'll be a quiet old curmudgeon in public, but I can watch Fil when you need to go out alone, and can help with his training. And I might even be able to help correct his homework."

"What's that?" Fil asked. Adam laughed.

Phoebe looked at Adam, her newly-narrowed face displaying a look of curiosity. "You seem very familiar, Adam. I feel like we've met before, from before we started planning everything that needed to happen on that night, and I felt that way even back then. Do I know you from somewhere?"

Adam shook his head. "Not some*where*, Phoebe. Some *when*."

XXIX
WAITING

2219 A.D.

Joshua Phillip Stark, known for many decades as Fil, sat at the edge of camp, his back against one of the giant trees forming the perimeter. He pulled his knees close and wrapped his arms around them.

It was something he'd seen his father do on a regular basis.

It had been an incredibly challenging two months, starting when they'd made the decision to rescue Will Stark from the pages of history, a history that said the man had vanished and was presumed dead following an explosion and inferno that consumed his home, and everyone in it.

Their conversation had been much like the staged conversation held to convince Will that he was the one who had rescued Josh and Hope from the house. Everything had been staged to get the man into the time machine, because they had all known he wasn't going back to the house. History said Will Stark would emerge from the time machine much earlier than that. They weren't sure that even Will would choose the path he would need to follow. If Will had known that his son was already here, he might never choose to leave. And if he'd learned that the morning of the fire, Hope Stark had discovered she was pregnant, and that the daughter he'd never known existed was in this camp... would he ever, willingly, go?

It was too risky to leave such an important element of history to chance in that fashion. And so they'd neglected to tell him about those details.

As for him, Fil's story had been completely true. He *had* viewed his father as a selfish man, perhaps embarrassed by his son's disability, a man who had no doubt decided that he'd simply give up on the boy and walk away. It didn't mesh with his memory of the man those first six years of his life, but when Hope had said his father needed to go and stay far away from them for their own protection... his young mind couldn't fathom that. He especially hadn't been able to fathom that the choice to stay away would be far more painful for Will than for his son.

He'd been somewhat more accepting of that reality when he'd become a father himself. The thought of being separated from his little girl was devastating, and yet if it was necessary for her survival he would have done so. The Hunters and Abaddon made sure that it was no longer necessary to speculate, however. He wished he had had the opportunity to punish Abaddon, but a few kicks at his predecessor, The Assassin, would have to do.

Over the decades that followed, he'd had plenty of time to forgive his father and himself for their self-imposed views of failure. Seeing the man again, just as he remembered him from nearly two centuries earlier, had brought back his old emotions and memories. He'd needed to keep Will from getting close; the man would recognize his own son for certain if given the chance. He'd grown to be a man, and his sandy blond hair was now the jet-black color of Will's own, so he was somewhat camouflaged. His eyes, though, hadn't changed, and he knew his father would recognize him through his eyes. He'd fashioned the sunglasses to ensure that his father would never see the eyes that would expose the truth of his identity, and thus make Will's choice to go back in time — *far* back in time — even more difficult. Why leave to save what was already there in front of you?

And so he'd gone along with the subterfuge, treating his own father as an unwelcome stranger, planting the idea in his mind repeatedly that Will would destroy his new family, that he'd lead to their destruction as well, for he knew Will Stark would do anything to avoid being a risk to anyone he even remotely cared for. In reality, all he truly wanted was to spend time with the man, before his father and his hero began his incredible journey. For he knew he might never see the man again.

Fil glanced at the backpack sitting on the ground next to him, the same bag he'd used to retrieve items from his childhood home on the trip back in time to rescue his father from death at the hands of the Hunters. He chuckled, noting the irony that Fil, the son, had rescued his father from punishment for the crime of enabling Fil to exist.

Inside the bag, he found a baseball. It was the ball he'd used to play catch with Smokey that morning all of those years ago, when his Energy stores had grown so immense that his mother had no longer been able to Shield them — or him. She was already too weakened from her early term pregnancy with Angel, who brought another set of Energy abilities for Hope to deal with.

Angel. His wonderful little sister. Her joy at seeing their father had been quite touching, and made it so much more difficult for him to maintain his feigned negative attitude. Angel had never met her father before, had never even seen him. She was so fearful of slipping up, of calling him Dad, that she'd insisted on the formal "Mr. Stark" for address, rather than "Will." She'd further changed her natural platinum-blond hair to red, trying and succeeding in fooling Will from seeing his wife's near-twin in his own daughter. Angel had learned of their father solely through the stories that their mother, along with Adam and others within the Alliance, shared, and though at times Fil thought they were embellishing a bit, he now wondered if perhaps they hadn't been restrained in their praise. Will Stark was a man who knew what he stood for, a man who knew the price he was willing to pay to support those principles and those he loved. The hero he'd worshiped as a six-year-old boy was even more mythic now, after he himself had grown, married, had a child and watched those loved ones murdered. When Will stated he was willing to stake his own life for even a chance to help Josh and Hope live, it was too much for him to take. He wished he had been given such a choice, for he knew that, like his father, he would have accepted any offer that would have altered the horrific outcome.

Adam sat down next to him. "We've done our duty, Fil. Now Will must do his."

"I know," Fil said. "The question is, when do we find out if he succeeded?"

"You're still here. So is Angel. That's the proof we need, and Will would say it's the only outcome that matters."

Fil rested his chin on his knees. "I know that's *his* definition of success. But I'd still like to see him again, when he knows the entire history of what we've all been through. That's my definition of the success of this mission. Seeing my father again. No acting, no drama... and no crazy sunglasses." He tapped the accessory.

"You do know that you don't have to wear those any more, right?"

Fil pulled the glasses off of his head, glanced at them, and put them back on. "Of course. I've grown rather fond of them, however. It's how my father knows me now. So, they stay. For him."

Adam said nothing.

"They'll still come after us, you know," Fil said.

"Who? The Hunters?"

Fil nodded. "They'll eventually stop waiting for Dad to do something foolish so that they can track us. They tried that the last time, gave it about twenty years, and then officially decided that he was dead. Now that they know he's not... it can't be good for your credibility for a man you've declared dead to show up, be hauled in for questioning, and then break his way out and possibly kill a Hunter in the process. No, they'll come after all of us as accomplices. And truth be told, we're just that."

Adam glanced at him. "You know, you could simply go to the island and eradicate them." It wasn't a question.

Fil nodded. "I know I could. Yet that would make me no better than them. Sometimes, the easy thing to do, the emotional response, is exactly the wrong thing to do. I know that if I did what you suggest, I'd not only get the Hunters and Abaddon and The Leader. I'd end up wiping out all of the Aliomenti there who are simply enjoying their lives, who don't truly wish us to be destroyed, but who simply lack the will to stand up and tell The Leadership to stop. Worse, I'd kill the humans working there. It would make me no better than The Assassin, who thought it fine to kill two good men that night to come after my mother." He sighed. "There are many easy solutions, simply none that I like." He glanced at Adam. "And it's not without precedent that my emotional responses, outside the faked ones the last few months, tend to turn out very poorly for a lot of innocent people. No, I'll make sure anything I do is targeted at those who come after me and my family directly."

The Mechanic, clad in his orange bodysuit, came over to them. "I take it the machine got away without fail?"

Fil and Adam nodded. "Everything went as planned," Adam said.

"I wonder how long it took Will to forgive us?"

"Immediately... and yet never, I'd imagine," the Mechanic said. "No doubt he'd understand the reasoning behind it and appreciate it. Yet I imagine he'd take a very long time to wonder why it was he was never given the chance to make an informed choice, to prepare himself for his journey." He glanced at Fil. "Or to say a very long goodbye to his son and daughter."

Fil nodded. "I know. Trust me, I've often wondered that as well. When I got the chance these past two months to see my father as he truly is, I couldn't help but fear the long goodbye might be one he'd never finish. That decision would have been rather complicated for my actual existence." He smiled. "Now, though? I'm pretty sure he would have left no later than he did, and I do wish we'd altered the plan. With the time machine gone, there's no chance to go back and change that decision, though."

"Will has his own difficult decisions to make in what will become his future, our past," the Mechanic noted. "He will understand that sometimes, just as the easy choice isn't the correct choice, sometimes the most difficult one is."

"I wish I knew what happened to him," Fil said. "Before he was, well, born." He chuckled. "That statement would get me institutionalized in many societies."

Adam laughed. "We'd be right there with you, since we'd nod along. But yes, the disappearance of the historical Will Stark, shortly before the birth of the man we just sent back in time, is quite the mystery."

The Mechanic glanced at him. "I don't know if I've heard this one."

Adam nodded. "As you know, Will Stark was well known among our kind for centuries. He eventually clashed with The Leadership over the establishment of roles for Hunters and Assassins, and that led him to leave the society he'd helped build to establish the Alliance, which believed that controlled assistance in human development of technology was not only acceptable, it was a moral imperative."

The Mechanic nodded. "This part I know."

"He became a hunted man, of course, and as such he'd disappear from any contact with Aliomenti — Alliance or otherwise — for years or even a decade or longer. But he always did come back, except the last time. He vanished in roughly the year 1994, a year or two before the man we went back in time to rescue was born. The newborn Will Stark lived and grew following his birth in the year 1995, and that Will Stark was lost to history in the year 2030, the year we pulled him *forward* in time to send him *back* in time. The mystery is this: why has that historical, pre-1995 Will Stark never reappeared, after the year 2030?"

"We can be fairly certain that if the Hunters or Assassin had gotten him, it would have been loudly trumpeted," Fil added. "His continual escapes were the source of great embarrassment, and probably encouraged a third of our membership to follow their convictions and move to the Alliance. Capturing or even killing him would be an emotional blow they'd want to celebrate. He's not vanished by their doing, that's for certain."

"Perhaps," the Mechanic mused, "he became so proficient at hiding that he simply stayed hidden."

"Perhaps," Adam agreed. "And if that is the case, then we must simply remain in waiting for him to choose to show himself again."

"I think he knows that the Elites are going to mount a large-scale attack on the Alliance at some point," Fil said. "And so he remains in hiding, letting them grow overconfident, and then he'll appear at a time that tilts the battle in our favor."

"Indeed," Adam replied, as the Mechanic nodded, thoughtful. "Yet they must know that *you* are still out there as well, Fil. And they can't underestimate your abilities. And Angel, though not quite as powerful as you... she's a total mystery to them."

"I'm what?" Angel asked, walking up to join the group.

Fil gave her a quick recap of the conversations, and Angel smiled. "He's out there, hiding in the shadows, protecting me, protecting Fil, and mostly protecting Mom, wherever she is. He'll reveal himself only if he feels it necessary to make sure that all of us are safe."

"Have you seen him?" the Mechanic asked.

"No, but I've sensed him, before, during, and after the time he was here with us from the past." She looked into the forest. "He's probably out there now, listening in, but making sure that the Hunters are heading in the wrong direction."

"And so," Fil said, "we will wait until he decides to show himself to us, and we will wait for the Elites to find us and attack. Until then?" He smiled. "We live, freely."

XXX
STEPS

Will was completely oblivious to his surroundings in the time machine for several minutes, lost in the shock of the events of the last few moments at camp.

He'd found his son. Josh had survived the attack and the fire. He'd grown into a man, had managed to meet up with and join the Aliomenti Alliance, and was a major force in their organization.

And Angel. He had a daughter? He'd had no idea. The only explanation that made any sense was that Hope had been pregnant at the time of the attack, and only recently so, if she hadn't told him yet. It wasn't something she'd keep to herself.

He'd found his children. They'd survived the fire. The Assassin who'd been sent after them had not killed them; he had, as he put it, failed in his mission. He'd only managed to burn the house down, but houses could be rebuilt. In the camp where he'd been living, buildings assembled and disassembled themselves on a regular basis.

Josh — no, Fil now — had survived. He was there. Almost two hundred years old, but he was there. And since Angel hadn't been born at the time of the fire — then Hope had survived as well, long enough, at least, to give birth to their daughter.

That meant his mission had succeeded. Or at least, it had succeeded in the last iteration of whatever time loop he was on. Time travel would certainly make your head spin.

He wished he'd gotten the chance to shake his son's hand, to tell him he was proud of him. Sure, Fil had been rather aggressive towards him, but he'd explained why. Left unsaid was the obvious: for a man like Will, knowing his children had survived — and had actually been with him the entire time he'd been in the future — might have been enough to dissuade him from getting in the time machine. He'd want to spend time with his children, to be sure. How long would it have taken for him to decide to leave, though? He could talk of duty and claim he'd do what needed doing, but that was a lot easier said when the desired result — healthy children, children who had survived an assault on their home — wasn't looking you in the eye.

The three of them — Adam and his two grown children — had manipulated him. They'd preyed upon his sense of duty, and Fil had ensured that at least one person in that camp made him feel unwelcome, that someone had wanted him gone, that someone would make him feel as if his mere presence would be the death of all of them. It was certainly easier to leave that type of environment, real or imagined, than one that mirrored the future he'd always wanted. They knew him well enough to play their parts and ensure he made the decision he needed to make. It didn't make him happy, but he understood their logic.

Yet in the end, they'd misjudged him. If he'd known that Fil was his adult son, and Angel the daughter he'd never known he had, he would eventually have left anyway. For there was one person he'd never seen in that camp while he'd been there.

Hope.

He would go back for her, even if everything else was as it should be. How long had she survived after the fire? Had she been hurt at all? Fil had said to focus on Hope, not him. That was disconcerting. Had she been gravely injured in Fil's memory of the day, living just long enough to deliver Angel, and then...? He didn't want to think of it, but he must.

The larger issue was that he didn't know if Hope had been invited into the Alliance culture, had gone through the Purge, had developed her Energy, and gotten the other treatments that enabled extreme longevity. She could have survived the fire, lived her life out, and died of old age. Perhaps Fil had been delivering that message: that Will needed to bring his mother home, or enable her to live. He didn't know the ingredients of the Purge, but he had a large batch of nanos.

She could certainly live long enough to meet him in the future if needed.

Something nagged at him, though. Something he was missing in the emotions of the moment, whether a sense of duty or a sense of shock.

His mission, as they'd discussed it, involved him going back to the night of the fire. He was to rescue Hope and Josh from The Assassin, from burning to death in the inferno he'd seen before the Hunters had jumped him and beaten him. Josh was saved. He'd grown into a man, becoming known as Fil, and had managed to live nearly two centuries before coming back to rescue his neophyte father. Likewise, his daughter Angel had been born, grown to adulthood, and like her brother had lived an impossibly long lifetime. She had joined her brother to risk her life traveling through time to save her father, a man she'd never met.

But they'd lived. More to the point: they'd *aged*. They'd existed throughout all of those two centuries between his disappearance in 2030 and his reappearance in 2219.

It meant the time machine had failed. He'd not, in this cycle of history, saved his children by returning them to the future. They'd reached the future by *living* their way to it. And now that he knew that, he certainly couldn't take young Josh and unborn Angel back with him.

Was he to wait until Angel was born and then return to the future with only Hope?

He would not do that to his children. He'd vowed that he would not. His birth parents had abandoned him emotionally when his older brother died suddenly at the age of five. Nothing Will did was satisfactory, compared against the idealized image of the older son they'd adored in life and idolized in death. He'd later heard the expression that the opposite of love wasn't hate, it was apathy, and he knew it to be so from living that truth growing up. It wasn't that his parents hated him; they simply didn't care about him at all. When they'd died in a car crash when he was sixteen years old, people had remarked how well he'd handled it, how mature he'd seemed. The reality was that his parents had been dead for years. He'd lived in poverty; his parents had directed their meager estate to anyone and everyone but him. And in that poverty he'd vowed that he'd be rich and that when he had children, he'd never leave them emotionally abandoned, or devoid of a loving household, as he had been.

No, he would not leave his children behind. Not without their mother.

Perhaps that was Josh's message to him as the adult Fil, though. He needed to rescue Hope, even if it meant leaving Josh in the past alone. How would Angel come to exist in the past then? Had he waited the months it would take her to be born before leaving for the future with just Hope?

If that was the plan for him, he'd prefer the machine get stuck in whatever time loop he was in and never emerge on the other side. They wouldn't send him back expecting him to make that type of decision, would they?

He became aware of a sudden hush inside the machine. The top became clear and vanished, and Will scrambled out of the craft and walked several yards away before he stopped and looked around.

He was not in a forest at all, but rather a field, cleared for miles around, with no sign of his neighborhood or the rest of the town, including the massive dome over the main city of Pleasanton, in sight. He supposed that when traveling back in time that the physical location on the planet might be only a secondary concern, so perhaps he was simply a few miles from his destination. The concern there was that he doubted he'd been given any excess time to travel to the neighborhood upon arriving in the past.

He had the ability to travel instantly, though he didn't want to do so. No sense alerting the Hunters to his location. But if he had to do it, he would.

He chose to teleport to his watching post in the forest behind his neighbor's house. He'd walked among those trees many times, and knew the area well. Perhaps that was why he'd been so drawn to the majestic trees near the Alliance camps; they truly reminded him of home. He concentrated on the image of that spot, and pictured himself traveling there.

Nothing happened.

Will frowned. He'd not had that happen before in his teleportation efforts. Perhaps he was much farther from the location than he thought he was.

He needed to go back to see the people in the Alliance about this. And while he was there, he would take the opportunity to truly see and speak to his children. To find out what, exactly, he was supposed to do in the past, knowing they needed to stay there and age their way to their present. Or perhaps there was a GPS device in the craft that could give him directions.

He turned back to the craft and froze.

It was gone.

Lying on the ground where he'd expected to see the time machine were several objects he'd not noticed in the craft, possibly items that had been stored in the trunk. One looked like a bag containing clothing. He opened a small pouch and was surprised to find a large supply of copper, silver, and gold coins. He closed up the pouch and examined a third item, which looked like a piece of paper. He flipped it over and noticed writing there, which moved as he touched the surface. It was a computer, the size and texture of paper, operated by a touch sensor. And the image of it being a letter was a correct one. Will read the note.

Will Stark —

You are reading this at the end of your journey in the time machine, no doubt wondering why the machine has disappeared, why you are in an open field instead of a dense grove of trees near your home, and why you have doubts about the actual nature of your journey.

You see, we've known since before we retrieved you from your backyard what your true journey would be, and we knew that, even for one as devoted to duty and family as Will Stark, that simply telling you what needed to be done would frighten any man into avoiding that duty. We say this not as an insult to you, but from the perspective of knowing how great the ask of you would be.

We knew that, in order to complete your journey, you needed to be adequately trained in Energy usage, be well-supplied with nanos, have a basic grasp of the history of the Aliomenti — and not have an Alliance tattoo on your palm. We also believed that you needed to make the decision to climb into the time machine, rather than being forced into it. Our actions since bringing you into the future have been designed to meet these ends. We realized that knowing the true identities of Fil and Angel would lessen the likelihood that you'd make that choice, and as such they hid their identities. Fil, against his every true desire, played the role of one seeking to push you away, invoking guilt and anger where necessary, to ensure that you'd be more eager to leave.

We created an elaborate story about the decisions you might need to make during your journey in time, knowing full well that you'd never need to make any of those specific decisions. But you needed to recognize that it was not a journey or a mission to take lightly, and thus we pushed various horrific scenarios at you to reinforce this truth.

On the night of the fire, you will, in fact, successfully teleport your wife and son away from an assassin and into a secret underground bunker beneath your home, a bunker created by your wife without your knowledge. She built that bunker for just that occasion, for she knew the attack was coming, and knew that she'd need to teleport the two of them to safety. In the face of the assassin, however, she froze, and but for your action they might have died. You do, in fact, save them.

How is it that Hope could plan to teleport anyone to safety? How did she know what would happen that night?

She knew because someone from the future told her. She could plan to save herself and her son because the woman you know as Hope Stark had been alive for nearly a thousand years before the assassin entered your house that night.

The woman you know as Hope Stark was born in the village where the earliest Aliomenti made their first homes, the first and only child ever born to at least one Aliomenti parent until Josh Stark was born many years later. Hers was not a happy childhood, Will. Her father decreed her to be the one subjected to all manner of experiments to find what exercises, substances, and foods would trigger the Energy they'd seen others use, the one to test if a given substance might be useful or harmful. Her mother fought for her, and the viciousness of that battle tore the village apart. Factions developed supporting husband and wife, but in the end, the greed — the desire of having another to absorb the pain needed to make progress — won out. Her mother died with a broken heart.

This left Elizabeth, as she was known, without a protector. Her health deteriorated, for no one loved her, and her own father watched his own power over the community grow in exchange for his daughter's suffering. She needed someone to save her, to remove her from her hellish existence. And her hero arrived one day.

Her hero was — and is — you.

You see, Will, the reason that the Hunters and The Leader and all the rest of the Aliomenti know of a mythic hero named Will Stark is because that man arrived in that first small Aliomenti village as Elizabeth celebrated her sixteenth birthday. Unknown to everyone in that camp, Will Stark had just arrived in their area from a different part of the world, and in their time from the distant future. That is why, Will, you are standing in a field in the wilds of England in the year 1018 A.D., armed with clothing and coins appropriate for the time and place. You will guard Elizabeth's life, not just in the near term, but for the next millennium, for she must survive to meet a young man named Will Stark in the twenty-first century. She must survive to give birth to Josh and Angel. And she must survive to ensure that the events of the night of the fire come to fruition, to ensure that Will Stark, a man born in the late twentieth century, is in a position to be carried into the future, trained, and sent to the past.

Would any man willingly make the decision to live a thousand years in the past, guarding the woman he loves yet unable to marry her, so that his future self can? We know of a man who did, though he was deceived into doing so. Yet we believe that his love for her was so genuine that he would choose to make that sacrifice. It is easy to give your life for those you love in death; it is far more challenging to give your living in the same cause. You may see our dilemma; we needed you to be prepared for a mission of great significance in the past relating to saving your wife, but we couldn't know if you'd make the decision if you knew the whole truth. We hope you forgive the deception. The decision needed to be made, for you, Will Stark, are a critical piece of history, and it is a mission you needed to undertake.

We have supplied you with clothing and coins appropriate to this region. This paper will periodically provide you with key information through your journey. Our first is this: the village with the early Aliomenti is in the forest to the north and west. Remember: you have yet to meet anyone in that village, no matter how familiar they might seem. You know nothing of Energy. And Elizabeth is not your wife. You must take the time to develop your back story, acclimate yourself to this time, and set out.

We have ensured that nothing visible or tangible from the future, save for this paper, remains behind. You do not have a gun or a flying craft. You do have a massive swarm of nanos, for your future clothing and the whole time machine are now part of your arsenal. Use them — and your hidden, Shielded skills — wisely.

We wish you well in your journey, Will Stark. We beg your forgiveness for our deception. And we look forward to speaking to you again in our present, your future, at a time of your choosing.

Adam, Angel, and Josh

P.S. Josh nailed the assassin with a fastball that night. He learned well. And yes, he does love baseball. Just like his father.

Will spent nearly fifteen minutes trying to process what he'd just read.

It explained his inability to teleport to his home, as the building wouldn't exist for a thousand years. He glanced at the bundle of clothes and the pouch of money. They'd at least prepared him with those essentials. The letter told him that he should travel to the northwest, into the forest there, for that was where Hope — no, Elizabeth — lived, and she needed his help.

For her, he truly would do anything, even live a thousand years to protect her from harm.

Will went to the pile of clothes, removing the nanos from his body. They joined his full original allocation, along with those which comprised the time machine. He donned the outfit in the bag, not without some difficulty as the style was completely foreign to him. He picked up his money pouch, and put his paper computer from the future in a pocket. Using the sun as a guide, he oriented himself to the northwest, toward his destiny, and towards Hope.

The journey of a thousand years would be taken one step at a time.

His mission established, his duty accepted, he moved forward. One step at a time.

FROM THE AUTHOR

Thank you for reading *A Question of Will*. I hope you enjoyed the story and are interested in continuing to read about Will Stark and the rest of the Aliomenti. Book 2 in the series, titled *Preserving Hope*, is available at many online retailers and in print.

If you enjoyed this book, please consider taking a moment to leave a review and rating at the site used to purchase it, or at sites dedicated to helping readers find books. Others will be very interested in your thoughts, and as an author it's wonderful to see feedback from readers.

If you'd like to contact me or find out when the next book is due, the best bet is to visit my website, http://www.alexalbrinck.com. While there, you'll find links to my Facebook fan page and Twitter feed. You can also email me at alex@alexalbrinck.com at any time.

I thank you again for your support, and wish you every success in your endeavors.

ALSO BY ALEX ALBRINCK

THE ALIOMENTI SAGA

Prequel: *Hunting Will* (December 2012)

Book 1: *A Question of Will* (September 2012)

Book 2: *Preserving Hope* (December 2012)

Book 3: Coming 2013!

To be notified of new book releases, sign up for my mailing list:
http://eepurl.com/o03Gv

Will Stark watched the villagers seal the lid of Elizabeth Lowell's coffin.

She had been the daughter of Genevieve and Arthur Lowell. Genevieve wasn't here to watch as the simple pine box holding her only child was lowered into the grave. Genevieve wasn't able to cry until there were no more tears to cry, nor was she able to curse her every breath as one stolen from the young woman buried that day. Genevieve had found her eternal rest three years earlier, and she now waited in silence as Elizabeth became her eternal companion.

Arthur, though, had to live through this event, not shielded from every parent's worst nightmare, the nightmare of burying your own child. For Arthur, the experience was far more profound, for deep down, he knew that his only child was dead before her twentieth birthday because of his own greed and selfishness.

At least, he should have known that.

Arthur had been part of a group of slaves who had escaped into the wilds of medieval northern England, revolting against a return to a life of servitude. The group had been forced to serve as human test subjects for a baron desirous of getting his slaves to live longer and work harder by freeing them of the diseases and ill health that lessened his return on his investment in human capital. If the experiments worked, they'd be healthy; if the experiments failed – as they had with earlier groups – then the slaves would die. The experiments with Arthur's group had succeeded, but had the curious side-effect of giving that group of slaves a thirst for freedom that could not be quenched. Arthur and the others had escaped, built up modest wealth, and had constructed a thriving village. There, they'd conducted experiments of their own choosing, seeking a far greater payoff than mere good health. The experiments were all conducted by a single "volunteer," a young girl "hired" each day to test out every possible "magical" substance reputed to provide a payoff of mythical proportions. Though she worked against her will and received none of the money paid for her services, the young girl – Elizabeth – was expected to freely share any breakthroughs with those who enslaved her.

In the end, though, the experiments had led only to the early and violent death of that girl. Two women had protested her treatment – Genevieve, and the woman who had come to be a second mother to Elizabeth – and those protests had led to those women preceding Elizabeth in death. For Arthur, these three deaths were a small price to pay to gain the knowledge and power he sought above all else.

Several of the men of the village pounded nails into the wood, sealing the box for eternity, just after Will caught a final glimpse of Elizabeth. Her hair was a flaming-red color like that of Will's daughter, Angel, but in death it lacked the same vibrancy. Elizabeth's hair now looked like the dying embers remaining from a once-great fire, the dirty hair matted against her head with blood and sweat. The bruises still marred her face, never having had the chance to heal before her bodily functions ceased. Her blue eyes, a window into the sadness of her life, were hidden behind eyelids sealed shut from the beating she'd endured. Her neighbors, aroused to a fearful passion aided by Elizabeth's own father, had exacted their final toll. After a decade of physical trauma and emotional neglect, Arthur had disowned his own daughter in her time of greatest need and peril, delivering Elizabeth to her early grave rather than standing up for the daughter he'd long ceased to show any fondness. Instead, the former slave had discarded his own child when she no longer served him any purpose.

Will bent to the ground and grasped one of the three long, wooden poles used to lift and carry the coffin. At a count of three, he joined the two women and three men in standing up, lifting the pine box off the ground for transport to the grave site. They walked in silence, pausing as Will momentarily lost his balance. There were no tears shed during this solemn time, for outside of one of the men carrying the coffin, they all bore a share of the guilt for the young woman's demise, a fatality that seemed predestined. No priest presided over the ceremony, for none of them wanted to be reminded of the terrible guilt they all shared.

The earth had already been removed from Elizabeth's final resting place. The dirt sat in a large pile atop Genevieve's grave, preventing anyone from stepping there. The pallbearers placed the pine box atop the open grave, where the wooden poles allowed the coffin to remain above ground. Will and two other men unrolled three coils of sturdy rope, which were fed under the coffin. The pallbearers lifted the box a few inches off the ground using the ropes, and one of the villagers removed the three poles from beneath the coffin. Inch by inch, the six lowered the box down into the grave, until it reached the bottom with a finality fitting for the end of a young life. They dropped the lengths of rope into the hole and stepped back.

Arthur Lowell stepped forward. As the father of the deceased, it was his duty to speak. "We have suffered a great loss. Elizabeth was a young woman of beauty, possessing a generosity of spirit rare among any I've ever met. She has uniquely contributed to the success of this community, and we mourn that she will be unable to continue to share in that success. In her memory, we must continue to move forward along the path she cleared, to see the sights she made available for all of us. In many ways, she epitomizes what we are striving to be, ever seeking to push the boundaries of human development. We will not let her death be in vain." There were murmurs of agreement and appreciation of his words.

Will looked around at the small assembly, incredulous. "That was a beautiful speech, Arthur. Why, if I didn't know any better, I'd think her death was of her own choosing. Let me offer my eulogy. Today, this young woman is laid to rest as a human sacrifice on the altar of greed and laziness and cowardice. She is mourned by those gathered here, not because they truly sorrow at her loss, but because they do not know where the next sacrificial victim will be found. They cry not because she is gone, but because they fear they'll be the next chosen to join her, the next innocent bludgeoned to death by so-called neighbors. None of you have any right to be standing on this ground; you all bear the guilt of her demise, regardless of the number of blows you delivered."

Most of the eyes in the gathering fell to the ground, their silence speaking volumes to the guilt they bore and the truth of his words. Arthur's eyes blazed in anger. "How dare you!" he hissed. "How dare you belittle her in such a fashion! My daughter worked harder than anyone here to unlock the secrets we know wait just beyond our grasp, teasing us with their potential, and you tarnish her memory before the dirt is in her grave?"

Will marched straight to Arthur, until he could lean down and stare directly into the shorter man's terrified eyes. "Get out of here now, Arthur." Will turned around, his gaze taking in all of those assembled. "All of you. Leave this place. You gave this woman no peace during her life. You failed to give her a childhood full of fun and play and laughter. You never gave her the love all children so desperately need. You feign interest in her now, as if you expect that to atone for the crimes you've committed against her. Her life is over; it's too late to seek forgiveness now. Leave, so that her final burial is performed by hands that didn't drive her into that grave."

Will turned back to Arthur and again stared down the shorter man, who finally withered under his gaze. Arthur turned and left the clearing, followed by the rest of the villagers, leaving Will alone with the coffin and the empty grave. Silence followed their departure, suggesting that he was alone, but Will knew that Arthur had not gone all the way back to the village with the others.

After a few moments of quiet contemplation kneeling by the coffin, Will stood and seized a shovel. He began pushing the dirt back into the open grave, covering the coffin and filling the hole. He worked without stopping, ignoring the sweat beading on his forehead and dampening his clothes. Once the grave was filled with dirt, Will located a small piece of rope on the ground nearby, and used it to fashion a small cross from two tree branches. He pushed the marker into the ground, and knelt down. He allowed the tears to flow, weeping over the tortuous life the young woman had lived. He wept at the love she'd so desperately sought from her father, love that the man had never reciprocated. He wept at her horror at the realization that that same man had permitted and encouraged her final end.

Will rose to his feet and marched into the trees, where Arthur stood, watching the entire scene.

"You loved her, didn't you?" It wasn't a question that Arthur directed at Will. It was an accusation, one designed to twist the emotional knife just a bit deeper, and perhaps locate a weak point for future exploitation.

Will fixed Arthur with a steady gaze, his eyes bright with malice toward the shorter man. "I will love her until the end of my days."

And then he punched Arthur square in the face, turned, and headed away from the village, ignoring Arthur's cries of pain.

He needed to get as far from this spot as possible. Only then could he determine if the woman lying in the box was still alive, or if he'd accidentally killed his future wife.

ABOUT THE AUTHOR

Alex Albrinck is a lifelong Ohio resident, where he lives with his wife and three children. When he's not trying to be in three places at once with his active youngsters, he's following local professional and collegiate sports teams, or possibly unscrambling a Rubik's Cube. In lieu of sleep, he writes fiction.

His debut novel, *A Question of Will*, explores themes of technological advancement, human potential (good and bad), and the love bonding a family together. It reached the Amazon Top 100 in Science Fiction -> High Tech less than a week after publication.

The sequel, *Preserving Hope*, follows Will Stark as he continues his epic quest to save and reunite his family against all odds, and continues the exploration of advanced technology and Energy skills.

He is currently working on the next novel in the series.

Made in the USA
Charleston, SC
08 April 2015